Forever and Always

Leigh Greenwood

sourcebooks
casablanca

Copyright © 2015 by Leigh Greenwood
Cover and internal design © 2015 by Sourcebooks, Inc.
Cover art by Gregg Gulbronson

Sourcebooks and the colophon are registered trademarks of
Sourcebooks, Inc.

Published by Sourcebooks Casablanca, an imprint of Sourcebooks,
Inc.
P.O. Box 4410, Naperville, Illinois 60567-4410
(630) 961-3900
Fax: (630) 961-2168
www.sourcebooks.com

Printed and bound in Canada.
MBP 10 9 8 7 6 5 4 3 2 1

To the Romance Writers of America:
Without this wonderful organization,
I wouldn't have had my career.

One

Chicago, June 1870

BRIDGETTE LOWE RUSHED INTO DR. JAMES PITTMAN's arms the moment the sitting room door closed behind him. At first glance, the room was elegantly and luxuriously furnished. Closer inspection would have revealed that the velvet covering on the daybed was thinning, that the curtains had begun to fade, and that the Aubusson carpet was frayed at one edge. Bridgette's elephant-gray silk and grenadine dress, however, was of the latest fashion. Her hair showed the attention of a well-trained maid.

"Thank goodness you came quickly," Bridgette said as she threw herself at the doctor. "I've been going crazy."

James disentangled himself from her embrace. "What is this about Elliot disappearing?"

Bridgette handed him the letter, which had been crushed in her hand. James took a moment to smooth it out.

Bridgette,

By the time you receive this letter, I will have left Chicago forever. Dr. Pittman has said I have only three months to live so I've decided to spend what time I have trying to find my brothers. From now on I'll be known by my birth name, Logan Holstock. Don't send anyone to look for me. You will receive notice of my death.

Logan

"Did he say anything else?" James asked.

"No," Bridgette fumed, "but he's done plenty." She reached for a newspaper and thrust it at him. "Read that!" But she didn't give him a chance to read the item she pointed to with a trembling finger. "He had this announcement put in the personals page. *Due to his declining health, Mr. Elliot Lowe has released Miss Bridgette Lowe from their engagement.*" She snatched the newspaper from James's hands and flung it to the floor. She strode across the room, took a large gulp from a glass of wine, and turned back to her visitor. "That's not all he's done. His lawyer paid me a visit before I had managed to swallow my breakfast. First, Elliot has put the company up for sale. Second, the company is under the sole management of his second-in-command until it's sold. Third," she practically shrieked the word, "he left no will."

"I don't see how that's a problem. You're his only relative."

"That's what I thought, but his bloodless lawyer informed me that Uncle Samuel never officially adopted Elliot. I'm not legally related to him. If he finds those brothers he's looking for, they'll get everything. We'll have been poisoning that medicine you've been having him take for nothing!"

James's complexion lost some of its color. "You've got to stop him."

"How? I don't know where he's gone."

"Where would his brothers be?"

"I don't know!" Bridgette practically shrieked. "His parents were killed somewhere on the Santa Fe Trail. I suppose they're out there somewhere." She gestured in a dismissive fashion, indicating somewhere in the direction she thought might be west.

"He must have said something about them. Think."

"I've been thinking all morning."

"You've been giving way to panic. That's not thinking. He must have said something about them at some time."

"Wait." Bridgette's hands flew to her temples, her brow wrinkled in concentration. "He said he'd read an article about a U.S. Marshal in Arizona named Holstock."

"Did he say where in Arizona?"

"Some new town."

"There's nothing in Arizona except new towns."

"Well, I can't remember. I'm not even sure what he said. I didn't pay any attention. He was always talking about looking for his brothers, but he never did anything about it."

"You have to look for him."

Bridgette looked at the doctor as though he'd lost his mind. "I'm not going out there. There's nobody out there but murdering Indians and criminals. I'd be lucky not to lose my scalp and my honor."

"Then hire a Pinkerton. They have an excellent reputation. They caught the Reno Brothers gang."

"Elliot's not a criminal you can locate by following his crimes. He's a wealthy man with enough money to live anywhere he wants. He could go to London or Paris."

"If he's looking for his brothers, he's gone west. That's why you need to hire a Pinkerton. They go anywhere and find anybody."

"Where do I find a Pinkerton?"

The doctor smiled. "That's easy. Their headquarters are right here in Chicago."

∽

Logan was so exhausted he hardly had the energy to wield the knife as he skinned the deer he'd just killed. Every day he seemed to lose a little more of his strength. Today was a good day, but he didn't know how long that would last. He just hoped he could get the meat back to his camp before he got sick again. There was a good reason native Indians had used deerskins for moccasins and coverings for their lodges. Deer hide was remarkably tough. He barely had the strength to peel it away from the meat underneath.

He couldn't decide how much of the meat he should take. He couldn't eat half of it before it spoiled, but it seemed a shame to leave it to be eaten by wild animals. He couldn't cure it, and he couldn't give it away. He hadn't been in the Arizona Territory long, but he'd made a point of staying away from other people. His plan was to find a place to set up a permanent camp. Then he'd decide when it was time to go into the town of Cactus Corner.

He had just cut away a large chunk of meat from the left flank when he heard movement in the brush.

Even as he reached for his rifle, he knew it had to be a bear. He would never have heard a wolf or a cougar. Yet when he looked up, he didn't see any animal. He waited several moments, but the silence remained unbroken. Placing his rifle within easy reach, he turned back to the carcass. Almost immediately, he heard sounds of movement. This time he scanned his surroundings slowly, being careful to study each patch of woodland before moving to the next. He'd nearly made the circuit when he saw what appeared to be a wolf or a coyote crouching beneath a scrub pine. He reached for his rifle but didn't pick it up.

Then he waited.

It wasn't long before the animal moved forward. Keeping his body so low to the ground he appeared to be lying down, he moved one step, paused, then moved another. It wasn't a wolf or a coyote. It was a dog.

Logan released his rifle. "What are you doing out here?" he asked the dog. "Are you as lost as I am?"

At the sound of Logan's voice, the dog dropped in its tracks.

"You don't have to be afraid of me," Logan said. "I doubt I have as much right to be here as you. What are you doing so far from home?"

Apparently deciding Logan wasn't going to hurt him, the dog started forward once more. He was a large dog with a tan coat. He had the powerful body, large head, and blunt face of an English mastiff. There was something else in him, probably bloodhound, but he didn't look large and powerful now. Each step was painfully slow, yet he kept coming. As he drew closer, what Logan saw turned his curiosity into fury. The dog was nearly skin and bones. He couldn't have had enough to eat for weeks. Worse were the sores that were scabbing over. Someone had beaten the dog so severely he could only move with great effort.

Logan surged to his feet. "What son of a bitch would do something like that?"

The dog dropped to the ground, bared his fangs, ears flat against his head, and growled deep in his throat. Despite his show of bravado, Logan could see fear in his eyes.

He took a step forward. "I'm not going to hurt you. I just want to look at your wounds."

But the dog started to back away.

Logan cut off a small piece of meat and tossed it to the dog. Despite its injuries, the dog pounced on the meat and swallowed it in one gulp.

"I guess the only reason you came this close is you're starved." Logan tossed a second piece of meat that was devoured just as quickly. "When I finish here, you can help yourself to what's left," he said to the dog, "but I'm taking all the good cuts with me. It's more than I can eat, so when you get finished with the carcass, you come to my camp. If you'll let me, I'd like to take a look at your wounds."

The dog's eyes never left him.

"You don't trust me, do you? I don't blame you. Some man did that to you. I know it was a man because no woman would do a thing like that. That kind of meanness takes years of practice. I'll feed you until you get well. Then I want you to go back and rip out the bastard's throat."

It took several trips for Logan to load the meat on his horse, which was tethered nearby. By the time he had finished, he was too exhausted to climb into the saddle. While he waited for his strength to return, he watched the dog attack the carcass. Rather than rip off and gulp down as much meat as fast as he could, the dog seemed to be pacing himself. He would eat then wait a bit before eating again.

"You're smart," Logan said. "You know as long as I'm here, no wild animal is going to take your meal from you. That gives your stomach time to get used to having food in it again." Logan wished it would work that way for him. He never knew when the seizures would take hold, and he'd wretch until he was too weak to move. "We have a lot in common," he said to the dog. "We should be friends."

Whatever the dog thought of Logan's offer, it wasn't enough to deflect his interest from his food.

"That's right. Don't waste your time on someone who'll die on you. Take what you can and move on."

The dog stopped eating.

"Better eat while you can. It won't be here in the morning."

Showing no sign of having heard him, the dog got up and made its way to a thin trickle of water about twenty yards away. It tore at Logan's heart to see the way the dog dragged his body to the stream where he sank to his belly and drank greedily.

"There's a special place in hell for the man who did that to you," he said. "I hope I meet him someday." But weak as he was, what could he do? It was better to forget the man and the dog. After all, they had a future. He didn't.

❧

Sibyl didn't look forward to her confrontation with Norman, but she couldn't put it off any longer. He'd stalled her every time she'd tried to talk to him at home. She hoped for more success if she cornered him in his office. Norman didn't like her coming to the bank. He would like it even less if she raised a fuss. He worked hard to project the picture of a happily married man, a facade he abandoned at home unless there was someone there other than Kitty. Sibyl only cared about the facade as it affected Kitty, and the effect on Kitty was what this was all about. The child was only six years old, but Norman had decided she should be sent away to school. He argued that it was impossible for her to receive a good education in Cactus Corner, but Sibyl knew that wasn't the reason.

She knew Norman wanted to send Kitty away because he didn't believe she was his daughter. Plucking up her courage, Sibyl opened the door and entered the bank.

The building had been designed to give the impression of substance, of success, of reliability. Its front was an impressive two stories high with large glass windows and the name "Spencer's Bank" printed in large flowing script. The spacious lobby was provided with comfortable benches and a writing table. The wood floor was oiled and swept each day. The tellers stood behind dark wooden counters topped by grilles that gave the illusion that a customer's deposit was safe from danger. Gas lamps suspended from the ceiling provided light on gloomy days. Cassie Greene, seated at a desk just inside the door, welcomed Sibyl with one of the brilliant smiles that did so much to draw male customers to the bank—and back again and again. "How are you doing this morning, Mrs. Spencer? It's been forever since I've seen you in here."

"I wouldn't be here now, but I need to speak to my husband." After seven years, the words still didn't come easily to her lips.

"You're here mighty early. We just opened the door."

"I wanted to catch him before he got busy. Is anyone with him in his office?"

"Not a soul. It's been quiet lately." She lowered her voice. "Dr. Kessling's bank has taken away a lot of customers."

Sibyl was acutely aware of that. Because two of Sibyl's cousins and their husbands were the biggest investors in the new bank, Norman seemed to think Sibyl could have stopped its formation if she'd wanted. He refused to believe it could have been due to any fault of his. Sibyl had no need to draw attention to his mistakes because customers leaving Norman's bank were only too ready to do it for her. Norman was so rich he didn't need to work another day in his life, but he fought tooth and nail for every new deposit. When he lost one, he was almost unbearable to be around.

"I shouldn't be long. Tell anyone coming in they shouldn't have to wait more than a few minutes." She hoped that would be the case, but she doubted it. Her knock on the door was greeted with a warm and friendly *come in*. Norman's eagerness evaporated the moment Sibyl walked through the door.

The office had been created to reflect Norman Spencer's image of himself. The room was spacious with large windows, thick carpets, and comfortable chairs, but the focal point of the room was a carved mahogany desk that was almost as big as most people's beds. Norman sat behind it like a potentate on his throne.

"What are you doing here? You know I don't like for you to take up my time when I'm working."

"You're not working now, and you refuse to talk to me at home." She walked to a chair across from his desk and sat down without waiting for an invitation. "It's entirely your fault that I'm here."

Since, in Norman's mind, nothing unpleasant was ever his fault, he had a lot to say. Sibyl made no response. She'd heard it all many times before. "I've come to talk about your plan to send Kitty away to school," she said when he stopped talking long enough to take a deep breath.

"We've been all through that."

"*You've* been all through it. You haven't listened to a thing I've said."

"It's for her benefit. If she stays here, she'll be as wild as Colby's twins. Do you know Esther rides her pony *astride*?"

"Everybody knows Esther rides astride, and nobody has a problem with it. She's only nine years old."

"I have a problem with it," Norman declared. "I won't have Kitty behaving like that. It's unbecoming to the Spencer name." Whatever Norman's private doubts about Kitty's parentage, he would have been horrified to know anyone else shared them. The Spencer name must always be above reproach.

"I'm perfectly capable of molding my daughter's character," Sibyl argued. "You can't point to a single instance when her behavior has embarrassed you." Since Norman rarely saw his daughter on any day other than Sunday, he knew very little about anything she did.

"As you pointed out, she's only six. Will you be able to say that when she's eight, twelve, or sixteen?"

"I have no objection to sending her away to school when she's fourteen. Right now, she's too young."

"Fourteen is too late. Her character will already be formed. About all any school would be able to do that late would be teach her French and a fondness for expensive clothes. She needs to go this year."

Trying to reason with Norman was a waste of time. Sibyl stood. "Let me make something very clear. You will *not* send Kitty to boarding school this year. There's no point in yelling at me or telling me that you control the money, therefore you'll make the decisions. This is one decision you will not make. If you try, I will stop you."

"How? There's nothing you can do." Norman was surprised by her defiance yet scornful of it.

"There is a great deal I *can* do, much of which you would find extremely distasteful."

"Don't try to threaten me. You can't—"

Sibyl heard raised voices in the bank, but she had more important things to think about than what might be happening outside Norman's office. Norman, on the other hand, seemed eager for a distraction.

"Something's wrong. Stay here while I see what it is."

Sibyl was furious he would use any excuse to avoid talking about Kitty's future, but she'd said what she'd come to say. She would deal with the future later. She was surprised when the voices became louder. Usually Norman's presence put a damper on things. Curious about what was happening, she got up and left the office. The sight that met her gaze caused her to freeze in her tracks. Cassie was struggling to escape from one man. A second man was talking to the teller. The third and fourth were confronting Norman. All four men were masked and holding guns.

They were in the process of robbing the bank.

The fourth man turned in Sibyl's direction. "Don't do anything foolish, ma'am, and you won't get hurt."

Sibyl was too shocked to do anything, foolish or otherwise.

"You can't rob my bank," Norman was shouting. "You won't get away with it." He started forward, but the man pointed the gun at his forehead.

"We're not greedy," the man said. "We'll leave you enough to buy food for your family."

Norman started to argue, and the man's voice turned hard.

"If you play it smart and shut your mouth, I'll leave you alive to make more money."

"We have a marshal now," Norman said. "He'll hunt you down."

"We'll be hundreds of miles from here by the time he gets back from Tucson."

"Colby Blaine can follow you like a cougar follows a deer," Norman boasted. "That man is better than an Indian."

Sibyl couldn't believe Norman was throwing around threats, which were bound to put the robbers' nerves on edge. Why didn't he shut up?

"If Colby doesn't come after you, I will." Cassie did her best to knee her captor in the groin, but he was too quick for her.

"How're you doing with the teller?" the man confronting Norman asked the bandit at the teller's window.

"I'm about done here. I've got all the money they keep up front. Where's the safe?" he asked the teller.

"In the office."

Sibyl couldn't blame Horace for revealing the location of the safe—not that a short search wouldn't have located it—but she was certain Norman would fire the young man the moment the bandits were gone. Jobs weren't easy to find for a young man with a wife and a small child, but Norman wouldn't take that into consideration.

The man holding a gun on Sibyl spoke. "While everybody out here remains quiet, why don't you show me where the office is so you can open the safe."

"I can't. I don't work in the bank. I was only here this morning to talk to my husband about a personal matter."

The man turned to Norman. "Give her the combination."

"I will not," Norman said. "A safe wouldn't be a bit of use if half the people in town knew how to open it."

The man struck Norman with his pistol. "Give her the combination."

"No."

The man struck Norman again before turning his gun on Horace. "You, open the safe."

Horace stammered so badly Cassie answered for him. "He doesn't know the combination. Nobody does except Mr. Spencer."

The robber whipped around to face Norman. "This is your last chance. Open the safe or I'll shoot you."

"If you kill me, you'll never learn the combination."

"I don't plan to *kill* you, just shoot you inch by inch until you come to your senses."

"For God's sake, Norman," Sibyl pleaded, "open the safe. The money's not worth getting shot."

"Listen to your wife," the man said. "She's a sensible woman."

"I haven't listened to a woman since my mother died," Norman declared, "and I don't mean to start now."

Sibyl didn't know much about holdups, but she had the feeling the robbers had been forced to spend more time inside the bank than they had planned. The longer they stayed, the more likely something would go wrong. The leader was getting angry and nervous. Still, she was shocked when he shot Norman in the leg.

"You've got five seconds to open that safe before I put a bullet in your other leg."

Norman was never sick, and he'd never been injured. He had never shown sympathy for others, often making light of their pain or discomfort. Now that he was injured, he was seeing things in a very different light. He screamed and fell to the floor, writhing in agony.

"I'll shoot your wife!" the robber screamed. "I'll shoot your teller and that pretty blond if you don't open that safe now!"

Norman was oblivious to anything outside his pain. The robbers weren't going to get anything out of him.

"Shoot the teller," the leader yelled at the robber holding the bag of cash.

Two

SIBYL GASPED AS ONE ROBBER POINTED HIS GUN AT Horace, and the other turned back on Norman. The sound of pistol shots was deafening. She expect to see Horace fall, mortally wounded. Instead, the robber crumpled into a heap. A second explosion, following so close on the first that it sounded like an echo, sent the robber who'd shot Norman to the ground. In the confusion, Cassie managed to break away from her captor. A third gunshot sent him into the next world after his fellow thieves. The remaining robber grabbed Sibyl to use as a shield.

Everything had happened so fast, it took a moment for Sibyl to realize three robbers were dead, and that a stranger with a gun in his hand was standing just inside the bank door. Cassie and Horace were staring at him with riveted gazes, their eyes wide from shock.

No one had seen or heard the man enter the bank. He was tall and thin, his face so bloated his eyes seemed to stare at them out of deep wells. Sibyl was certain she'd never seen him before. It would have been impossible to forget such a face. At the moment, however, she didn't have time to wonder who he might be. She was standing between two guns, one held by the stranger and one by the outlaw. She could be the next one to die.

"Let her go," the stranger said. "You can have the cash."

"I'm not a fool. If I let her go, you'll shoot me."

"I'll shoot you if you don't."

"Don't do anything foolish," the man growled at Sibyl.

Sibyl could tell by his shaking voice that he was as stunned by the unexpected turn of events as she was. "You'd better take your own advice," she responded. "If you shoot me, you will die for sure."

"We're getting out of here together. There's a back door."

Sibyl wasn't willing to trust her safety to this man. As soon as he tried to pull her back toward the rear door, she went limp. The bank echoed with the sound of a shot, and the robber and Sibyl tumbled to the floor. It seemed the stranger was at her side the moment she hit the floor.

"Are you okay?"

Sibyl was so horrified by what she'd just witnessed—and the blood spatters covering most of her upper body—she couldn't get a word out, but she did manage to sit up.

Cassie wasn't similarly handicapped. "I'm sure glad you got here when you did," she said to the stranger. "That son of a bitch who grabbed me smelled bad." She looked around at the bodies and the blood. "You made a real mess. I hope nobody's expecting me to clean it up."

Sibyl didn't know whether to laugh or take the easy way out and faint. Instead, she took the hand the stranger offered. For a moment she was afraid he didn't have the strength to help her up. Just as she was about ready to call for Horace, the stranger grimaced and pulled her to her feet. The effort so exhausted him that he staggered.

"Are you okay?" she asked. "Have you been shot?"

"No. I'm just a little weak," the man said. "I haven't been well lately."

He looked so unwell, she looked for signs of a wound anyway—maybe he was in shock and didn't realize he'd been shot—but she saw no blood. She raised her gaze to his face. Despite the distorted features, she was stuck by the intensity of green eyes that were like fiery emeralds, backlit until they glowed even in the light of day. They gave evidence that the man inside this emaciated body still held to life with a tenacious grip, that his spirit was as vigorous as his body was frail.

"Are you all right, Mrs. Spencer?" Horace had gotten over his shock and come out from behind his teller's window.

The sound of his voice shattered Sibyl's focus on the stranger. She didn't know how to answer that question, but after having survived an Indian attack, she wasn't going to let a little blood be her undoing. "I'm fine, Horace. We'd better see to Mr. Spencer. His leg will need treatment."

Before she could move, the bank doors were flung open, and people wanting to know what had happened began to stream in. She quickly lost sight of the stranger in the confusion.

Cassie pointed to the dead robbers. "They tried to rob the bank. Fortunately for us, that stranger showed up and shot all four of them. I've never seen anything so brave since Colby swam that swollen river three times."

"I need to check on Norman," Sibyl repeated.

"Norman's dead," someone said.

They were mistaken. Norman had been shot in the leg. He had screamed a lot, but it hadn't killed him. But when she reached Norman, he wasn't moving. The reason was obvious. There was a large bloodstain on his shirt over his heart, with a small hole in the middle. She didn't know when it happened, but Norman had been shot a second time.

For a moment, she couldn't take it in. For seven years, Norman had been as constant in her life as the sun in its orbit. She and Kitty had been the satellites that revolved around him. Every thought, every deed had been in response to him and his wishes that were often delivered like commands. She had been catapulted into a vacuum without a stabilizing force.

"Are you all right?"

Sibyl managed to focus her gaze on Dr. Kessling's kind face.

"I think so. I mean, yes."

"Of course she's not all right," Cassie declared. "She just watched her husband get killed."

"Did they get any money?" someone asked.

Cassie held up the bag with the cash. "Not one dollar. Your money is safe."

"I have my money in the doctor's bank. I just wanted to know."

"I'll take care of Norman's body," the doctor said.

Naomi pushed her way through the crowd. Sibyl had never seen her look so frightened. "Peter said you'd been shot by robbers."

"This isn't my blood. I'm okay, but Norman was killed."

The crowd parted enough for Naomi to see Norman's body. "What happened?"

"I think it's better to save the questions until the marshal gets back," the doctor said. "Right now, Sibyl needs to go home."

Sibyl struggled to pull herself together. "I can't go. Who's going to take care of the bank now that Norman's dead?"

"You need to be thinking about yourself," Cassie said. "The bank's not going anywhere. Horace and I can take care of things for the time being."

She hadn't meant right now, this very minute. She meant in the future. Norman had made sure she knew nothing about running a bank. She pushed that worry aside for the moment. She needed to find the stranger and thank him. He hadn't been able to help Norman, but he'd saved Horace's life. Probably hers and Cassie's as well. She looked through the crowd but didn't see him.

"Cassie, where is the stranger?"

"I don't know. He left through the back as soon as he knew you were all right."

"Do you know who he is?"

"I never saw him in my life."

She had to find him. It wasn't just that she needed to thank him for what he'd done. In the brief moments when he'd faced the man holding her, she'd seen something in his eyes that startled her. At first she'd thought it was fearlessness. It certainly fitted with the way he'd waded in with no visible concern about the consequences. But now she decided it was hopelessness. He had no fear because death didn't frighten him.

Maybe he welcomed it. As odd as it seemed, she had the feeling he was reaching out to her—at least reaching out to someone—in hopes of finding a reason to live. Unexpectedly, in a few moments saturated with desperate struggle and fear bordering on panic, she had been able to absorb so much about this man.

Though she knew she'd never seen him before, there was something familiar about him. She knew it wasn't possible, but she couldn't shake the feeling. What had caused his features to become so distorted? He must have had to endure public ridicule on occasion. Was that the reason he seemed unafraid of death? Who was he? Where had he come from, and what was he doing in Cactus Corner?

She had to find him.

❧

Logan was bent double, his body racked by dry heaves. His stomach had been emptied long ago. There was nothing left to throw up, but he knew from experience it would be a long time before the abdominal pain and spasms stopped. He should have been used to this by now. One of the worst times occurred when he was on a riverboat traveling up the Missouri River from St. Louis to Independence. The boat had just pulled away from the little town of De Witt at the junction of the Missouri and Grand Rivers. Most of the passengers were on deck waving good-bye to the small group that had performed for them. Logan had been standing back from the rail when the attack hit him without warning. Rather than spatter the deck, himself, and those nearest him, he thrust aside several people who were leaning against the rail and emptied the contents of his stomach in the murky waters below. Their anger turned to sympathy when his agony seemed to have no end. If Logan had had the strength, he would have been mortified. As it was, he could summon only enough energy to be grateful when the spasms ended. After that, he kept to himself until the boat docked in Independence.

The trip to Santa Fe had been long and increasingly arduous. He traveled as part of a wagon train, but he rode his own horse and slept apart. The nausea and spasms gradually grew worse, but it was the weakness that affected him most. Some days he felt fine. Other mornings he hardly felt able to go on. He wondered why he bothered. What was at the end of the trail for him but more sickness and a lonely death? Wouldn't it be better to stop now and get it over with?

Yet he was driven by the need to try to find at least one of his brothers before he died. The death of the adopted father he had loved left him feeling alone in the world. His uncle had disliked him, had tried to turn his father against him. He felt only a slight affection for the cousin he was supposed to marry. He believed her feelings for him were just as tepid—so lukewarm he'd preferred to die alone rather than in her arms. That's how he'd ended up camped on the edge of the Mogollon Rim waiting to die. That's how he'd ended up in the bank while it was being robbed.

He'd never thought of himself as a gunman. He'd never even carried a gun until he left Santa Fe, but he knew how to shoot. Target shooting was a hobby, but he'd never shot at anyone. He hadn't expected to shoot all the robbers before one of them shot him. In fact, he'd *expected* to be shot. What did he have to lose?

In truth, he hadn't stopped to think at all. Whatever lines of reasoning had gone through his head had traveled so fast he had no conscious memory of them. All he could say for certain was he didn't intend for that woman to be taken hostage.

He could see her as clearly as if she were standing before him now. Her youth and beauty were obvious to anyone who wasn't blind, but it was what he saw in her eyes that struck him. There was no fear, only a steely determination to survive. And stunned surprise seconds later when the robbers were all dead.

He'd used people rushing in from the street as an opportunity to escape. He didn't want to be noticed nor did he want to be thanked. He'd been so weak he'd had trouble climbing into the saddle. He'd made it back to his camp before the nausea overcame him.

Finally, the worst of the nausea faded. Using what little strength he had, Logan dragged himself to the trickle of water that ran a short distance from his campsite. He always felt better after drinking as much water as he could hold, but the relief never lasted long. Nor did the third prescription Dr. Pittman prescribed work any better than the first two. Still, he continued to take it. He couldn't make himself relinquish even one minute of his life.

Dragging himself back to his tent consumed the last of his strength. He propped himself against a tree and waited for his strength to return. He was staring at the woods that surrounded him, his gaze blurry, his thoughts as clear as mist, when he noticed movement among the trees. Moments later the head of a dog emerged from a tangle of underbrush.

Logan gave a weak chuckle. "I see you came

looking for me. I bet a cougar or a bear took the carcass from you."

The dog crawled from the cover of the underbrush. He was walking a little better, but he didn't approach Logan. Instead, he crouched down to watch.

"You don't have to stare like that," Logan said. "I haven't always looked like a puff pastry. But I don't suppose you care what I look like. I bet you're wondering if I have any of that deer left." Logan reached for the meat he'd planned to cook for his supper. "I got plenty more hanging from that tree over there. Don't plan on letting a bear steal my supper." He tossed a chunk of meat to the dog.

He gobbled up the meat but not with the urgency of the day before.

"A full belly feels good, doesn't it?" Logan asked. "Are you planning to hang around as long as I feed you?"

The dog answered by eating the second piece of meat Logan tossed to him.

"I'm not much company," Logan said, "but I'm the best you're going to find around here, so you might as well hang around."

The dog continued to watch from a safe distance. Logan figured he might never overcome his distrust of men.

"I'll make you a deal," Logan told the dog. "I'll feed you if you'll watch my campsite. I'm not expecting you to take on any bears, wolves, or cougars, but I'd be mighty pleased if you could keep the squirrels away. One of them chewed through a practically new saddlebag. The danged fool tried to use it for a nest."

The dog turned his head to one side as though he was really listening.

"You probably think I'm nuts talking to you like this. Maybe I am, but I don't care." He tossed the last piece of meat to the dog. "I'm too tired to be hungry and too weak to cook anything, so I'm going to sleep. You can stay if you like. Try not to bark unless you see a bear trying to get our food. I don't feel like going hunting just yet."

The dog responded with a low whine, but his gaze never left Logan. Logan didn't know whether the dog would go or stay, but he was too tired and too miserable to care. He'd feel better tomorrow.

As Logan lay there waiting for sleep to come, he thought back on his decision to undertake this final journey using his birth name rather than Elliot Lowe, the name he'd used for the last thirty-one years of his life. Elliot Lowe fitted the man he'd been in Chicago, but he'd left everything about that life behind. He wanted to be Logan Holstock for the time he had left. It's where he'd begun. It's where he wanted to finish.

❧

Sibyl loved her family and friends. She deeply appreciated the love they had for her and Kitty and their concern for her in the wake of Norman's death. However, at this moment, all she wanted was to be left alone with her cousins. Naomi would worry about her, but she wouldn't suffocate her. Laurie had lost her first husband, so she understood what Sibyl was feeling now. Sibyl felt a little guilty, but she feigned exhaustion so the people wouldn't linger. There would be plenty of time for them to commiserate with her at Norman's funeral and the reception afterward.

It would be held in her home, the frame house Norman had built as a monument to his importance. It was bigger than any house in town, was on a larger lot, and was in the central part of the street. A wide porch afforded entrance to a hall with large parlors opening off each side. Floor-to-ceiling windows offered views out to the street—passersby could see in as well—a reason why Sibyl preferred a sitting room at the back of the house. Stiff-backed Victorian furniture—Norman's choice—filled each room. Several large mirrors as well as family portraits hung over walls covered with white wallpaper featuring gold fleurs-de-lis. Sibyl disliked both rooms and entered them as seldom as possible.

"I'm really okay," she told the doctor. "It was a shock, but I'm over the worst of it. I just need some rest."

"You know they're here because they're worried about you."

"I'll be better by tomorrow. If they want to know what happened, they should talk to Cassie. She never misses any detail."

"Okay, I'll run everybody off, but they'll be back with enough food for a church supper before nightfall."

"Laurie and I will take care of that," Naomi said. "I don't want Sibyl to do anything but rest."

Not everyone took kindly to being told to leave, but it was hard to argue with the doctor. Within ten minutes, everybody was gone, leaving the three cousins alone.

"Do you think it was wise to leave Cassie and Horace in charge of the bank?" Naomi asked.

"Who else could I have asked? Either one of them knows more about it than I do."

"Norman was just like his brother," Laurie said. "I know I shouldn't say this, especially under the circumstances, but you should feel relieved to be out of that awful marriage. Everyone in town knows you were miserable."

Sibyl had never wanted to marry Norman. But after the events of a particularly tragic night, she'd been nearly out of her mind, and so emotionally distraught she'd given in when her father had threatened to disown her if she didn't marry Norman. At that moment, she hadn't cared what might happen to her. During the following seven years, she'd had plenty of opportunity to wonder if being disowned wouldn't have been better. It was humiliating to have to be ashamed of her husband, horrible to feel she had to hold her tongue in public when he'd done something disgraceful. Norman had some good qualities, but they never came close to compensating for the character traits that had made him the least liked person in Cactus Corner.

It was ironic that now Norman was dead, she should feel guilty. If he hadn't been so anxious to avoid talking to her at breakfast, he might still have been at home when the robbery started. But no, Norman would never have allowed the bank to be opened or closed by anyone else.

"I'm not going to allow you to feel guilty just because you're glad Norman is dead," Naomi said.

"I'm not glad," Sibyl objected. "He was a terrible husband and worse father, but I can't be glad he's dead."

"Then I'll be glad for you," Naomi said. "I'm not afraid he'll rise from the grave and come after me."

All three women laughed. Shocked at her behavior, Sibyl sobered quickly.

"But now that Norman *is* dead, what are you going to do about the bank?" Naomi asked.

"I have no idea."

"You could sell it," Laurie suggested.

"I don't even know enough to do that."

"You could combine it with Papa's bank," Naomi suggested.

"Which would put Cactus Corner back in the position of having just one bank."

"You don't think Papa will cheat anybody, do you?" Naomi loved her cousin, but she wouldn't allow anyone to criticize her father.

"Of course not, but I think everybody has been better off with a choice."

"I agree with her," Laurie said.

"So do I," Naomi countered, "but Sibyl doesn't know a thing about running a bank."

"I could hire Ethan to teach me."

"And what is Papa going to do while Ethan's helping you? He can't be the town's doctor and its banker."

Sibyl was tired of this conversation. "I don't know what I'll do, but the bank will stay closed until after Norman's funeral. That will give me time to think of something."

The women talked about funeral arrangements and what food the neighbors could bring for the wake.

"Now that I'm thoroughly depressed, I think I'll go home," Laurie finally said. "Jared and Steve are wonderful with the children, but I don't like to leave them too long. They tend to forget they have a ranch to take care of."

Naomi laughed. "Colby is just as bad. We shouldn't have needed any more proof that they were brothers."

Everyone in town knew Laurie and Naomi's husbands adored their children. That's why it had been so painful to have everybody know Norman had wanted so little to do with Kitty that he had planned to send her away to school at the tender age of six.

"Did anyone find out what happened to the stranger who stopped the robbery?" Naomi asked Sibyl.

"I asked everyone I talked to, but nobody saw him leave. With all the confusion, he probably just walked away."

"That's too bad. People have been saying we ought to stop depending on the soldiers at the fort and hire our own sheriff. From the way you said he handled a gun, that man sounds like a perfect candidate for the job."

He might appear on the surface to be the perfect candidate thanks to his fine shooting, but even though she'd shared only a moment with the stranger, Sibyl was certain *that* was something he'd never do.

❧

Logan brought his horse to a stop near his new camp—his permanent camp, he hoped. He'd pitched his tent in the pine forest that lined the Mogollon Rim. The small stream flowing nearby plunged noisily into one of the many brush-and-rock choked canyons that carried water from the Rim to the Verde River below. A series of sun-filled meadows offered forage for his horse while the forest provided all the meat he could eat. After dismounting and stripping his horse of its saddle, he led the animal to the creek to drink. A short distance away, a Hereford cow accompanied by her yearling calf was enjoying the cold, clear water. From her size, Logan expected she'd drop another calf any day now. She was late. All the cows he'd seen already had calves at their sides. He figured they belonged to the people living in the big house he'd seen when he was looking for a suitable place to camp. He'd spent two days observing movement around the ranch before choosing a site he hoped they wouldn't find before he had time to die.

He grinned when he saw the dog appear at the edge of the clearing. "If you've followed me again, I guess you're not afraid of me."

The dog watched Logan intently.

"It's not supper time yet," Logan said. "You're going to have to wait."

After staking his horse out to graze, Logan started a small fire to make coffee. For years he'd matched his adopted father drink for drink, but he stopped altogether when he decided to leave Chicago. He didn't want anything to cloud his memory or his appreciation of his last days. He wanted his experience of each moment to be crystal clear, every detail remembered, every minute savored. He'd always known in the back of his head that he would die someday, but he'd assumed he wouldn't need to face his mortality for decades to come. Learning he had only a few months left had been such a shock it had knocked him out of the pattern of living he'd occupied for most of his life. Nothing would ever be the same again.

Taking his coffee, he headed toward the Rim. The dog followed. A thick carpet of needles still damp from yesterday's rain muffled his footsteps. The tangy scent of pine filled the air with a crisp, clean fragrance unlike anything he'd experienced in Chicago. The air under the pines was cool and invigorating. It made him wonder why he'd given up working outside to spend his days in an office. Yet he knew the answer.

The business. It had always been about the business.

He'd cared so much about it that he'd let it crowd everything else out of his life. But what good did that do him now? While it was thriving, he was dying. He was a wealthy man who wouldn't live to spend a tithe of the money he'd worked so hard to acquire.

He reached the edge of the Rim and looked out over the valley two thousand feet below. The Verde River was a thin ribbon that meandered through the valley, collecting water from various streams and canyons as it went. Cottonwood leaves hung breathless in the still air, waiting for the monsoon rains to reinvigorate the landscape. The white faces and red bodies of fat Herefords were scattered as far as he could see, some in small groups, others singly, still others accompanied only by their calves. It was a peaceful scene, yet one that thrummed with a vitality whose power to impart life lay in quiet strength rather than raucous noise. He'd never seen that before. Would he have time to learn to understand it?

The dog had followed Logan at a safe distance until something caused him to turn and run back into the surrounding forest. A moment later, Logan heard the sound of a horse's hooves. He turned to see a young man riding toward him. It was pointless to attempt to hide. Maybe he could convince the young man to keep his presence secret. He wanted to preserve his solitude. He wanted no witnesses to his bouts of weakness and nausea. Pulling himself up to his full height, he prepared to meet the stranger.

Three

As HE DREW CLOSER, LOGAN REALIZED THE MAN WAS no more than a teenager. He appeared determined to discover the reason this interloper was camping on his grazing range, but he was cautious about approaching a stranger alone. Logan decided to make it easy for the boy. "Get down and have a cup of coffee. I just made it, so it's still hot. I'm sure you want to know who I am, what I'm doing here, and how long I plan to stay."

The boy looked uncertain. "I didn't know anybody was up here until I saw your smoke."

"It looked like a nice place to set up camp for a bit. Water and graze for the horse, and plenty of game for me. Don't worry about your cows. I'd never shoot one of them."

"My uncle paid a lot of money for them," the boy said. "We take looking after them very serious."

"And you should. The coffee's good. You really ought to try it." Logan was careful to make it clear he wasn't carrying a weapon and didn't plan to approach his tent.

"I appreciate the offer, but my uncle would knock

me upside the head if I did anything so stupid without knowing something about you."

"Well, let me try to set your mind at rest. My name is Logan. I come from Chicago."

"You mean the Chicago in Illinois?" The boy was obviously impressed.

"It's the only Chicago I know. Anyway, I was tired of working in an office all the time, so I decided to come west. This seemed like a nice place to settle for a bit, so I did. While I expect you'll tell your uncle about me being here, I hope you won't go spreading it around. I'll go into town maybe every week or so, but I like to spend most of my time alone. I won't bother you for long. Now tell me your name and what you're doing here."

"I'm Steve Smith. My uncle and I own the Green Valley Ranch."

"You're mighty young to be a ranch owner."

"I'm old enough." The boy seemed defensive. "We sold our ranch in Texas and came out here. Uncle Jared says it's like changing one desert for another."

Jared! That was the name of one of his brothers. Was it possible this was the Jared Smith he'd read about? It wasn't likely that a Jared Smith from Texas could be his lost brother, but he couldn't ignore the possibility. Wanting to see his brothers before he died was the whole reason for coming west, but he didn't plan to reveal his identity because he didn't want to leave them mourning. Just seeing them and getting to know a little about them would be enough.

"I understand the rainy season will start soon," Logan said. "It is a little dry."

"The rain won't last long. It's usually just enough to keep everything from drying up and blowing away.

I appreciate the offer for coffee, but I've got to be going. You might want to be careful. Some gang tried to rob the bank yesterday. Some guy showed up and shot every one of them dead, but there might be more robbers hanging around. They'd be mighty desperate."

"I'll make sure to keep a careful watch. Who was the man who shot them?"

"Nobody's ever seen him before. He just walked into the bank, shot the robbers, and then disappeared. You'd think he'd want to stay. There might be a reward for those guys."

"Was there?"

"I don't know, but there might have been."

Logan recognized the eagerness of a young man for an exciting adventure to relieve the humdrum nature of his life. He wanted to tell Steve he was more fortunate than he knew, but he knew the boy wouldn't believe him. "I hope it's all right if I stay here awhile. I'll even help watch your cows. Tell your uncle I said to drop by anytime. If I'm not at the camp, I won't be far away. This is beautiful country. There's a canyon a little ways from here I'm looking forward to exploring."

"If you get hurt in some of these canyons, nobody will ever find you."

"I'll be careful. You, too. It's a long way down to your ranch."

"I know an easy way down. Maybe I'll show it to you if you're here very long."

"Thanks. I'd like that."

As Logan watched the boy ride away, he felt a pang of regret. He could have had a son like that boy. As it was, he was going to leave this world with no one to mourn or remember him. Not even Bridgette. He'd known from the beginning she was only marrying him for the money.

For some reason, that made him think of the woman in the bank. He didn't know why he should be thinking of her now. The moment he'd entered the bank he'd been focused on the robbers. He'd barely had time to remember what she looked like before people started rushing in from the street. Still, there was something about her that stood out even amid the confusion. Maybe it was the way she remained calm when the robber tried to use her as a shield. Maybe it was that she was sensible enough to appear to faint so he could have a clear shot. Maybe it was something as ordinary as her beauty, the way she dressed, or the way she wore her hair. He didn't know what it was, but the impression was no less powerful for lack of a reason.

She was not an ordinary woman.

It was a foolish waste of time to be thinking about her or any other woman. He was a man without a future. He had begun to mark off the days. It was the only way he had to guess how much time he had left. Though he'd traveled as quickly as boat and horse could take him, the trip from Chicago had taken more than a month. He'd been such an unpleasant traveling companion people avoided him. Traveling on horseback had allowed him to keep his distance. He'd chosen this spot to set up his camp for the same reason, but he hadn't been suffering quite as much lately, with the exception of a few bad spells. Maybe it was the clean air and release from the strain of running a large and successful business. Maybe it was the hours of peaceful sleep or the physical exercise. Whatever it was, he was grateful to be feeling better even if it was a false security. Each good day was a gift he intended to enjoy to the fullest.

He looked up when the dog emerged from the trees. "I thought you'd be back. Not willing to give up the free meals yet? Don't worry. I won't quit until you're able to hunt on your own." He swallowed the last of his coffee. "I guess it's time to go hunting again. It takes a lot to keep you fed."

Maybe he'd head into town tomorrow. The robbery had kept him from conducting any of his errands. Setting up an account with the bank could wait, but not the purchase of some staples, the most important being more coffee. He expected he'd soon receive a visit from Steve's uncle. Hospitality required that he offer his guest something to drink. Besides, he wanted to convince the man to let him stay on his land. He liked it here. It was nothing like the life he'd led in Chicago. Much to his surprise, that had a strong appeal to him. Being away from the city and his life-consuming work had forced him to confront himself, to see who he *really* was. Much to his surprise, he had no idea.

He knew he'd been adopted at five after his parents died from a mysterious fever. He knew he had two younger brothers. He'd been taken in by a man who traveled the Santa Fe Trail before concentrating his business in Chicago. As far back as Logan could remember, he'd worked alongside his father. Being without children of his own, Samuel Lowe had treated Logan as his own son, had given him his own name. In turn, the boy had bonded with his father so firmly his only interests had been his father's interests.

Now every part of the only life he'd known had

been left behind. His slate had been wiped clean, and his image had disappeared from the mirror. In its place was a man he didn't know. Instead of a three-piece black wool suit, stiff cotton shirt, and ascot, he wore faded denim pants and a plaid shirt. His topcoat was now a rain slick. His bowler hat had been replaced by a wide-brimmed hat with a flat crown, his square-toed shoes by boots. His house with its fifteen rooms and servants had been exchanged for a tent and sleeping bag, his carriage for a single horse. His kitchen was a coffeepot, two pans, and a Dutch oven.

The price for all this freedom had been the loss of who he was. It hadn't taken Logan long to realize he didn't regret it. It had been a surprise at first, but he'd been so consumed with the problem of getting as far as possible from Chicago as *quickly* as possible that he hadn't had time to do more than face the inevitability of his death. Once he had done that, what he'd left behind didn't matter any longer. He intended his death to be private and to take place in beautiful, peaceful surroundings. There were few better places for that than the Verde River Valley.

He hadn't intended to develop an interest in anyone, but already that was a danger. He'd been intrigued by the woman at the bank. There was something about her that wouldn't allow him to forget her.

Then there was Steve. Maybe it was what Steve stood for rather than the boy himself, but he could see himself in the boy's shoes, proud in the saddle, on the cusp of manhood, his whole future before him. In a way he represented the family Logan had never had. Bridgette had never spoken of wanting children, and he'd been too busy to give it any thought.

It was time to stop thinking about what might have been. He didn't know how he was going to fill his remaining days, but he couldn't spend them dwelling on the past or a future he wouldn't have. The present was all he had. He had to find a way to make the best use of it. He'd been feeling better today. He'd ride into town in a day or two. He didn't have many good days. He didn't want to waste them.

"Keep on the lookout for squirrels while I'm gone," Logan told the dog. "I never knew how much I disliked the damned little critters."

⁓

Sibyl sat on the front pew, her hands clasped so tightly her knuckles had turned white. Kitty sat next to her, her body rigid, her eyes staring straight ahead. Sibyl wished she could have spared her daughter, but there were certain rituals in small towns that couldn't be avoided and which required slavish adherence to the rules. Funerals ranked near the top of the list. Only immediate family was allowed to sit in the front pew. They must all wear black.

Sibyl wore a black dress, hat, and veil, but Kitty wore her navy blue Sunday best. If that wasn't good enough, it was too bad.

The clapboard church was small with bare walls. The wooden pews had straight backs that made sitting in them uncomfortable. They kept the parishioners awake and eager for the end of the service. All the windows along the side of the church were of plain glass, but the two behind the altar were stained glass scenes of Christ's birth and crucifixion. Norman and his brother had given them in memory of their parents. Sibyl and her cousins had paid for the piano that made the singing bearable.

Sibyl had asked for an open casket. She and Kitty had stood next to it as what must have been every person in Cactus Corner above the age of twelve—and quite a few younger—came to offer condolences. That was fine. What she found difficult to bear was the extravagant praise being offered from the pulpit by Reverend Simpson. To hear him talk, you would have believed that Norman had been kindhearted, generous, fair, loving…it was useless to go on. He'd been none of those, and everyone in town knew it. She thought it a sacrilege to mouth such untruths about a man just because he was dead. It had to be even more difficult for Kitty to hear a man who'd treated her so brutally praised so lavishly. She unclenched her fists, took her daughter's hand, and gave it a squeeze. Kitty didn't look up, but she could feel her daughter's tension ease.

After what seemed like an eternity, Reverend Simpson brought the service to a close. The pallbearers came forward—Jared, Horace, and her cousins Ethan and Ben—to carry the casket in the procession to the cemetery. Sibyl and Kitty followed close behind. Her cousins Naomi and Laurie came to walk on either side of them.

Laurie whispered, "It'll soon be over."

Laurie understood better than anyone else. She'd been married to Noah, Norman's brother. There hadn't been much to choose between the two men.

Sibyl would have been content with *ashes to ashes, dust to dust*, but the reverend hadn't exhausted his bag of fulsome praise. By the time he finished the grave-side service and invited the mourners back to Sibyl's house for a collation and a chance to express their sorrow in person, she was squeezing Naomi's hand so hard it had to hurt. But the formal part of burying Norman was almost over. Sibyl promised herself that once the last person left her house tonight, she'd never again pretend that Norman had been anything but the bastard he was.

❦

Logan hadn't intended to attend Norman Spencer's funeral service, but the town had closed down for the occasion and he found himself swept along by the townspeople despite any protest he might offer. He couldn't do any of the things he'd come into town to do until the reception at Mrs. Spencer's house was over and people returned to their jobs. He didn't really mind the delay. He was impressed that apparently everyone thought so highly of the banker. If only half of what the minister said was true, Norman Spencer must have been an outstanding man. His death would be a great loss to the community.

His widow's behavior appeared to support that view. She looked to be in such deep shock she was unable to show any emotion. Their daughter appeared to be in such distress she clung to her mother and the woman who walked on her other side. Coming from Chicago where he knew hundreds of people, Logan found it awkward being in a small town where his only speaking acquaintance was a teenage boy. He drifted toward Steve when the graveside service ended.

"I had expected to see your uncle before now."

Steve recognized him immediately, but no one else did. He'd escaped through the back door before anyone else saw him. "You would have if Aunt Sibyl's husband hadn't been killed. Laurie's been staying with her, which means we've been looking after ourselves and eating leftovers."

"Who's Laurie?"

"She's my uncle's wife and Sibyl's cousin. She's the blond woman holding Kitty's hand. The other woman is Naomi. She's also Sibyl's cousin. Colby is her husband."

Logan didn't attempt to keep all the names and relationships straight. It was a small town. It was inevitable that many people would be kin. "I'm glad she has a lot of family to support her. It's tragic to lose a husband, especially one as outstanding as Mr. Spencer."

Steve cussed. "I don't know why the preacher had to carry on like he did. Norman was a bastard and just about everybody disliked him. He was the richest man in town, and he never let anyone forget it. People had to beg for loans. Then he'd stick his nose in their business until they paid him back. It got so bad people got together and opened a new bank. Norman got a lot nicer after that, but nobody forgot what he used to be like. I couldn't stand him. He was hateful to Sibyl."

Logan doubted he'd ever seen three more beautiful women in one place, but Sibyl had the kind of classic beauty that could start a man to having embarrassing fantasies. He couldn't imagine any man being hateful to her.

"Sibyl was forced to marry Norman," Steve explained. "She didn't like him one bit. You can ask anybody. I don't know what got into the preacher. I'm going to ask Martha if her father's been sampling his communion wine."

Logan lost interest in the lengthening catalog of names without faces. "Taking over the running of the bank is going to be a difficult undertaking for Mrs. Spencer," Logan said. "I hope some of those men you mentioned can help her."

"Norman never let her go near the bank so she has no idea what to do," Steve told him. "He didn't like Colby or Jared, either."

Small towns were worse than big ones for people letting their family conflicts spill over into their business relationships—and big towns were bad enough. Logan had witnessed such a clash between his father and his uncle firsthand. So Mrs. Spencer would be on her own. Surely there was someone in Cactus Corner who knew something about banking or business, at least enough to help her until she got on her feet.

"Are you going to the reception?" Steve asked.

"No. I only went to the funeral because everything in town is closed, and people seemed set on everyone being there."

"You ought to come. You could meet my uncle."

"I'd feel too uncomfortable not knowing anyone." Nor did he look forward to the curious and pitying looks he was sure to receive.

Steve laughed. "My uncle didn't know Laurie when he went to her husband's funeral, but they ended up getting married. Now I've got a little cousin with another just arrived."

That certainly wouldn't happen to Logan. He didn't intend to strike up any friendships. He was wary of even casual acquaintances, excepting Steve. "I think I'll look around town for a bit. I may wait for stores to open or come back another time."

"If you want, you can come by the ranch to see my uncle," Steve said. "We're babysitting while Laurie stays with Sibyl. That means I have to run all the errands while Jared stays home."

There was that name again. Logan wouldn't get his hopes up, but it was something he was going to have to check into sooner or later.

One of his reasons for leaving Chicago had been to find his brothers, but they were grown men with lives of their own that had no place for him. It was probable that the money he could leave them could make a difference, but he didn't have to do it in person. He could leave money in his will. That way they could benefit without having to watch him die.

Even if he hadn't been looking for his brothers, he was glad he'd left Chicago. He hadn't realized his work was taking so much there was virtually nothing left for himself. Now whatever was left was his. He no longer had to plan. He no longer had to worry about the consequences of what he did. For the first time in his life, he was completely free.

❧

"Are you sure you don't need me to stay with you tonight?" Laurie asked Sibyl. "Jared and Steve won't mind. They fight over who gets to take care of the baby."

Sibyl moved through the two parlors plumping pillows, straightening doilies, and repositioning chairs. She would have to decide tomorrow what furniture to move to make room for the reception. She might remove some of it permanently. She'd never liked it because it reminded her too much of Norman's mother, who had crocheted every doily in the room.

"Go back to your family. If I need anything, there are a dozen people close by itching to bring food, provide comfort, and try to find out what I plan to do with the bank."

"Forget about the bank. You're *free*. And don't pretend you don't know what I mean. You don't have to follow his orders or swallow your pride because you don't want people to know your husband treats you like an unpaid servant. You don't have to wonder if he can tell what you're thinking."

Sibyl didn't pretend she didn't know what Laurie meant. "After seven years, it's going to take some getting used to. I never wished Norman dead. I know you find that hard to believe, but I didn't. I just wished I could find some way to be free of him. I even considered stealing enough money to run away." She laughed. "That just shows how desperate I had become. I thought we'd worked out ways to put up with each other until he took it in his head to send Kitty away to school."

Laurie's expression registered shock and anger. "The child is only six. What was he planning to do? Send her to a convent?"

"I don't know. He wouldn't talk about it at home, so I had gone to the bank to confront him when the robbers entered. You should have seen him. He acted insulted, like he could just order them out and they'd go." Her mouth twisted. "Sometimes I wondered if he was really sane. His mother gave him a completely unrealistic view of the world." Sibyl sighed. "I never liked her. She was a stiff, proud woman. After being compared unfavorably to her for seven years, I started to hate her."

"I know how you feel. Noah did the same to me. Now if you really don't need me, I think I will go home. I miss having my husband's arms around me at night."

"I'm glad Jared is such a wonderful husband. It's your reward for putting up with Noah."

"You should start looking around for a man you can love, one who could be a real father to Kitty." Laurie took Sibyl's hands in hers. "He'll have to be a real prince charming to make up for the man you loved disappearing, and those years with Norman."

Sibyl felt the bottom drop out of her stomach. She hoped Laurie believed her reaction was due to Norman's death, not the horrific night that still haunted her dreams. "I'm not interested in men or marriage. As you pointed out, I have enough money to support Kitty and myself. I don't have to subject myself to a man ever again."

"That's how I felt when I met Jared. It didn't take long for me to change my mind."

"There aren't any more men like Jared and Colby."

"They have a brother."

"The chances of him showing up here are about one in a bigger number than I can imagine. Even if he did, there's no assurance he'd be anything like his brothers."

"Wouldn't that be something? Three cousins marrying three brothers."

"Go home, Laurie. You've been out in the sun too long."

Laurie grinned. "I know it's a silly idea, but it got your mind off dreary thoughts. Naomi will check on you tomorrow, but if you need anything, don't hesitate to let me know."

Sibyl sighed with relief when she closed the door behind Laurie. She loved her cousins, was thankful for the support of other relatives, but she needed quiet and to be alone. Her life had taken a dramatic turn, one she was unprepared for regardless of the years she'd spent dreaming about it. This wasn't about the bank or even about Kitty. It was about herself. She was twenty-three years old, yet she'd never lived by herself or been allowed to make her own decisions. No one had asked her opinion or encouraged her to have one. She'd spent years trying not to think, not to have opinions or ideas because it made life easier. Every time she'd become so frustrated and angry she was tempted to rebel, she thought of the effect it would have on Kitty and swallowed her resentment.

That had changed when Norman decided to send Kitty away to school. She had been prepared to fight for her daughter's future. Now she had one question that needed an answer.

What did she want to do about her own future?

Sibyl caught herself wishing Naomi had chosen this evening to pay her a visit, but she knew she had to handle this by herself. If she was ever going to stand on her own two feet, she had to begin with her parents. Her father was striding about the parlor like he owned it while her mother studied the furnishings with envy. Sibyl thought she just might tell her mother to take her pick. It would give her an excuse to buy furniture of her own choosing.

"You know you can't run the bank," her father was saying. "You must turn it over to me. If I can't find the time to manage it, I'll sell it for you."

Sibyl thought she must have loved her father at some point in her life. Surely a young girl would love the man who protected her, made her feel safe and loved. Only he'd never made her feel loved and not even particularly safe. He was unhappy that she was his only child. He was even unhappier she was a girl. She couldn't recall that he'd ever put his feelings into words. Looks she caught before he turned away, things not said or shared, times she was ignored or considered deficient of understanding, being left entirely in female company—all of these spoke to his belief that she was a disappointment to him. She could probably have accepted all of that because that was the way most men thought of women.

But all of that changed when he killed the man she loved and forced her to marry one she didn't.

"You wouldn't want to be thought the forward kind of woman who would go into business," her mother was saying. "It's very unladylike."

Her mother conveniently glossed over the fact that her cousin Mae Oliver owned a millinery shop, Polly Drummond ran a bakery, and Amber Johnson worked in the mercantile. But making hats, baking bread, and selling household goods were considered suitable work for women. Setting herself up as the head of a bank—a job that would put her in competition with men—was something else entirely.

"Naturally I'll handle all your financial matters," her father said. "Norman didn't take me into his confidence on all his dealings, but as his lawyer, I have a good understanding of his holdings. You're a wealthy woman. You don't have to worry about anything."

"I don't want to be left out of all the decisions," Sibyl said.

"You owe a debt of gratitude to your father," her mother said.

"Why?" Sibyl asked.

"Norman's will," her mother said. "As bad as it is, it would have been worse without your father's influence."

"How do you mean?" Sibyl asked her father.

"Naturally Norman didn't believe he could leave you to handle any of his business interests. After Noah died, he planned to tie everything up in a trust to be handled by a distant cousin. I managed to convince him that it would be impossible for a man living in Pennsylvania to understand anything about life in the Arizona Territory. He filled the will with a lot of tedious and, I believe, unfair restrictions, but I managed to convince him to name me the executor."

"He never signed that will," Sibyl said.

"Why not?" her father asked. "How do you know?"

"He made the mistake of leaving it out on his desk," Sibyl told him. "I figured I had a right to read it since I was his wife. When I read what he wanted you to do, how he intended Kitty and me to live, I got so mad I tore it up. You don't have to look at me like I've committed a crime," Sibyl said to her father's stunned reaction. "He hadn't signed it."

"He said he was going to sign it as soon as he read it over one more time."

"He probably wanted time to see if he could think of more ways to humiliate me."

Her father ignored her. "But that means Norman died without a will."

"No, he didn't."

"He tore up the will leaving everything to Noah," her father said. "I saw him."

"He never destroyed the will you had him make when we got married," Sibyl said. "That one leaves everything to me."

"He said he lost that will when we left Kentucky."

"I took it," Sibyl confessed. "I knew he intended to make a new will. I kept it in case I ever needed it."

"That makes it very easy to turn everything over to your father," her mother said.

"I don't want to do that."

"But you can't handle everything by yourself. What if you should lose everything? Think of your future. Think of Kitty."

"I am thinking of the future," Sibyl insisted, "of both our futures, but I don't see why that means I have to give up control of my own property. Laurie has kept control of the store, and she's doing just fine."

"She has a husband to take care of everything for her."

"They make all decisions about the ranch together, but Laurie manages the store by herself."

"She has her father to help."

"That man is such a terrible businessman he forced his daughter to marry a man she disliked so he wouldn't lose his share of the store."

That was so close to what her parents had done that neither spoke.

"I intend to handle my own affairs," Sibyl told them. "If I need help, I'll ask. But no one is going to tell me what to do with my property or my daughter. I've spent seven years married to a man who didn't want to be married to me and who disliked my daughter."

"That's because—" her mother began.

"I *know* why," Sibyl said, "but no one is ever going to put the reason into words. I can forgive you for forcing me to marry Norman—it wasn't a good solution, but it was probably the only one possible—but I will not forgive you *that*." She realized she was so angry she was shaking. She had to calm down. She would never convince anyone she could handle her own affairs if she couldn't control her emotions. She'd done that for seven years with Norman, and she could do it now.

"Now I want you to go home. I've had a very difficult few days, and I need time to get back to normal. I still don't know how this is going to affect Kitty. Tomorrow I have to go to the bank. I can't let Cassie and Horace lose their jobs."

"I can help," her father offered.

"I want to do this by myself. All my life I've been treated as though I can't do anything beyond keep house. I think I can do more. Starting tomorrow I intend to find out."

❧

"You didn't have to come back so soon," Cassie said to Sibyl. "Horace and I could have handled things until you felt up to it."

Sibyl was unhappy to find Cassie waiting when she came to open the bank. She had hoped to spend the day alone in Norman's office. It was time to decide if she would sell the bank or try to manage it herself.

"I'm not opening the bank," Sibyl said. "I don't know anything beyond unlocking the door at the start of the day and closing up at the end."

Cassie laughed. "Some days that's about all we do. The new bank has taken away a lot of business."

"Norman never talked about that, but I knew. I guess I'll have to get familiar with the accounts. Do you know where they are?"

Cassie laughed again. "Of course not. Everybody knows Norman only hired me because he thought my looks would bring in customers. He thought I was dumber than a mule deer. You could have cut out his tongue before he would have told me where to find anything in his office."

"All I have is the combination to the safe. I found it in his wallet."

"Do you have the key to his desk?"

Sibyl extracted a ring of keys from her pocket. "I'm hoping it's one of these."

Cassie sighed in disgust. "How did Norman expect you to deal with his affairs when he died if he didn't tell you anything?"

"I don't believe Norman thought he would die, and certainly not before me."

"No point in fretting about what can't be changed. If you're not going to open today, what will I tell people who come by?"

"That we're closed."

"When will you reopen?"

"I don't know."

"It's better to have a specific date. You can always change it later."

Sibyl didn't know why Norman hadn't given Cassie more responsibility. The young woman was as capable as any man when it came to common sense. "Tell people three days from now. I ought to have made up my mind what to do by then."

"I hope you decide to keep the bank," Cassie said.

"It's about time people in this town learned a woman can do more than cook and take care of babies."

"I'm not interested in setting any precedents, just doing what's best for Kitty and me."

"That's staying here and running this bank." Cassie grinned broadly. "And making sure Horace and I still have jobs."

Sibyl had already thought of that. Cassie and Horace weren't the only ones who depended on the bank for a job. But if she kept the bank, it was quite possible she would ruin it, and no one would have a job. It was enough to make her wish Norman were still alive—as long as she wasn't married to him.

"Don't worry about me," Cassie said before Sibyl could think of a suitable reply. "I can always get a job, but you need to think of Horace and the others."

"I intend to think of all of you," Sibyl assured her. "Now I'd better see about getting started."

She told herself it was silly to feel uncomfortable walking into Norman's office, but she couldn't shake the feeling that she was intruding. She had no doubt he wouldn't have wanted her here. She could feel the disapproval emanating from all around the room.

"You might as well get used to it," she said to the antagonistic space. "I'm going to be here for a long time."

But was she? She didn't know anything about running a bank, and she had no assurance she would like it or have a talent for it if she did. Right now, she was going through the paces. Once she got over the shock of Norman's death, she could begin to sort out how she truly felt about things.

She tried five keys before she found the one that

unlocked his desk. Norman had one of those hand-crafted desks where one lock secured all the drawers. She found nothing of interest until she opened a deep drawer that contained several large volumes. She took out the one on top and opened it. A brief scanning of the pages proved it to be a meticulous record of the loans Norman had made, the amount of the repayments, and the dates on which they were made. The only thing remarkable about it was that there were so few. Business was worse than Norman had led her to believe. Was the bank making enough money to pay its employees? Was Norman too proud to admit he was losing money?

Other volumes in the drawer did little more than confirm that the new bank had taken away much of Norman's business. If the situation was so bad, was there any point in keeping the bank open? She'd always assumed Norman was rich, but was he? She went through all the volumes in the desk without finding an answer. Maybe there was something in the safe. She had to work the combination three times before she could get the heavy door open. When she did, she couldn't believe what she saw.

Sibyl had rarely handled money. All her life, she'd gotten what she needed from one store or another, and her father or Norman had settled the bills. She had handled a few gold and silver coins, but she'd seen paper money so rarely it seemed like something children would play with. There were stacks of it in the safe, many with very large numbers written on them. Sacks covering the bottom of the safe contained more gold coins than she'd thought existed in the whole town.

There was no way this could be right. Unless…

She stared at the contents in horror. She knew where Norman had gotten that money, and the knowledge made her blood run cold. Instinctively, she backed away. What could she do? She didn't want to keep it, but it would be impossible to give it away. She was so distracted she almost didn't hear the knock on the door. Without a second's hesitation, she slammed the safe shut and spun the dial. On shaky legs she managed to get to the chair at the desk and sit down before her legs gave out.

"Come in." Her words came out in a whisper. She cleared her throat. "Come in." When Cassie entered the office, a single glance told Sibyl the young woman was dancing with excitement.

"There's a man here to see you."

"I told you to tell everyone the bank wasn't open today."

"I did, but he wants to see you anyway."

"Who is it?"

"The stranger who shot the bandits."

Four

"WHAT DOES HE WANT?" SIBYL ASKED.

"I don't know," Cassie answered. "He asked to speak to you."

"Tell him to come in."

He was probably hoping for a reward. He didn't look prosperous. She had no idea how much to offer him. What did you give a man for saving your life? Money seemed like a poor substitute, but she had plenty of it. If that's what he wanted, it's what he'd get.

When he walked into her office, his appearance shocked her all over again. It wasn't just the swelling that had distorted his features. He had the look of a man who was seriously ill. He looked to be well over six feet tall with the bones of a big man, but his body had wasted away to the point that he looked like a skeleton. His walk was slow and effortful. Only his eyes showed the vigor she guessed must have filled his body in the past. Stepping from behind Norman's huge desk, she moved toward him, her hand extended.

"My name is Sibyl Spencer. Norman Spencer was my husband. I want to thank you for saving my life. Cassie's and Horace's as well. You were extremely brave."

"I don't want any thanks. It's what any man would have done in my position."

"Nevertheless, you're the man who did it. You're a hero. Cassie hasn't stopped talking about you, and Horace's wife has added you to her nightly prayers. I give thanks for you at least once every hour."

The man looked upset, maybe like he was sorry he had come. She thought for a moment he might leave, but he seemed to reach a resolve.

"I'm not a hero, and I don't want anyone to think of me like that. I'm grateful you didn't tell anyone who I was. I don't want attention, I don't want any thanks, and I don't want to intrude on anyone's prayers or thoughts. I would rather leave than have to face that."

Sibyl found it difficult to understand how anyone could feel that way, but he appeared quite sincere. "I'm sorry, but that's impossible. I'll remember you for as long as I live. Because of you, I'll get to see my daughter grow up." He looked so frail she was afraid he might collapse. "Won't you have a seat and tell me how I might help you?"

The man hesitated before taking the seat she offered him. Sibyl circled her desk and sat down. "I want to offer you a reward," she said as soon as she was seated. "I don't know how much is appropriate—"

"I don't want a reward!"

The words came out with such force, Sibyl was shocked into silence.

The man struggled to get himself under control before saying, "I didn't come here for money. I have more than enough for my needs."

"One can always use some new clothes or a nice

meal in a restaurant." Sibyl was surprised when he glanced down at his clothes then looked up and smiled.

"I dress this way because it's comfortable. Really, I don't want any money. I came here to offer my help."

He could hardly have said anything that would have surprised Sibyl more. How could this man who looked like a vagabond help her? She struggled to keep her shock from showing in her face. When his smile widened, she knew she had failed.

"Let me introduce myself. My name is Logan Holstock. I've only just arrived in the Arizona Territory. I was coming to the bank to open an account when I surprised the robbers."

"Why did you choose our bank?"

"It was the first one I saw. The building was so impressive I figured it must be a successful bank."

Of course it was impressive. Norman wouldn't have had it any other way.

"Is there another bank I should investigate?"

The more Mr. Holstock talked, the more confused she became. He didn't talk like a vagrant, and he didn't act like one. He intended to open an account, but he looked like he'd spent his last dollar weeks ago. He was clearly very ill, but he appeared to be ignoring it. "There is another bank," Sibyl said, "but I hope you will choose ours." She couldn't say *mine*. It didn't seem right. "Servicing your account will give me a chance to thank you for keeping us from being robbed."

"I wish you wouldn't mention thanking me again." He reached into the pocket of his thin jacket and pulled out a wallet. She knew very little about men's wallets, but she could tell expensive leather when she saw it. How would such a man have such a wallet?

Her surprise was even greater when he withdrew a handful of bills and handed them to her. A quick count added up to over five hundred dollars.

"I hope this will cover my needs for the next two months or so."

She had trouble finding her voice. "It would be more than adequate for all but the most extravagant spender."

"I'm not a spendthrift. Now to the other reason I'm here." He paused as though looking for the right words. "I've been told your husband kept you ignorant of the workings of the bank. I can only imagine how daunting taking over his position must be, so I want to help any way I can. I haven't always been as you see me now. I was in commerce for a long time. I know how to handle difficult customers and build a business. I know how to read a ledger and balance books. I understand income versus expenses."

Sibyl didn't know what to say. She was irritated that anyone in town had thought it was acceptable to talk about her to a stranger. Cactus Corner was growing rapidly, but it was still a small town. People stuck together, especially those who were related. They didn't give out that kind of information to just anybody.

But someone had. It would be foolish to ignore an offer of help just because she was irritated. Yet it seemed impossible that he could do all he said. Where would he have learned it? If he knew so much, how could he have ended up as he was now? She knew nothing about him. Could she trust him? There was no one to vouch for him. She didn't even know enough to be able to tell if he was doing the work correctly. Apparently, he guessed what was going through her mind.

"I know I'm coming to you without references. You don't know if you can trust me or whether I can do what I say. But unless I'm mistaken, you don't have the experience to know what work needs to be done or how to do it."

He was a stranger, an unknown entity, and a man whose appearance was against him. So why did she feel she could trust him? "You have gauged my situation exactly," she told him, "so you can understand why I'm reluctant to accept your offer."

"What have you got to lose? If you can't learn how to manage this bank, you'll go broke. If that's the case, I can't see anyone wanting to buy it. Your only alternatives are to sell it immediately if you can find a buyer, or settle in and learn how to run it."

Sibyl thought of the money sitting in the safe. Was it enough to last for the rest of her life? She had no idea. Even if it was enough for her, what about Kitty's education? Boarding school would be expensive. Was it possible to find a buyer quickly? Even so, her customers would need access to their accounts. She couldn't just close up and wait for a buyer to show up.

"Are you on good terms with the owners of the other bank?" Mr. Holstock asked.

"Yes. The biggest investors are my cousins and their husbands."

"Do you feel you could ask any one of them to take the time to teach you?"

She'd already thought of that. The only person deeply involved in the management of the bank was her cousin Ethan, and he didn't have the spare time to teach her how to be his competition. Nor did she feel it was fair to ask him now that she'd had time to consider the matter in more detail. "No, I don't. We're a close family, but we're all responsible for ourselves."

"Do you think he could spare the time to look at my work and tell you if I'm honest and capable?"

Ethan was very busy, but maybe Colby or Jared could help in a pinch. They had their own businesses, but they would be sure to know if Mr. Holstock was cheating her. "You say your name is Holstock. One of my cousins is married to a Jared Smith, but he was born a Holstock. He came from Texas."

"I'm from Chicago, so I'm sure there's no connection."

She hadn't thought so, but Holstock was an unusual name, and Jared and Colby had a missing brother somewhere. But beyond having a big-framed body, Logan Holstock didn't bear the slightest resemblance to them. "Sorry. I seem to have wandered from the problem at hand." She took a deep breath and made her decision. It didn't make sense, but she felt drawn to this man. Maybe it was just that he'd saved her life, but she was curious to know more about him. "I have no way of knowing if you're honest, if you can balance a ledger, or even if you can read. I wouldn't know anything about you except that you're very brave and an excellent shot. But you could very easily have backed out of the bank and left us to our fate. Because you didn't, I'm going to take a chance that you can help me. I have to be honest and say I would never have considered this for one minute if I weren't desperate."

She did need someone to explain the mysteries of all those figures that filled so many books, but maybe "desperate" wasn't the right word. Maybe she was fearful she would fail on her own. Maybe she just needed to feel that she wasn't facing this battle alone. Maybe it was the feeling there was more to this man than met the eye, and she was curious to find out what it might be.

"I understand," Logan said. "If I do anything to upset you or cause you to question my honesty or my work, just tell me, and I'll leave."

"That goes without saying. Now about your wages."

"I don't want to be paid."

That was completely unexpected. "Why not?"

"I have enough money for the time I'm going to be here."

"You're already planning to leave?"

He took a moment to answer. "Let's say I'm not *planning* to leave but *expecting* it."

"I would feel better paying you."

"Why don't we wait to see if I'm worth being paid?"

That seemed a reasonable, if unexpected, request. "I have to tell you the bank isn't doing a lot of business. My husband was a very arrogant man. He offended so many people they opened a new bank so people wouldn't have to endure his rudeness any longer."

"I'm sure things will change now that you're in charge. I need to ask one favor. Don't tell anyone I'm the one who shot the robbers."

"Why?"

"I don't want people staring at me. I—" An abrupt change came over him. He looked uncomfortable, maybe even unwell. He got to his feet. "I need to be going, but I'll be here first thing in the morning. I know accepting the help of a stranger is a big gamble for you. I promise you will not regret it."

With that, he turned and left her office with quicker

steps than he had entered it. He could have hardly gone through the front door when Cassie knocked and entered without waiting to be invited.

"What did he want? Did he ask for a reward? How much did you promise to give him?"

"He didn't ask for a reward, and he refused one when I offered."

"Why? He looks sick, not crazy."

"He says he has experience in business. He has offered to help me learn how to manage the bank."

"You didn't believe him, did you? I bet the closest he's been to any business is begging for handouts."

Sibyl picked up the money Holstock had given her and handed it to Cassie. "He was coming to the bank to open an account the other morning. Here's the money he wants to deposit."

Cassie counted the money in half the time it had taken Sibyl. The total caused her eyes to grow wide. "What'd he do? Rob a bank?"

"I doubt he would foil a robbery if he were a thief himself. I don't know how he came by the money, but there's more to that man than meets the eye. You only have to talk with him a few minutes to realize he hasn't always looked like he's living hand-to-mouth."

Cassie was more blunt. "He looks like a bum."

"Bum or not, he'll be starting work here tomorrow morning."

"You can't do that. He'll scare away the customers."

"He'll be working in the office with me."

"Does Naomi know about this?"

Even Cassie didn't believe she knew enough to make decisions for herself. "I have great respect for my cousin's intelligence and ability to judge people, but if I'm going to learn to run this bank, I have to start making decisions on my own."

"I can help. I've been here five years."

"Norman didn't tell you any more than he told me. There's more here than either of us knows. If Mr. Holstock can't help me, I may have to sell the bank."

"You can't do that. You'll never get a decent price when the other bank has taken so many customers. I can't smile brightly enough to bring them back."

"I know. But even if I could get a decent price, I wouldn't want to sell. I want to prove I can run this bank just as well as Norman did."

❧

Keeping his eyes closed, Logan leaned against the tree until he felt his strength begin to return. He didn't care that he'd lost the little breakfast he had been able to eat. He was just thankful he hadn't been sick in Sibyl Spencer's office. He was aware of a growing attraction to this woman. It wasn't just appreciation of her beauty or empathy over the loss of her husband. He couldn't put his finger on it, but there was something more that seemed to reach out to him, something that compelled him to think of her almost constantly, to compare her to every woman he'd ever known. It mortified him for anyone to see his weakness, especially Sibyl. It was useless vanity, but he'd always been in perfect health, immune to the ailments that plagued other people, and practically tireless. He supposed he'd taken pride in his good health, but mostly, he'd take it for granted. When you've always had something, it didn't seem special. Losing it had shown him how badly mistaken he was.

He didn't know where he was. He'd run from

the bank and headed for the first group of trees he saw. There wasn't a lot of privacy—the desert being unlikely to produce a lot of growth even in the rainy season—but everyone was busy with their morning chores while it remained relatively cool. Before it got hot, he'd be back at his camp on the ridge, safely hidden among the trees and about two thousand feet above the town.

"Are you all right, mister?"

Logan opened his eyes to find a little girl staring up at him with concern in her eyes. She was a beautiful child—blue eyes, corn-silk blond hair, and skin that would shame a peach. Her dress was slightly dirty, but her face and hands were clean. He hadn't heard her come up. He didn't want to lie to the child, but he wanted to cause her to lose interest in him and go back to playing. "I'm just a little tired. I'll be fine in a minute."

"You don't look fine to me. I think you look sick. Want me to take you to the doctor? I know the way."

So she wasn't going to lose interest in him, and she wasn't going away without a better explanation. "I don't need a doctor. I just had a weak spell. It won't last long."

"What is a weak spell?"

He wasn't in the mood for explanations. Why couldn't she have been a grubby little boy he could have run off without a qualm? "It's when you feel tired all of a sudden and have to sit down."

"Aunt Naomi said she felt like that a lot before Annabelle was born."

Logan smothered a smile. "Well, I'm not going to have a baby."

"Men can't have babies. Only ladies."

A serious girl who didn't see the humor in Logan's answer. "And it's a very good thing. I don't believe men would make very good mothers."

"Men can't be mothers. They have to be fathers."

He was clearly out of his depth here. He had no idea what to say to a child this young. It was clear she didn't like anything he'd said. "You're a very smart little girl. I'm sure your mother is very proud of you."

"Mama says she gives me all her love because she doesn't have anybody else now."

Now he placed the child. She'd been sitting on the front bench at Norman Spencer's funeral. He'd been too far back to get a good look at her. "I don't have a mother. I had a father, but he died several years ago."

"Do you miss him?"

"Very much."

"I—"

"Kitty! What are you doing here?"

"I'm talking to this man."

A boy a few years older, maybe about ten, and several inches taller had pushed his way through the undergrowth with the energy typical of a child who spent most of his life outside. He was a handsome young man, but unlike the little girl he appeared to be unconcerned with his looks or the condition of his clothes. His hair looked like he'd come through a bush backward, and his clothes were snagged and dirty at the knees. He approached Logan.

"What's wrong with your face? It's puffed up like bread dough."

Kitty turned on the boy like an avenging angel. "That's a mean thing to say, Peter Blaine. If I was to tell your papa, he'd tan the hide right off you."

Before Peter could reply, a blond girl a few years older than Kitty and looking remarkably like Peter burst into the clearing. "Here you are," she exclaimed, out of breath. "It's not fair for both of you to leave without telling me where you were going."

"I wasn't going anywhere," Peter said. "I was looking for Kitty. She's talking to this man." He indicated Logan.

"Oh." She reacted like she hadn't been aware of Logan until Peter pointed him out. "Who are you? What's wrong with your face?"

"My name is Logan Holstock, and I'm resting in the shade."

"He's sick," Kitty informed her.

"I'm feeling much better," Logan insisted.

The girl didn't look convinced. "You don't look like it. We can take you to the doctor."

"I already told him," Kitty said. "He says he doesn't need a doctor. I'm Kitty Spencer," she told him. "Peter and Esther are my cousins. We'll take care of you until you feel better."

The sincerity in the girl's voice touched Logan. "I'm feeling much better now, but thanks for the offer."

"You don't look a lot better," Peter challenged.

"Don't pay any attention to Peter," Kitty said. "Aunt Naomi says Uncle Colby is letting him grow up as wild as a longhorn steer."

Since Logan had never seen a longhorn steer, he wasn't exactly sure how wild that might be. It was clear, however, that all three children felt free to speak their minds.

"I have to be going," Logan said. "And I imagine your mothers are wondering where you three might be."

"Mama says somebody always knows where we are," Kitty said. "She says that's what comes of being related to half the people in town."

Logan couldn't imagine what it would be like to have such a large family. It had always been just him and his father. His uncle only caused trouble, and Bridgette preferred to spend her time with her friends. It made him wonder if he and his brothers would have been like these three children if their parents hadn't died. But finding them now wouldn't be the same. They would have jobs, families, and responsibilities. Life had been good to him, but he was realizing he'd missed far more than he'd ever guessed. And now it was too late to do anything about it.

"You're very fortunate to have so many people who love you," Logan said.

"Mrs. Oliver called Peter a hellion." Esther giggled then turned to her brother. "If you tell Mama I said that, I'll tell her what you said about Preacher Simpson."

"I'm no snitch," Peter said, incensed his sister would accuse him of such treachery. "Are you sure you're all right?" he asked Logan.

"Yes, I'm sure."

"Then we gotta be going. Kitty is only six. She can't stay out playing as long as we can."

Logan watched the children head off, all three talking at once. Why had he never known children could be like that? He would have given anything to have had two or three of his own. Why was he learning everything when it was too late?

❦

The next morning, Logan stared at his saddled horse and cursed himself for a fool. Why had he offered to help Sibyl? She was related to half the people in Cactus Corner. Any one of a dozen people could probably do everything he could. The dog rose from where he'd been resting at the edge of Logan's camp. He'd come a little closer each day.

"You've had a rotten turn of luck, too," Logan said to the dog. "What do you think I should do?"

The dog whined softly.

"Tell me to unsaddle the horse, take my rifle, and go hunting."

The dog inched closer, then paused.

"You're no help. Some bastard practically beat you to death, and you're willing to trust me because I feed you. You're as foolish as I am."

Logan had argued with himself ever since he got back to his camp. He had as many reasons to stay away from Sibyl as he had to help her. He didn't really know anything about her, but he found himself attracted to her. She was a lovely woman. Beautiful in fact. Any man would be attracted to her. She was a young widow with a small daughter to provide for and a business she knew nothing about. Everything about her situation was bound to arouse the protective instincts of any man. He wouldn't be surprised if, before the end of the week, half the men in Cactus Corner had offered to help her. The fact that she was a rich and beautiful widow was guaranteed to bring her to the attention of men—some handsome and charming—who would try to take advantage of her. Was that why he offered to help, to protect her? She had family to do that. She didn't need some stranger who would live for only a few more months.

He felt a genuine desire to help, but was that all?

Last night he'd dreamed of her. And there was nothing altruistic about those dreams. If he hadn't already felt so rotten, he'd feel embarrassed. How could he say he had a selfless desire to help, that nothing more than that had prompted his offer, when he had erotic dreams? He'd never dreamed about Bridgette like that. He wasn't sure he'd ever dreamed about Bridgette at all.

"It's a rotten piece of luck," he said to the dog. "I finally meet a woman who makes me have dreams I'd be embarrassed to share with anyone, and I'm a dead man walking. You ever met a female who made you dream like that?" Logan struck his forehead with the base of his palm. "What the hell's wrong with me? Not only am I asking a dog for advice, I'm asking him about his dreams. If I were back in Chicago, they'd lock me away in an asylum for the permanently insane."

The dog whined and crept closer.

"If you had any idea what I've been saying, you'd turn tail and head for the woods. I must be crazy. Whatever has made my face look like it's about to bust must have invaded my brain. Maybe I'll soon be running through the woods barking like you." He laughed, then sobered. "Only you don't bark. Are you afraid that man will find you? I ought to be hiding, too, yet I'm going into town to teach Sibyl Spencer how to run her bank. After that…well, we know what comes after that. You'd better look around for someone else to feed you. Maybe that boy who came by a few days ago. He seems like the kind of young man who'd take real good care of a dog like you. You think about it. You can't depend on me forever."

The dog's eyes never left Logan.

"If you insist on staying, you can crawl inside the tent. It gets right hot in the afternoon."

With a sigh signifying the acceptance of the inevitable, Logan mounted his horse. Gathering the reins, he headed toward the trail leading down the rim and into town. He'd known from the beginning he was going. Maybe that's why the dog hadn't said anything. No point in giving advice that would be ignored.

⤺

"Elliot Lowe?"

The sound of his forgotten name caused Logan to stiffen. He had been wary when Cassie informed him that a man in the bank lobby had asked to speak to the man with the puffy face.

"Who are you?" he asked. "And why would you expect me to respond to that name?" The man didn't appear disconcerted by Logan's unfriendly manner or the nature of his question.

"Is there somewhere we can speak in private?"

"Here is fine." The bank was empty except for Cassie and Horace. "My name is Logan Holstock. You have followed the wrong man."

"I don't think so." The man looked pleased rather than disconcerted. "I'm a Pinkerton agent hired by Miss Bridgette Lowe to find you and take you home. I followed you from Chicago."

Realizing this was a conversation he couldn't avoid, Logan said, "Let's go out back."

He wasn't surprised Bridgette had tried to find him. Her father had done nothing to help his brother build his businesses. Nevertheless, she believed she should have been the one to inherit her uncle's money. Now her only way to get it was to marry Logan. "How did you find me?"

"Your looks made it easy to follow your trail."

That shouldn't have surprised him. Everyone he'd encountered between here and Chicago probably remembered the sick man with the bloated features. "You've wasted your time and Bridgette her money," he told the agent. "Tell Bridgette I'm not going back because I have no reason to go back."

The agent cocked his head. "I understood you were engaged to marry Miss Lowe."

He didn't know what Bridgette had told the agent, but he wasn't going to discuss his personal life with a stranger. "I have to go back to work, and you have a long way to travel. You should get started."

"I would like to talk to you again," the agent said.

"I don't want to talk to you. Now I have to leave. I have work to do."

The man seemed reluctant. "I'll be in town for a few days."

"Enjoy the scenery."

"If you change your mind—"

"I won't."

After a pause, the agent left. When Logan reentered the bank, Horace pretended to be busy. Making no attempt to hide her curiosity, Cassie looked directly at him.

"I knew you couldn't be a bum," she said. "You talk too nice."

"There are lots of bums in Chicago."

Cassie's curiosity couldn't be diverted so easily. "I bet there aren't any with Pinkerton agents looking for them. You aren't a criminal, are you? No, you wouldn't be," she said, answering her own question. "Not with some rich woman wanting to marry you. Why don't you want to marry her? Has she seen your face?"

He'd only known Cassie for a few hours, but he knew the only way to stop her was to satisfy her curiosity. "Yes, she's seen my face."

"She must really love you."

He wasn't going to get into that. "It wouldn't be right for either of us."

Cassie regarded him with open skepticism. "There's something else, isn't there?"

Horace poked his head through his teller window. "Leave the man alone. If he's got secrets, it's none of your business."

"I'm not interested in *knowing* his secrets," Cassie said. "I just want to know they won't hurt Mrs. Spencer." Her gaze zeroed in on Logan. "What about it?"

"My secrets won't hurt Mrs. Spencer or anyone in Cactus Corner," Logan said.

"I'll hold you to that," Cassie said.

"I'd prefer it if you didn't tell Mrs. Spencer about this. No need to worry her."

"Only as long as I think it's best for her not to know," Cassie said.

"Fair enough. Now I'd better get back to work. I don't expect Mrs. Spencer would like her employees standing around gabbing."

"Why should she care? Horace and me don't have any customers, and you're not being paid."

"I care," Logan said. "I made an offer, and I mean to stand by it."

❧

Sibyl was having trouble getting over her astonishment. Logan had interpreted the contents of Norman's ledgers as though it were something he did every day. He had worked though the books so quickly she could have believed he'd written down the figures himself. Even more amazing, she could understand his explanations. What Norman had always insisted was a complex system that required a long apprenticeship, as well as great intelligence to master, was simply a matter of common sense. Once she knew what the figures were intended to represent, it was like coming on the answer in a flash of understanding.

"The bank doesn't seem to have been doing much business," Logan told her. "I find that surprising considering the prominence of the building."

"That was built when this was the only bank," Sibyl told him. "Norman was so obnoxious people opened a second bank. Nearly everyone went there."

"Why are all these loans so large?"

"The other bank has limited resources. If anyone wanted to borrow a lot of money, they had to come to Norman."

"What did he do to lure them back?"

"Nothing."

He looked at her like she hadn't understood his question. "He must have done something. Any businessman would."

"You would have to know Norman to understand. He didn't believe it was his fault. If anyone left his bank, it was *their* fault."

"Well, *you* must certainly attempt to regain their business. There must be lots of things you can do. The first thing we have to do is analyze your competition to learn their strengths and weaknesses. Once we know that, we'll be in a position to attack them."

Sibyl was feeling very uneasy. "I don't think I'd like that."

"Why not?"

"The people who own the bank are all related to me."

"So?"

"I expect it's hard for someone without a family to understand how I feel."

"I have a family. I just don't know where they are."

There was such sadness in Logan's voice that Sibyl wanted to reach out and comfort him. She'd often felt she had too much family, had longed for the chance to live her life without having to consider how it would affect people she loved. There had to be a sense of freedom to owe allegiance to no one—no explanations, no excuses.

"You don't know where they went, what happened to them?"

"No."

She waited for him to explain, but he said nothing. She took that as a sign he didn't want her to pry. "I'll be happy to lend you some of mine. I've got more than enough for both of us." She was relieved to see him smile.

"I had an adopted family." His smile vanished. "I'll trade you."

"I think I'll keep mine even though they think they can run my life better than I can. It can be annoying, but it's a comfort to know they're concerned about me and Kitty." She smiled. "Though I'm not sure letting her play with Colby's twins is a good idea. Colby is happy to let them run around like two ragamuffins."

Logan's eyes lit up. "I met all three of them yesterday." He laughed. "The oldest can't be more than ten years old, yet they wanted to take care of this old man. They insisted I should see the doctor. Kitty even offered to take me there."

Sibyl knew about the meeting because Kitty had told her about it. She had spent all of supper talking about Logan. She knew Logan's health was none of her business, but she couldn't let such an opening slip by. "I agree with them. Dr. Kessling is an excellent physician."

Logan's gaze locked on her. "I've consulted the best doctor in Chicago. There is no help for my condition. If my looks upset you, I won't come here again."

"It's not that," Sibyl hastened to assure him. "It's just that you're clearly not well, and I don't think seeing the doctor would hurt."

"There comes a time when the only thing left is to accept what can't be changed."

Sibyl wanted to say more, but she decided against it. "Where are you staying? I'd hate to see you use all your money paying for lodging. I'd be happy to give you a wage. You've more than earned it."

"I have a camp up on the Rim," Logan said. "It's all I need."

The idea of camping out in the wilderness appalled Sibyl. Memories of the trip by covered wagon from Kentucky still gave her nightmares. A campsite on the Rim was no place for a man as sick as Logan. "You've got to move into town. I know of a number of places you can stay inexpensively."

"I don't want to move into town. My tent is warm and dry, and I can find plenty of meat by hunting. I like my solitude. It gives me time to think. It also spares people having to look at me and pretend nothing is wrong with my face." His smile was wintry. "Not like the children. They asked me right off what was wrong."

"I'm sorry for that."

"I'm not. I would find it much easier if everyone would acknowledge that I suffer from weak spells and my face looks like it's about to explode. Despite all this, I can take care of myself and prefer to do so without bothering anyone else."

"It wouldn't be a bother."

"Of course it would. Let's not pretend otherwise."

Sibyl felt like a child who had been chastised. "All right. It would be a bother, but I'd rather be bothered than have you living in the woods surrounded by wild animals." She didn't know how a smile from that face could be endearing, but it was.

"The only wild animals up there are cows that are too lazy to do anything but graze, and deer that do their best to stay far away from me."

"Jared says there are cougars, wolves, and bears."

"Probably, but they stay even farther away."

"You're not going to let me talk you into moving into town, are you?"

"Your appeal was presented very charmingly, and your concern does you credit, but I'm going to resist despite your nearly irresistible smile."

Sibyl felt herself blush. Norman had never complimented her, and no man who wasn't related to her had dared. She was disconcerted to realize she found his words very agreeable, even that she wished he would say a few more. She attempted to chastise herself for vanity, but it did no good. It felt absolutely wonderful to be told that a man found her charming and nearly irresistible.

"I wish you would reconsider. It worries me to know that you're sleeping in the woods. I wouldn't be able to close my eyes."

"I sleep better than I ever did when I lived in a house. Who would have expected that?"

He had never said much about his life before he came to Cactus Corner. "What kind of house was it?"

"It was large and quite comfortable, but it never felt as welcoming as my tent."

Apparently he wasn't going to tell her anything about his past. "Either you had a very strange house, or you have a very unusual tent."

"I don't think it has anything to do with the house or the tent. I'm sure the difference is in me."

"How is that?"

"I'm not sure. If I figure it out, I might tell you about it."

"But you might not."

He became very serious. "No, I might not." He seemed to gather himself and put whatever thoughts that were in his head behind him. "We'd better get back to those books. This bank isn't going to run itself."

Considering how little business they had, there was nothing happening that Cassie and Horace couldn't handle. However, it was clear Logan wasn't going to share any more confidences. She would have to contain her curiosity as best she could. Maybe he would tell her more about himself in the coming days. She couldn't tell his age, but he'd obviously done more than wander around the West. What kind of man could effortlessly unravel the mysteries of bank ledgers yet be so good with a gun and prefer living in a tent in the woods to a large, comfortable house?

She was surprised by the extent of her curiosity, as well as her comfort with a man who was a virtual stranger. It wasn't merely that he'd saved her life or that he was helping her learn how to run the bank. She was interested in *him*, the person behind the swollen face and periodic bouts of weakness. It wasn't just about his illness or where he lived. She wanted to know where he'd lived, what he'd done, the people he had loved, his reasons for coming to Cactus Corner. How old was he? Had his face always looked like this? Where did he learn to understand ledgers? Had he ever been in love? Had anyone loved him? What happened to his family? Had he tried to find them? Did he *want* to find them?

What made him offer to help her? What did he think of her? Did he think she was a helpless female who couldn't do anything without a man looking over her shoulder? Would he get bored and disappear in a few days? Why was she afraid he might disappear? He was a stranger who had no place in her life.

"Are you all right?"

Logan's words startled Sibyl out of her abstraction. "Of course I'm all right. What made you think I wasn't?"

"I spoke to you, but you didn't respond."

"Sorry. I was thinking."

"It must have been something really important. I hope they were happy thoughts."

She couldn't answer that question because she didn't know the answer. "I'm not sure. I guess time will tell."

"You don't have to go back to work if you're not ready. I can go over the rest of the books and report what I find."

"Thanks, but I need to go over them with you. That's the only way I'll know what's in all of them. You don't mind, do you? I know I ask a lot of questions."

"It's your bank. You have the right to ask any questions you want."

She didn't feel like it was her bank. She could practically feel Norman trapped in his grave howling in protest that she would be brazen enough to enter his office, sit in his chair, believe she could understand how to manage *his* bank. She was a mere woman. She couldn't expect to be able to do the work of a man. Yet that voice in the back of her head made her more determined than ever to learn everything Logan could teach her. Norman would never know that she had succeeded, but she would. And that was all that was important.

She returned Logan's gaze. "I'm ready when you are."

∾

Logan was glad his horse knew the way to his camp. He'd been so preoccupied with his own thoughts he could have been headed in the opposite direction and he wouldn't have known it. He badly wanted to know what had occupied Sibyl's thoughts so completely that she hadn't heard him when he spoke to her. Being around her had forced him to realize he didn't know much about women. He'd always been so busy working he hadn't had much time for them. Besides, it hadn't seem important when he expected to marry Bridgette, despite the fact that their fathers— brothers who looked as different as they were unalike in personality—rarely spoke to each other except to argue. He was honest enough to know he didn't love Bridgette—he knew she didn't love him—but he needed a wife, and she was the logical choice. He had to admit she'd endured his lack of attention with a degree of acceptance few women would have been able to equal. He had seen it as a promise that their married life would be without the arguments and stresses he saw in the lives of the men who worked for him. She never entered in the arguments between her father and uncle. She'd said she was happy to leave all business decisions to the men in her family. Logan had thought that was an admirable attitude. Now he wasn't so sure.

He had never met a woman like Sibyl. To be honest, he wasn't sure he looked carefully enough to know what any of the women he'd known were like. He'd lumped them into this anonymous group that was always attached to some man, who gained their identity through that man, who depended on men to make all the decisions in their lives. He'd taken it for granted that all women felt that way.

Sibyl was completely different. She had no intention of leaving the business decisions to anyone. She was determined to learn how to run the bank herself. She wasn't interested in impressing anyone. Nor did she look for approval. He didn't know anything about her family. Did she have a father, brothers, uncles? Logan wondered how the men in her family had reacted to her decision. Did the women in her family agree with her decision, or did they believe she ought to stay home and let—

He heard the dog growling before he saw the man.

Five

"STEVE DIDN'T TELL ME YOU HAD A WATCHDOG," THE man said to Logan when he rode up. "He won't let me dismount."

"He's a stray," Logan said. "Somebody beat him so badly he could hardly move. I've been feeding him."

The man laughed easily. "Looks like he's decided *you* belong to *him*. Do you think you could convince him I'm not here to steal anything?"

"I don't know," Logan said. "This is the first time anybody's come to my camp since he followed me here. Take it easy," he said to the dog that had planted himself in front of the tent. "I don't know who this man is, but I think he's friendly."

"I'm Jared Smith, Steve's uncle. You met him a few days ago."

Jared Smith, who'd been born a Holstock. He'd been looking forward to meeting the man. He was disappointed he didn't see any similarity, but that didn't mean the man couldn't be his brother. "If you've got time to sit a spell, I'll make some coffee," Logan offered. "Quiet, dog. Go sit in the woods if you don't like company."

The moment Jared's foot hit the ground, the dog bared his teeth and growled deep in his throat.

"Stop it!" Logan commanded. "If you're going to stay here, you've got to be polite to company when I'm here. If I'm gone, you can lay into anybody who comes nosing around."

The dog stopped growling and moved to a spot about a dozen feet from the tent.

"He still doesn't trust me," Jared said.

"He was hurt real bad when I first saw him. I'm not sure he'll ever trust anyone."

"He seems to trust you."

"We have something in common. I'm not in much better condition myself."

"Steve said you looked sick."

That was a tactful way to put it. "I've been better. You two don't look much alike," Logan said to change the subject.

"We're not blood kin. I was adopted."

His name was Jared Holstock and he was adopted. If he hadn't come from Texas, Logan could have been certain. But for now he should get on with making the coffee and not try to find connections where there may not be any.

"Of course, I wasn't born in Texas, and my name wasn't Smith."

Logan hoped Jared didn't notice that he'd almost spilled the coffee. "Where were you born?"

"I don't know, but my name was Holstock. That's one of the reasons I had for coming to see you. My parents died on the Santa Fe Trail. I had two brothers who were also adopted. I found my younger brother Colby right here in Cactus Corner. His name was Kevin, but he goes by Colby Blaine. I have no idea what happened to my older brother. When I heard your name was Holstock, I had to see for myself even though I knew it was only one chance in a million that you were my brother."

Logan forced himself to say, "I've spent my whole life in Chicago."

Jared shrugged in disappointment. "I knew it was a long shot, but I had to ask."

Logan struggled to calm his thundering pulse. "Do you know his name?"

"No. He was adopted and gone before my parents adopted me. If they ever knew, they forgot."

Logan had no doubt that he'd found his brothers, but despite the joy that surged through him, he told himself to be cautious. He would wait until he met Colby so he could be sure. Even though he didn't intend to reveal his relationship, there was no reason why he shouldn't learn as much about them as possible. It wouldn't be the same as being accepted as a member of the family, but friendship was far more than he could have hoped for.

"I hope you like your coffee strong. My father taught me to drink it hot and black."

"Is there any other way?"

Logan had often thought about finding his brothers, but he'd never really considered what they'd be like. He'd assumed they'd be like him, but why should they? They were different men raised by different families with very different lives. Consequently, he was surprised and pleased when Jared settled without hesitation on the fallen log Logan had been using.

"You've got a comfortable little camp here," Jared said. "How long do you plan to stay?"

"I don't know."

"You're welcome to stay as long as you like. I would appreciate another pair of eyes on my cattle. I can't afford to lose any to cougars."

"I haven't seen any cats. I expect the dog would keep any from staying around."

Jared looked at the dog, who was still unhappy about his presence. "Do you know if the calves are safe from him? He looks pretty big."

"I'm sure they will be, but right now he's too weak to chase anything faster than a three-legged rabbit."

The coffee had started to boil, so he rifled through his tent for two cups. "I don't have anything but tin," he told Jared. "Crockery was too heavy for travel."

"I was in the army," Jared told him. "I didn't eat off of or drink from anything but tin for seven years."

"What made you decide to go into ranching in the Arizona Territory?"

Jared blew on his coffee. "My last army posting was Camp Verde, which is about twenty miles upriver. I was raised on a cattle ranch in south Texas, which isn't a lot different from here. So when the Green River Ranch came up for sale, buying it seemed the thing to do. Besides, I was looking for my brothers. My parents went back east, but I figured at least one brother came farther west. It was just luck that I ended up close to Cactus Corner where Colby lives."

"Did you recognize each other?"

"I was sure when I saw Colby, but he wasn't convinced. He wouldn't even consider it until he got proof after his parents died."

"Are you close now?" Could brothers who'd spent nearly all of their lives apart regain that closeness?

Now that he'd found them—*if* he'd found them—it would be easier just to watch than have his offer of friendship rejected.

"I can't say we're close, but we're good friends. We don't live near each other, but that's not the real reason, either. We're just different people who are busy with our own lives and families. My wife and I own the ranch, and she owns the mercantile in town. Colby transports stuff all over the Territory and as far away as Santa Fe. Still, it's nice to know I've found one brother. I'd hoped to find both, but that was always more of a wish than a possibility."

Logan wondered how he'd feel if he knew this disfigured stranger was his brother.

"How long ago did you find each other?"

"About two years ago."

"There's plenty of time to catch up."

"I don't know. Every time we think about doing something together, one or the other of us is too busy. Other times our children are sick, or our wives have a new baby. It looks like we won't have time until we're old men and can sit around reminiscing while our grown children do all the work."

If they hadn't managed to build a relationship in two years, how could Logan expect to accomplish anything in just a few months? His father and his uncle had never been able to build a relationship, and they had spent their lives in near daily contact. Logan was a commodities dealer who had bought and sold products without ever seeing what he bought and sold. What would he have to share with a rancher or a teamster, men who spent their lives outdoors and in direct contact with the fruits of their labors?

"I didn't mean to bore you with all this talk about myself," Jared said. "I just wanted to meet you and tell you that you could stay here as long as you wanted. Do you get into town very often?"

Apparently Sibyl and the others had been able to keep the secret about him shooting the robbers, but he figured it was best if everyone knew he was working with Sibyl. Too much secrecy would only cause problems.

"I plan to go in every day for a while. Mrs. Spencer needed some help understanding her husband's books. I've done a little work in an office, so I offered to do what I could."

"Is she planning to sell the bank once she figures everything out?"

"I think she's planning to run it herself."

Jared grinned. "Good. I hope she's successful. That will put her father in his place."

"Why's that?"

"He has as poor an opinion of Sibyl's ability to understand business as her husband did. He expected Sibyl to hand everything over to him to run or sell as he saw fit. I hope you have more than *a little* experience, though. I hope you're a genius who can turn the bank around. Norman was a good businessman, but he was also an arrogant, interfering snob who managed to alienate just about everybody in town."

Apparently no one had a good word for Norman Spencer. Why would Sibyl have agreed to marry a man so unlike herself? Surely her father couldn't have forced her down the aisle, and he didn't believe Sibyl would have married him just because he was rich. Norman hadn't been unattractive, but he wasn't so handsome a woman would lose her head over him.

Jared swallowed the last of his coffee and stood. "I'd better be getting back. I hope you're able to help Sibyl. I'd like to see her succeed, but she'll need to find a way to win back some of the customers Norman drove away."

"She wants to succeed, but she doesn't want to compete with the other bank."

"That's because one cousin runs it, and another cousin's husband is the primary investor. Sibyl is very loyal to her family."

Logan valued loyalty to family, too, but it shouldn't determine how you do business. If his father had been so loyal to his brother that he'd refused to go against him, their company would have been bankrupt years ago. He'd have to help Sibyl understand that. She owed it to herself, her daughter, and her employees.

"Where do you have your accounts?" Logan asked Jared.

Jared grinned sheepishly. "With the competition. Norman was particularly cruel to my wife when her first husband died. That's the main reason the new bank was formed. Neither she nor I would do business with Norman."

"But Norman is dead, and Sibyl is your wife's cousin, isn't she?"

Jared's gaze narrowed. "What are you getting at?"

"Since both banks are owned by your wife's cousins, wouldn't it be a gesture of goodwill to use both banks equally?"

Jared's features relaxed. "I'd never thought of that."

"That's not surprising with Norman's death being so recent. But now that you have, I hope you'll consider it."

Jared favored Logan with a speculative gaze. "I get the feeling you're a very clever man. I hope you're an honest one as well. I'll talk with my wife about your *suggestion*, but I hope you know that everyone in Cactus Corner loves Sibyl. They would be very upset if your efforts to help her were to have any negative effects."

Logan smiled inwardly. Jared might not have been able to develop the brotherly relationship with Colby he'd hoped for, but he clearly had developed a protective feeling for his own wife's family.

"I know I don't look like an upstanding citizen. I live in a tent in the woods with an abused dog as a companion. I'm not in good health, and no one knows who I am, where I came from, or why I'm here. All I can tell you is that my time is my own. I have nowhere to go and no place to be. I offered my help because Sibyl needs it, but I have no plans to stay here. In fact, I'll be gone before the end of summer."

"I'm not trying to run you out of town," Jared said. "Steve likes you, and Sibyl obviously trusts you. And if you've managed to win Cassie's approval, that's good enough for me. She comes across as flighty sometimes, but that woman can smell a bad apple hidden at the bottom of a barrel. I just want you to know that people will be watching you."

"Good. I'm glad everyone is so concerned about Sibyl. And I hope you'll encourage people to give her bank another chance. They'll get a very different reception."

"I can't appear to favor one cousin over the other."

"I wouldn't expect you to do that, but it would help if you'd let it be known that things are going to be very different now."

"No one doubts that. They're just waiting to see

what happens. As much as everybody loves her, they don't know if she can successfully manage the bank."

"She'll do fine," Logan said. "You just wait and see."

"Will she let people know that you're responsible for some of that success?"

"I'm just helping her figure out what everything means. All the decisions will be hers."

Jared seemed skeptical. "If you're as good as I think you are, she might benefit from your advice."

"What makes you think I know anything about banking?"

"There's something about you that doesn't fit. You live like a hobo yet you speak with the confidence of a successful man. You've already talked me into thinking about supporting both banks equally. Besides, I trust Sibyl and Cassie's judgment." He glanced over his shoulder at the dog that was still watching him with unfriendly eyes. "On top of all that, you've got a dog with plenty of reasons not to trust anybody defending your campsite like it's his own. I'd say that speaks well for your character."

Logan ached to tell Jared they were brothers and that he'd do everything in his power to be worthy of his respect and friendship, but he didn't want to start something he couldn't finish. He would do everything he could to help Sibyl. When they learned after his death who he was, they'd have reason to think well of him without having to deal with his illness and death.

"I'll talk to my wife about your suggestion tonight," Jared said. "I may be able to let you know tomorrow."

"Tell Sibyl, not me—but don't let her know I had anything to do with it."

"Why?"

"I feel more comfortable not taking credit for something she would have thought of once she got over the shock of the robbery and Norman's death."

Jared looked like he was about to say something when a thought made him stop and regard Logan with a curious expression. "You wouldn't be the stranger who shot all the thieves, would you?"

His question stunned Logan. "Why would you think that?"

"Sibyl says he was a stranger who disappeared before everyone came rushing into the bank. She says she was so shocked she never really got a look at him. As far as I know, you're the only stranger in town."

"Do I look like a gunman to you?"

"I doubt he was a gunman. I'd say a marksman was more likely."

Logan was glad to know his brother was intelligent, but he didn't like what Jared was doing with that astuteness at the moment. "No doubt you're right," Logan said. "That means it was probably someone who'd been in the army. You said there was a fort not far from here."

"I never met a soldier who wouldn't have been eager to take credit for a feat like that. They'd have been after a reward, too."

"Maybe it was a retired soldier who didn't need the money or want the notoriety."

"Or maybe it wasn't a soldier at all. Sibyl, Cassie, and Horace say they can't describe him, but I don't think they're telling the truth."

"What makes you think that?"

"Sibyl and Horace can tell a lie with a straight face,

but Cassie is as transparent as glass. A child could tell she was lying."

"Why would they pretend they couldn't describe him? You'd think they'd be eager to tell everyone what the man looked like and who he was."

"That's what you would think, which makes them doing the opposite intriguing."

"Well, I'm sure they have their reasons. When the time is right, I expect they'll tell you what they know."

"We'll see. In the meantime, keep an eye out for a stranger who's handy with a gun. Until then, I'll be keeping an eye on you. A friendly eye," Jared added. "Like I said, Steve likes you, and I trust the boy's instincts."

"I liked him, too," Logan said. "He seems to be a fine young man."

Jared turned to the dog, who had never taken his eyes off him. "Have you given him a name?"

"He's not mine. Why should I name him?"

"I think *you're his*," Jared said. "You might as well give him a name. *Dog* seems an unappreciative way to refer to such a staunch friend."

Jared mounted up. "Why don't you drop by the ranch sometime? I'd like you to meet my family."

"Why?"

"Why not? Do you have anything against meeting new people? My wife loves company. She says the ranch is too far out for most people. She keeps threatening to move back into town."

"I'll think about it, but it's usually late by the time I get back from the bank."

"Then come for supper. Laurie is a great cook. That's the main reason half my men still work for me."

"I'll think about it."

"I'll send Steve to persuade you." He rode away before Logan could respond.

Logan watched him go, pensive.

Jared had too much of what Logan had missed in life—a wife, children, friends, and a focus in life other than work. He wondered if his father had missed those things. Did adopting a son make up for everything else? Would he have gone through life thinking of little beyond work if he hadn't gotten sick? Was one of the reasons he had been willing to marry Bridgette— despite knowing she didn't care for him—that she wouldn't distract him from his job? He couldn't answer those questions, but he did know that getting sick had changed all the answers.

"I suppose being beaten so badly changed things for you, too," he said to the dog. "Otherwise you wouldn't be willing to spend your time in the woods with me."

The dog whined and moved closer. He didn't appear ready to come within reach, but he seemed willing to trust Logan. At least as long as he fed him.

"Would you like a name?" he asked the dog. "I suppose you already have one, but I don't know what it is. I guess a new life deserves a new name. What do you think?"

The dog whined and crept a little closer.

"How about Trusty? It's not very imaginative, but it's something that's important to both of us."

The dog dipped his head and whined, but he didn't move any closer.

"I don't blame you. I'd never hurt you, but I'm not the person I thought I was. I wonder if any one of us is."

The dog just watched him.

"How about I fix something to eat? After that, we can go hunting. Would you like that?"

The dog's tail thumped against the soft earth.

"I thought you would. Always thinking about your belly. Come on. I've got a little deer meat left."

He headed to where he'd stored the meat in a bear hang, the dog padding after him.

&

Bridgette waved a telegram in Dr. Pittman's face. "The Pinkerton we sent found him just like you said he would, but he refuses to come back."

"I didn't expect he would."

James had come to take her to the opera. For the occasion, Bridgette was wearing her new Worth gown made of pink silk. The skirt and muslin overskirt were trimmed with a plaiting of white French muslin headed with a Valenciennes insertion. It had a cuirass bodice and muslin sleeves. It had cost her far more than she could afford. If Elliot couldn't be convinced to return to Chicago and marry her, she'd soon be out of money.

"Why not?" she asked. "What reason could he have for staying in a place like Cactus Corner? That sounds like a desert."

"I doubt it matters to him where he is," the doctor said.

"But he's got one of the biggest houses in Chicago. He's got a cook, maids, a butler, and goodness knows how many more people to look after him. Who will take care of him in a place like that?"

"He thinks he's going to die. Maybe all that doesn't matter as much to him now."

Bridgette frowned. "You sound like you sympathize with him."

"I'm only trying to put myself in his shoes, imagine what he is thinking."

Bridgette flounced across the room, dropped onto a sofa, and fanned herself vigorously. "While you're at it, *imagine* what will bring him back to Chicago."

"I don't think anything will except you."

"Me! Why not you?"

"You're the one he was supposed to marry."

"*You're* his doctor."

"He doesn't have any faith left in medicine. If he had, he wouldn't have left Chicago."

"What am I supposed to do?"

"Go after him?"

"Go after him!" Snapping her fan closed, Bridgette sat ramrod straight, her voice rising to a near shriek. "You can't seriously think I'd go to a place called Cactus Corner."

"You will if you want him to come back to Chicago."

Bridgette's pouting had never worked on her uncle or Elliot, but it always worked on James. At her hurt look, he dropped down on the sofa next to her and took her hands in his. "Forget about him," he pleaded. "I'm rich enough to give you anything you want."

Bridgette jerked her hands away. "What I *want* is the money that rightfully belongs to me," she said from between clenched teeth. "I will not let it go to that *foundling*. I'm the only living relative Uncle Samuel had."

"He's going to die. Even without a will, I'm sure the courts will give you the money."

"He won't die unless he keeps taking the poisoned

medicine you gave him. Besides, who knows who he might meet out there? In his condition, some clever woman night convince him to leave everything to her."

"The telegram says he's camping in the woods and living like a tramp."

"That won't make any difference. I expect everybody in Cactus Corner looks like a tramp." She turned on the charm and smiled at James. "Won't you go after him for me?"

Much to her surprise, James proved surprisingly unhelpful. "I can't go. It would take months. What would I do about my practice?"

"All those old biddies would still come flocking to you," Bridgette snapped. "You're the handsomest doctor in Chicago as well as the best."

"I have several patients undergoing serious treatments. I couldn't possibly leave even if I wanted to."

Bridgette was surprised she couldn't bend James to her will this time, but she had spent her life living with uncooperative men. Her father, uncle, and fiancé had all been stubborn, unfeeling men who'd shown a callous disregard for her desires. Her father had never provided her with the kind of house or the style of clothes she deserved. Her uncle had always preferred his adopted son to his blood kin, and Elliot had insisted they had plenty of time before they needed to get married.

That's why she'd had to talk James into poisoning him.

If James hadn't been besotted with her, he never would have agreed. Even then, it had taken her the better part of a year and the threat of seeing her married to another man to make him relent. She didn't have that kind of time to convince him to go after Elliot.

"Give up trying to get your uncle's fortune," James urged. "I never thought it was a good idea to try to poison Elliot. Let him give his money to anyone he wants."

"I can't!" Bridgette practically shouted. "It'll drive me crazy knowing he left *my* money to perfect strangers. I've got to stop him."

"I don't see how you can do that."

Bridgette took a deep breath. "I'm going to Cactus Corner. That's how I'm going to stop him. Unless you'll change your mind and go for me."

"I've done all I'm going to do, and that's more than a man with a conscience would have done."

"Are you saying I have no conscience?"

James backed down. "I was speaking only of myself."

"I'll need more of the medicine."

"There's no point in giving him more. He already has enough to kill two men."

❧

Logan stared at the figures in the book. He had no trouble understanding what he saw. They just didn't make sense. Money didn't materialize out of nowhere. It had to come from somewhere. All of the other books made sense. Why should this one be different?

He had no reason to be looking at these books. They reached back to the days when Norman Spencer lived in Kentucky, but Logan had been bored. Kitty had come down with a cold, and Sibyl had decided to stay home with her. With nothing specific to do, Logan had decided to leaf through some of the books Norman had kept in his safe. He'd been surprised at the number of loans Norman had negotiated five years ago, as well as the extremely low interest rates. He'd been told that Norman was a hard, unforgiving person who tried to wring every possible cent from his clients. If that was true, why had he handed out loans practically for free? It was none of his business, but it didn't fit with everything he'd been told about Norman.

But it was the large sum of money that suddenly appeared on the books that confused him. He wasn't exactly surprised at the appearance of such a sum, but there was no explanation, not even a hint of its origin. The timing intrigued him as well. The year was 1863, in the middle of the War between the States. Confederate and Union forces battled for control of Kentucky, but it was unlikely that either army would have agreed to buy anything they could take by force. It must have been the sale of property or an inheritance from Norman's father.

He was putting the books away when Sibyl entered the office.

"I thought you were staying home today," Logan said.

"I was, but Kitty is so much better she begged to go out and play. I wasn't going to let her, but Naomi said she was no longer infectious."

"You should have stayed home and rested."

Sibyl removed her hat and placed it on a table next to the door. "I'm not tired."

"You sat up with Kitty for two nights. You've got to be worn out."

"I thought I would be, but I got so fidgety I decided I might as well go to work. What have you been doing while I was gone?"

"Looking over some old ledgers from the years in Kentucky. I'm surprised Norman kept them this long."

Sibyl hung up her lightweight jacket and turned to her desk. "Norman kept everything. Did you find anything interesting?"

"A couple things were curious."

Sibyl sat down at her desk and turned to face Logan. "Like what?"

"Norman made an unusually large number of loans five years ago. I know that's when the town was established, but it looks like he lent the money with so little interest it hardly mattered. That doesn't sound like the Norman who was so disagreeable and controlling that people banded together to start a new bank."

"Things were different then. Norman changed later." Rather than face Logan, Sibyl fiddled with things on her desk.

"Why were things different?"

"It's a long story."

"We've got all afternoon. There's not likely to be any business Horace can't handle." It looked like Sibyl wasn't going to say anything more. It was obvious she didn't want to. "I don't mean to press. I was just curious."

"It's not a secret," Sibyl said, still not facing him. "Not everyone wanted to leave Kentucky. It was just after the war, when it was virtually impossible to sell property for anything like its real value. People turned their property over to Norman on condition that he give them money to start over."

"That couldn't have been it. The money appeared on the books two years before everyone left Kentucky."

"Why are you so interested in what happened so long ago? I told you Norman never discussed business with me."

The sharpness of Sibyl's tone startled Logan. "I was just curious."

Logan didn't doubt that Norman kept all knowledge of his business dealings from his wife—his uncle would never have thought of discussing his business with Bridgette—but Sibyl suspected something, and it was something she didn't want to talk about. "I didn't mean to sound like I'm demanding answers. It was just something I didn't understand."

Sibyl took a moment to compose herself before turning to face Logan. "My husband was not the man I thought him to be when I agreed to marry him."

Logan thought that was an unusual choice of words. Either a woman said *when I fell in love with him* or *when he asked me to marry him.*

"Both of our grandfathers founded Spencer's Clearing, but Norman's family always had more money than anyone else. Maybe it came from his mother. She was certainly disagreeable enough to have been born rich. In any case, all that money convinced Norman he was better than anyone else. He did many things that embarrassed me, some so appalling that Colby and others had to take a hand. It got to where I didn't want to know anything about the bank. Money was something Norman used to hold over people. Sometimes I almost wished we were poor."

Logan could see that it was hard for her to admit this to him. He started to stop her, but she indicated that she had more to say.

"I'm sure there was something not quite right about that money, but I do know he wouldn't have granted those loans on such easy terms if my father hadn't known something Norman didn't want known. Whatever it was, Norman did what he promised even though it made him as cross as an old maid jilted at the altar. Now I've told you all I know. I hope you're satisfied."

Logan wasn't satisfied any more than he believed Sibyl had told him all she knew, but whatever it was had happened long ago. Since Norman was dead, there was probably no way to learn the truth.

"I didn't mean to upset you," he said. "There can be many perfectly acceptable explanations. I shouldn't have opened any of those ledgers without asking your permission. I was just trying to fill up the time until you returned. I apologize."

Sibyl deflated almost immediately. "I shouldn't have gotten so upset. It bothers me that I don't know what Norman did over the years. It feels like I have something I don't deserve."

"You're not responsible for anything your husband may have done," Logan assured her. "From what I've seen of the people here, they feel the same way."

"But I *feel* guilty."

"You shouldn't. If we find a situation you can correct, I know you'll do it. Would your father have done any better?"

"My father is nearly as bad as Norman." She caught herself. "I shouldn't have said that."

"Why not? My uncle was a liar and a cheat. He was also a drunk and an abuser of anyone who wasn't as strong as he was. Should I think differently about him because he was my uncle and he's dead?"

"Of course not. It's just that it's hard when it's your father or your husband. You think you ought to have done something to change things."

"You will if you find something that needs changing.

You would deprive yourself before you'd do anyone an injustice." Worried he'd said too much, Logan hurried on. "Now, what do you want to do today? I think we've done all we need to with the ledgers for the time being. At this point, I think we ought to start trying to come up with strategies to find new depositors and win back old ones. How do the other bank's funds compare to yours?"

"We have several times their assets."

"Good. Then we have the advantage with anyone looking for large loans. Also, we can offer them lower interest rates."

"I don't know. Colby says he's not interested in making a lot of money, just giving people a fair deal."

"That's a perfect motto for you."

"I can't steal that from Colby."

"Has he used it?"

"No, but he doesn't run the bank. Naomi's brother Ethan and her father do."

"Have they used it?"

"No."

"Then it's fair game. I think we ought to print flyers with that slogan across the top as a banner. We can also advertise a range of interest rates lower than Ethan's. We can hire Colby to have his wagon drivers distribute them throughout the valley. Who handles the fort's accounts?"

"We handle the payroll, but the soldiers don't often come into town."

"Then we'll open a branch at the fort that's open one day a week. I think Cassie would be perfect for that."

Sibyl looked like she'd been steamrolled. A moment later she burst into laughter. "You're scaring me half to death. Nobody's ever done anything like that, not even Norman."

"It's good to be ahead of the game."

"Everybody will think I'm crazy."

"No, they won't. They'll think you're the smartest businesswoman in the Territory."

"But they're not my ideas. They're yours."

"They're mine now, but you'll soon start coming up with more and better ideas. You just need to get your feet wet."

"Wet! I feel like I'm drowning."

"You're a strong swimmer. Now don't be faint of heart. Find a pen and paper. We've got some planning to do."

Logan was delighted to see Sibyl so excited, so ready to throw herself into the job. He planned to do everything he could to keep her excited, but he wouldn't forget about that money. Something was wrong, and he was determined to find out what it was. Nothing—not the past, present, or future—was going to harm Sibyl Spencer as long as he could do anything about it.

❧

"I don't know why you hide when you eat lunch," Cassie said to Logan. "Nobody would make fun of you."

Logan had taken to having his lunch in a shady ravine just outside of town. It had the advantage of being away from the prying eyes of adults and being one of the children's favorite haunts. They were curious about his face, but they accepted him just the way he looked. They thought Chicago was an exotic place, but lost interest when they discovered it was just a bigger version of Cactus Corner. They were concerned if he suffered a weak spell, but they forgot about it as soon as it was over. They would talk to him when they were bored or ignored him when playing was more fun.

And the things they told him! Several people would be shocked to know what the children had to say about them. Logan remembered everything and stored it away on the off chance he could use it to Sibyl's advantage.

"I'm not exactly hiding," Logan replied. "I just like being with the children."

"Little Abe likes your stories. Do you make them up?" Cassie's house was on the edge of town closest to the ravine. She had fallen into the habit of walking back to the bank with Logan.

"Only parts of them," Logan confessed. "My father and I used to travel the Santa Fe Trail several times a year. I heard most of the stories from him or one of his friends. We didn't stop traveling until I was in my twenties." He didn't like lying, which made it difficult to know how much to tell and how much to leave out. Cassie was a lot more perceptive than people expected of a woman with flashy good looks, so Logan tried to be careful what he said around her.

They turned into the dusty main street. Colby had convinced everyone to plant trees in their yards and along the road, but they weren't tall enough to provide much shade. Cassie used a parasol to protect her delicate skin. "Do you miss your home?"

Logan had been careful to give as little information as possible about his family. "Not really. After my father died, I didn't feel any attachment to it."

"Don't you have friends back home who worry about you?" Cassie asked.

The men who worked for him cared only about their jobs and the income it provided. Bridgette wanted access to her uncle's money and was willing to marry him to get it, but did any one of them truly care for him? "No one who would miss me for very long."

"That's sad," Cassie said. "I didn't know any of the people who were in my father-in-law's wagon train when we left Independence. I wasn't very nice to them, but they didn't hesitate to take care of me when he and my husband were killed. After we got here, they made sure I had a house and a job. If I didn't show up at work, a dozen women would be on my doorstep wanting to know what was wrong. My own sisters couldn't have cared more for me." She laughed. "Naomi loves me even though she wanted to strangle me when she thought I was after her brother."

Just more proof of the emptiness of his former life. After his father died, all he had left was work. Had he ever been as cared for or as lighthearted as Cassie? She had lost her father-in-law, her husband, and was left to raise her son alone, but she was always cheerful, willing to help, and vigorous in defense of her friends. Had he ever felt that strongly about anything or anyone other than his father?

"What made you come to Cactus Corner?" Cassie asked. "It's got to be about as far from Chicago as you can get."

It was easy to say he'd ended up there by chance, but Cassie was never satisfied with answers that didn't ring true. She had a way of pressing for information that was as hard to resist as it was difficult to resent. He was prevented from coming up with a suitable answer by the sound of a wagon approaching at a dangerous speed. He turned around, but the vehicle was out of sight around a bend in the road.

"Who can that be?" Cassie asked. "Nobody I know is dumb enough to drive that fast coming into town."

Logan turned in the direction of town. He was horrified to see several children playing a game of hoops in the middle of the street. Like all children, they were so engrossed in their game they were paying no attention to their surroundings. If that wagon wasn't stopped, some of them could be hurt.

"It's a runaway!"

At Cassie's exclamation, Logan turned again to see a wagon pulled by two horses heading toward town at a gallop, a look of panic and fear in their eyes. There was no driver holding the reins, no one to stop their headlong flight down the center of the street. Throwing the remains of his lunch to the ground, Logan ran toward the oncoming wagon.

"Stop!" Cassie screamed. "You'll be killed!"

Logan had never tried to stop a team of runaway horses, but that didn't deter him. If he didn't stop them, some child would surely be hurt.

He couldn't run as fast as he used to, but he had to try. He couldn't fail to intercept the horses. The food he'd just eaten sat in his stomach like a solid weight. Cassie was running up the street, screaming at the children ahead. He hoped she would have time to warn them, but he couldn't take the chance. He had to reach the team of horses. Drawing on all his energy, he flung himself at the head of the horse nearest him.

The horse tried to veer away from him but was

prevented by his teammate, who couldn't see Logan. That was the only reason Logan was able to grab hold of the leather strap running from the horse's collar to the singletree that connected with the wagon. Logan was immediately pulled off his feet and dragged dangerously close to the pounding hooves. Had he been younger and stronger, he might have been able to pull himself up and mount the horse, but that was out of the question. He would have to catch hold of the bridle to have any real chance of slowing the horses before they barreled into the center of town.

He cursed his weakness as he reached for and got a grip on the horse's collar. An agonizing pain shot through his leg where one of the horse's hooves struck him. For a moment he thought he was going to lose his grip, but he fought the pain. It didn't matter what kind of injury he might suffer. The children were more important than a leg he soon wouldn't have any use for.

He didn't know if he had any strength left. His weight had managed to slow the horse perceptibly, but it wasn't enough. Somehow he had to find the strength to reach for the bridle. Flecks of foam from the horse's mouth hit him in the face, blinding him. He couldn't free a hand to wipe it away. Blindly he reached for the bridle but only encountered the horse's sweat-soaked neck. He tried to dig his toes into the cut-up soil of the street, but the horses were too powerful. Terrified he would fail, he found the strength he needed to reach for and finally grab hold of the horse's bridle. The horse screamed in fury and slewed around so abruptly he pulled the second horse against him. That caused the wagon to swing in the opposite direction. The wheels caught in the dry dirt, and the wagon pitched onto its side, spewing its contents into the street. The horses, slowed abruptly by the overturned wagon, squealed and plunged about in their harnesses.

Fearful of being trampled, Logan held on to the bridle despite being tossed about like a rag doll. As he desperately tried to find the strength to fling himself out of range of fear-crazed animals, an iron-shod hoof struck his leg again. Gasping at the searing pain, he felt his grip on the bridle begin to slip. Frantically, he groped for the horse's collar, but he couldn't get a grip on it. He was falling. He was going to be trampled to death.

In the same moment he lost his hold on the bridle, he felt hands grab hold of him and pull him from under the hooves of the frantic horses.

"Are you insane?" the man asked. "It's a miracle you weren't killed."

Logan wiped the foam from his eyes and looked up into the face of his birth father.

Six

FOR A MOMENT, LOGAN THOUGHT HE MUST HAVE passed out. He had been four years old when his parents died, but his memory of them was vivid despite the passing of so many years. Though he was no artist, he'd tried to draw their portraits so he'd never forget them. They had invaded his dreams on nights when he'd felt particularly alone.

"Is he okay?" a woman asked.

"I can't tell," the man said. "I've never seen anyone who looked like this."

"Out of the way! Let me through!"

It was Cassie. Logan would recognize that voice anywhere.

"Logan! Logan, speak to me. Can you hear me?"

Logan pulled his attention from the man in front of him, focusing. "I'm all right, but I think my leg is broken."

He could feel someone's hands on his leg.

"It's not broken, but you've got a nasty cut. I'll take you to Dr. Kessling."

By now the street was full of people, most of them talking at once, but Logan was interested only in the man who'd just examined his leg. "Who are you?" he asked.

"I'm Colby Blaine," the man said. "Do you have a death wish? You've got to be the craziest man I've ever met."

Logan focused on the pain in his leg, the noise of the crowd, anything to prove he hadn't passed out or was dreaming. The face swam before him, taunting him with hope.

"He's not crazy," Cassie declared. "He's the bravest man in the world. Those horses could have run over Little Abe if he hadn't stopped them."

"He wasn't the only child in the street," some woman said. "Without him, half the town would have been in mourning."

Logan tried to get to his feet, but Colby restrained him. "You're not walking on your own until the doctor takes a look at that leg. His office is just up the street. I'll carry you."

Logan tried to protest that he could walk, but he was unceremoniously picked up and carried in arms that were stronger than his own even before his illness. The adrenaline of excitement and exertion combined with the shock of seeing a man who looked like the memory of his birth father collided to make him feel dizzy and disoriented. The commotion around him just made it worse.

"Does anyone know who this man is?" Colby asked. "He looks like a drifter. What's his name, and what's he doing here?"

"I don't know why he's here," Cassie said, "but his name is Logan Holstock."

Logan could feel Colby's body tense.

"Holstock?"

Logan could only nod his head.

"That's my birth name," Colby told him. "Where are you from? Who are your parents? Where is the rest of your family?"

Forestalling his curiosity, Cassie said, "He's from Chicago. He used to do something important there. He's helping Sibyl learn how to run the bank."

"I was never important," Logan managed to say. "I just know a few things that can help."

"Sibyl swears he's a genius," Cassie said. "She says she doesn't know what she would have done without him."

Logan wanted to contradict Cassie so he could sink back into obscurity, but the weakness hit him so hard he had difficulty remaining conscious.

"I'm going to tell Sibyl," Cassie said. "She'll want to know."

Despite the dizziness, the weakness, and the confusion around him, he was acutely aware that he was in the arms of his brother. And Colby was Jared Smith's brother.

That meant Logan had found both his brothers.

The impact of that was so enormous it threatened to deprive him of what little mental capacity he had. Against all odds, he'd succeeded. He barely had time to process this information when he was carried inside a building and found himself facing another man he didn't know.

"He's got a bad cut on his leg," Colby told the doctor. "He didn't break anything, but he probably needs stitches."

Logan could tell that Kessling was the kind of

doctor who inspired confidence in patients by his kindness as well as the intelligence in his expression. He just hoped his skills were equal to the promise of his demeanor.

"Let me look." For a moment, the doctor's attention was more on Logan's face than his leg. "I'd like to talk to you about that," he said before turning his attention to Logan's leg.

The cut proved to be deep enough to require stitches but not bad enough to immobilize him. He'd just managed to endure having the wound sewn up when Sibyl came hurrying into the doctor's office.

"I don't know why I have doors," the doctor said. "They don't keep anything out but the flies."

Sibyl ignored the doctor's sarcasm. "Are you hurt?" she asked Logan. "Cassie said you managed to stop a runaway wagon by yourself."

"He was foolishly brave." Colby had stayed while the doctor cleaned and sewed up Logan's leg. "Or crazy. I haven't decided which. And he still hasn't answered my questions about his family."

Sibyl ignored him. "Weren't you afraid of getting killed?" she asked Logan.

"No." That might sound like a lie, but it was the truth. It would have saved him a lot of suffering. In the same instant, he knew he didn't *want* to die. He knew beyond a doubt now that he had found his brothers. He wanted the chance to learn as much as he could about them and their families, even spend some time with them. It wouldn't be the same as letting them know he was their brother, but secrecy would allow him to be around them without the fear that they would see him as an unwelcome burden.

"I think he's crazy," Colby said. "Anybody who tried what he did had to know he could get killed."

"Why did you do it?" Sibyl asked.

"There were children in the road. There was nobody else to stop them."

The doctor finished bandaging his leg. "You're fine to go now. Just take care of that leg and keep the wound clean. I'd like to see you in a couple of days. You don't look to be in good health, so the wound might have some trouble healing."

"I'll be fine."

"I'll make sure he's here," Sibyl told the doctor before turning to Logan. "You *will* be here if I have to find your camp and drag you into town."

"I'll help you," Colby offered. "Peter and Esther were also in the street. Fortunately they had the good sense to look up when they heard Cassie's screams."

Logan didn't waste his energy arguing. He was trying to gather the strength to walk out of the office on his own.

"I'd like to talk to you about that swelling in your face," the doctor said.

"There's no use," Logan said. "I've seen the best doctor in Chicago." He could tell the doctor wasn't going to let it go at that, so he summoned his energy and struggled to his feet.

"Do you want some help?" Colby asked.

"I'm a little weak, but I'm fine."

"I'll make sure he gets back to the bank," Sibyl said.

"Why the bank?" Colby asked.

"That's where I work."

"See that he doesn't chase any more runaway horses

until that leg heals," Colby said with a grin. "And I still want some answers to my questions."

"Make sure he gets some rest," the doctor said. "He doesn't look good."

Logan managed to walk out of the doctor's office, where he was immediately set upon by a noisy crowd who were eager, one by one, to tell him how much they appreciated what he'd done. If he had his hand shaken and received tearful thanks once, it happened a dozen times. It didn't do any good to try to escape. He was surrounded.

"It's no use trying to act like you did nothing more important than catch a loose dog," Sibyl said. "You saved several children from serious injury or worse."

"Colby said they heard Cassie's screams."

"Even if every child got out of the street in time, that doesn't diminish what you did," one woman said.

"That's right," said another. "We'll be thankful for what you did for as long as we live."

Naomi came striding up. "Colby just told me what you did," she said to Logan. "He may act like he thinks you were out of your mind, but he would have gone crazy if anything had happened to either of the twins. They'll be lucky if he lets them out of the house for the next week."

"He'd better lock the windows and seal off the attic," Logan said. "The Peter I know will try to take the side off the house to get outside."

Naomi laughed. "He is a little wild, but he was so repressed before he came to us, we don't have the heart to keep him inside."

Several women offered their opinions on Peter's high spirits. Not all of them were complimentary.

While Naomi was making it clear no one was going to criticize her children within her hearing, Logan and Sibyl were able to slip away.

"I hear you're a hero," Horace said the moment the bank door closed behind them. "I could never have done anything like that."

"If you'd been where I was, you could have, and you would have," Logan said.

"My brother, maybe, but not me."

"No man knows what he's capable of until he's faced with a challenge where he has no choice."

"Are you sure you're okay?" Sibyl asked when they reached the small room Logan used for an office.

"I'm just tired."

"Why don't you go home? There's nothing you have to do today."

"I just need to rest a bit."

"I'm afraid you won't get much rest here. Now that everybody knows where you work, they'll be coming in all day. Some to thank you, others just to get a look. They'll insist on talking to you, thanking you, and telling you stories about their children or brave deeds they've performed or they know about. Today you're the most interesting person in Cactus Corner. It'll probably stay that way until something *more* interesting happens."

"I don't like to leave before I've done my work. Besides, this will be an opportunity to try to convince people to deposit their money in your bank."

"Logan, I'm not desperate enough to take advantage of you like that."

"You won't be taking advantage of me but of the situation."

"You can't talk your way around me that easily. I

will not make money off your celebrity. I'm *ordering* you to leave early. If you feel guilty, we can figure out something else for you to do, but you're done for today. If you don't feel better tomorrow, take as much time as you need."

Logan hated to admit it, but being ordered to leave was a relief. Now that the excitement had worn off, he felt too weak and exhausted to think. Besides, his leg was painful. It embarrassed him to be around people when he felt this way, especially Sibyl. It was foolish to worry about how he looked in her eyes, but that was something he couldn't change.

"Cassie is more responsible than I am for keeping those children safe."

"Nobody's going to believe that as long as Cassie is doing her best to convince everybody there would have been a bloody tragedy if you hadn't stopped those horses. You might as well get used to it. You're a hero, Logan. Of course, you were already a hero to me."

Logan was shocked when Sibyl reached out and grasped his hand. His gaze flew to hers, only to be stunned at what he saw. Yet he had to be mistaken. It was impossible that she could be attracted to him. His heart was beating so rapidly he was sure she could hear it. Fearful his feelings might betray him, he gently pulled his hand away. "I'm not a hero. I only did what anyone else would have done."

"I know how you feel about people thanking you, but I get chills down my spine when I think Kitty could have been hurt. You are a remarkable man whether you believe it or not. Now go back to your camp and rest. I don't like to see you looking so exhausted."

He wasn't remarkable. His hobby was target

shooting. Before his illness, he'd practiced several days a week since he was a boy. As for the wagon, anybody could have done that. He just happened to be the one who was there, but he didn't have the energy to argue. Maybe he'd stay away for a day or two. That would give people time to forget him and think of something else, but he would come back soon. He didn't know how many days he had left, but he was beginning to realize he wanted Sibyl to be part of as many as possible.

⤫

"Who is that man?" Colby asked Sibyl. "And don't tell me he's a man named Logan Holstock."

"I can't tell you much more," Sibyl said. "He's been very secretive about his past." She laughed. "I think the children know more about him than I do."

Sibyl had spent the afternoon answering questions about Logan from at least half the inhabitants of Cactus Corner. Nearly all went away unsatisfied. She had dropped by Naomi's house to pick up Kitty on her way home. That's where Colby cornered her.

"He doesn't look strong enough to get out of his own way," Colby said. "I can't imagine where he found the strength to stop those horses."

"Neither can I, but he continues to surprise me."

"Jared said he's living in a tent on the Mogollon Rim with some half-starved dog for company."

"I've tried to get him to move into town, but he refuses."

"I doubt he has the money."

"He deposited over five hundred dollars in cash when he arrived. I know almost nothing about his past, but I'm sure he's not a thief or a vagrant. He's been a successful man in the past. I believe the illness that has distorted his face so badly is the reason he left Chicago. I know it's the reason he avoids people."

"Then he'd better stop doing things that are bound to bring him attention," Naomi said. "One more, and they'll erect a statue of him."

"Naomi says you let him work in the bank with you. Are you sure that's safe?"

"How can you ask that after he saved my life and possibly the lives of your children?"

"I can ask that about any man I know nothing about."

"When he found out I knew nothing about running a bank, he offered to help me figure out Norman's books. I don't know what he used to do, but he reads those figures as easily as if he wrote them himself. He already has several ideas for how to reclaim some of our customers. In fact, he wants you to help."

"How can I help when I'm the majority owner of the competition?"

"He just wants your drivers to distribute leaflets."

"What kind of leaflets?"

Sibyl couldn't repress a smile. "One that will show why a person will get better terms at my bank than yours."

"It's not my bank."

"You have the biggest investment in it, and your father-in-law and brother-in-law run it."

"It's still not my bank."

"That doesn't matter. Will you have your drivers distribute the leaflets?"

"I'll have to think about it. It's a matter of family loyalty."

"If you want to talk like that, both banks are in the family. That's even more true since Jared decided to divide his business equally between the two banks."

Naomi's surprise was clear. "Why did he do that?"

"You'll have to ask him, but it was Logan's idea. He said it wasn't fair to favor one cousin at the expense of the other."

"I think I'd better get to know more about this man," Colby said. "For a stranger, he's made an unusually strong impact in a short time. I'll drop by the bank tomorrow."

"I've told him to take some time off," Sibyl said. "I don't know what's wrong with him—he won't talk about it or agree to consult Dr. Kessling—but he's a very sick man. He has frequent bouts of weakness and nausea. You can see what it's done to his face. Sometimes I feel guilty for letting him work for me, but it seems to lift his spirits."

"Are you sure it's not *you* who lifts his spirits?" Naomi asked.

Sibyl refused to be discomfited by Naomi's question. "I make no secret of the fact that I admire him. He refuses to accept any pay though he works as long and hard as any of us. I think he's a man of character, but if you want an enthusiastic endorsement, ask the children. Kitty talks about him all the time."

"Peter's just as bad," Naomi said. "He insists on telling me all of Logan's stories, sometimes two or three times."

"Now I know I've got to find out more about him," Colby said. "I can't have my son thinking more of a stranger than of his own father."

Both women laughed. "That's not likely to happen

as long as you continue to spoil him," Naomi said. "He leaves the discipline to me," she told her cousin.

"I'm gone too much," Colby said. "Besides, you're much meaner than I am."

Naomi pinched her husband so hard he yelped.

"I think it's time for Kitty and me to go home," Sibyl said. "I'll check in tomorrow morning to see who's the winner."

"It'll be Naomi." Colby gave his wife a kiss. "I can't deny her anything."

Sibyl left quickly. Watching Naomi and Colby act like lovesick teenagers made her jealous. Why couldn't she have found a man to love her like that? He didn't have to be as big and outgoing as Colby. He could be a man like Logan—kind, thoughtful, and sweet despite being a hero. She could so easily have loved a man like that.

Or did she already?

❧

"Is Logan going to die?" Kitty asked her mother as she was being tucked into bed.

Sibyl wasn't sure how to answer this question because she didn't know how Kitty was dealing with Norman's death. She hadn't asked any questions after being told what had happened in the bank. She hadn't asked any questions about the funeral. Once she knew she wouldn't be sent away to boarding school, she seemed to forget about Norman. She had always liked Colby and was learning to be comfortable around Jared, but her relationship with Logan was different.

"Why do you ask that?"

"He's sick," Kitty said. "I wanted to take him to

the doctor, but he won't go. Peter says he's going to swell up and bust."

Sibyl tucked the single sheet around her daughter and smoothed her hair from her forehead. "You know better than to listen to what Peter says."

"Esther says Peter is just telling stories because I'm little and will believe him."

"Esther's a smart little girl."

"I didn't believe Peter. Does that make me a smart little girl, too?"

Sibyl laughed. "It certainly does. And you're a very thoughtful little girl to be so worried about Logan."

"I like him, but he seems sad. Do you think he's sad?"

"Yes, I do."

"Do you know why?"

Naomi said Peter always had to know the why of everything. It used to worry Sibyl that Kitty never asked why about anything. She had attributed that to Norman's influence. She was relieved to see that now Kitty might be coming out of her shell.

"I expect it's because he's sick."

"Esther says it's because his face is swollen."

"I'm sure she's right. How would you feel if your face looked like that?"

"Peter said if his face got all puffed up, he'd run away and become an outlaw. He said it would scare people into giving him their money."

Sibyl thought Peter was an amazing little boy, and she was happy to let Kitty play with him and Esther, but she thought it was about time he had a little more supervision. "Peter likes to exaggerate."

"Do you think Logan is going to die?" Kitty asked again.

"I don't know," her mother replied, "but I hope not. He's a very nice man. Now go to sleep and stop worrying about him."

"Peter says he's going to die because he's too old to be chasing wagons."

"He was tired. All he needs is a couple days of rest, and he'll be as good as new."

"Peter says—"

"I've heard enough of what *Peter says*. You need to stop paying attention to everything he says." She had to lower her voice. There was no point getting angry over anything Peter had said, and she had no right to be upset at Kitty. They were just as worried about Logan as she was.

"I like Peter," Kitty said. "He's funny."

Forcing herself to speak calmly, Sibyl said, "I like him, too, but he's a silly little boy to speak every outrageous thought that comes into his head." She kissed her daughter on the forehead. "Sleep well. I love you."

"I love you, too, Mama."

Those were the sweetest words in the world, and Sibyl never tired of hearing them. She already regretted the time when Kitty would grow up, marry, and move into her own home. She'd never thought much of what would happen when that day arrived, but Norman's death had caused her to think of many things for the first time.

Having washed up after supper and put everything away, she had nothing she had to do, but it was too early to go to bed. She didn't feel like visiting even if she'd been willing to leave Kitty by herself. She wouldn't think about the bank until morning, and the house was clean and dusted. She was restless, her mind unable to concentrate, her nerves feeling jumpy. Was it because of Kitty's question?

She supposed she'd accepted that Logan would die. It was unlikely a man as sick as he appeared to be would recover his health, but it was something she hadn't thought about. He was a stranger, an unknown, someone with whom she had no connection.

But that had changed. Every day she spent working with him, everything she heard about him, all the things he did without thinking they were unusual, the way he accepted his illness without complaint or expecting special consideration—it all came together to create a man unlike any she had known. As unlikely as it would have seemed two weeks ago, she had started to think of him as someone she cared about. Yet it was the way she cared about him that was taking her by surprise.

She'd started to have feelings for him. She didn't bother trying to convince herself it was just friendship. They were *feelings*! How could she have expected that? How could it have happened? She had no doubt he was a man of character, but she was a recent widow, so recent she still found herself expecting Norman to walk in the door and tell her she'd been dreaming. And despite what she believed, she actually knew nothing about Logan. He could be married, the father of half a dozen children. He could be escaping punishment for some kind of improper activity, running from debts, fleeing for his life. He could really be a drifter or a small-time thief. It didn't matter that she didn't believe any of these things. It only mattered that she had no proof they couldn't be true.

Restless, she needed to go outside for a breath of air. She couldn't sit on her front porch because somebody was bound to come along and want to talk to her. She needed solitude, quiet, time to think. Kitty would be fine if she was gone only a few minutes.

Most of the houses in Cactus Corner had been built off the main street with the Mogollon Rim rising in the distance behind them. Towering cottonwoods vied with sycamores while junipers and willows hugged closer to the ground. The early evening was punctuated by the sounds of birds seeking a roost for the evening and the sounds of human voices floating from the main street and neighboring houses. Their presence was comforting, their distance soothing. Sibyl took a seat on a bench built in the center of what would someday become a shady grove of oak trees. The dry night air was disturbed by drafts sweeping down from the rim that created eddies of cool mixed with warmth. An occasional breeze wafted through the trees, but the night was almost eerily still. And in that stillness she felt like an island, adrift with no port in sight.

Had she been so dominated by Norman she had no thoughts of her own? No, but her whole existence had turned into a day-to-day struggle to find ways to survive her life as his wife. Now that he was gone, the life she knew had disappeared. So had the person her marriage had forced her to become. Who was she now, what did she want, and what was she going to do about it? Was it that uncertainty that had caused her to think of Logan as more than just a man who was helping her? Was she reaching for a steadying influence, a kind of guidepost for what to do with the rest of her life? Did she want a relationship with a man, even one that was no more than friendship?

She couldn't be sure about the answers to any of those questions, but she was sure her feelings for Logan were rapidly moving beyond friendship. Maybe it was the contrast between him and Norman. Except for being a knowledgeable businessman, he was everything Norman hadn't been. He was kind, quiet, competent, generous, and giving to a fault. And that didn't take into account acts of bravery that seemed to show complete disregard for his life. There was a goodness about him that found its way in everything he did. That was something the children had noticed before anyone else. Oddly enough, his disfigured face and weak spells generated her sympathy rather than antipathy. She knew what it was like to feel that her life had slipped beyond her control.

But that wasn't entirely true. At the time of her marriage to Norman, she hadn't cared what happened to her. She had melodramatically declared that she wanted to die, but she hadn't meant it. She was in such pain she couldn't think. Marrying Norman hadn't seemed such a bad thing. It was only later that she'd discovered how wrong she had been.

Logan's wife would have had an entirely different life. Sibyl had dreamed of how wonderful it would be to wake up next to the man she loved, a man who loved and valued her for herself rather than how well she could cook or manage a household. Norman hadn't cared about love, only his position as a married man. He would probably have been happier with a housekeeper. In reality, that's all she'd been.

After the first year, that's all she'd wanted to be.

Disgusted with herself, she got up and walked back to the house, but she stopped when she'd mounted the steps. She leaned against the post and turned back. The night was so quiet, the Rim in the distance so peaceful looking. That should have quieted some of the turmoil inside her, but the sheer beauty of it made her unhappiness weigh more heavily. She was twenty-three years old, and she could barely remember being happy. Or feeling loved. Her father had always wanted more children, specifically sons. Her mother had been unhappy because her sister had produced two boys. Sibyl had never been able to understand why Aunt Annabelle having two sons should be Sibyl's fault, but her father's coldness had made her feel that way. Things had only gotten worse when they disapproved of the man Sibyl fell in love with.

But he had been killed, and Sibyl had been talked into marrying Norman.

She'd done all she could to push those old memories from her mind. She'd been mostly successful until Norman's death. Now everything had come streaming back to bedevil her over events she couldn't control. She even felt guilty about the ones she hadn't seen coming.

She wondered if her interest in Logan was simply an exercise in wishful thinking, imagining how her life could have been if she'd married a man like the man he seemed to be. There was no logical reason for this attraction. Regardless of how she might feel about him, she could only guess at the quality of his character, the depth of his integrity, the steadiness and dependability of his nature. Because of his illness, there was little about him that was physically attractive, yet she *did* find him attractive. She knew that didn't make sense, but knowing it didn't change anything.

Maybe it was that she liked the person she saw inside. Norman had been a handsome man on the outside, and a vile one on the inside. Could she be intrigued because Logan was the opposite?

She had no answers, and trying to find some was giving her a headache. She turned and went inside, being careful to lock the door behind her. Norman had insisted it wasn't necessary, that there was no one in Cactus Corner who would be a danger to them, but Sibyl was alone now, something that weighed heavily on her mind. Even though she didn't get along with her father and had disliked Norman, the men had been protection against potential danger. Maybe it was all a matter of changing her thinking, but she felt uneasy. She'd made the journey from Kentucky to the Arizona Territory, surviving Indian attacks, lightning storms, flooded rivers, and physical exhaustion. She'd lived in a wagon, cooked over an open fire, and worn clothes permeated with dirt because there was no way to wash them. Yet during all of that, there had always been a man around who was responsible for protecting her. Now there was no one.

Did she need protection? Or did she just want someone by her side?

Tired of all this fruitless thinking, Sibyl turned down the wick on the lamp in the parlor and picked up the smaller lamp on the hall table. She ascended the stairs with slow but firm steps. Norman's death had turned her life upside down, had forced her to assume responsibilities for which she was unprepared, but she wasn't going to back away. She had something of great value that she'd never had before—control of her own life. It might take a while to learn how to manage it, but she intended to make the most of it.

❧

Logan absently rubbed the dog's head. A week ago, he'd waked to find Trusty sleeping next to him inside the tent. When he reached over to pat the dog, he responded by snuggling closer. From that moment on, the dog had never left his side until he got to the edge of town. At the end of the day, he was waiting for Logan in the same spot

"This is a nice place up here," he said to Trusty. "Quiet, cool, and nobody to bother us."

The dog moved closer to give Logan better access.

"You're a slut," he told the dog. "You'll do anything for food and a little scratching. You gotta have more pride."

Trusty whined, looked up with complete trust in his eyes.

"I know," Logan said. "It's nice to have a friend, even if it's only for a little while."

Is that how he felt about Sibyl—that she was a friend he would have only a little while? He knew better than to ask the question, but he'd decided not to be afraid of the answer. It was safe to let himself feel anything he wanted, imagine anything he could, hope for everything he lacked because no one would ever know about it.

"Except you," he said to the dog. "It's good to have someone to talk to who won't argue or tell me I'm a fool. Outcasts deserve to have some of what we want even if it's only in our imaginations."

Trusty's stare remained unbroken.

"Nobody's as good as you think I am," Logan said. "I fed you because I had food I didn't need. I let you stay because you used to guard the camp before you started hanging out in town waiting for me to come home. You ought to stay here. Think of all the squirrels you could chase. You could even do the hunting. It would be nice to come home and find a couple of rabbits all ready for the cook pot."

Trusty whined and smacked his lips.

Logan laughed. "I swear you know when I'm talking about food. Makes you hungry just to think about rabbits, doesn't it? It does sound pretty good. Maybe I'll—"

Pain and nausea struck together, causing Logan to double over with a groan. Forcing himself to move before he fouled his camp, he attempted to get to his feet only to stumble when a paralyzing pain gripped his body. Desperate to get away from his camp, he headed toward the stream. When he couldn't walk, he crawled on hands and knees. When that was no longer possible, he crawled on his belly. He could hear Trusty next to him, whining piteously, but he focused on reaching the stream.

Nausea overwhelmed him before he got there, but he kept going. By the time he reached the water's edge, he'd emptied his stomach of its contents. Glad for even that modicum of relief, Logan dropped his head into the water, relieved to wash the sour taste from his mouth. Even though it was summer, the water was deliciously cold. It did more to revive him than the gradual retreat of the nausea. Trusty was lying next to him when he finally raised his head. The dog whined and crawled closer.

"Not ready to give up on me yet, huh?"

The dog's anxious whine moved Logan more than human commiseration could have.

"Thanks for the concern, but I'm afraid there's not

much either of us can do about it." He sat up, but his head spun so rapidly he didn't try to get to his feet right away. "I hope you know how embarrassing this is. I'm only letting you stay because I know you can't tell anyone. I feel weak as a baby."

Logan came to his hands and knees before he was able to stand using a nearby tree for support. His legs were shaky, but he managed to get back to his tent and cleaned himself up and changed clothes. "I'm going to have to do laundry," he said to the dog, then laughed. "Wouldn't Bridgette love to see me washing clothes in the creek in this wilderness? She'd take it as proof that I'm the low-class foundling she always thought me to be. Maybe I'll throw everything away and buy some new clothes. It's not like I'm going to have a lot of use for my money."

He dug out his medicine and took a dose.

"I don't know why I bother," he told Trusty. "It doesn't make me any better, but maybe it'll help me live a little longer." His laugh was bitter. "Live longer so I can regret I missed the chance to marry a woman like Sibyl Spencer. I haven't told you about Sibyl, have I?"

Fortunately Trusty wasn't able to tell him he'd talked about little else.

"She's beautiful. I know a man of character wouldn't be overawed by a woman's looks, but he would if he saw Sibyl. If there's such a thing as a perfect woman, it's Sibyl. I would describe her physical attributes, but I don't want to cause you to blush. Let's just say they're enough to cause a man to get down on his knees and thank God for making him a man. Yet she dresses modestly and behaves as though she's an ordinary woman. I don't think she has any mirrors in her house. Do you think we should buy her one?"

Trusty shook his head to rid himself of a mosquito.

"You're right. She's not the kind of woman to preen in front of a mirror or spend time worrying about whether others think she's attractive. She's more concerned with her daughter, the fate of the bank and its employees, and her family. Sometimes I think she worries about me, too." He looked at the dog. "You probably think I'm fooling myself."

Trusty didn't move a muscle.

"Okay, don't say anything, but I can guess what you're thinking. Who'd spend even five minutes worrying about a man who spoke as little as possible, avoided people when he could, kept getting sick, and who looked scary enough to give people nightmares? But that's exactly the kind of thing Sibyl would do. Sometimes I swear she looks right past my face to what she thinks she sees inside. Don't ask me what she sees that makes her worry about me. I never thought there was anything about me to attract a woman but looks and money. When I lost one and gave up the other, I expected to die forgotten and alone. That's part of why I came west. I never really thought I'd find my brothers. I'd even decided I wouldn't look for them. Instead, I believe I've found both brothers and a woman I could love. My father used to say, *What one hand gives, the other can take away.* Doesn't seem fair, does it? Is that what happened to you? Did you start out with someone who loved you and end up with someone who'd rather kick you than give you a scratch?"

Trusty wiggled forward until he could lick Logan's hand. It brought tears to Logan's eyes.

"If we ever run across the son of a bitch, I hope you rip his heart out. Now I'm through feeling sorry for myself. It doesn't do any good, and I have to go to work tomorrow and act like nothing's wrong. We'll keep this between the two of us, okay? People in Cactus Corner are really nice. They'll be concerned and ask if there's anything they can do, but they'll be relieved when I say *thank you, but I'm fine*. There's no point in saying anything else. There's nothing anybody can do."

Logan crawled into his tent and lay down on top of his sleeping bag. The evening temperature was perfect for sleeping, not too hot and not too cold. He'd hardly gotten settled when Trusty crawled into the tent and lay down beside him.

"You're hot," Logan complained. "Why don't you sleep outside? That way you could watch for bears."

Trusty shifted his body so he could be a little closer to Logan.

Logan reached over and put his hand on the dog's back. Then with a smile no one would ever see, he drifted off to sleep.

⸎

"That horse bucked and jumped every which way he could," Logan said to his attentive audience. "Squealing like somebody was taking his hide off a piece at a time, he went to bucking, spinning, fishtailing—"

"What's fishtailing?" Kitty asked.

"It's sorta like his head's going in one direction, and his rear is going another."

"How can a horse do that?"

"Who cares?" Peter complained. "Did your pa fall off?"

"No," Logan said.

"Did he get away from those bandits?" Little Abe asked.

"He might not have," Logan told him, "but all that ruckus—especially the squealing—got the other horses so riled up the bandits couldn't catch them. He was able to run off the horses so the bandits couldn't follow him. He caught a couple, which he sold later."

"My pa could do that," Peter said. "He's got this big old horse he won't let anybody ride, but I bet I could."

"You come near that horse, Peter Blaine, and Pa will take your hide off an inch at a time," Esther warned her brother.

"I'm not going to mess with that old horse, but I *could* ride him," Peter insisted. "Now come on. Ma said if we were late for lunch, we'd have to stay inside all afternoon. I'm not staying cooped up inside for nobody."

Peter ran off. Esther and Little Abe followed, but Kitty stayed behind. "Did your father really ride that horse?"

Logan tried not to smile. "Do you think I make up stories?"

"I don't know. I think Uncle Colby can do all those things, but Aunt Naomi says there's nobody else as good as Uncle Colby in the whole world."

"I'm sure my pa wasn't as good as your Uncle Colby, but he did ride that horse, and he did capture two of the bandits' horses, which he sold later."

"I suppose it's okay to take bandits' horses. They're not nice people. They killed my father." A furrowed brow indicated Kitty wasn't entirely sure of herself.

"It's good to take horses away from bandits," Logan said. "That stops them from doing bad things to people."

"I wish somebody had taken the horses from the bandits who killed my father."

Logan had never seen any sign that Kitty missed her father. The other children all called their fathers *Pa*, but Kitty always said *my father*. From the things Cassie said—and she said a great deal—Norman hadn't loved anyone but himself. Logan didn't understand how any father could not love Kitty. She was as pretty as a picture, and as sweet as could be. She seemed shyer than the other children, but she had backbone. Not even Peter could run over her.

"You'd better catch up with the others," Logan said. "I don't want you to be late for lunch."

"I don't mind staying inside. If I offer to play with baby Annabelle, Aunt Naomi will read to me. Annabelle will cry if Jonathan doesn't want to play with her. She was named for Aunt Naomi's mother."

Another name he didn't know. Logan wondered what it would have been like to live in a village where people knew everyone who'd lived there during the last hundred years. "Still, you'd better hurry. Your lunch will be cold."

"Your lunch was cold," she said. "Wasn't it good?"

"It was fine, but it doesn't matter what an old man like me eats. You're young. You need lots of good, warm food so you'll grow up big and strong."

"Will it make me grow up like Peter?"

Logan chuckled. "No. You'll grow up to be just like your mother. Now run away. I have to go back to work."

"I'll see you tomorrow."

"I'll be waiting here as usual."

Kitty turned to go, but instead of walking or

running, she skipped. There was something about skipping that made it seem like the child hadn't a care in the world. Logan had never felt like that. He wondered if he ever could.

"I've been wondering what you did when you disappeared down this ravine. Now I know."

Seven

THE SOUND OF AN UNEXPECTED VOICE CAUSED LOGAN to spin around. Sibyl had stepped from behind one of the large boulders some ancient flood had washed down from the Rim above. He flushed from embarrassment.

"Peter and Esther like my stories," Logan explained. "Their father doesn't like to talk about his experiences, so they get to imagine all the things he's done by listening to me."

"What about Kitty? Does she also crave excitement?"

Logan wasn't sure how to answer. "She listens, but I think she's more concerned about my health. She studies me very carefully each day."

Sibyl's smile slid away. "She's worried about you just like the rest of us. She's afraid you're going to die."

"What did you tell her?"

"I told her I hoped not because you're a very nice man, and we're all very fond of you."

Fond seemed such a miserably insignificant word when he wanted something much stronger. He knew better than to hope, but knowing better couldn't stop him wanting. It was a cruel trick of fate that something he'd never missed had become the one thing he wanted most.

"You shouldn't waste your time on me. One of these mornings, I won't show up at the bank because I'll be gone."

Sibyl moved closer. "I hope not before saying good-bye. We'll miss you."

She stood in the dappled shade of a towering cottonwood. Its rustling leaves caused light and shadow to play across her face, making it difficult to see her expression. He wanted to look away but couldn't. He was fearful of what he would see—or what he wouldn't.

"I was never going to be here long. If I hadn't entered the bank when I did, you'd never have known I existed."

"That doesn't matter now."

"Why?"

"Because I do know you exist. So does Kitty. And Cassie. And Horace. And half the children in town."

"They'll forget me soon enough." He'd never worried that people might not remember him, so why should it bother him now?

"We never forget people we come to know and like, even when they disappear from our lives. They become part of who we are, what our lives have been."

Logan didn't want to be responsible for anyone's sense of loss, even if it was brief and painless. If this was how Sibyl felt after such a brief acquaintance, it was all the more reason not to reveal himself to his brothers. Still, he liked the idea that someone would remember him if only briefly. Maybe it was only natural to want to leave some trace of having been on this earth. Bridgette would remember him, but it would be with anger. Peter would remember his stories. Kitty would remember his illness. Trusty would remember him because he fed him, but how would Sibyl remember him?

"I will remember you because you saved my life," Sibyl reminded him. "Every mother with a child in the street the other day will remember you, too."

"It was Cassie who—"

Sibyl came closer. "You can object all you want, but we know what we saw. No one has been louder in declaring you a hero than Cassie."

"*I'm not a hero!*" He hadn't meant to shout. "It's not heroic to do what any other person who was standing where I was would have done."

"I couldn't have done it. Half the men in this town can't run fast enough or aren't strong enough. The fact that you could do both while being so sick is amazing. You'll have our eternal gratitude whether you want it or not."

Logan felt some of the steam go out of his anger. "I don't know how I did it. I just know I couldn't let anything happen to those children."

"That's because you love them."

"I don't...I can't—" He couldn't think of anything to say. Did he love those children? Could he love anyone after such a short acquaintance? Did he even know what love was? He'd always thought he loved his father, but might it have been gratitude and admiration instead?

"You can't convince me you don't love those children," Sibyl said, "not after I saw the way you looked at them."

"I've never been around children," Logan said. "I didn't know what to do with them. They asked too many questions. That's why I started telling them stories. Kitty wanted to take me to the doctor that first day." He smiled at the memory. "She offered to go with me so I wouldn't get lost."

"She worries about you. We all do."

"Don't. Everything that can be done for me is being done." He gathered up the remainder of his lunch. "It's time I went back to work."

Sibyl didn't move. "Why do you work so hard? It's not like I'm paying you or that you're in danger of losing your job."

"I like having something to do. Working in a bank is something I've never done. I find it interesting."

"What have you done?"

"Nothing important. I worked for my father."

"What kind of work?"

"Anything he needed done."

"You're not going to tell me, are you?"

"Why do you want to know? I'll vanish as suddenly as I appeared. In a couple of years you'll hardly remember I was here."

"There are reasons why that will never happen, but there's no need to repeat them. I didn't follow you just to spy on you. I have a request for a rather large loan. I'd like your opinion on what to do about it."

"You don't need my opinion."

"Maybe not, but I would like it. You may find it difficult to accept, but I value your opinion. You have a greater knowledge of the world of finance than I do. I want to succeed on my own, but I don't want to jeopardize mine and Kitty's futures."

"Is it that big?"

"No, but it's large enough that I feel like it is."

Logan couldn't help but feel sorry for Sibyl. After spending her whole life dealing with sums that rarely exceeded ten dollars, she was now faced with requests for loans that ran to the tens of thousands of dollars. That would be enough to cause any normal person to panic. "I'll help you as much as I can, but the final decision will have to be yours."

Sibyl seemed to relax. "I know that. I know nothing about the business this loan is for. Despite your attempts to claim otherwise, I think you do."

It was getting harder and harder to keep his distance from Sibyl. There were so many things he wanted her to know. That he thought she was the most beautiful, admirable, and courageous woman he'd ever met. That she shouldn't be afraid of freedom, that rather she should embrace it. That she should never invest all her energy in her work, or she would end up looking back on a life full of barren years. That she should hold close to family and friends because freedom from connection to others was a form of slow death.

You just didn't know it until it was too late.

He wanted to tell her how much he wanted to reach out to his brothers, how much he'd missed by not having children, how he'd been given a glimpse of what life could mean just as his own was drawing to a close. He wanted to tell her that he thought he might love her, something he'd never said to another human being, not even his father.

But he would say none of that. He didn't have the right.

"I'll do what I can, but your family probably knows more about the man's business than I will."

"I'll talk with them, but I still want to go over it

with you. I'll walk back with you unless you're afraid of being seen with a widow."

He wondered if she'd sensed his slight hesitation. "I don't mind if you don't."

Sibyl's gaze softened. "I'm proud to be seen with you. I doubt there's a finer man in all of Cactus Corner."

If he'd met Sibyl earlier in his life, he might have had a chance of becoming the man she thought him to be. He wasn't a hero, and he wasn't fearless. He simply wasn't afraid of death.

"Whose idea was it to open a teller's window at Camp Verde?" Naomi asked.

"Logan's," Sibyl replied. "You didn't think I'd come up with an idea like that, did you?"

"Why not?"

"Because I was so afraid of being responsible for the bank, I couldn't think. How would you feel if you were faced with a business you knew nothing about?"

"I'd run straight to Colby," Naomi confessed with a laugh. "Why didn't you?"

"Because he wasn't here. Besides, he's the biggest investor in your bank."

"Community Bank isn't *our* bank."

"You're the biggest investor, and your father and brother run it. It's *your* bank."

"You still could have asked any one of us. We'd have been glad to help."

Sibyl couldn't describe the tangle of emotions or explain the complex feelings that had kept her from asking anyone for help.

"By the time I was ready to tackle the job, Logan

was there to help. I don't know what I would have done without him."

"For a man who materialized out of nowhere, he certainly has made a strong impression on this town. I wish we knew more about him."

"I do, too, but he seems determined to protect his past."

"Doesn't that make you nervous?"

Sibyl's laugh sounded nervous, even to her. "It probably should, but it doesn't. Every time I tell myself I must be crazy, I remember that Cassie trusts him as well. I know all of us sometimes wonder if Cassie isn't a little bit crazy, but her instincts are never wrong. Besides, all the children adore him. Kitty keeps asking me if he's going to die."

"I wish he'd see Papa."

"I do, too, but he says all that can be done is being done."

"What does that mean?"

"I don't know. Maybe he has some medicine up at that camp."

"From what I can tell, he's not getting any better."

"No. He's getting worse."

"Does he have any family? Who are we to notify if he dies?"

"I don't know, but he keeps saying he won't be here long. I get the feeling he'll leave before that happens."

"Where will he go? Who'll take care of him?"

"I don't know that anybody will."

"Well, we can't let that happen. He may be a stranger, but this town owes him a debt of gratitude. We won't let him die alone. You've got to convince him to stay with us."

Naomi had the bit between her teeth. Once she made up her mind, there wasn't much that could stop her. Sibyl would talk to Logan, but she didn't know that she could convince him to change his mind. She hoped he would. She wouldn't put it past Naomi to tie him to his sickbed.

"I'll talk to him, but he's not very persuadable."

"If you can get him interested in more projects like the office in Camp Verde, he might forget about leaving. What are you going to do about opening an office there? Who would run it if you did?"

"We haven't made any definite plans yet. I'm going to drive up there tomorrow and—"

Naomi made no attempt to hide her shock and disapproval. "You can't go to an army camp. It's too dangerous. There's still a threat from renegade Indians. Besides, a woman alone has no business in an army camp."

"Logan is going with me."

"We're worried the man could take to his deathbed any minute, and you're depending on him to protect your life and your honor? Have you gone mad?"

Sibyl couldn't help but laugh. "Have you forgotten the time you rode out in the middle of a terrible thunderstorm to look for our missing mules and oxen? Your father was scared to death, and Colby was livid, but you didn't back down from either one."

Naomi had the decency to look abashed. "Okay, maybe that wasn't the smartest thing I ever did, but Colby used to make me so mad I'd do anything to prove him wrong."

"Well, I'm not fighting mad or trying to prove anyone wrong, but if I'm going to consider opening an office at the camp, I've got to see it for myself and talk to the commanding officer."

"Ask Jared to do it. The camp was his last army posting."

"I need to do it myself."

"At least talk to him. He might be able to tell you all you need to know."

"Logan says it's unwise to make any business decision without learning everything you can firsthand."

It was obvious Naomi wasn't pleased. "I'm beginning to think you're placing too much reliance in Logan and his opinions."

"Norman used to say the same thing. How many times have you heard people complain that he wanted to know things that were none of his business? As obnoxious as he was, he didn't make bad business decisions."

"Why don't you wait until Colby can go with you? He goes to the camp all the time."

"Do you wait for Colby to come home before you make decisions?"

"Of course not. If I did, nothing would ever get done."

"Did Laurie ask our permission before she took the job on Jared's ranch?"

"No, but she should have."

"If she had, we'd have told her not to go, and she'd have missed falling in love with the perfect man for her."

"This is different."

"So you're saying it's all right for you and Laurie to make your own decisions, but not for me. Why not? Do you think the two of you are smarter than I am?"

"Of course not. You're probably smarter than either one of us."

"So what's wrong with me?"

"Nothing. You're beautiful, and sweet, and I adore you."

Sibyl didn't feel mollified. "But you don't think I can take care of myself?"

Naomi sighed and admitted defeat. "I think you're smart enough to do anything you make up your mind to do. I'm all for you opening an office at the camp, one in Preston, and in Tucson, if you want. I just don't want you to do anything dangerous."

"Laurie drove to Jared's ranch every day."

"But Steve was with her."

"Logan will be with me, and he's not a teenage boy."

"Okay, okay. Go to Camp Verde, and convince them they'd be crazy not to let you set up an office there. But if you tell me you've decided to operate the office yourself, I'm going to lock you in your own house."

Sibyl laughed, all tension gone. "I'm thinking about asking Cassie. One look at her, and they'll probably give her an army escort."

The two cousins put their arms around each other and had a good laugh.

"I just want you to be safe," Naomi said when she released her cousin and sat back.

"I will be."

"And happy and successful and married to a man who adores you."

Sibyl's smile faded. "Being married to a man who adores me might be a bit much. I'll settle for happy and successful."

"Don't you dare. Laurie found Jared. You'll find someone."

Sibyl was afraid she'd already found someone. And she could hardly have made a more unfortunate choice.

❦

"There's a dog in the bushes," Kitty said to Logan.

Peter jumped up from where he was drawing in the dirt. "Where? I don't see him."

"He hid when you jumped up," Kitty said. "I think you scared him."

"He's not much of a dog then." Peter tossed his stick away. "I'm going to the livery stable. Ted says they're getting some new horses today. Want to come?" Little Abe and Esther were quick to join him.

"I'll stay," Kitty said.

"Why? Logan's not going to tell another story."

"I just want to," Kitty replied. "I don't like horses."

"Ma says she used to be afraid of horses, but she's not anymore."

"I'm not afraid," Kitty said. "I just don't like them."

"I do," Peter said. "When I get big, I'm going to have a dozen horses all my own."

"Uncle Colby won't give Peter a dozen horses," Kitty told Logan after the others had left. "He says horses are for work, not for play."

Logan was sorry he wouldn't have much time to get to know Colby. From what everyone said, his younger brother was quite a remarkable man.

"The dog's back," Kitty said.

Logan looked to where Kitty was pointing. He wasn't really surprised when Trusty pushed his way through a juniper thicket and sidled up to him. Logan ruffled the dog's fur affectionately. "Just couldn't stay away, could you?"

"Is that your dog?" Kitty asked.

"No. He's just a friend."

"Would he be my friend?"

"I think so. Why don't you ask him?"

"How do I do that?"

"Hold out your hand. Let him sniff it."

Kitty held out her hand to Trusty, but he didn't move.

"Why isn't he sniffing?" Kitty asked.

"People haven't been very nice to him."

"What's his name?"

"I don't know, but I call him Trusty."

"I won't hurt you," Kitty said to the dog.

After hesitating a moment, he started toward her. The next moment he disappeared into the juniper thicket. The reason was apparent when Sibyl came into view.

"I thought I'd find you here," she said to her daughter. "Why aren't you at the corral with the others?"

"I wanted to stay here. Logan has a dog named Trusty for a friend. I think he wanted to be my friend, too, but you scared him away."

"Somebody beat him very badly," Logan explained when Sibyl turned to him. "He only took to me because he was starving."

"Where is he?"

"In there," Kitty said, pointing toward the juniper thicket.

"Are you sure he's safe?" Sibyl asked.

"He's nice, Mama," Kitty said. "I know he is."

"Then maybe he'll come back another day. You need to go stay with your aunt Naomi. Logan and I have to go to Camp Verde."

"I thought we were going to do that later," Logan said.

"So did I, but Naomi spoke to Laurie who spoke to Jared who is at the bank right now waiting to talk with us."

"Then you don't need me," Logan said. "If Jared worked there, he'll be far more help than I would be."

"I want you to go with me. Opening an office there was your idea. In any case, Jared isn't a banker. He's a rancher. What kind of advice could he give me?"

"Very sound advice, I expect. A man has to be a good businessman to be a successful rancher."

"Maybe, but I still want you to go with me."

"Why?"

"I already told you."

"But you don't *need* me."

"If I said I *did* need you, would you go with me?"

Logan didn't know what to say. The words that nearly tumbled out of his mouth would have been the worst possible response. He would rather suffer greater pain than he'd yet endured than have Sibyl turn away from him in disgust.

"Don't you want to go with Mama?"

Kitty's question brought Logan to a crossroads. Answering the question truthfully would subject him to the misery of spending an entire afternoon next to the woman he knew he could never have. A false answer would send him back to his camp cursing himself for giving up the chance to spend a few more precious hours in her company. "Yes," he said to the little girl, "I would like to go with her."

"Why didn't you say that in the beginning?" Sibyl asked.

Another question he couldn't answer truthfully. "I thought I'd be in the way."

"Nonsense. You know I depend on you to help me understand all sides of a decision before I make up my mind."

"Mama thinks you're brilliant. I heard you say it to Aunt Naomi," Kitty told her mother when she looked put out. "You also said you thought he was a wonderful man."

Sibyl turned crimson. After a brief glance at Logan, she turned to her daughter. "I did say both of those things, but it's not always wise to tell everything you know."

Logan would never know what Kitty might have said to her mother because just then Trusty stuck his head out of the juniper thicket. "Look!" she exclaimed, no longer interested in whether Logan would go with her mother. "Trusty's back. Do you think he'll sniff my hand now?"

Logan struggled to turn his attention from Sibyl. He longed to ask how she could think he was a wonderful man. He wanted to ask if she really meant it or was just saying it. He didn't believe she would lie, but neither could he imagine she could think he was wonderful. What had she really said? What were the *actual* words? Had she said he was wonderful, or had she used terms like nice, agreeable, pleasant, polite, or good-natured? They were all good words, but they weren't the same.

If she really had said he was wonderful, just what did she mean by it? Was he wonderful at figuring out Norman's books? Was it wonderful of him to spend so much time telling the children stories? Was it wonderful that he'd stopped the runaway horses? Was it wonderful of him to offer to help her without being paid? He tried to convince himself there were too many ways what she had said could be misinterpreted, but he couldn't dismiss the chance that she had used that word because she meant it.

"Look, he's licking my hand."

Logan pulled his wits together. "He likes you," he told Kitty. "He wants to be your friend."

"Mama, let him sniff you."

Sibyl looked as uncomfortable as Logan felt, but she extended her hand to Trusty. After a moment's hesitation, she inched forward until his nose touched her hand.

"He's got scars," Sibyl said.

"He was badly beaten, but he's recovering."

"It takes a particularly awful kind of person to beat an animal that way. I'm glad you've taken him in. It's time for you to go to your Aunt Naomi," she said to Kitty. "Logan and I have to go to Camp Verde. We can't keep Uncle Jared waiting any longer."

She hadn't looked at Logan, but Logan didn't need to see her face. The tone of her voice, the way she enunciated each word as though it were an enemy, told him she was unhappy about the confession her daughter had forced from her. The ride to Camp Verde was going to be all business and nothing else.

◦≫◦

"Are you sure it was a good idea to let the dog come with us?" Sibyl and Logan were nearing Camp Verde. "He doesn't like me as much as he likes Kitty."

"He doesn't dislike you," Logan said. "He just doesn't trust you yet. Anyway, I don't know how I could have left him. At camp he either sleeps next to me or sits at my feet. He follows me to town and waits outside the bank or in the grove where I eat lunch. He doesn't like to let me out of his sight. I'm not sure whether he's trying to protect me or depending on me to protect him."

Trusty ran alongside. When he'd followed them out of town, Logan had tried to coax him up into the buckboard, but he'd balked at the sight of Sibyl. His easy stride was a welcome sign he'd regained much of his strength. He was starting to look like a real dog, not a badly chewed piece of hide stretched over some bones.

"I think he likes me because I feed him."

Sibyl looked down at the dog. "His attachment to you is a lot more than like. He's yours as long as you'll have him."

Logan had already realized that was going to be a problem. He hoped he could talk Sibyl into adopting Trusty after... He didn't like putting his future into words. Saying it, hearing it, even thinking it, made it seem too real, too imminent. Facing his illness day after day was enough. He preferred to spend what energy he had left enjoying being with the people who'd become important to him. Horace came to him for practical man-to-man advice. Cassie was trying to turn him into a surrogate father for Little Abe. The children came to him for stories of adventure and excitement. Sibyl came to him... Well, she hadn't exactly *come* to him for anything, but she'd started to turn to him when she wanted to talk, even when it was about things that didn't concern the bank.

At first he tried not to become too invested in their lives, but he quickly gave up. He *wanted* to become involved with them. Doing so gave his remaining days meaning. He didn't want to be a pathetic man just sitting around waiting to die. There, he'd thought it.

He was going to die, but he wasn't going to give up. And there were things he'd been thinking about Sibyl that he couldn't go a moment longer without saying. It had all built up too strong inside.

"I've never been to Camp Verde," Sibyl said. "I have no idea where anything is."

"I don't expect you'll have any trouble," Logan had told her. "One look at you, and half the men will be fighting each other for the chance to take you anywhere you want to go."

"Only half?" Logan chuckled at the gleam in Sibyl's eye.

"The other half will be staring out their windows after being locked inside by their wives."

Sibyl chuckled delightedly. "If I didn't know both Laurie and Naomi are prettier than I am—not to mention Ted's wife Martha, who's absolutely beautiful—I could become rather vain."

"You're the most beautiful woman I've ever seen. And there are a lot more attractive women in Chicago to be compared with than Cactus Corner."

Sibyl's humor dried up. "I wish you wouldn't say things like that."

"That's how I feel," he said quietly.

"That's an even better reason. We shouldn't...we can't...I don't know. It just makes me uncomfortable."

"Then I won't *say* it again, but I will continue to *think* it."

"I wish you wouldn't."

"Why not? Do you object if I say Kitty is the most charming little girl I've ever met?"

"Of course not. She's my daughter. I think she's perfect."

"A perfect daughter requires a perfect mother. Did you adopt her or find her under a cabbage leaf?"

"Now you're being ridiculous."

"Good. I'm glad we've settled that because we've reached the camp."

Jared had described the camp for Logan. Instead of a wood stockade, twenty-two adobe and wood buildings had been built along the four sides of a large open square that served as a parade ground. The officers and their families lived on one side. The regular soldiers who had to survive on fifteen dollars a month lived in barracks scattered among buildings such as the hospital, the sutler's store, general storehouses, and wagon sheds. The fort had one cavalry unit and one infantry unit. Their job was to provide protection for the settlers from attacks by the Apache and Yavapai Indians. The original camp had been moved about a mile from the river because of malaria.

"Where do we go?" Sybil asked.

"Jared said we should talk to the commander. He'll be the one to decide if we can start a bank here."

There was a lot of movement about the camp, but no concerted action. Soldiers moved in random groups or singly, some on horseback, but most on foot. Children played under the watchful eyes of their mothers. Logan was headed toward what appeared to be the largest of the houses when Trusty's deep-throated growl caught his attention.

"What's wrong, boy?" he asked. "You won't find any bears or cougars here."

Trusty's response was to bare his teeth and snarl menacingly.

"Something or somebody has upset him," Sibyl said. "What's he looking at?"

"I can't tell, but he seems to be looking at a group of soldiers lounging against that building." The building appeared to be a barracks, and the soldiers were standing around, laughing and passing the time. A couple of dogs had flopped down under the shade of a cottonwood tree. Logan snapped his fingers at Trusty. "Get up in the buckboard," he said. "We're trying to do business here, and getting into a fight with the local dogs won't help."

Trusty's growls were unabated.

Logan snapped his fingers again. "Get up here, or I'll do it myself."

After a slight hesitation, Trusty jumped up in the buckboard only to start barking and growling with greater ferocity.

"I've never seen him act this way around other dogs," Logan said. "He usually pays them no attention."

One of the men who wasn't wearing a soldier's uniform, his interest apparently caught by Trusty's barking, left the group and started toward them. Trusty's growls and barking swelled in a crescendo. The hair on the back of his neck stood up, and he crouched as though ready to attack.

"There's something about that man," Sibyl said.

Logan agreed, and he was sure he knew what it was. His suspicion was confirmed by the first words out of the man's mouth.

"Where did you find my dog?" the man asked. "I lost him some weeks ago. Thanks for bringing him back."

Eight

LOGAN PUT HIS HAND ON TRUSTY'S BACK, BUT THAT didn't calm him. "I don't know who you are or why you think you have a claim on this dog," Logan said, "but Trusty is mine."

"His name ain't Trusty," the soldier said. "It's Brutus, and he's my dog. I'd recognize him anywhere."

"Then you can't be his owner. He didn't look a thing like this when I found him. He was starving, barely able to crawl, and covered with wounds from several savage beatings."

"You gotta beat a dog when he don't behave," the man said. "In any case, he's mine, and I want him back."

"He's mine now," Logan said, "and I intend to keep him."

"Now, see here," the man began, "you can't go around stealing a man's dog and get away with it."

"He found me, not the other way around," Logan said.

By now, their exchange had attracted the interest of the soldiers, and they approached the wagon.

"Looks like your dog, Wat," one of them said.

"That's what I been telling this man," Wat said, "but he don't believe me."

"I believe he *was* your dog," Logan said, "but you mistreated him so badly he ran away."

"That don't make any difference. He's my dog, and I'm taking him."

Wat reached for Trusty. With a startled yell, he drew back a bloody hand, his palm ripped open. One of the soldiers reached for the bully stick he carried at his waist, but it was shattered by a gunshot before he could raise it in the air. He stared at the gun in Logan's hand.

"No one touches that dog except to pet him, and then you'd better ask first. Is that understood?"

"He ripped my hand open," Wat exclaimed.

"You can't expect that dog to like you after what you did to him," one of the onlookers said. "I'm surprised he didn't try to tear out your throat."

The pistol shot had attracted attention, and almost at once they were surrounded by soldiers with arms drawn. "This is not how I expected things to go," Logan said to Sibyl.

Explanations were made and blame placed by both sides. They all ended up in front of the camp commander.

"If you told me a fight started over that woman," the commander said after giving Sibyl a thorough looking over, "I'd have no trouble believing you. But over a dog?"

"I'm sorry to have caused any trouble," Logan told the commander, "but I only fired my pistol to keep that man from hitting my dog with a bully stick."

"He's my dog," Wat complained.

The commander ignored him. "Who tried to hit your dog?"

Logan pointed to the offender, who the commander ordered to step forward and explain himself.

"That dog ripped open Wat Pfefferkorn's hand when he reached to take him," the soldier explained. "I was afraid he might jump out of the wagon and attack him."

"Why were you trying to take this man's dog?" the commander asked Wat.

"He's *my* dog," Wat insisted. "I was just trying to get him back."

"What dog rips open his owner's hand when he reaches for him?" the commander asked.

"One that's been starved and so badly beaten he's nearly dead," Logan told him. "He approached me up on the Rim at a deer kill. He was so badly wounded he could barely crawl. I fed him and took care of his wounds."

"Did you beat him?" the commander asked Wat.

"Only when he wouldn't behave," Wat answered.

"He did a lot more than that," a soldier said. "I warned him to stop before the dog turned on him."

"He did turn on him," the man with the bully stick said. "Just look at Wat's hand. He's vicious."

"He is not." Everyone turned to Sibyl in surprise. She hadn't spoken except to give her name. "I've seen him with children, including my six-year-old daughter. He lets them pet him and will eat out of their hands. He follows Logan wherever he goes. No one in town is afraid of him. Not even the other dogs."

"He's still my dog," Wat insisted, "and I want him back."

Trusty had kept up an undercurrent of growls and snarls all during the exchange.

"What do you propose to do with him?" the commander asked. "He clearly hates the sight of you."

"I don't know yet, but he's my—"

"I don't think we need to hear that again," Logan said to Wat. "You may own the dog legally, but he's never going to be yours." Logan handed Wat a twenty-dollar gold piece. "I trust this is adequate compensation for your loss."

"That mutt's not worth two dollars, much less twenty," a soldier said.

"He's worth every bit of it to me," Logan said.

"Then it's settled," the commander said before Wat could respond. "Now all of you get out of here, and go about your business. The fort could be under attack, and we wouldn't know." After the soldiers had withdrawn, the commander turned his attention to Logan. "Aside from firing a pistol in the middle of the parade ground, what's your reason for being here?"

"I'm just accompanying Mrs. Spencer. She owns Spencer's Bank in Cactus Corner. She would like to provide the same services for your soldiers."

The commander turned an appreciative eye on Sibyl. "If you're planning to provide these services personally, I can assure you of complete success."

Logan kept telling himself the commander was showing no disrespect by the way he looked at Sibyl, but he had to clench his jaw to keep from saying something while the commander and Sibyl talked terms. He could understand why the commander's gaze never left Sibyl, but he didn't have to like it. He just made himself a promise that as long as he had anything to do with it, Sibyl would never come back to Camp Verde. Nor would he send Cassie. The soldiers would have to make do with Horace.

❧

"Don't you like Logan?" Kitty asked her mother.

They were eating supper. Since Norman's death, Sibyl had started serving meals in the kitchen rather than the dining room. It was more convenient, cozier, and a distinct break from the torturous formal dinners they'd both suffered through under Norman's disapproving gaze. Kitty was happily eating her favorite meal, chicken in gravy with rice. Sibyl had no appetite.

"I like Logan very much," she told her daughter, "but that's not what I'm talking about. You can't tell people everything I say about them, especially not when it's the person I was talking about."

"Why? You didn't say anything bad."

Sibyl had known this was going to be a difficult conversation, but it was turning out to be harder than she'd expected. With no one to frown at her or show resentment that she'd ever been born, Kitty had virtually bloomed since Norman's death. She talked like she had to make up for years of silence. She ran where she'd previously walked with trepidation, and she had even come back from playing with dirty clothes. Equally important in Sibyl's eyes, she'd struck up a friendship with Logan. It wasn't the same as her relationship with Colby and Jared or her cousins Ethan and Ben. She liked all four men and enjoyed being around them, but there was something a little reserved about their time together. She was supposed to like them, to feel safe around them, because they were related to her.

That wasn't true with Logan. Kitty had pursued the friendship from the day she met him. She was the one who made certain the children joined him every day at lunch. She was the one who asked for his stories despite Peter insisting his father could have done everything better and faster. She still worried about his health and tried to convince him to see the doctor. She could talk to him about anything, ask any question. Sibyl didn't want to damage that friendship. It was the first time Kitty had opened up to anyone other than her mother.

"It's not a question of whether I said anything bad," Sibyl told her daughter. "It's just that when you say something in confidence, it shouldn't be repeated."

"What's a *confidence*?"

Sibyl didn't want to wish her daughter's life away, but she'd be relieved when Kitty was older. Talking to a six-year-old was difficult. They knew so much and so little at the same time. "It's like a secret," Sibyl explained.

"Is everything you say to Aunt Naomi a secret?"

"Just when we talk about people."

Kitty thought for a moment, her fork poised between her plate and her mouth. "Is everything *I* say about people a secret?"

"If you want it to be."

She was thinking again, her brow creased. "Even when I told Peter he was mean?"

Sibyl laughed at her daughter's concern. "Especially what you say about Peter. We wouldn't want to hurt Aunt Naomi's or Uncle Colby's feelings."

"It didn't make Peter mad when I told him. Why would it make Aunt Naomi and Uncle Colby mad?"

How did she explain that parents were very sensitive about their children, that they didn't take criticism well even when it was deserved? "Peter's parents love him very much. So it hurts them if someone says something unkind about him."

"Would it hurt you if someone said something bad about me?"

"I'd be furious. Everybody knows you're a very nice little girl who would never intentionally do anything wrong."

"Peter says I'm a goody-goody."

"There's nothing wrong with that," Sibyl said with a reassuring smile. "I like you just the way you are."

Kitty finished her supper. "I don't want my dessert."

"Why? It's apple pie, one of your favorites."

"I want to save it for Logan. He can't make a dessert in the woods."

And with that, Sibyl was catapulted right back into the miasma of conflicting emotions that assailed her every time she thought of Logan. How could she possibly keep him out of her thoughts when Kitty kept putting him back? "It's nice of you to think of Logan, but maybe he doesn't like dessert."

"He likes apple pie. I asked him."

This from a child who wouldn't speak to an adult unless they spoke to her first. What kind of magic had Logan worked on Sibyl and her daughter to keep him foremost in their thoughts? Logic and common sense said it should have been just the opposite. "You can take him some apple pie. I'll wrap it up for you, but there's enough for you to have some, too."

"If I eat a piece of pie now, the piece I give Logan won't be from me."

The logic was flawed, but Sibyl didn't try to refute it. Logan had installed himself as firmly in Kitty's thoughts as he had in her own. She would have to talk to him. She didn't know what either of them could do at this point, but she didn't want Kitty to be broken-hearted when Logan disappeared as he said he would.

And what about her own feelings? Would she be brokenhearted? Maybe not, but there was no use denying she would feel a terrible loss.

"If you've finished, it's time to get ready for bed. I'll be up to tuck you in as soon as I'm finished in the kitchen."

But as Sibyl moved about the kitchen putting away food and washing dishes, her thoughts were wholly absorbed with her feelings for Logan. What was she going to do? She couldn't stop thinking about him ever since the trip to Camp Verde. The drive there had been the most enjoyable of her life. He was a fascinating man, and not because he kept so much of his past to himself. He could talk about anything, but he could also listen, something she had once believed men found impossible to do. Then there was his faith in her. He had let her do all the negotiating with the commander. When he said he couldn't have done any better himself, she thought her insides would melt.

She wouldn't forget how he stood up for Trusty. She couldn't imagine paying twenty dollars for a dog, but she had no doubt he believed the dog was worth it. If Wat hadn't agreed, she had no doubt he would have paid more. What kind of man paid that kind of money for a mongrel dog just to keep him from being abused?

A man who valued trust and loyalty, one who wouldn't see even a stray dog mistreated. One who believed money wasn't the most important thing in life. What a change from Norman.

She could be mistaken, but she was certain his regard for her was very much the same as hers for him. That pleased and frightened her. She was vain enough to admit she enjoyed having men find her attractive, but if she was right, Logan's regard went deeper than that. Just knowing that caused her feelings for him to struggle to free themselves from her restraint. What was the harm in admitting how she felt? She was a grown woman, and she was free to bestow her favors wherever she pleased.

Yet she'd learned as a teenager that life and love weren't as simple as that. Every action had conse-quences, some dire enough to cause a woman to deny herself what she wanted most. She wasn't sure she was in love with Logan—it seemed impossible that it could have happened so quickly or have happened at all—but she had controlled her feelings to protect herself. Now she had to worry about Kitty. Should she ask Logan about his plans? He'd always said he wouldn't be around for long. Would he change his plans if she asked? Were his feelings for her strong enough to make him *want* to change?

If it came down to that, were *her* feelings strong enough to do any of that? Her husband of seven years had been dead only a short time. Now she found herself free to order her life as she wished, but she also found herself in charge of a bank people depended on for a living. Suddenly she was responsible for their livelihoods, herself, and her daughter. She was feeling overwhelmed. It was possible she was so emotionally overburdened she couldn't make good decisions, that her feelings for Logan were little more than an attempt to hold on to something steady while she learned to navigate these new and difficult waters. She would probably feel quite differently a year from now.

Her heart said her feelings wouldn't change, but her brain asked how could she know that. She'd spent years learning not to feel, deadening her heart and blunting her thoughts. How could she now be sure she knew what she *really* felt or what she *really* thought? And if she *was* sure of what she thought and felt, why was she unwilling for anyone to know? Was it because illness had distorted Logan's features so badly or because no one really knew anything about him? Was it because she was embarrassed to admit she could have fallen in love so quickly? Was she reluctant because of the explanations that would be needed to justify herself? Did she think it was unsuitable for a recently widowed woman to fall in love so quickly?

It all came down to the fact that she couldn't be sure, but she would figure it out soon. She wasn't going to miss the chance to be with Logan, even for a short time, because he embodied all she'd come to value in a man.

"There's no point in hiding in your office or trying to sneak back to your camp," Cassie said to Logan. "Everyone turns out for the Fourth of July celebrations. It would be unpatriotic not to."

"Cassie's right," Sibyl said. "Everybody in town will be there. It's especially important to the children. You wouldn't want to disappoint them."

Logan didn't want to attend the Fourth of July celebrations, or celebrations of any kind. Hundreds of people would be there. Most of them had never seen him. *All* of them would stare. There would be hordes of children who, in their innocence, would point to his face and ask what was wrong with him. He had no assurance he wouldn't have an attack of nausea and a weak spell, either of which would attract unwanted attention. It was hard enough accepting that he was going to die while he was in the prime of his life. It was too much to ask him to do it in front of a whole town.

But those weren't the only reasons. After the trip to Camp Verde, Sibyl had turned distant. She didn't physically avoid him, nor did she fail to treat him with her usual kindness and understanding, but there was a barrier between them now. Barely perceptible—even Cassie hadn't picked up on it yet—but it was there. The fact that the barrier existed gave him hope that she really did feel something special for him, but her reaction showed it was a feeling she was uncomfortable admitting and one she didn't intend to let develop into anything beyond friendship. He should have been flattered that she thought so well of him and relieved it wouldn't go any further.

Instead he was frustrated with her and angry with himself. He wanted her to admit her feelings even though he knew it wasn't good for either of them. He had no right to want that when he didn't intend to be equally open about his feelings. But how could he when he knew there could be no future for them?

But things had changed today. All trace of the chill had vanished, leaving Sibyl more open and charming than before. It was as though she was trying to apologize for her earlier behavior and wanted to get back to where they used to be. Logan wanted to be close even though he knew it wasn't good for either one of them. Maybe he should just let things happen. It would all come to an end soon enough.

"I'll go if you go with me," he said to the two women.

"Of course we'll go with you," Cassie said. "Little Abe likes you, and Sibyl says Kitty can't stop talking about you. We'll be like one big, happy family."

The word *family* made Logan feel guilty. "I shouldn't have asked that," he said, turning to Sibyl. "You'll want to spend time with *your* family."

"I have so much family I'll be running into them all day. Besides, I've never had a guest for the celebration. It will give me a chance to play hostess."

"Well, let's not hang about here," Cassie said. "Horace is already gone. All we have to do is lock up."

Sibyl locked the bank doors then turned to Logan. "I should have asked if you're feeling well enough to spend the afternoon in a noisy crowd. You didn't say anything, but I know you were sick soon after you got here this morning."

Logan hated that Sibyl worried about his health. There was nothing she could do to make things better. "I'm feeling much better. I'll make sure to take my medicine when I get back to camp."

"I know it's none of my business, but I wish you'd move into town," Sibyl said. "If anything happened to you while you were up on the Rim, we might not know until it was too late."

"Keep after him to be sensible," Cassie said. "He won't listen to me."

"I like staying at my camp," Logan said. "It

reminds me of camping along the Santa Fe Trail with my father."

"I wonder if he ever met Colby and Jared's parents. They died on the trail."

"My father said thousands of people traveled the trail every year. Some wagon trains were so large they could have been in the same one and still not have met." He hadn't meant to mention the Santa Fe Trail, but it was getting harder and harder to avoid dropping details of his life. It wasn't that he wanted to hide his previous life. It was just that it would cause too much curiosity and too many questions.

"I don't want to be reminded of anything about the Santa Fe Trail," Cassie said.

"It wasn't a good time for me, either," Sibyl added.

They were walking along the boardwalk through the center of town, which was deserted. A variety of sounds came from an area south of town where the valley widened into a flat, grassy area normally used to graze milk cows. The young people had been given the task of cleaning it up so it could be used for the celebration.

"Are you going to compete in anything?" Cassie asked Sibyl.

"I was arguing with my father about that very thing. He said it was disgraceful for a woman to participate in any competition except food. He said he was certain I hadn't considered anything so foolish."

"That sounds like half the men in Cactus Creek," Cassie said in disgust.

"I told him I thought it would be okay for a woman to enter the three-legged race. To hear him talk, you'd have thought I'd said it was okay to ride through the streets in my nightgown. He made me so angry I told him I *would* enter the three-legged race, and that you'd be my partner." Sibyl hesitated. "You will, won't you?"

"I'd be happy to, but I've got a better idea. Logan can be your partner."

Caught off guard, Logan turned to Sibyl. "I don't know—"

"No excuses," Cassie said. "It's hardly more than a fast walk."

Sibyl turned to Logan. "It's usually a lot of fun, but don't do it if you don't feel up to it."

It wasn't the race that worried Logan. It was being that close to Sibyl. He'd seen three-legged races before. The couple ran shoulder to shoulder the entire distance. How could he do that and control his reaction to her presence?

"Come on," Cassie pleaded. "Any man who can stop runaway horses can manage a three-legged race."

"All right." Logan hoped he didn't sound harassed, but that's how he felt. "I don't want anyone to think I'm lacking patriotic spirit."

"Good. Now what are you going to try after that? There's shooting, horseback riding, foot races, wrestling…"

It seemed there were enough activities to keep everyone in town busy for the next two days.

"Then there's the food," Cassie continued. "I'll have a time keeping Little Abe from eating himself sick."

❦

Logan figured Chicago had celebrations like this, but he'd never gone to one. After the first hour, he realized he'd missed something important. People came from as far away as fifteen or twenty miles. Children covered the grounds as thick as fleas on a hound dog. Running from one event to another, their shrieks and shouts could probably be heard all the way to Prescott. Grown men, almost as excited as the children, congregated in groups, each preparing to exhibit his skills in one competition or another. The women—bless their souls—had the impossible task of keeping a watchful eye on their children and a stern eye on their husbands gathered around the beer barrels while dishing up food for the hungry crowds. Judges inspected courses set up for foot races, while others put together rope corrals for bronco riding and calf roping. The one thing that interested Logan most was the target shooting.

It was to be the first event of the day. The men were already gathering, comparing their pistols and rifles, each explaining why his chosen weapon would give him the advantage. Logan practically itched to enter that contest. Target shooting had been his only hobby. It had been his relaxation, the way he was able to put aside his job for a few hours. His father had taken pride in his ability. That drove Logan to become even better until he was the acknowledged champion of Chicago. However, winning would bring unwelcome attention. He turned away, but not fast enough. Jared Smith had spotted him and immediately headed toward them.

"I'm glad to see you're not hiding at your camp," he said when he approached Logan.

"He wanted to," Cassie said, "but we talked him out of it. We even talked him into joining the three-legged race with Sibyl."

Jared turned to Sibyl, his surprise evident. "Wait until Laurie hears this. She'll be green with envy."

"I'll probably regret it," Sibyl confessed, "but my father made me so angry I've decided to show him. He's already sure I'll fail with the bank."

"From what I hear, you and Logan are doing fine. I came over to see if I could talk Logan into entering the shooting competition. If he can participate in the three-legged race, he can certainly shoot," Jared insisted.

Logan knew Jared suspected he was the *stranger* who'd foiled the bank robbery. Doing well in the shooting contest would prove it in his mind. One more reason for turning him down.

"I'm not sure—" Sibyl began.

Cassie cut her off. "I think it's a great idea." She looked directly at Logan. "It's about time people found out you can do more than chase runaway horses."

"Oh, he doesn't have to worry about winning," Jared said. "Colby will beat him by a mile. He always wins."

Logan's father had often said that confidence in one's ability made a good businessman, but pride in that ability could cloud your judgment. Now would have been a good time to heed that advice, but Logan turned his back on it. He was tired of feeling sick, of being nauseated, of avoiding people to keep them from staring at him. If they were going to stare, at least they'd have something to think about besides how ugly he looked.

"I might as well sign up since there's no danger of winning. No one pays attention to the losers."

"Are you sure?" Sibyl asked.

Logan knew she really was asking if he was ready to face the notoriety if he won.

"No, I'm not, but it looks like every male big

enough to hold a gun is entered. I'd hate to be the only holdout."

"Good for you," Cassie said. "Now I'd better find Little Abe. He's far too fascinated with guns to suit me."

"I'm going to look for Naomi," Sibyl said. "Kitty is with her and the children."

"Maybe Jonathan and Annabelle," Cassie said, "but I'll bet you a dollar Peter and Esther are following in Colby's shadow."

Fortunately Sibyl didn't take Cassie's bet, for when Jared led Logan over to sign up for the competition, he saw both children with Colby.

"Where's your rifle?" the registrar asked Logan.

"I didn't bring it with me. I guess I'll have to drop out." It was a disappointment but also a relief.

"You can use mine," Jared said. "I'm tired of getting beaten by Colby."

"So is everyone else," the registrar said. "They've been practicing all year in hopes of getting good enough. Not that it's ever worked before," he added.

"You don't have to give me your rifle," Logan told Jared.

"I don't mind."

The rifle wasn't the same as Logan's own, but it was solid and well balanced.

"You'll need to get used to the rifle," Jared said. "Everyone is given a little time to warm up."

That *little time* sounded like a small war. It seemed every man had to fire his rifle as many times as possible. Logan tested his by firing just once, aiming at the far edge of the target, and calculating how far he missed. Then he sat back and waited.

Nine

LOGAN WAS THE LAST TO SIGN UP SO HE WOULD BE THE last to compete. Everyone was eager for his turn. Each was anxious to show that, even if they couldn't beat Colby, they'd improved. The targets were placed a hundred yards away, far enough that no one was sure of how well he shot until the target was brought to the judges' stand. There were several arguments over whether a shot had touched a line or was safely inside a circle. There was a lot of jeering when a shot missed the target and just as many cheers when a shot hit the bull's-eye. The judges measured and conferred before assigning each contestant a score. No one was completely happy with his score, but the judges' decision was final.

Unlike many others, Jared's nephew was delighted with his score.

"Steve spends nearly all his spare money buying ammunition to practice," Jared told Logan. "That's his best performance ever."

Over the last hour, Logan had witnessed some very impressive shooting. Even the youngest competitors managed to find the edge of the targets at least once.

The way their eyes would light up when they managed a really good shot reminded Logan of himself, and the praise from their fathers of the praise Logan had received from *his* father. He missed him often, but the ache was particularly acute today. Maybe it was seeing all these happy families, especially the close bonds between fathers and sons.

The arrival of a noisy group attracted Logan's attention. He turned to see Sibyl and Cassie approaching, accompanied by two other women and several children. Colby was with them, Peter and Esther clinging to him like burrs. They settled in the shade of an enormous cottonwood tree a short distance away.

"You didn't think the women were going to miss Colby shooting, did you?" Jared said to Logan. "Naomi's enormously proud of her husband. The others, my wife included, are nearly as bad."

Every time Logan saw another piece of evidence of the invisible web that held these families together, he felt more and more desolate. Why had he waited so late to learn what was really important in life?

Seeing Logan, Peter broke away from the group. "My papa's next," he announced loud enough for everyone within fifty yards to hear. "Nobody's better than him."

"You shouldn't say that," Colby said to his son.

"Why not?" one of the contestants asked. "Everybody knows it's the truth."

"It's not that. It's just that I don't want him to think that makes me better than anyone else."

"Even if you are?" someone asked, their tone of voice biting.

"People like Colby," Jared whispered to Logan, "but they're jealous, too. He's rich, has a family that adores him, and a beautiful wife he loves as much as she loves him. On top of that, he's the real mayor of the town even if there's no official title. Everybody goes to him for advice."

Much to Logan's surprise, he felt his heart swell with pride. It was *his* brother everyone envied and admired. It was *his* brother who had a wife and children who adored him. It was almost as though he could share his brother's success and good fortune.

By the time Colby finished shooting, Logan had more reason to be proud of him. All three shots had landed in the bull's-eye, close enough to be covered by a silver dollar.

"Now you see why nobody beats him," Jared said. "He never misses the bull's-eye."

"The competition is over," the judges announced. "According to the scores, the winner is—"

"There's one more contestant," Sibyl called to the judges. "Logan Holstock hasn't shot yet."

Seeing the pride his family took in his achievements, Logan didn't want to do anything to diminish Colby in their eyes.

"I don't have to shoot."

"Yes, you do," Jared said. "Sibyl has brought you to the attention of the judges so you don't really have any choice. Now get up there and shoot. I'm anxious to see if you do any better than I would have done."

He could still refuse, but one look at Sibyl changed his mind. He didn't know the true extent of her feelings for him, but he knew she cared for him and wanted to do anything she could to see he got the recognition she believed he deserved. She would understand if he didn't shoot, but she would be disappointed in him. As long as it was possible, he would never do anything to disappoint Sibyl.

Now that his mind was made up on that point, he had another question. Did he shoot to win, or did he let Colby get the trophy?

It was a short tussle, but it wasn't really hard. He could choose not to compete, but he couldn't throw a contest. Maybe it was pride more than principle, but that didn't change the way he felt. If Colby was the kind of man Logan believed him to be, he wouldn't want anyone to give him something he didn't deserve.

Accepting the consequences of his decision, he got to his feet. He appeared unsteady as he walked up to the line. He could hear murmurs, people wondering if he was okay to shoot. They didn't know that once he came to a stop, he would be as steady on his feet as anyone else.

"You have three shots," a judge told him. "Take as much time as you need." From his expression, Logan figured the judge thought he'd need a long time just to stop shaking.

They didn't know that walking up to the line, a rifle in his hands and a target in the distance, invoked habits acquired by years of practice. His body relaxed, his breathing slowed, and his concentration zeroed in on the target in the distance. Slowly he raised the rifle, took careful aim, and gently squeezed the trigger. His ability to see things at a distance that others couldn't told him all he needed to know. He squeezed off two more shots so close together that most of the men stared at him in surprise. Some shook their heads. Others smiled knowingly.

Logan turned, walked over to Jared, and handed

him the rifle. "It's an excellent rifle. If you ever want to sell it—" He had started to say he'd want to buy it, but what did a dying man need with a rife? Instead he said, "Make sure you get a good price for it."

"I think I'll keep it. How do you think you did?"

"We'll see in a moment." Now that the competition was over, the energy and force of will that had steadied him melted away, and he was tired. As much as he didn't want to admit to weakness in pubic, he had to sit down.

Apparently, being seated some distance away didn't prevent Sibyl from sensing his distress. "Come sit with us," she called. "Laurie has been wanting to meet you."

"I'd like for you to meet the rest of my family," Jared said. "This is the first time Laurie has come to town with the new baby."

The pride in Jared's voice was matched by the brightness of his eyes when he turned toward his wife. Logan didn't know why he'd ever thought he could marry Bridgette. He could never have looked at her with a fraction of the love and happiness that was written large across Jared's face. He wasn't sure he'd believed such profound feeling could exist between anyone other than parent and child. Another lesson to add to the ones that had come too late.

Steve had gone to meet the man bringing Logan's target to the judges. After looking at the target, he turned and ran up to Logan. "You got one dead in the center," he said, "but the others were clean misses. Why did you fire so quickly?"

"That doesn't make any sense," Jared said.

"There's only one hole in the target," Steve said. "Go see for yourself."

"I will. Logan can come with me."

"I'll wait here with everybody else. You can tell me what you find."

"Getting one in the center is very good," Sibyl said after Jared left. "I'm sure you used to be even better."

She meant before his illness.

"I was hoping he would put them all in the center," Cassie said. "It's about time somebody gave Colby some competition."

"What's wrong with Colby winning?" Naomi demanded.

Cassie wasn't intimidated by Naomi's steely gaze. "Nobody admires Colby more than I do. I doubt any of us would be here if it weren't for him, but it's not good for anyone to win everything all the time. It causes a lot of hard feelings."

"Are you saying Colby shouldn't compete?" Naomi asked.

"Of course not. I just wish someone could give him a run for his money."

Sibyl looked to where the judges were studying the target. Jared and Colby were huddled with them. One judge looked over at Logan, a strange look on his face, before turning back to the target.

"I wonder what's taking so long," Sibyl said. "Steve said there was only one hole in the target."

"It looks like Colby and Jared are arguing with the judges," Naomi said. "There's something going on here, and I want to know what it is."

Sibyl reached out to restrain her cousin when she started to rise. "Jared and Colby will tell us what they've decided. The judges won't appreciate you questioning them."

"Do you know any man who appreciates being questioned?" Laurie asked. "Jared doesn't, and I don't know a fairer man."

"Colby doesn't like it, either," Naomi said of her husband. "We argued almost the whole length of the Santa Fe Trail."

"They're coming this way," Steve said, "and the judges are bringing the trophy."

"Why?"

"I'm sure it's for Colby," Naomi said. "He had the highest score."

"Then why haven't they given it to him?" Steve wondered.

Jared was leading the group coming toward them, and the grin he wore told Logan all he needed to know.

"What's going on?" Naomi asked when the group reached them. "Why haven't you given Colby the trophy?"

"Because I didn't win it," Colby said. "Logan did."

As every eye turned to Logan, Steve asked the question on everyone's mind. "How? Only one shot hit the target."

"All three shots hit the bull's-eye," Jared explained. "They were just so close they looked like one."

Cassie jumped up and threw herself at Logan so hard they both tumbled on the ground. "I knew you could do it," she exclaimed.

Logan managed to right himself in time to see Sibyl's smile of happiness. That was more than enough to compensate for the embarrassment of being soundly kissed by Cassie in public.

"I don't believe it," Steve said. "I saw the target. There was only one hole."

Jared held the target up so everyone could see. "If you look closely, you'll see a slight indentation here where the second bullet hit the edge of the hole made by the first bullet. Over here, you'll see a similar indentation made by the third bullet. They were so close together we were almost ready to agree with Steve, but Colby has better eyesight. He's the one who insisted all three shots hit the center."

Steve studied the target intently before turning to Logan with wide eyes. "Well, I'll be a long-eared coyote. I wouldn't have believed anybody could do that."

"It's the most amazing piece of shooting we've ever seen," one judge said. "We're proud to declare you the winner. We're going to post the target. Everyone is going to want to see it."

"I don't know what you're so surprised at," Cassie said. "That ought to be easy as pie for a man who can shoot four robbers quick as you can say jackrabbit."

Logan's feeling of panic wasn't helped by the reaction of those around him. Everyone started talking at once, but they were all looking at Logan—some even pointed.

"Cassie!" Sibyl exclaimed. "You promised not to tell."

"It's about time everybody knew he's the man who saved my life, Horace's life, and probably yours, too. Besides, everybody knows there haven't been any strangers around here for weeks. There's never been one who can shoot like Logan."

Logan's sudden notoriety wasn't as bad as he had feared, partly because Sibyl's family closed around him. Sibyl positioned herself at his side, deftly turning aside any intrusive questions. Cassie, who considered herself part of the family by adoption, was more than capable of running interference with those most curious and least easily satisfied with the limited information Sibyl was willing to give. Peter, momentarily stunned by his father's loss, was quick to proclaim his special kinship, telling them that Logan had accomplished almost as many amazing feats as his own father. Colby occupied himself with his two youngest children, but several times Logan found him looking at him with a puzzled expression.

Jared grinned like a man with a secret. "I'd already figured you had to be the stranger who shot the bank robbers neatly between the eyes," he murmured under the cover of a particularly noisy exchange between Peter and a boy who didn't believe anybody could put three bullets in the same hole.

But no amount of exciting news could occupy everyone's attention for long. A wide variety of events were scheduled for the rest of the day. Everyone wanted their chance to snatch a little of Logan's glory. There was food to eat, friends to see, gossip to exchange, and children to watch who had little interest in the winner of a shooting contest. Over the next hour, children played games and took naps in the shade. Some mothers nursed babies while others discussed their favorite recipes. It was completely unlike anything Logan had ever experienced.

"I'm sorry Cassie went back on her word," Sibyl said to Logan after everyone had wandered away to other activities, "but I'm glad people know. Are you angry?"

Was he angry, or was he just upset at being thrust into the limelight? Before his illness, he'd have taken pride in it. Now he'd let his illness, especially his swollen facial features, turn him into a recluse. He didn't want to die, but that was no reason to act like a coward. He had seen men show great courage in the face of death. He was shocked that it should be happening to him so young, and he was embarrassed at the changes it had caused, but it was time he stopped running away. He ought to make the most of the time he had left. Besides, he had people he'd started to care about. He didn't want them to remember him like this.

"No, I'm not angry. I've finally realized that I shouldn't let my illness dominate the rest of my life. At least now there's something more interesting about me than my face."

"I've always known that."

He wished he knew if she was more interested in him as a man than in what he'd done in the past. He'd thought about answering her questions, but there were only two things that were important now—his feelings for her and that he'd found his brothers. He couldn't talk about either, so it seemed pointless to mention the rest.

"Other than being mobbed by curious people, are you having a good time?" Sibyl asked. "I know you didn't want to challenge Colby, but I was glad you did. I was very proud of you for winning."

"That's the only reason I did it," Logan said.

Sibyl looked uncomfortable. "I don't want you to do things just for me."

"It wasn't just for you. It was for me, too. I like pleasing you. I don't think you've had enough occasions to be happy."

Now Sibyl was looking decidedly uncomfortable. "My life hasn't been all terrible."

"You were forced to marry a man you didn't love and who didn't respect or value you as he should. How could it have been anything else?"

"Who told you? If it was Cassie, I'll wring her neck. There's not a mean bone in her body, but she never knows when to keep quiet."

"I didn't need Cassie or anyone else to tell me your husband didn't deserve you. Any man worthy of calling himself a man would have been more worried about protecting you than losing his money. I'd have given up every cent I had before I'd let anyone harm you."

Logan didn't need Sibyl turning an unflattering shade of purple to know he'd said too much. Yet he couldn't be sorry. Now that he'd decided to stop living in the shadow of his illness, he was hard pressed not to say even more. What could it hurt? She'd never been valued as she ought. He'd want her to know he thought she was beautiful, that she was noble, that she was what every man looked for in a woman. She was warm, thoughtful, and caring.

Despite the illness that ravaged his body, being near her, thinking of her, desiring her, caused his blood to warm in his veins. She was slim, tall, and elegant, but her body had a roundness that only maturity could bring. Thinking of holding her in his arms had ruined his sleep on several occasions.

"I think I'd like to get something to eat," Sibyl said. "You must be famished by now. There are several wonderful cooks in Cactus Creek. They always outdo themselves on occasions like this."

Sibyl wasn't ready to hear what he had to say to her, but she'd invited him to eat with her. That was enough for now. The time wasn't right, but he couldn't wait much longer. He was determined to say everything in his heart before it stopped beating.

❧

Logan hadn't enjoyed any day half this much since his father's death. He and Sibyl had spent the afternoon sampling food from nearly every table, meeting all of her family, and watching Kitty have the time of her life. He even got to hold Jared's infant son. He didn't take a deep breath until the child's mother took him back. He teased Peter when he lost his foot race to a girl, and commiserated with Little Abe when his wagon broke during his race. It took him a while to realize no one was put off by his face. If they asked about his illness, it was out of genuine interest. He received stern admonitions to see the doctor and offers of homemade remedies that might cure him within weeks. All in all, it seemed people had accepted him as part of the community.

"Why wouldn't they?" Sibyl asked. "You're a very special person. We're proud to have you here."

Logan knew he'd been fortunate to have a good life. He'd never felt special, but he liked that Sibyl thought so.

"Now you're going to have to put yourself on the line once more. I think it's about time for the three-legged race."

The words had hardly left Sibyl's mouth when Cassie came running up. "It's time for the race. I bet Little Abe you'd win. He's pulling for the Hill boys."

"You'd better see if you can get your money back," Logan advised.

"My money's on you. I remember you chasing down those horses."

"If we lose, it'll be my fault," Sibyl said.

"You're not going to lose. Now come on."

Halfway there, Kitty came running up to them.

"The race is starting, Mama. You've got to hurry." She took hold of her mother's hand to pull her along.

"They won't start without us," her mother told her.

It seemed everybody in Cactus Corner had come to watch the race. Both sides of the course were several rows deep with spectators. A dozen sacks had been laid on the ground at the starting line. Couples were already beginning to pair up.

Naomi came over to them. Peter and Esther followed with Jonathan and Annabelle in tow. "I'm pulling for you in this race," she said. "I tried to get Colby to enter with me, but he said he'd rather wash dishes for a week."

"You can't be shy in this race," Cassie counseled Logan. "The couple that looks the most ridiculous is usually the one that wins."

"Are you going to win?" Kitty asked her mother.

"I doubt it," Sibyl said. "We just want to have fun."

Peter weighed in with, "It's not fun unless you win."

"That's not true," Naomi said to her stepson. "It only important to win when you have something valuable to lose."

"Like my dignity," Logan mumbled.

"If I don't lose mine, you won't lose yours," Sibyl told him. "Now let's line up."

Once they were at the line, Sibyl turned to Logan. "I don't care if we win," she said in a whisper, "as long as we finish ahead of my father."

Logan looked to where her father and Tom Hale were figuring out how to get their legs into the sack. "He was furious when I told him I might enter the three-legged race with Cassie."

He smiled. It was impossible for Logan to stay in

poor spirits. If the contestants weren't laughing at themselves as they tried the get their legs into the sacks, the spectators were doing it for them. One pair tumbled down in a tangle before they could line up. Their being a young married couple only added to the merriment. The only serious faces in the crowd belonged to the Hill brothers, who were determined to win the race. According to their mother, they'd been practicing for a week.

"I don't know how a woman is supposed to participate in this race without exposing her legs," Sibyl complained.

"Then we won't compete," Logan said. "I'd never do anything to embarrass you."

"I'm not embarrassed," Sibyl protested, "just frustrated. I never thought I'd see the day when I wished I was wearing pants."

Logan was thankful that day hadn't come. The thought of Sibyl's body clearly outlined by a pair of pants made him weak in the knees. He nearly stumbled getting his leg into the sack. When it came into contact with Sibyl's leg, he was in danger of collapsing on the spot. But that was only the beginning. Seconds later, their bodies were touching from knee to shoulder. Logan felt a dizzy spell coming on, but he didn't know if it was due to his illness or Sibyl's nearness.

"They're about to start," Cassie shouted. "Look lively."

This was no time to have a dizzy spell. If he did anything to cause Sibyl to fall, he'd never forgive himself. The idea of a woman of her character being tumbled in the grass was nothing short of a nightmare.

"Are you ready?" Sibyl asked him.

"Yes. You?"

"I'm excited," she said. "Norman would never have let me do anything like this. He would have said it was disrespectful of his mother's memory. I don't remember that woman very well, but my mother says she was stiff and disagreeable. I never could understand why both her sons practically worshipped her."

Logan could barely remember his mother. For the first years after he was adopted, he missed her a lot, but his father took him everywhere he went, got him involved in everything he did. Gradually, Logan didn't have time to miss his birth parents. That used to make him feel guilty. After a while, even that feeling went away.

The starter's pistol sounded before any more memories could resurrect themselves.

"I've changed my mind," Sibyl said as she charged forward. "I want to win this race. I'm not sure I've ever wanted to do anything more in my life."

Logan would have done just about anything to make Sibyl happy. Winning a three-legged race might not seem like much, but he had a feeling it was more that his illness-ravaged body could accomplish. Still, he'd chased down a runaway team of horses. Surely running a three-legged race would be easier.

If he hadn't been so busy concentrating on avoiding failure, he might have been able to enter into the spirit of the event. Everyone on the sidelines was loudly cheering on their favorites. The contestants exhorted each other to make a greater effort to win the race for the honor of…well, it didn't matter if there was no one or nothing to honor. Winning was enough.

"Come on," Sibyl hollered to Logan over the noise

of the crowd. "We've got to catch the Hill boys. We can't let two children beat us."

Those two *children* were healthy, active teenage boys who were moving as though they'd walked on three legs all their lives. That week of practice was paying off.

"We've got to match our strides," Logan said to Sibyl. "Those boys are running like they really do have only three legs."

It was hard to do at first, but once they got the hang of it, it was surprisingly easy. Before long, they managed to pass all the other contestants except the Hill boys.

"Faster," Sibyl encouraged. "We're gaining."

Only because the Hill boys' sack had caught on a stump or a root, and they had stumbled. Quick as a flash, they were up again. It would take another stumble for Sibyl and Logan to win, but that was no reason not to try. His breath was coming in painful gasps, and his head felt like it was about to explode, but he ignored it. Sibyl wanted to win this race. He was going to win it for her if it killed him.

The boys stumbled again. Apparently, having lost their rhythm, they were having trouble getting it back.

"We're gaining!" Sibyl exalted. "A little faster, and we'll win."

It probably said something unflattering about Logan's character, or his upbringing, but he was surprised by Sibyl's athleticism. The women he knew rarely left their homes for anything other than shopping. Walking too fast was considered unladylike. Running was simply never done. Yet here was Sibyl, as much a lady as any he'd ever known, not only running this race, but straining to win. He had to pick up his pace, or he'd be the reason they didn't win.

Logan didn't know where he found the extra energy or the will to fight the agony he was putting his body through, but somehow he did. Maybe it was some hidden reserve, some part of his mind that didn't care about pain. Maybe it was his last chance to achieve something before his body failed him. It didn't matter. It was only a few yards to the finish line. He would give it everything he had. He would have eternity to rest.

It sounded as though the whole town was cheering for them to win. He could hear the childlike soprano of Kitty cutting through the only slightly lower sopranos of Peter and Esther. Naomi and Cassie's voices fitted somewhere in the middle between Steve's tenor and the baritones of Jared and Colby. There were many voices he didn't know, including a bass that rumbled across the field like distant thunder.

"Only a few more strides, and we'll have it," Sibyl exclaimed between gasps for breath.

Logan wanted to see where the Hill boys were, but he was so tired his eyes were losing focus. All he could see was the line just a dozen feet away and the blur that was the cheering throng. Calling on the last of his energy, Logan and Sibyl hurtled toward the finish line—at which point they stumbled and fell into a tangled heap.

If Logan had had the energy, he would have been caught between the need to disentangle himself from Sibyl as quickly as possible, and the desire to prolong their nearness as long as possible. As it was, he was incapable of doing anything beyond drawing painful breaths into his exhausted body. His head was swimming, his senses overladen. How then—when he felt nearer to death than ever before—could his body be reacting to Sibyl's nearness? It was impossible for his pulse to pound any louder in his head, for his heart to beat any faster, for his breath to be any shorter, yet he could feel that physical pull, the heady sensation, that comes when a man is close to a woman he desires.

Sibyl was laughing, her body relaxed against him. "Who won?" she wanted to know.

"It was close," Naomi told her. "The judges are trying to decide."

Sibyl made no attempt to move. "I refuse to get up until they tell me who won."

Logan couldn't move. Sibyl's body covered two-thirds of his own body. She'd spun when they fell until she was facing him. He could feel her breast pressed against his heaving chest, her breath warm on his neck.

"Are you okay?" she asked.

Somehow he managed to collect himself enough to nod his head.

"I'd get off you," Sibyl apologized, "but we're so tangled I need help."

He felt like he was about to expire. But if he had to die, this would be a wonderful final memory. Yet he couldn't keep her in this position just because he wanted to enter the afterlife with the memory of her practically in his arms. Fortunately, his help wasn't needed. Jared took hold of Sibyl while Colby took hold of him. The two men lifted Sibyl and Logan onto their feet. The sack slid to the ground, and they were able to step out.

"You won!"

Peter's shout in his ear nearly caused Logan to lose his balance.

"Are you sure?" Sibyl asked.

"He must be right," Naomi said. "The Hill boys don't look happy, and the judges are heading this way."

Sibyl turned to Logan, the most beautiful smile in the world on her face. "We did it!" she exclaimed.

"I knew he could," Cassie said. "He just had to stop remembering he was sick."

"I think it's even more amazing because he *is* sick," Sibyl said. "He always manages to rise to the occasion. I think he's quite a remarkable man."

The collusion of exhaustion and elation over their win caused Sibyl's words to reduce Logan to near incoherence. He would never have believed it was possible, but this was just about the happiest moment of his life. But he didn't have time to indulge in this wonderful daydream. The judges had reached them.

"This is quite unexpected," one announced to Sibyl. "This race is always won by young people. I'd been certain the Hill boys were a shoo-in."

A beaming Sibyl turned to Logan. "You can never depend on the expected when this man is involved. This is another example of—"

A scream cut through the excitement surrounding them. Logan turned to see a woman bending over a man who'd been one of the contestants in the three-legged race.

"He's dead," she cried. "My husband's dead."

Ten

AFTER TWO DAYS OF NEAR AROUND-THE-CLOCK attendance to her mother, Sibyl was finding it difficult to generate any sympathy for the newly widowed Alma Edwards. Sibyl's mother was a sister to Alice Hale, Laurie's mother. Her other sister, Annabelle Kessling, Naomi's mother, had died shortly after the birth of her third child. The sisters had never been so close as their children. Thus it was Naomi and Laurie who supported Sibyl through the trying time of arranging her father's funeral and supporting her mother through the process of readying the body for burial. Laurie's mother stayed away because Laurie refused to be in the same house with her.

"I'll sit with your mother for a while," Mae Oliver said to Sibyl. Mae and Alma were second cousins, but Mae had been cool toward Alma ever since Sibyl's marriage to Norman. "Go outside for a while. It's a nice evening. You don't want to waste it."

"Thank you," Sibyl said. "I could use a little fresh air."

Sibyl and her mother could hardly have been more different if they'd been unrelated. Alma had married young and taken every word her husband spoke as gospel. Her one disappointment in life was not being able to give him the sons she felt every man deserved. If there was ever a difference of opinion between Sibyl and her father, Alma took her husband's side. She believed no woman should ever question her husband. She had never understood why Sibyl wasn't happy being married to Norman. She had believed, and stated on occasion, that the fault was Sibyl's.

"Would you like for me to come with you, or would you rather be alone?" Naomi asked.

"Please," Sibyl said. "I can do without my own company."

"You've got to forget what your father did," Naomi said once they were settled on the bench in the grove of cottonwood saplings. "Not forgive him. Just forget."

"You know, I can forgive my parents for forcing me to marry Norman. There are reasons you don't know why even I thought it might be the best thing. What I *can't* forgive is the way they never believed anything I said about Norman. They thought he was perfect, that our marriage would be idyllic if I would just act like a normal wife."

"No woman's life could be idyllic married to that man. I tried to tell your mother how Norman treated you, but she wouldn't listen."

"Everybody tried to tell her, but she wouldn't listen because my father wouldn't listen. I don't know what she's going to do now. She doesn't have a thought in her head that my father hadn't put there."

"She'll get along fine once she recovers."

"I can't have her move in with me," Sibyl said. "I don't care if it's a completely unnatural way to feel. I don't care if every person in Cactus Corner thinks I'm heartless and selfish. I won't have her in my house. It would be like living with Norman all over again."

"Why don't you consider hiring a housekeeper to live with her?"

"That's what Logan suggested."

Naomi was suddenly alert. "I didn't know you'd seen Logan."

"He's taking care of the bank for me. Of course I see him."

"When?"

"He comes by at night after everyone has gone."

"Do you mean that man has to climb the Rim every night in the dark? There are times I'm not sure he's going to take the next step without falling down."

"I tried to convince him he didn't have to come by. Cassie can tell me anything I need to know." Sibyl chuckled. "She tells me all that and a lot more."

"Are you sure it's safe to trust Logan? I mean, we don't really know anything about him, and he has access to everything in your office. At least your money's safe. He can't open the safe."

"Of course he can. How do you think he handles deposits and withdrawals?"

Naomi favored her cousin with a stern look. "I know he's half in love with you, but I didn't think you were equally out of your mind."

"I don't have to be in love with a man to trust him. I trust Colby implicitly, and I'm not in love with him. I also trust Jared, your father, Ethan—"

"You don't have to list all the men you *do* trust. I just want to know why you feel you can put so much trust in Logan."

Sibyl had no idea how to answer that question. She couldn't say why, but she'd trusted Logan from the beginning. Maybe it was because he risked his life to save her. Or because he stayed to make sure she was okay before he escaped. Or because he offered to help with the bank. Maybe it was the way he looked at her, like she was the most beautiful and wonderful person in the world. Maybe it was because he worked so hard despite his sickness. Maybe it was his way with the children. Maybe it was his heroic effort to stop the runaway wagon, or an equally exhausting effort to help her win the three-legged race. Maybe it was that Cassie and Horace felt they could turn to him with any question they might have. Maybe it was the way he never wanted credit for the things he did.

It was all those things, but there was more, more that had to do with feelings rather than facts. It sounded silly to say there was something in Logan's eyes that spoke to her. How could anyone else see anything but his distorted features and the pain so often reflected there? Yet she had from the first day. That something had caused her to accept his offer to work with her and had caused her to open up to him as she had to no one else. There was a quietness about him that spoke more of confidence than shyness. There was also an element of resignation she didn't quite understand.

"I suppose it started when he saved my life," Sibyl told Naomi. "He didn't have to come into the bank. He could have backed out, and no one would ever have known. Knowing how sick he is, no one would have blamed him."

"I would have."

Sibyl laughed. "You have very high expectations of everyone."

"Of course I do. We're talking about a man you trust."

"He didn't have to refuse being paid to help me. Nor did he have to work on days when he was too sick to have left his camp. He's constantly coming up with ideas to bring in customers. Besides, the children trust him. So does Cassie, and no one has better instincts."

"Okay, you trust him, but how about the other feelings you have for him?"

"What feelings?"

"That's what I want to know. And don't try to deny it. Laurie has noticed your interest in him, too."

Sibyl would have preferred to keep silent, but she needed to talk to someone about her confused feelings. She certainly couldn't talk to Logan. "I don't know what to say," she began. "There are times I'm certain it's no more than gratitude for what he's done as well as admiration for the courage with which he faces his illness. You ought to see him. I've seen him go dead still, turn white from pain, and never say a word. He won't ask for help, and he refuses to let anyone pity him. He has to be lonely. And as sick as he is, it's dangerous to be alone, but he insists upon staying up on the rim with only that dog for company. I used to think it was because of the way he looked, but after spending all day at the Fourth of July celebrations, I don't think that's it."

"He ought to see Papa."

"Even Kitty has tried to get him to go to the doctor, but he says all that can be done has been done."

"What does that mean?"

"He has some medicine he takes, but I can't see that it does any good."

"Well, you can't take responsibility for him."

"Why not? No one else is."

"He's a grown man. He can take care of himself."

"That's just it. I don't think he can."

"Maybe not, but why should you do it?"

"Because I want to." That was the clearest statement Sibyl had made about her feelings for Logan. *Because I want to.* That answered many questions she didn't have answers to, but it didn't explain *why* she wanted to care for him. That was Naomi's next question.

"Why?"

"Maybe because he's the first man to think I'm capable of more than keeping house. Because he cared enough—I have no idea why—to help me learn how to run a bank. Because my daughter likes him and is afraid he's going to die. Because I think he's lonely and needs someone to care whether he lives or dies."

Naomi's expression softened. "That sounds like a woman falling in love. Considering everything, that's not a smart thing to do."

"Marrying Norman wasn't the *smart thing to do,* yet I survived it."

"You didn't love Norman."

"I don't love Logan—at least I don't *think* I do—but I care about him. Seeing the way he looks at me has made me feel like a woman for the first time in years. I haven't told anyone this, but Norman never touched me after Kitty was born."

"Why?"

"He never told me."

"Do you think he was in love with someone else?"

Sibyl's laugh was derisive. "Norman didn't love

anyone but himself. I was never sure why he agreed to marry me."

"He *agreed*? That sounds like he had to be convinced."

Sibyl had come too close to divulging something she'd sworn to keep secret. She was closer to Naomi than anyone else, but she intended to bury that secret with her father. "Maybe he thought it would be good for the two founding families to be joined in marriage."

"Only if he thought it would make him richer." Naomi paused. "Are you sure Logan's not interested in your money?"

"He said he'll be gone before the end of the summer."

"Where's he going?"

"He won't say. I worry that it's not something good. He came from Chicago. You only have to talk with him a short time before you realize he's a sophisticated man. He's very careful in what he says, but little things slip out now and then. He mentioned a play he'd seen. He talked about a mayor like he knew the man. He dresses like a hobo and lives in a tent, but he knows women's clothes. He has a wallet made of expensive leather. Horace said his boots were made by a fancy boot maker in Chicago. The day the robbers showed up, he was coming to the bank to deposit over five hundred dollars in cash. Cassie swears he was rich and important and has come out here to die."

"Well, you can't let yourself become too attached to a man who's going to die."

"You, of all people, should know you can't dictate who you love. I remember when you thought Colby was an army spy come to arrest you for murder."

"Okay, I was wrong about Colby, but I don't want you to fall in love with a man who's going to die or disappear. After putting up with Norman, you deserve someone really special."

"I don't expect to be as lucky as you and Laurie."

"Maybe the third brother will show up."

Sibyl turned thoughtful. "You know, it's weird that a drifter named Holstock would show up here. It's obvious Logan can't be the third brother, but it still seems weird."

Naomi laughed. "I agree. It was incredible that Jared was able to find Colby. Finding the third brother would be too much to expect."

"Even if he did show up, there's no guarantee he'd be as wonderful as his brothers."

"Nobody is as wonderful as Colby," Naomi stated, "but I'd be happy if you could find a man who is."

"I have a feeling I'm never going to marry again."

"Don't say that."

"It's not that I don't *want* to marry again. I'd love to give Kitty a father who could love her as she deserves, but I'm not sure she could like any man as much as she likes Logan. She takes him dessert and prays for him every night. She's still trying to convince him to see the doctor. She even tried to talk your father into going to see Logan."

"He told me. He said it was the sweetest thing he'd ever heard."

"She adores him. I'd be tempted to marry Logan just for her even if I didn't like and admire him."

Where had that come from? She'd never thought of marrying Logan for any reason. It wasn't that she found the idea repugnant, just that it hadn't occurred to her. Yet now that it had, it didn't shock her.

Surprise, yes. Shock, no. That in itself was a surprise. Why wasn't she shocked? He was a stranger, a man she knew little about. He kept to himself and lived in the woods. He was sick and disfigured. Her whole family—indeed, the entire town—would be stunned and dismayed. They would do everything in their power to change her mind. So why would something that was so wrong in everyone else's eyes be acceptable in hers? She was not an adventurous woman. She'd never wanted to do anything to shock people. She'd even covered up the truth about her marriage to avoid gossip and scandal. So how could she see herself doing something that would cause an uproar?

Because she no longer cared what people thought about her. She wasn't sure how it had happened, but her father's and Norman's deaths had released her from constraints that had bound her all her life.

"I hope you won't ever marry anyone for Kitty's sake," Naomi said. "She'll grow up, and you'll be stuck with him for the rest of your life."

"I'm a wealthy widow," Sibyl said. "I don't ever have to marry a man I don't love." As far as she was concerned, no man measured up to Logan—and despite her momentary lapse, she couldn't marry him—so there was no danger of her marrying anyone. She didn't like the idea of facing the future alone, but being married to Norman had taught her there were worse things than loneliness. Besides, she would always have family.

Mae Oliver appeared at the back door. "Your mother is calling for you."

Sibyl heaved a sigh. "All my life she's told me I was going about everything the wrong way. Now she can't let me out of her sight for half an hour."

"She feels lost and lonely," Naomi said. "You're all she has left."

"Both our husbands were stubborn, controlling men who treated us more like servants than wives. Why should I feel liberated when my mother feels lost?"

"Because you're stronger and smarter," Naomi said.

At the moment, Sibyl didn't feel strong or smart. The futures of so many people depended on her. She wondered if she could handle such a responsibility without Logan's help.

"I'll take your mother home with me," Mae offered. "She needs something to occupy her mind. She can't help you with the bank, but she can work with me in the dress shop. No one knows more about hats or clothes than your mother. She's been critiquing what all of us wear for as long as I can remember."

Relief washed over Sibyl. "I don't know how to thank you. It's just that I have so much to do right now."

"Don't apologize. Everybody knows you've undergone your own tragedy. You take care of yourself and your daughter. I'll take care of your mother. I never liked how she forced you to marry Norman, but she is my cousin. I suppose I should forgive her now."

Sibyl wondered if she'd truly forgiven her mother.

⸎

Logan was ill at ease. He'd been invited to Jared's home for supper. He'd tried to beg off, but neither Jared nor Steve would leave his campsite until he'd agreed. He wondered if Jared's insistence that Laurie and their children wanted to see him hadn't been what changed his mind. He didn't know why children had become so important to him, but getting to know Kitty and the others had been a revelation.

Steve had come to get him. He said he wanted to make sure Logan knew the way to their ranch. Logan suspected they feared he would change his mind at the last minute, something he'd considered at least once an hour since the invitation.

"Is your dog coming?" Steve asked when he noticed a dog trailing them at a distance.

"He goes everywhere with me," Logan explained.

"Laurie doesn't allow dogs in the house."

"Trusty stays well out of sight of people he doesn't know. He wouldn't go inside the house if I asked him."

"The house is new," Steve told Logan as they rode into the ranch yard. "There was hardly enough space for two people in the old one." He pointed to a small house sitting some distance away and closer to the river. "Jared turned it into a bunkhouse. He ripped out the floor of the old bunkhouse and made it a barn and henhouse. Coyotes ate the chickens, and everything wanted to eat the pigs."

"I didn't know ranchers bothered with pigs."

"Laurie grew up in Kentucky where everybody had their own fresh milk, eggs, and pork. She said she didn't see any reason why she couldn't have them here, too. As long as she cooks like she does, Jared will do anything she wants."

"The way to a man's stomach…"

"My stomach, too." Steve stood about six feet with wide shoulders, but he was whipcord thin. "I nearly starved before she came to work for us. I would have married her myself if I'd been older."

Logan couldn't remember being interested in girls

at Steve's age. Looking back, it seemed his whole life had been about work. That was because his father's life had been about work, and Logan had done everything he could to be close to his father, to win his praise as well as his love. He supposed that came from being adopted and feeling he had to earn his father's love, but he had been too young to see that, and it was too late to worry about it now.

"It's a big house," Steve said, "but Laurie said she wants lots of children." He laughed. "She only has two, but I think it's enough. I love both of them, but one or the other always needs something. Laurie hardly has time to do anything besides cook and take care of them." He laughed again. "I think Jared misses the time before they were born."

The house could have been set just about anywhere in the eastern half of the United States. It was a big rectangle made of wood with a porch across the front and a second story. Jared was waiting at the bottom of the steps. Logan noticed the buggy tied to the hitching post. He supposed it could have been for Laurie's use, but Logan was certain he'd seen it before.

When he and Sibyl went to Camp Verde.

"Glad you didn't change your mind," Jared said as he came down the steps to greet Logan. "Laurie would have been very disappointed."

"Is that why you sent Steve to get me? I appreciate the invitation, but a man in my condition is not the ideal guest."

"I know about your condition, and I don't care. Now come inside. Laurie is anxious to see you again."

Logan was relieved when Jared didn't offer to help him up the steps, but he got a firm grip on the railing.

He was not feeling his best, but he was determined he would do nothing to embarrass himself.

The interior of the house wouldn't cause any excitement in Chicago, but Logan thought it was sensible as well as attractive. The rooms were large and airy with big windows and high ceilings. The wallpaper in the broad hall was decorated with a pattern of green ferns on a white background. The paper in the parlor was covered with bouquets of blue and pink flowers. Not the kind of room he would have expected for a ranch house, but exactly what he would have expected of the woman who rose to greet him. If a woman could be said to exude sexuality, Laurie Smith was a prime example. It in no way changed his preference for Sibyl—who he was not surprised to see sitting across the room—but he'd have had to be dead not to be affected by the lushness of her figure, the sensual mouth, and skin that could cause a peach to cry from envy.

"I'm so glad Jared was able to convince you to come. I've been anxious to see you again."

If velvet had been able to speak, it would have spoken with Laurie's voice.

"I'm pleased to see you again, too, but I'm afraid I'm going to have to be rude and sit down. I don't travel very well."

"Do whatever makes you comfortable. Could I get you something to drink?"

"No. I just need to sit. You have a very nice home. Not quite what I expected."

Laurie laughed. "Jared wanted something smaller, but I was determined to spend as much of my first husband's money as possible."

"He was Norman Spencer's brother, wasn't he?"

"Yes, and neither one of them thought women could be trusted with money." She laughed again. "Norman would turn over in his grave if he knew Sibyl was sitting in *his* chair behind *his* desk in *his* bank."

"You don't have to talk about me like I'm not here," Sibyl said. "And the only reason I'm doing well is that I have Logan to help me."

Logan knew Laurie and Sibyl were cousins, but he was sure she'd been invited for him. Did Laurie or her husband have any idea of his feelings for Sibyl? They must not because they couldn't possibly approve.

"Considering Norman never wanted you even to enter the bank, you'd be doing well if you could only handle a deposit or withdrawal," Laurie said.

Sibyl laughed. "I don't have to do anything as complicated as that. Cassie draws the customers in, and Horace handles their transactions. All I have to do is come up with ideas, which Logan transforms from the far-fetched to the practical."

Logan was uncomfortable being given so much credit. "That may have been true in the first few days, but not any longer. You should have seen her talk the Camp Verde commander into letting her set up a bank there. He was practically ready to hand over the whole payroll."

Now it was Sibyl's turn to appear uncomfortable. "You give me too much credit. It was you who talked Jared into dividing his business between the two banks."

"It seemed a good idea," Jared said. "To keep peace in the family."

Everyone laughed but Logan and Steve. Logan

didn't know whether he contributed to or against peace in the family, and Steve was distracted by Kitty entering the room while leading Jere.

"You were supposed to keep him in the play-room," Laurie said.

"I wanted him to meet Logan," Kitty explained. "He's my friend."

Logan stiffened. The little boy was hardly more than a baby. He toddled across the room on short, stubby legs. Logan had no idea how the child would react to his face. If the boy was frightened or cried, it would bother his parents more than it would Logan.

"He's not quite two," Jared said. "I can't under-stand a thing he says."

"You don't have to understand," Laurie said, "because I can."

Jared rolled his eyes.

"I can't make out most of his words," Laurie con-fessed, "but I usually know what he means."

Jared held out his arms to his son, but Kitty steered him toward Logan. When the child came to a stop, he peered up at Logan and made a sound that no one appeared to understand.

"He wants to talk to you," Kitty said, "but you're too high up."

Logan was completely out of his depth. He could understand why the child would want him on his own level. It was something he'd never considered, but he eased out of the chair and settled down on his knees.

"You don't have to do that," Jared protested.

Logan ignored him. "Is this better?" he asked the boy.

Jere came a step closer. The child had his mother's eyes and his father's hair. It was a toss-up as to who his chubby features would favor when he grew up. To the chagrin of his parents, he reached out and pushed Logan's nose with his stubby index finger. Then he giggled.

"He likes you," Kitty said.

How she figured that was a mystery to Logan.

"Say something to him."

Logan had rarely been around children of any age. If he hadn't been able to tell stories, he didn't know what he would have had to say to Kitty and her friends. But what did you say to a child still shy of his second birthday? His tongue lay like a stone in his mouth.

"Ask him what his name is," Kitty prompted.

Logan did, but the response he got could only be interpreted as *Jere* by someone as besotted as his mother. Jere promptly poked Logan's nose again and giggled.

Laurie got to her feet. "That's enough. I won't have my child poking my guest then laughing about it."

"I don't mind," Logan said.

"That's as may be, but I mind very much. It's time he was put to bed. Please excuse me. I need to check the baby, too. Do you want to help me?" she said to Kitty.

"Can I hold the baby?" Kitty asked.

"Of course." With that assurance, Kitty followed her aunt from the room.

Feeling a little guilty for causing the child to be put to bed early, Logan pushed himself up and back into his seat.

"Don't let it bother you," Jared said. "I don't know what to say to him, either, so I just pretend he understands me and talk to him like I talk to everyone else."

"You ought to hear them," Steve said with a laugh.

"Both jabbering away and neither having the vaguest idea what the other is talking about."

"He makes about as much sense as you half the time," Jared said to his nephew.

Logan listened, slightly shocked as the men traded insults with all the enjoyment of two children. Logan had loved his father and had enjoyed a close relationship, but they had never done anything like this. He couldn't even imagine it happening.

"They don't mean a word they're saying," Sibyl whispered. "They couldn't love each other more if they'd been brothers."

Odd. They were saying very much the kind of things Logan's father and uncle had said to each other, and they fought all the time.

"Stop it," Sibyl said to Jared. "You're giving Logan a very odd idea of our family."

"Sorry," Jared said to Logan. "Laurie says we act like children."

As it happened, that exchange set the tone for the evening. It seemed everyone had a funny story to tell about the others. Even the characters of Norman and Noah Spencer served as fodder for laughter. Events that must have been difficult to live through took on entirely different aspects as everyone seemed to find humor in just about anything. By the time the evening was over, Logan had probably laughed more than he had in his whole life. An added benefit was that he'd managed to forget his illness for much of the time. He almost felt normal again.

But there was something else, something barely perceived. In some way, they'd managed to make him feel like a part of their community. Despite being a virtual stranger, despite his illness and being disfigured, he belonged. More important, he *felt* like he belonged. How different from Chicago.

The evening came to an end when Laurie rose and said it was time for her to go to bed. "I have to get up and feed the baby while everybody else gets to sleep." Sibyl and Kitty were going to spend the night, but they had to get up early because it was a long ride into town. "They can't return tonight because it's too far for Jared to make the round trip, and it's not safe for them to make the drive alone at night."

There was nothing left except for Logan to take his leave. To his surprise, he was reluctant to go. He hadn't felt this good for this long in months.

"Thanks for the invitation," he said to Laurie. "I was reluctant to come, but I don't know when I've had a more enjoyable evening."

"I can ride to your camp with you," Steve offered.

"Thanks, but you have to be in the saddle tomorrow. All I have to do is sit at a desk."

"You don't have to do that if you don't feel like it," Sibyl reminded him.

"I'm fine. I'll see you tomorrow."

"Do you have time for a drink?" Jared asked. "I have a nice bottle of Napoleon brandy I think you'll enjoy."

Logan had drunk nothing but water once he got ill, but it hadn't made any difference. And he did enjoy a good brandy. "That sounds good."

They moved to what must be Jared's office, a room that was dominated by dark wood and leather. Logan smiled to himself, thinking how much his father would have enjoyed such a room. He settled into a deep chair even though he might need help getting out of it. The brandy Jared handed him had a deep golden color. He breathed in the heady aroma, letting it arouse his taste buds. Next he took a sip, rolled it around on his tongue, and sighed. "I've missed this."

Jared smiled. "Come back any time. Brandy is best when it's enjoyed with a friend."

That word hit Logan hard. They were much closer than *friends*. They were brothers, and Jared didn't know.

"I've been wanting a chance to speak with you alone," Jared said after he'd sampled his own drink. "I wanted to thank you."

"Why? I haven't done anything for you."

"You've helped Sibyl. That would have been more than enough."

"She didn't really need help. She just needed information. Now that she has that, she won't need me or anyone else."

They were silent for several minutes. It was a companionable silence even though Jared stared at Logan as though he were trying to see inside Logan's head. Logan wondered what questions he wanted to ask, what answers he would give.

It was Jared who broke the silence. "I knew you were the stranger who shot the bank robbers," he said. "I thought it might be you even before the shooting contest. After I saw the target, I was positive. There can't be one man in a hundred thousand who can shoot like that."

"Target shooting was my hobby. That doesn't mean—"

"I don't know why you would want to deny it."

"I don't like to draw attention to myself."

That caused Jared to laugh. "Then you'd better

not stop any more runaway horses or win any more shooting contests. People stare at that target and go away shaking their heads."

Logan didn't know what to say, and another silence ensued. It, too, was broken by Jared.

"Sibyl says you're planning to leave in a month or two. Why don't you think about staying?"

That was exactly the kind of thing Logan didn't want to hear, because it's what he most wanted to do. But there was a long list of reasons why he shouldn't, and he couldn't forget them. "I never meant to stay this long. I have places to go."

"Forgive me if I don't believe you," Jared said. "You're not well, and you're not getting better. You need to be under a doctor's care. And you need people around you who care about you, who will do whatever they can to help you get well."

Logan tried to speak, but he couldn't get past the lump in his throat.

"You know Kitty prays every night that you'll get well. Sibyl says she doesn't know what she'll do without you, and Naomi says Peter looks up to you almost as much as he does to his father. Hell, even a stray dog follows you about like a slave."

"Trusty follows me because I feed him, and Peter is impressed by tall tales and a fast gun."

"Is that what impresses Kitty?"

Logan could only shake his head. "Kitty is an incredible little girl. She'll grow up to be a remarkable woman."

"Wouldn't you like to see that? What about Peter's aim to be exactly like his father? I think Esther will be as pretty as Kitty. All three will miss you."

Logan couldn't find the words to say how much he'd

like to share the future with these children. And with Sibyl. Jared could have no inkling of how hard it was not to blurt out that they were brothers, that he could wish for nothing more than to spend his last months with siblings he hadn't seen in thirty years. The words were on the tip of his tongue before he could pull them back. "I would like that very much, but I can't. Don't ask me why." He swallowed the last of his brandy and got to his feet. "I've enjoyed being with your family. You have a beautiful wife who adores you and two beautiful children. You are a fortunate man. Now I'd better go."

Jared followed him outside. "Are you sure you wouldn't like me to ride with you? Since I'm the boss, I can sleep late."

"I'll be fine. It's not a long ride, and I'm used to riding at night. I sometimes walk for hours when I can't sleep." Jared's look of concern made him wish he hadn't mentioned that.

"All of us wish you would see the doctor," Jared said. "I know this is a small frontier town, but he's as good as you'll find anywhere."

"I'm sure he is, but all that can be done has been done. I have enough medicine to last for months. Trusty is waiting for me. He'll make sure I get home okay."

It took several minutes before Logan could convince Jared that he would be fine to ride home with just the company of a dog. It would have been a relief when Jared went into the house if Sibyl hadn't emerged from around the corner.

"What are you doing here?" he asked.

"I was hoping to catch you before you left."

"Why?"

"To tell you not to come in to work tomorrow.

The swelling seems to have gone down a little, but you aren't looking very strong."

Something inside him gave way. It was a moment before he realized it was his resolve to keep his distance from this woman who obviously cared for him a great deal. He was sure she believed the swelling had gone down because she *wanted* it so badly. Knowing that removed the final barrier, and he reached out to take Sibyl's hands. It was almost too much for his self-control when he received an answering squeeze.

"How could I have been so lucky to find someone to care as much as you and Kitty?"

"We wouldn't care so much if you weren't so wonderful."

The sincerity in her voice was his undoing. Any shred of restraint vanished. Before he knew what he was doing, his arms were around Sibyl, and he was kissing her with an ardor all the more intense for having been denied so long. When he realized she was responding just as eagerly, it was nearly too much. Still, he fought to keep control. It almost wouldn't matter if he dropped dead afterward. He would have had this one moment of indescribable happiness.

Finally, Sibyl broke the kiss. "You've got to take better care of yourself. You may not care what happens to you, but *I* care very much. Now before I say something I can't retract, I'm going back inside." She kissed him again—quickly this time—then turned and almost ran back around the corner of the house.

Logan was unable to move for several moments. His life had taken a turn so abrupt that it had thrown him off balance. Did Sibyl love him as much as he loved her? It seemed impossible that could be true.

Still, she had responded to his kiss and kissed him again. Surely she wouldn't have done that out of mere sympathy. The euphoria started to wear off, leaving him feeling weak and shaken. Needing to sit for a few minutes, he walked over to the steps and sank down. Trusty approached and whined softly.

"I'm not going to fade out on you yet," he told the dog. "In fact, once I get my strength back, I'm going to do everything I can to live. I might even see that doctor. I never knew holding a woman in my arms could make me feel like I've been half asleep for my whole life." So many possibilities of what life could be like flooded his mind that he didn't hear the door open behind him.

"Are you okay? I knew I shouldn't have agreed to let you ride home alone."

Logan turned to see Jared coming down the steps toward him. "I'm fine, really. I just had something I needed to think about, and I didn't want to be on a horse when I did it."

"That's when I do some of my best thinking," Jared said.

"Too many distractions. I like to sit still and close my eyes."

"I left you just minutes ago. There's nobody here but your horse and your dog. How could anything so important have happened?"

"It's just something that occurred to me unexpectedly."

Jared sat down on the step next to him. "I hope it's not about your health. I'm sure Dr. Kessling could find a cure if you'd just give him a chance."

"I'm thinking about doing just that."

"Good. I know Sibyl thinks a lot of you, but you're important to all of us."

It was all Logan could do not to blurt their connection. "Why? I'm just a stranger who wandered into town a few weeks ago."

Jared chuckled. "After all you've done, you're not *just a stranger*." He sobered. "There's something different about you. I don't know what it is, but I feel there's a connection between us, and not just because we have the same last name. I have from the beginning. It's almost like you're part of our family." Jared got to his feet. "Now I've talked enough nonsense for one evening. Give me a few minutes to saddle a horse, and I'll ride with you."

"There's no need. I'm perfectly fine. My horse knows the way, and Trusty will make sure nothing attacks me."

Jared shook his head. "It's almost like you're related to us. You're just as stubborn as Colby. You'd better arrive home safely. If anything were to happen to you, Sibyl would never forgive me."

Logan appreciated Jared's concern, but he wished he wouldn't bother about him. His worry made it hard to keep from telling Jared they were brothers. The odds against finding both Jared and Colby had been so great it was hard to believe he hadn't made a mistake somehow. But as much as he was tempted, he couldn't. He would stay as long as he could, spend as much time with them as he could manage, but he would leave before he died. Both men had worked hard for their happiness. He would not be responsible for bringing sadness into their lives.

But his thoughts didn't stay dark. As he thought

back over the evening, he remembered some of the stories they'd told, and he found himself laughing at them again. How was it that he and his father had never laughed like that? Why should this be another aspect of life he'd missed? His life had been successful and rewarding, but had it been fun? He'd thought success itself was sufficient reward, but now he wasn't sure. When he looked back, he couldn't remember he and his father ever doing anything just for fun. Everything had been about work. He'd always enjoyed what he did, never thought he might be missing out on anything, until now. As far back as he could remember, life had been a serious matter.

In the beginning, he was afraid his new father wouldn't be proud of him, might even regret having adopted him. He'd done everything he could to make sure that wouldn't happen. He didn't know when he'd started to be comfortable, probably not until he was nearly twenty, when he started to feel his contribution was equal to his father's. Building the business had been hard, had taken all their energy, and required all their attention. Trips to Santa Fe had been long and dangerous. There always seemed to be a challenge in front of them, another obstacle to overcome. He believed his father had come to love him—he certainly loved Samuel Lowe—but their love had lacked the joy, the sheer fun, he'd experienced this evening. He'd spent his free time shooting at targets. His father had spent too much time arguing with his brother.

Had he known love could include joy? Until now, he'd thought of it as a duty, a responsibility, a loyalty—maybe even a return for what he'd been given. It had been his father's duty to be responsible for his brother and niece. His engagement to Bridgette showed his loyalty to the family that had adopted him—as well as a return for what he'd been given. It had seemed so ordinary then, so *natural*. Why did it seem so unnatural now?

Because of Sibyl. Because of the kiss. He'd never come close to feeling this way about any woman. Why did it have to happen when he had so little time left? It seemed like an unusually cruel twist of fate.

"Be glad you're not a man," he said to Trusty, who trotted alongside his horse. "All you need to be happy is a full stomach, a dry bed, and someone to snuggle up to at night." He laughed at his own words. "Who am I kidding? That's about all a man needs, too."

About all. That was the crux. It was that little bit more that made the difference.

≈

"You're looking mighty chipper this morning," Cassie said when Logan entered the bank. "It must have been a really good party."

"It wasn't a party," he explained. "Just dinner."

"Whatever it was, it agreed with you."

It had agreed with him so well he'd gone straight to bed without taking his medicine. As a precaution, he'd taken a double dose this morning. He felt better than he had in a long time. He wanted to make it last as long as possible. He felt so good he was even reconsidering his decision to leave without telling Colby and Jared that they were brothers. Maybe he was getting better. Maybe the clean air, clear water, and plenty of rest was making a difference.

But that wasn't the only change. For the first

time, he had begun to feel a connection with people. He'd thought he been connected before, even with Bridgette and his uncle, but he'd come to realize he was only going through the motions. He cared—or thought he cared—because he was supposed to, because they were his father's family. He cared about the people who worked for him because that was something else he was expected to do. He asked about their children, about their health, but had he really been interested? Did he remember their answers a day or a week later?

He could remember every conversation he'd had with Sibyl. He replayed them on his rides to and from town. They even invaded his dreams. He cared about Kitty, Peter, Esther, and Little Abe. He worried Cassie would never fall in love again, wondered if Horace was completely happy working in the bank. He absorbed every detail he could about Jared and Colby. He wanted to feel a part of their lives, even if only from a distance. It was as though someone had turned a mirror around, and he saw everything in ways he'd never imagined. For too long he'd been going through the motions, doing what was expected, *feeling* what was expected. It had taken a life-threatening illness to open his eyes. He hoped it wasn't too late.

"Mrs. Spencer is driving in from her cousin's ranch this morning," he told Cassie. "I don't know when she'll arrive."

Cassie laughed. "She's already here. She said she hoped *you* would be coming in late." Cassie tilted her head, her curiosity easy to see. "It seems the evening agreed with both of you. What did Laurie cook? Did she have any leftovers?"

Logan knew Cassie had something very different from food in mind, but he wasn't going to satisfy her curiosity. His love for Sibyl would remain unspoken. It was a relief to admit the nature of his feelings to himself. Now he was free to let his feelings go in any direction they wanted. He could feel, hope, dream—as long as he never put his feelings into words.

"Last night's dinner was excellent, but I imagine Jared's cowhands will have eaten every last scrap for this morning's breakfast. Steve could probably have eaten it all himself."

"He's a nice boy," Cassie said. "He's got his eye on Opal Sumner, but they're both too young to be doing much more than making eyes at each other."

About all Logan knew of Haskel Sumner's family was that his oldest daughter, Amber, had married Horace's brother Cato. He wondered how young people went about *making eyes* at each other. At seventeen he'd been too busy to think about girls. Besides, being on the Santa Fe Trail a couple times a year didn't give him much opportunity.

"Did you get to see Laurie's new baby?" Cassie asked. "He's beautiful."

"Laurie had fed him and put him to bed before I got there, but Kitty brought Jere in to see us. He looks like both his parents."

"I'd like another baby," Cassie said, "but I need to find a husband first. Do you know anybody you could suggest?"

Logan knew she was teasing him, but it made him uncomfortable. "A lovely young woman like you must have lots of suitors."

Cassie frowned. "Not the kind I'm looking for." She

broke into a sexy smile and winked at him. "Now if you were to ask me to marry you, I'd jump at the chance."

Logan thought the sudden queasiness that came over him was due to Cassie's unexpected comment. No beautiful young woman could be romantically interested in him, so he couldn't understand why her teasing should affect him so. He started to say something, but a dizzy spell caused him to lose the thought. He was about to be very sick.

Eleven

SIBYL HAD JUST REACHED FOR HER COFFEE WHEN SHE heard Cassie scream for help. Leaping to her feet, Sibyl rushed from her office. The sight that met her eyes sent her heart into her throat. Logan lay on the floor unmoving. Cassie was kneeling beside him.

"What happened?" Sibyl asked.

"I don't know," Cassie said. "We were talking. He was in good spirits. Next minute he seemed to have some kind of seizure, then he just fell down. I didn't know what to do," she wailed. "Horace has gone for the doctor."

Sibyl knelt next to Logan. He had lost all color, but his heartbeat was strong. Too strong. It was tumultuous. Sibyl could see it pulsing through the veins on his neck. Was he having a heart attack? A stroke? She wished the doctor would get here soon. She felt so helpless. A racking spasm gripped Logan. He came to his knees, a look of desperation on his face.

"Uh-oh." Cassie scrambled to her feet, ran to her desk, emptied a bowl of candy she kept to give children and new customers, and ran back just in time to place it on the floor next to Logan. He pulled it toward him and proceeded to empty his stomach. The paroxysms shook his body so violently Sibyl almost expected him to expire right in front of her. She was weak with relief when the spasms finally stopped. She moved closer to Logan and put his head in her lap.

"No," he managed to say, but his resistance was weak.

"The doctor will be here soon," she told him. She took the handkerchief from her pocket and wiped his mouth.

"You shouldn't do this." He tried to pull away, but he didn't have the strength. He was exhausted, his brow covered with perspiration.

"Lie still." Cassie brought her a basin of water. Using Cassie's handkerchief, she bathed his forehead. He tried to push her hand away, but Cassie gripped his hands and pushed them down to his side. He groaned, and his resistance ebbed.

Horace burst through the bank doors. "The doctor is on his way," he told them between gasps for breath. "There are people outside waiting to get in. What should I tell them?"

Sibyl didn't look up. "Tell them the bank will open an hour later than usual. Make sure the doors are locked. Cassie can open them for the doctor. I want you to find Colby. I need him to move Logan to my house."

"I can go back to my camp," Logan protested. "I'll be all right after a while."

"You're too intelligent to make such a ridiculous statement," Sibyl told him. "You haven't been all right from the moment you arrived. You are a very sick man. Are you going to depend on your dog to take care of you?" She didn't wait for an answer but turned back to Horace. "If you can't find Colby, tell

Naomi. She'll know who to get. And tell her I intend to put Logan in Norman's bedroom."

"I can't put you out of your own bed," Logan said.

"You won't. I haven't slept in that room since Norman died."

A loud rattling of the door caught her attention. "See if that's the doctor," she told Horace. Moments later Dr. Kessling came bustling in, muttering about people craning their necks to get a glimpse of what didn't concern them.

"I wish you'd come to see me before now," he said to Logan. "Then I might have some idea of what's wrong with you."

"I'm dying. That's all you need to know."

"Well, you're not dead yet, so let's see what I can do to put that off a while longer. That is, of course, if you're not set upon dying. If you are, just say so, and I'll get back to my breakfast. I hate cold coffee."

"Don't be absurd," Sibyl said.

"I'm not being absurd. I'm just irritated. This man's been walking about for weeks looking like his next breath might be his last, and he has refused all entreaties to get himself looked at. Now he collapses, and he expects a miracle cure."

"I don't expect a cure," Logan told him. "I was treated by a doctor with a reputation for being able to identify any disease and formulate a cure. After several months, he told me my case was hopeless. I have only a few months to live."

The words hit Sibyl like a physical blow. She had known Logan was sick, but she'd assumed he would get well. He said he was taking the medicine his doctor had prescribed. He had even been looking and acting better. He'd had the strength to catch runaway horses, the steadiness of hand to win the shooting contest, and the energy to help her win the three-legged race. How could she have believed a man who could do all of that was facing death? He had to be mistaken. Dr. Kessling would find out what was wrong. He wasn't a fancy Chicago specialist, but he was a fine doctor.

"Well, there's still hope," Dr. Kessling said. "What I have to do now is get you to a bed where you can get some rest. After that, I'll see about getting a little food in you. Maybe a clear broth. If you can keep that down, I'd say there's hope for you yet."

"It's a waste of your time," Logan said.

"Well, it's my time, so I guess I can waste it any way I want."

Sibyl had always admired Dr. Kessling—he was the only doctor she'd ever known—but she was doubly grateful he refused to be put off by Logan's pessimism. It wasn't like Logan *wanted* to die. It was more like he'd given up hope. That was something Sibyl couldn't understand. Several times her life had taken a tragic turn, but she'd never given up hope that she would someday find happiness for herself and her daughter. That was the only way she could face each day.

"How long have you been like this?" the doctor asked Logan.

"How do you mean *like this*?" Logan asked. "Being sick, passing out, or having my face look like it's about to explode?"

"Any or all of the above," the doctor replied.

Logan struggled to sit up. Sibyl pressed him down until his head rested in her lap again.

"You can get up when Colby gets here," she told him.

"I can sit up now."

"But you don't have to."

"Don't fight her," the doctor advised. "I've learned never to argue with a woman unless absolutely necessary. And then you should think twice before doing it."

"You argue with Naomi," Cassie said. "I've heard you."

"I haven't in years. And even then, it didn't do much good. But don't distract me. I want to hear what this man has to say."

"It started at least six months ago," Logan said. "Sometimes, I think it had begun even before that, but it was hard to tell."

"Why?"

"At first I was just more tired than usual. I'm thirty-five. I ought to be in the prime of my life. I'd always been able to outwork any man in our company. I was stronger and had more stamina. The stamina was the first to go. My strength went next. I thought I was just working too hard. My father had died, and I was trying to do the work of two men. Occasionally, I would forget something I'd planned to do or when I was supposed to be somewhere, but I credited that to a lack of sleep. I used the same excuse when I started forgetting things I considered minor details."

"Even men in their prime can suffer from the stress of overwork," the doctor said. "The mind compensates by blocking out what it can't handle."

"That's when I started to get sick and have dizzy spells," Logan continued. "The doctor changed my medicine, but I got worse. He tried several prescriptions, but nothing helped."

"Did this *outstanding* doctor come up with a diagnosis?" the doctor asked.

"He had several explanations but nothing that fit a specific disease or illness. When my face started to swell, he changed my medicine again. When the swelling didn't go down and my other symptoms got worse, I asked him how long I had. He said only a few months. That's when I decided to leave Chicago. I didn't want people to remember me like this."

"Why did you choose Cactus Corner? Why did you think people here wouldn't care how you looked?"

His hesitation was only brief, but Sibyl got the impression he was trying to think of an answer that was only part of the truth.

"I'd seen a picture of Jared Smith in a newspaper. It was about his appointment as marshal. The writer implied Jared had gotten the job because of his military experience, but that he'd really taken it so he could pass it on to his foreman, a man who'd served in the Union army under his command. The article went on to describe Cactus Corner. It sounded like the kind of town I'd like to know more about."

"Sounds like a pretty slim reason to travel a thousand miles to a place you'd never been."

"What else was I going to do with my time? Sit in a corner and feel sorry for myself?"

"Now that's the kind of thinking I like," the doctor said. "You don't sound like a man who's ready to give up."

"He can't give up," Sibyl said. "He has to teach me how to run this bank."

"You're doing just fine," Logan said. "Now it's

about time I went back to my camp and let everybody get back to what they were doing."

He tried to sit up, but he didn't have the energy. It was all Sibyl needed to make up her mind. "We're taking you to my house, so there's no use arguing. You're not well, and you need someone to take care of you. After all you've done for me, it's the least I can do. There's no use arguing," she said again when he started to protest. "If you're too weak to sit up, you're certainly too weak to ride a horse."

"What was I just telling you about arguing with a woman?" the doctor asked. "You don't learn very quickly, do you?"

"I'm not used to being helpless," Logan said. "I don't like it."

"No man does, but it's nice to be looked after once in a while." He winked at Sibyl. "You might as well relax and enjoy it. It doesn't last."

A knock on the door drew their attention. Horace opened the door for Colby. The Sumner brothers followed, carrying a mattress.

"You can give us a hand after we get Logan on the mattress," Colby said to Horace. "Naomi's at your house," he said to Sibyl. "She said she'd have the room ready by the time we got there."

When they lifted him to put him on the mattress, Logan insisted he was well enough to go back to his camp, but no one paid him any attention. The Sumner brothers could have carried him between the two of them, but Sibyl was sure Logan would be more comfortable on the mattress. The men had him out the door in a jiffy.

It was a strange procession that wound through the

streets. People who'd been standing outside the bank followed in a shapeless gaggle, asking questions and offering suggestions. People came out of stores, shops, and homes to ask what was going on. The children, never ones to miss a bit of excitement, ran alongside cutting up. She didn't see him, but she was certain Trusty was following as well.

They were not more than halfway home when Logan was shaken by violent tremors.

"Put the mattress down," the doctor ordered.

Sibyl watched breathlessly as the doctor tried unsuccessfully to ease Logan's distress.

"Bring him into the shade," the doctor said.

Colby and the other men carried Logan to the shadow of the mercantile. They placed the mattress on the ground, but the tremors seemed to have subsided.

"What do you want us to do?" Colby asked.

"Take him to the house. I don't know what else to do. We can't have him lying in the street with everybody gawking at him."

People were staring, but they watched because they cared. Most remembered that Logan had stopped the runaway horses. Others admired his gallant effort in the three-legged race. Everyone had sympathy for the illness that had robbed him of his strength and turned his face into a caricature. A second onset of tremors caused many to offer words of sympathy and promises of help. By the time they reached the house, Sibyl felt like she ought to invite the whole town inside.

But there were too many inside already. In addition to the four men, Naomi, and Cassie, who'd followed as soon as she'd locked the bank, Kitty had insisted that Peter and Esther had to be allowed to see

Logan. Fortunately, Garnet Sumner was taking care of Naomi's other children and Little Abe, or they'd have been there, too. Mae Oliver had wedged her way inside. She insisted that Sibyl couldn't be expected to take care of Logan by herself. Since the doctor agreed with her, Sibyl had given in.

The men weren't anxious to linger, but the children wouldn't leave. Kitty stood at the head of the bed, out of the way but as close as possible to Logan. Esther stood next to her, but Peter planted himself next to the doctor and pummeled him with questions. Beset with worry about Logan, it was difficult for Sibyl to control her irritation at Peter, but it was obvious the boy was as concerned about Logan as she was. Esther looked confused, but Kitty was solemn, her little face devoid of animation. It was the doctor who finally cleared the room.

"Okay, children, it's time to undress Mr. Holstock and put him to bed, so you'll have to leave."

"Come on," Sibyl said to the children. "You can come back to see Logan when he's had time to get some rest."

Colby stayed to help the doctor undress Logan.

Once downstairs, Naomi gathered the children and took them home with her. Feeling helpless and needing something to do, Sibyl moved to the kitchen to make some coffee. This had always been her favorite room, in part because Norman had refused to enter it. His mother had told him it was undignified for a man to enter the kitchen. Being unable to take all of one's meals in a dining room indicated a loss of status.

"Are you sure you'll be all right?" Mae asked Sibyl.

"I can stay until Frank comes home from work. I can come back after I give him his supper." Ever since the death of her only child in an Indian attack, Mae had never wanted to be home alone.

"I won't know what I'll need until after the doctor has had time to give Logan a thorough examination. I'll send Kitty over if I need anything."

"How is he doing?" Cassie asked.

"Nothing has changed, but the last seizure wasn't as bad as the one before it."

"What about his medicine? He never brings it to the bank."

"I wouldn't know what to tell you. The doctor might decide to change the medicine."

"I wonder if he has any better clothes," Cassie said. "I can't believe he's always dressed like he doesn't have two bits to his name."

"I expect he's going to be in bed for a while," Sibyl said. "We have plenty of time to worry about clothes."

"What about Trusty?"

Sibyl turned to see her daughter standing in the doorway to the kitchen. "I thought you went with your Aunt Naomi."

"I was going to, but I saw Trusty hiding under the front steps. We have to feed him while Logan is sick."

Sibyl wasn't ready to think about adding a dog to her responsibilities, but it was obvious Kitty was. "Run ask the butcher if he has any bones."

Kitty looked upset. "We can't feed Trusty bones."

Sibyl grinned at her daughter's frown. "I meant bones with some meat on them. I'll ask the Hill brothers what they feed their dogs. In the meantime, ask the butcher if he has any scraps."

"I'll go with Kitty," Mae volunteered. "You don't want her coming back with nothing but fat."

"Why did you bring Logan here?" Cassie asked as soon as the door closed behind Mae and Kitty. They were standing in the front parlor, a room as uncomfortable as Sibyl felt under Cassie's questioning.

"Where else could I have taken him? I couldn't send him back to his camp in the woods."

"Nobody's saying anything now, but they've got to be wondering why a single woman, and one who's recently widowed, would bring a single man into her home. Are you going to look after him?"

"Of course. Who else should do it?"

"I don't know, but why does it have to be you?"

Sibyl felt like she was being backed into a corner, and she didn't like it. "He works with me. I couldn't have managed the bank without him. He's become a good friend."

"If you ask me, I'd say it was more than that."

"Well, I didn't ask you, and I'd be grateful if you didn't say anything like that again."

"It won't matter if I say it or not. Others will soon enough. What are you going to tell them?"

"No one I respect will ask such a question."

"That's ridiculous. I'm sure Naomi's wondering the exact same thing right now."

Sibyl was certain of it. She had seen the question in Naomi's eyes. Mae's curiosity had been even more evident. "I expect she is, but she won't think less of me."

"No one who knows you could ever think badly of you, but you own a bank. The public are your customers. That means you're a public figure. People are going to want to know what kind of person has charge of their money. They'll think if you're honest in your private life, you'll be honest with their money."

"That's absurd. They have nothing to do with each other. Norman was a miserable person in his private life, but he was an excellent businessman."

"But you're a woman. They're going to look at you differently."

Sibyl was worried about Logan's health. She was wondering how she could run the bank and take care of him. She worried how it would affect Kitty if he died. She didn't have time to worry what the people of Cactus Corner would think of what she'd done. "Why are you asking these questions?"

"You're a wonderful woman and will be a good bank president, but you're naive when it comes to people, especially people you think are your friends. Being Norman's long-suffering wife and his widow has brought you widespread sympathy, but all of that will change now. Your situation is a lot like mine. You're a beautiful single woman who's rich and owns a bank. That makes you the most envied person in Cactus Corner. Women are going to be jealous of you. Men are going to think you're above your station. Unconsciously or otherwise, they're going to try to bring you down to their level. Any tidbit of gossip will be nurtured and passed along. Everyone will have their own versions of why you do what you do. Most of them won't be flattering."

"I can't believe people will be that malicious."

"I do because I know what people say about me. I'm young, single, and beautiful. I'm paid to smile to bring customers into the bank, but many people think I smile to coax them into my bed, even though everyone knows I've led a depressingly blameless life ever since Abe was killed."

Sibyl had to admit Cassie was right because she'd heard what people said. Nothing she had said had been able to make any difference. Men saw a beautiful, unattached woman as a temptation, and women saw her as a rival. "Everybody knows Logan isn't well. They won't be upset when they know I brought him here rather than let him return to his camp in the woods. He could die out there, and no one would know."

"What if he dies anyway?"

Sibyl refused to face that possibility. "The doctor will figure out what's wrong. He'd probably be well by now if he'd gone to the doctor when he got here."

Cassie walked over to where Sibyl was staring out the window and gently turned her until they were facing each other. "Are you in love with him? I wouldn't blame you if you were. He's a wonderful man."

The question wasn't as much of a shock as Sibyl had expected. "Of course not. Why would you ask such a question?"

"Because he's going to die, and I'd hate to see you lose the first man you could really love."

Too late. I already lost the first one! Sibyl refused to think about that handsome, young Union soldier and banished his image from her mind. "Whatever happens, I have to do everything I can to make sure Logan gets well. He's always said he wouldn't stay here long. Why would I let myself fall in love with a man I knew was going to leave?"

"Because we can't control who we love. And I think you love Logan. You've just been denying it. After being married to a man like Norman, who wouldn't love Logan?"

Sibyl wasn't ready to admit her true feelings. "I do have strong feelings for Logan. I like and admire him very much. I'm also immensely grateful for the help he's given me with the bank and for teaching Kitty how to laugh. I know some people wonder how I could be so fond of a man with such distorted facial features, but I hardly see that anymore. I just see the kind of person he is underneath all that. That's who the children see, too."

"I just don't want you to get hurt. You deserve a wonderful man who can give you love and more children."

"So do you."

Cassie sighed. "All men ever see is my face. What will happen when I get old?"

"You'll always be beautiful."

"Well, you're beautiful and rich. How can you tell if a man loves you for yourself?"

"I don't know." But what about a man who'd fallen in love with her against his will, a man who was sure he was going to die? She could trust his love, couldn't she? Logan had never put his feelings into words, but she could see them in his eyes, feel them in the sound of his voice, sense them in his presence. It was in the very air that hung between them. She had been the one to hold back her feelings.

The creak of the stairs told her that the doctor had finished his examination and was coming down. Both she and Cassie faced him eagerly.

"I don't know what to tell you," the doctor said without waiting for them to speak. He looked tired, frustrated, even angry. "I can't find anything wrong with his vital organs, but it's clear he's dying. It's almost as if he's being poisoned."

"But that's impossible," Sibyl said. "He gets his food at the mercantile in town or from hunting. He feeds his dog the same things, and the dog is thriving."

"That's what he told me," the doctor replied, "but something is causing a steady decline. I wish I knew what his doctor prescribed for him."

"Colby can get his medicine from his camp."

"Good. I'll ask him to go tomorrow."

"Can I see Logan now?"

"He's sleeping, so I wouldn't bother him until he wakes up. When he does, give him nothing but clear liquids. He doesn't have enough strength to keep throwing up everything he puts in his mouth. I'll be back later this evening. I need time to see if I can find something that will explain what's happening to him."

"I'd better go find Little Abe," Cassie said. "He's going to be upset when he hears about Logan. He likes to pretend it could have been his grandfather in Logan's stories."

"Peter pretends it's himself when he grows up. I don't know what kind of magic he has with children, but they all adore him."

"It's not confined to children," Cassie said. "You and I admire him, and Horace takes everything he says like it's gospel. Even Colby and Jared are impressed by him, and that's not easy to do."

"Everybody likes him," Sibyl added. "He *can't* die."

But he would unless the doctor could find out what was wrong.

Sibyl had seldom entered Norman's bedroom since his death, but Logan's presence had changed the feeling of the room. The four-poster bed took on the character of a shelter rather than a throne. The dark, imposing furniture had become sentinels rather than aristocrats looking down their noses at her. Even the size of the room was no longer intimidating. The mossy green wallpaper was soothing rather than gloomy, the heavy brocade curtains reassuring rather than stiff and formal.

She didn't know how long she'd sat by Logan's bed, but it was long enough for the bowl of clear beef broth to have gone cold. It was long enough that the twilight of evening had turned into the dark of night. Kitty had been asleep for hours. Trusty lay outside the bedroom door, occasionally whining for the man separated from him by a wood barrier. Sibyl was certain the bedroom door was badly scarred where Trusty had scratched trying to get in.

Sibyl wished she could whine or do something that would release the terrible pressure that weighed on her like a huge boulder. Logan had lain in a deep sleep ever since the doctor's first visit. He hadn't waked during the second visit or when Kitty came to tell him good night. Sibyl's heart nearly broke when her daughter knelt beside Logan's bed and prayed that he would get well. The child who had never done anything wrong in her life promised she'd do whatever God wanted if He'd just make Logan better. Naomi and Colby had come by to offer to do whatever they could. Mae had brought the beef broth and promised to bring another bowl first thing in the morning. The stream of visitors had been steady all afternoon. It was a relief to lock her door after posting a note that she'd gone to bed.

But she hadn't gone to bed because she knew she wouldn't sleep. So here she sat, staring at Logan's unresponsive body, and praying silently a prayer much like the one offered by her daughter hours earlier.

She didn't promise to be good in return for Logan's recovery. That was a foolish thing to do, yet she felt the urge to make a bargain with some unseen power. There must have been a reason why such a healthy man was taken mysteriously ill. If that was true, there had to be something that could be offered in exchange for sparing him. She kept telling herself not to be foolish, but she couldn't drive the thought from her mind. Had Logan done something terrible? Had *she* done something so terrible that a man she hadn't known should be made to suffer?

She had to be losing her mind. She'd never acted like this before. Is that what love did to a woman who'd given up hoping she would ever experience it again? The first time she'd been in love, she was too young to know what it meant. It had been exhilaration over a future so fantastic that it brushed aside reality. It had been promises given without thought of consequences. It had been blind faith that this was how her life was meant to be, and neither her parents nor the war that was tearing a country apart could change that.

But she was older now. She'd lived with the reality of crushed dreams. She'd experienced the emptiness of promises given by those who never meant to keep them. And she'd learned that many things much less powerful than parents or war could rip a life asunder. Which made what she was feeling for Logan all that much more important.

She loved this man. There was no reason why she should. She knew little about him because he hid his past from her. He was neither rich nor handsome. He was very ill and could easily die. Most important of all, he'd never said he loved her. There was absolutely no reason she should have fallen in love with him. But she had, and it was time she admitted it.

But even as her mind accepted that, she wondered if she really knew what love was. Her parents hadn't loved her, or they'd never have forced her to marry Norman Spencer. Norman hadn't loved her. She was just another possession to bolster his image of himself. Her daughter and cousins loved her, but that wasn't the same as a man's love. She even wondered if she'd been in love with her handsome soldier, or whether she'd just been in love with the excitement of rebellion.

She couldn't compare her feelings to Naomi's for Colby. They were devoted to each other, but they were fiercely independent. Her feelings weren't like those of Jared and Laurie, either. They could barely keep their hands off each other for as much as half a day. Her feelings for Logan were a quiet thing, though no less powerful for its lack of visible energy. Looking at him now, she just wanted to be able to sit next to him, to hold his hand, to have him put his arm around her. It wasn't much, but it would be more than she'd ever had. It would nourish a soul that felt as barren as a desert.

"Why?" she asked aloud, but she hardly knew which question she looked to answer first. Why had he contracted an illness no doctor could identify? Why had she fallen in love with him? Why had he found his way to Cactus Corner if he was just going to die once he got here? Questions bombarded her like a blizzard. She felt defenseless before the onslaught. She wanted to run away, but there was no way to hide from herself.

Without warning, Logan's body began to convulse so violently the bed shook. Sibyl's first impulse was to call for help, but there was no one to call. The next was to go for the doctor, but she couldn't leave Logan unattended. What if he died while she was gone? His eyes flew open, and a thin line of drool ran down his chin. Unable to do anything else, she tried to wipe his mouth, but his head moved from side to side too quickly. Then just as suddenly, the convulsions stopped. The relief that flooded through her turned to horror.

Logan had stopped breathing!

Twelve

"No!" THE WORD BURST FROM HER UNBIDDEN. A feeling she would be unable to explain later—that the death of Logan somehow stood for everything that had been denied her—took her firmly in its grasp. Rage surged through her with the speed of a flash flood. This was brutally unfair, and she wouldn't stand for it. Balling up her fist, she hit Logan squarely in the chest.

"Don't you dare do this to me!" she shouted. "I didn't ask for you to come into my life! I didn't want you to be so wonderful my daughter would pray for you, or that some flea-bitten stray would be lying outside the door whining because he thinks you're dying. I didn't want to fall in love again, not with you or anyone else." She hit him again. "It's not fair!" The futility of what she was doing overcame her, and she pounded out her anger on Logan's chest.

A wall inside her broke, and all the emotions she had held back for years came spilling out like water from a broken dam. She abandoned the restraint she'd practiced for so long it had become second nature. She forgot to care what anyone, not even her own self, would think of her at this moment. Hers weren't the tears one sheds after the death of a near stranger. They weren't even the tears of a grown woman who'd experience many sorrows in her life. They were gut-wrenching cries brought forth by the crushing loss of hope, the unbearable weight of loss, and the nearly physical pain of despair. Falling across Logan's body, her own body shaking from the force of her heartbreak, she sobbed out her misery.

"Mommy! Please don't cry. It scares me."

Sibyl's sob ended in a hiccup. Regardless of her own pain, she couldn't hurt her daughter. Struggling to pull herself together, she wiped away the tears that streamed down her face. With eyes still swimming with tears that nearly blocked her vision, she stumbled to the door and opened it. She was aware of Trusty slipping by her into the room, but her only concern was for her daughter.

"I'm all right," she reassured Kitty.

"Why were you shouting? You sounded mad at Logan."

She was angry at him for leaving her, but she didn't think Kitty would understand that. "I wasn't mad at Logan. I was just upset that he..." She'd almost said *that he'd died*. Kitty had to be told sometime, but not while she was still upset. "I didn't mean to shout. I'm sorry I woke you."

"I wasn't asleep. I was waiting for you to tell me Logan was better."

Sibyl had thought she would choke on her own sadness. Now she realized her daughter's loss would be just as great. "I'm sorry, darling, but Logan isn't better."

"Why not?"

"He had a seizure. I'm afraid it was a very bad one."
She was a coward. Why didn't she just come out and
tell her daughter that Logan had died?

"Why is Trusty licking his face?"

Sibyl had forgotten about the dog, but what harm
could licking the face of a dead man do? Then it struck
her. *Dogs don't lick the faces of their masters after they've
died. They howl their own sadness.* Not knowing what
to think, she turned and hurried to Logan's bedside.
What she saw nearly caused her to swoon.

He was breathing. The faint rise and fall of
his chest was unmistakable. She thought she had
exhausted her tears, but they flowed again, even
more rapidly than before. She didn't know whose
prayer had been answered, but it didn't matter.
Logan was breathing. She wanted to tell Trusty to
stop licking his face, that it was unsanitary, but she
was too weak with relief to form the words. Kitty
did it for her.

"Dr. Kessling said you have to stay outside," she
told the dog. "He said you might have something
that would make Logan sicker. You want him to get
better, don't you?"

Sibyl didn't know whether or not the dog understood, but he let Kitty push him from the room and
close the door on him.

"I want to stay with you," Kitty said to her mother.
"That way you won't be so sad."

Words failed Sibyl. Instead she pulled her daughter
into a tight embrace. She tried to hold back her tears,
but she was so overcome by a multitude of emotions
that she couldn't stop.

Troubled, Kitty asked, "Why are you still sad?"

"I'm not sad," her mother told her. "I'm happy Logan is still alive, and I'm thankful to have a wonderful daughter like you."

"I don't cry when I'm happy and thankful. Is that bad?"

"No, darling. Most people laugh when they're happy. Some even sing or dance. But there are some who need quiet to enjoy their happiness. Then there are a few, like your mother, who cry because they're so thankful they can't stand it."

"Will I cry when I grow up?"

"Probably not."

"But I want to be like you. Peter says he's going to be exactly like Uncle Colby. Aunt Naomi says he's already much worse."

Sibyl laughed, this time without tears. "You're a wonderful little girl, and you're going to grow up to be a wonderful woman who's not a bit like her sentimental mother."

"What's *sentimental*? Why wouldn't I like to be it?"

This time when Sibyl laughed, she really felt like it. She wondered how she would ever have survived without her daughter. "You're too practical. You're a lot like your Aunt Naomi."

"I love Aunt Naomi, but I'd rather be like you."

"Well, I want you to be exactly like yourself. Now I want you to go back to bed. I'm not sad anymore, so you don't have to stay with me."

Kitty turned her gaze to where Logan lay in the bed. "What will we do if he doesn't get better?"

Sibyl knew the answer to that question—go on living because they had no other choice—but she chose not to face it yet. "I'm sure he's going to get better. Dr. Kessling is working very hard to find out what's wrong with him."

"I love Logan. Do you think he loves me?"

"I know he does, and he'll do everything he can to get well and make you happy. Now you have to go back to bed. Tomorrow we have to work very hard to take care of Logan."

"Can I take Trusty with me?"

"If you think he will go."

But despite Kitty's entreaties, Trusty refused to leave his position outside the door. Sibyl knew how he felt. She couldn't imagine leaving Logan's bedside until the doctor returned. She had no idea why his heart had stopped beating, and she understood even less why it should have started beating again—it *had* stopped. She was sure of it—but she couldn't leave because it might happen again. So she would stay. Wasn't that what a woman in love would do?

She no longer questioned her feelings for Logan nor did she bother to ask how it could have happened. Her reaction when she thought he'd died left no room for doubt. Now she had to do everything she could to make sure he got well. She had something very important to tell him.

❧

Logan woke to find Sibyl staring straight into his eyes. Where was he? What happened? How did he get here? The enormous room was completely unfamiliar. The four-poster bed he lay in was as big as a small room. The dark, imposing furniture was as heavy and gloomy as the brocade curtains. Only the mossy green wallpaper kept the room from feeling like a dungeon.

"How are you feeling?" Sibyl asked.

"Extremely weak. I can't lift my head. What happened to me?"

"You had several seizures. The doctor has been to check on you twice, but he can't figure out what brought them on."

"Where am I?"

"You're in my house. Taking you back to your camp was out of the question, and I didn't think sending you to the hotel was any better."

Logan tried to rise, but he was too weak. "I can't stay here. It's not right."

"Why not? You're sick, and you need someone to tend you. I have the time, and I have plenty of room. I can hire a nurse and someone to cook for us. It seems like the most logical arrangement to me."

Logan could barely summon the energy to keep his thoughts straight, but he knew he shouldn't be in Sibyl's house. "I can't stay here."

"Well, no one is going to remove you, and you're not strong enough to leave on your own. So I suggest you concentrate on trying to get better."

"But what will people say?"

"Half of the town has made a pathway to my door. They all want to know how you're doing and asked if they can do anything to help."

"I can't let you turn yourself into a nurse for me."

Sibyl smiled so brightly he thought he might pass out. "You're in no position to do anything about it, so you might as well accept it. Trusty is outside the door. He's been whining all night. I hope you can assure him that you're doing better. He should go outside. I doubt he's housebroken. Kitty was the only one of the children I let in to see you, but I doubt I can keep Peter out much longer. And if I let him in, Esther and Little Abe will want in, too. They're very worried about you."

Warmth and embarrassment battled inside Logan, but warmth won out. "I'd like to eat something first. But as soon as I can sit up, I want to see the children."

Sibyl stood. "I'll go warm up the broth. Kitty can keep you company until I get back."

"Where is she?"

"She's been keeping vigil outside your door since she got up."

Logan had always felt his father cared about him, but he realized he'd never known what love was like until he came to Cactus Corner. Of all the unexpected places to find it. "I don't know how to thank you for what you've done."

"Then don't try." Sibyl opened the door.

Someone had found a rope and put it around Trusty's neck. He practically pulled Kitty into the room, but she kept him from reaching the bed.

"Mama said I couldn't bring him in unless I had a rope on him," she told Logan. "He licked your face last night." Trusty kept trying to reach Logan.

"I'd better take the dog with me," Sibyl said. "Otherwise you'll spend all your time trying to keep him off Logan. I don't know what you did to him. I've never seen such loyalty in a dog. It shouldn't take more than ten minutes to heat up the broth."

After Sibyl and Trusty left, Kitty moved the chair next to Logan's bed and seated herself. "Mama said you were very sick. She thought you died, but I knew you hadn't. I prayed you would get well. The preacher says if we're sincere and want something good with all our hearts, that it will come true. That's why I knew you wouldn't die."

Logan couldn't think of anything to say, but it wouldn't have done him any good if he had. He was so choked up he couldn't speak.

"Peter said I was a fool. Peter can be very rude sometimes. He said you were going to die, that they'd put you in the ground, and you'd rot like a dead carcass. But I could tell he didn't want you to die. He just said it because he was afraid."

"Thank you for your prayers. I'm sure they helped."

"Mama prayed, too. She didn't say anything, but I know she did."

"How could you tell?"

"I wasn't asleep. I heard her shouting. She said she didn't want to fall in love with you, that it wasn't fair. Then she started crying real loud. I got scared so I came in to stay with her. Trusty started licking your face, and Mama started crying again, but this time she said she was crying because she was happy you hadn't died. She says grown-ups sometimes cry when they're really, really happy. Do you cry when you're happy?"

Logan could hardly collect his thoughts enough to say, "No. I don't."

Sibyl loved him. It was almost impossible to believe, but surely she wouldn't have said something like that if she hadn't meant it. But why would she love him? How *could* she? He was a stranger who'd avoided telling her anything important about himself. He was dying, and he looked like a gargoyle. He dressed like a hobo, he'd just collapsed in front of her, and he'd made a mess in her bank foyer. What could there be to love about that?

"Do you love Mama?"

Shock riveted Logan's mind. "Why would you ask that?"

"I asked Mama if she thought you loved me, and she said she was sure you did."

"Of course I do," Logan said, relieved to have sidestepped the question. "Who couldn't love a sweet little girl like you?"

"Peter says I'm a goody two-shoes. Is that bad?"

Logan almost laughed. "Peter is just jealous he isn't as nice as you."

"No, he's not. Peter *likes* being bad."

"I don't think Peter is really very terrible."

"I heard Aunt Naomi say he was a *bête noire*. I asked her what that meant, but she said to ignore her, that she was just out of temper."

"I think it means Peter had tried her patience."

"Aunt Naomi says Peter tries everybody's patience. One time she threatened to send him back to Santa Fe. Peter was good for almost a week."

Logan had been so afraid his new father might be sorry he adopted him that he hadn't done anything bad *ever*. He was nearly an adult before he could sleep without fear of what might happen the next day. He could understand how Peter felt.

"Do you love Mama?"

Logan hadn't known a child's mind could be so tenacious. He'd been certain Kitty had forgotten all about her question. "Why do you want to know?"

"If Mama loves you, you have to love her back.

Then she will be really, really happy. But I won't like it if she cries all the time."

"I'm sure she won't cry all the time. You mother likes to laugh and have fun."

Kitty shook her head. "Mama never did that."

"Why not?" Logan thought of Sibyl on the day of the celebration. She'd been full of high spirits, even dragging him into a three-legged race, something he could never have imagined her doing when he first got to know her.

"Norman didn't like levity. I asked Aunt Naomi what that meant. She said it meant laughing and having fun. Norman didn't like fun, either."

"Did you love your papa?" Logan regretted the question the moment it was out of his mouth. "I'm sorry. I had no right to ask that."

"I didn't like him because he made Mama sad."

"Why did you call your father by his name?" Another question he shouldn't have asked.

"He wanted me to."

Odd. Why wouldn't a father want his daughter to acknowledge their relationship? Even a very formal person should have wanted to be called *father*.

"Norman wouldn't let me talk at the table," Kitty told him. "If I forgot, I had to go to my room."

The more Logan heard about Norman, the more he disliked the man for what he had done to his wife and child. No man in his right mind could fail to find Sibyl beautiful and desirable. And he couldn't imagine having a more perfect daughter than Kitty. He couldn't imagine anything better in life than being able to come home to such a wife and daughter. He would have traded all his wealth and success for such a chance. Fortunately, before he could fall into a deep depression, Sibyl returned with the broth.

"I hope Kitty hasn't tired you," she said as she sat in the chair her daughter had vacated for her mother.

"Kitty could never tire me," Logan said. "None of the children do."

"Don't say that too loudly. If Naomi hears you, she'll hire you to look after Peter."

Logan tried to laugh, but it came out as a cough.

"Don't try to talk," Sibyl said. "Just eat."

He *wanted* to talk, but he had so many things to say he didn't know where to start. So he concentrated on eating. Sibyl fed him the broth one spoonful at a time while Kitty watched silently from across the room.

"Who's looking after the bank?" he asked when Sibyl paused.

"I had Cassie post a sign saying we were closed until further notice."

He started to argue, but she shoved a spoonful of broth into his open mouth.

"The bank is a day-to-day business. You can't ignore it and stay here with me."

"I can if I want." Sibyl fed him more broth.

"But you shouldn't. I don't want you to."

Sibyl gave him a fierce look. "Look me straight in the eyes and tell me you don't want me to take care of you, that you'd rather be in the hotel, that you'd rather be surrounded by strangers than people who'll do everything they can to see that you get well."

There was so much intense emotion behind that statement that Logan knew Sibyl was asking for something far beyond what her words conveyed. Could her feelings for him be even a distant cousin to his feelings for her? Had she meant the words Kitty said she uttered, or was it just the consequence of an excess of emotion? He couldn't make himself believe Sibyl could love him, but he wasn't willing to discount the chance.

"Of course I'd rather be here than in a hotel. I can't understand why you would want to be the one to take care of me, but I am grateful that you do. Still, I wish you wouldn't."

Sibyl gave him a spoonful of broth then subjected him to a quizzical glance. "Why do you feel you can't ask for what you want? Don't you feel you deserve it?"

He'd grown up being reluctant to ask for anything for fear it might not be what his father wanted. Later it didn't matter because they wanted the same things. But it was different with Sibyl. What was the point of telling her that he loved her? It would be even worse if she loved him. He hoped Kitty had misunderstood what she heard. He loved Sibyl too much to want her to suffer even a little.

"It's not that I feel I can't ask for what I want or that I don't deserve it. It's that I have no right to ask it of you."

"You saved my life at the bank. You've been at my side every step of the way as I've tried to learn how to manage it. I owe you a great deal, much more than I can repay by sitting by your bedside or feeding you broth."

Before he could stop himself, he said, "I don't want you to sit here because it's an obligation. I want you here because you *want* to be here."

There was silence as both seemed to be shocked by his words. He'd said more than he intended but much less than he wanted. He wondered how Sibyl would respond. Would she take his words with their surface meaning, or would she look for the feelings behind them? He wanted her to know exactly how he felt even as he hoped she would never know. He wasn't used to being at odds with himself. He didn't know how to handle it. He hadn't wanted to marry Bridgette, but he hadn't *not* wanted to marry her either. This time he did care. He cared so much he couldn't decide what to do.

"I do feel an obligation to take care of you," Sibyl said. Before he could despair, she added, "But I'm here because I want to be. I hoped you would be glad of that."

Of course he was glad. He could hardly keep from confessing his love before the last words were out of her mouth. Still, he felt guilty. Was it better to admit his love and make the most of the time they had together, or keep silent so she wouldn't be hurt? But if she wanted to be here, wouldn't she be hurt anyway?

"I am glad," he said. "Only a fool wouldn't be happy to have a beautiful woman by his bedside."

He could have kicked himself for a fool as soon as the words were out of his mouth. Now he would have to say more than he wanted, but he couldn't let Sibyl believe he cared only for her looks. "I'm sorry. That's not why I'm glad you're here. There are so many reasons that have nothing to do with the way you look." He couldn't start listing reasons. It would sound clinical. Besides, he would be avoiding saying what he needed to say.

"Kitty said she thought she heard you say you loved me. I hope she misunderstood. I would hate for you to have such feelings for a man who hasn't long to live, but I need you to know that I do love you. It wasn't something I planned. I should have made sure it didn't happen, but I didn't fight it because being with you gave me so much pleasure. Since I intended never to tell you of my feelings, I was free to indulge them as much as I wanted. And I did. I felt like I had found a home here, a place where I could spend my last days in nearly complete happiness. I had you, my work at the bank, and the children. What more could I possibly want?"

"You could want to live."

He sighed. How did he explain that at some point he had had to face the inevitable? "I *do* want to live, but there comes a time when you have to stop denying a truth that's staring you in the face. I intend to make the most of every minute of every day. I never realized how much I've missed until I came to Cactus Corner."

"There's even more to discover."

"Don't you think I've tried? I did everything the doctor told me. I took every prescription exactly as I was supposed to even though I only got sicker. I only left Chicago when the doctor said I only had a few months left. I wanted to..." He was about to say he wanted to see if the man he read about in the paper might be his brother, but that was something he intended to keep to himself. He had made a connection with Sibyl that would cause her pain. He didn't want to do the same to Colby and Jared. "I didn't want people who'd known me all my life to be unable to recognize the man who'd died."

"Anyone who had known you would see you as you used to be, not what illness had done to you."

Maybe that's how things happened in Cactus Corner, but people in Chicago were only interested in what was happening now. What used to be meant nothing to them. "Maybe I left because *I* didn't want to see me. There were too many mirrors in Chicago."

"I can't believe you've ever been afraid of anything."

He hadn't used to think so, but being told he was dying had caused him to be afraid of loving, of being loved, of finding his family. He hadn't had much to live for when he left Chicago. It had been easy to accept the inevitable, to hide in the shadows until the lights went out. But that wasn't true now. He didn't know how much time he had left, but now was no time to hold back on anything. There was no time to waste. Even tomorrow might be too late.

"I've been afraid of loving you, and more afraid of what you might do if I told you," Logan added.

"Why?"

"You're a beautiful woman. How could anyone think you could be attracted to a man like me?"

"Norman Spencer was a handsome man. The first man I fell in love with was even better looking, but neither man's character matched his appearance. I finally learned to look inside the man. What I found in you makes you handsome in my eyes. Kitty feels the same way."

"Kitty is a child who likes me because of my stories. She could fall in love with a bedraggled mongrel because he had sad eyes."

When Sibyl laughed, it softened her eyes. "You do have sad eyes, and you are a bit bedraggled, but I would never call you a mongrel. I think you're beautiful inside."

Logan couldn't decide whether he was speechless from the shock that Sibyl would think he was beautiful in any way or from the emotion welling up in his throat. He could never remember feeling anything this strong except fear his adopted father wouldn't keep him. It defied imagination that this woman would love him. He had nothing to offer even for the short time he would be with her.

"I never imagined you would love me. I hoped you wouldn't."

"Why? Because you think you're going to die?"

"I *am* going to die. If you loved me, my death would cause you pain, and I don't want that."

"I've suffered pain for a lot of wrong reasons during my life. It would be a joy to suffer pain for something as wonderful as loving you."

She said it! She actually said the words. It was no longer a supposition, a hope, even a forlorn dream. As incredible as it seemed, it was real! His heart beat so thunderously he could hardly catch his breath. The impossible had happened. It shouldn't have happened. Reason said it couldn't happen. Yet it had. He didn't understand it. He found the words hard to accept, yet he didn't have to depend on words. It was in the sound of her voice, the look in her eyes, the softness in her expression. And her touch. Could anything feel more wonderful than her hand in his or the gentleness with which she soothed his fevered brow?

He had to live. He didn't know how, but he had to find a way. It was no longer just his happiness at stake.

❧

"Colby said there was nothing left of your camp," Sibyl told Logan. "He said it looked like a bear had pawed its way through everything. He couldn't find any trace of your medicine."

Logan looked to where Trusty was sprawled in a corner. "That was your job," he said to the dog. "What good are you hanging about here? Now Sibyl has to feed both of us."

Realizing that his master was talking to him, Trusty got up and came over to Logan and licked his hand. He would have licked Logan's face if he had been allowed to get up on the bed.

"You can't get around me that easily." Logan's words meant nothing to Trusty. It was the tone of voice that mattered, and Logan knew he didn't sound angry.

Sibyl chuckled. "I don't think he cares about your camp. Kitty can hardly get him to go out long enough to stretch his legs and take care of his business. The minute he finishes eating, he wants to come right back to your room. What are you going to do about your medicine?" she asked. "Do you have a way of getting more?"

"Not without going back to Chicago." That was out of the question. He had no intention of spending one minute of his remaining time outside of Cactus Corner.

"Maybe Dr. Kessling can prescribe something."

"Maybe." Logan doubted it would do any good. If his doctor in Chicago couldn't find a medicine to cure him, how could he expect a doctor in the Arizona Territory to find one? What was the point? The medicine always made him sick without curing him. Wouldn't it be better to enjoy his remaining time without seizures and a stomach that couldn't keep down half of what he put in it? He still felt very weak, but he felt more clear-headed, and that was extremely important. He didn't want to miss a minute of his time with Sibyl.

"The doctor promised to come by this morning,"

Sibyl told him, "but first you have several children waiting for their story. Peter reminded me that you have missed two days."

Logan laughed. "Where are they?"

"Downstairs. Naomi said Peter could hardly finish his breakfast, and you know how that boy likes his food."

"Send them up. Maybe I can think up a rip-roaring tale to make up for lost time."

"Kitty says you're not to let Peter cause you to make up stories. She wants them to be real ones."

"She doesn't miss anything, does she?"

"Not where you're concerned. She loves you like the father she never had."

Logan took her words to mean that Norman had never been a real father to Kitty, but Sibyl looked stricken, like she'd said something she shouldn't have. She left the room so abruptly, Logan was certain there was something troubling behind her words. He didn't have long to wonder what it might be before Peter came pounding up the stairs and burst into the room. His entrance was so abrupt, Trusty came to his feet with a low growl. Esther was right behind. Both children stared at him with wide eyes.

"What's wrong?" Logan asked. "Do I look that different?"

"I heard Papa tell Mama you had died," Peter said. "Did you see God?"

"You can't see God," Esther told him. "Our first Mama said he was a spirit."

There seemed to be no end to the ways these children could thrust Logan out of his depth. "I must have stopped breathing, and your Mama thought I had died, but I'm fine now."

"You don't look fine," Peter said. "I'll ask the doctor to give you some pills."

"He's going to get better because Mama's taking care of him," Kitty said.

Logan thought that was a far better prescription for getting well than some new pills.

"Mama said we couldn't stay long," Esther told Logan. "She said putting up with Peter and me would wear down a saint."

"What's a saint?" Kitty asked.

"I don't know," Esther said, "but Mama said she wasn't one."

Logan didn't know where he found the energy, but he laughed. If he could have had children, he would have wanted them to be just like these three. He was far from a saint, but he would have happily put up with them for as long as possible. Peter told him the news, and Esther corrected him when he wandered too far from the truth. Kitty just watched him. Peter and Esther were visitors, but she belonged there. That gave her an ownership the twins couldn't claim. Peter was in the middle of a story about riding his favorite horse when the doctor arrived.

"All of you, out!" he declared with a wink and a grin that had the children laughing.

"Logan needs pills," Peter told the doctor.

"He stopped breathing," Kitty informed the doctor. "It made Mama cry."

Logan figured the doctor already knew he'd stopped breathing, but there was something about his expression that said he'd learned something that upset him.

"I have to examine Logan," he said to the children. "You can come back later."

"Will you make him well?" Kitty asked.

"I'll try," the doctor replied.

"That's what Mama says when she doesn't want to do something. Don't you want Logan to get well?"

"Is it that important to you?" the doctor asked.

"I love Logan," Kitty said. "I want him to get well so he can marry Mama."

The doctor had looked upset before, but now he looked deeply disturbed. "I'll do the best I can. Now you children run along."

Once the door was closed behind the children, the doctor turned to Logan, his expression having nothing to do with his usual bedside manner. "What do you mean by putting such a stupid notion into that child's head?"

"Kitty wants a father, but I've done nothing to make her think I can be that for her. If you want my opinion, and I doubt you do, I think it's a result of how badly Norman Spencer treated his wife and daughter. If anybody's to blame, it's this town for letting him get away with it."

The doctor's anger eased. "The situation was complicated."

"They always are, but that doesn't mean something couldn't be done about it."

"Sibyl wouldn't stand up for Norman, but she wouldn't speak against him. He was her husband and the father of her child. She might not respect him, but she respected his position in her life."

"Why did she marry him?"

"Many of us have asked that question for years. Her only answer was that it was her choice."

"I believe she was forced to marry him."

"I don't see how. Now let's talk about you."

"Before we do, I want to make one thing clear. I do love Sibyl, and she loves me. I can tell by your shocked look you find that unbelievable. So do I. I sometimes worry that I'm dreaming and will wake up in my tent on the Rim. I've never said anything to Kitty, and I'm sure Sibyl hasn't. We haven't spoken of marriage and never will. Sibyl refuses to admit it, but I know I'm dying. My only desire is to spend what time I have left with her."

"If she does love you, how can you cause her that kind of pain?"

"I asked her the same question. Can you guess what she said?"

The doctor shook his head.

"I've suffered pain for a lot of wrong reasons during my life. It would be a joy to suffer pain for something as wonderful as loving you."

The doctor looked crestfallen. "It was her father's doing, and nothing will convince me otherwise. But that's past doing anything about. If Sibyl does love you, the best you can do for her is get well. What are we going to do about that?"

Sibyl was waiting anxiously when the doctor came down from Logan's bedroom. He looked tired and unhappy. "How is he? He hasn't gotten any worse, has he? Do you have any idea what's wrong with him?"

The doctor settled into a chair next to her. "He hasn't gotten any worse. In fact, he seems better today. His eyes are clearer, and his breathing is easier, but his pulse isn't good. If he hadn't been under a doctor's care, I'd say he'd ingested some kind of poison."

"He got sick before he left Chicago. That was weeks ago."

"I don't understand the randomness of the attacks," the doctor said. "One day he has the strength to stop runaway horses and the next he can't sit up in bed. He makes a recovery, and the cycle starts all over again. It's like he's still being poisoned but only erratically. It doesn't make any sense."

"It can't be poison, so it must be something else. You've got to find out what it is."

The doctor's demeanor changed abruptly. "Why? What makes the health of a stranger so important to you?"

Sibyl was unnerved by the tone in which he voiced his question. "I'd be concerned about anybody who worked for me. I don't know what I would have done without his help at the bank."

"So what are you going to do when he dies? If I can't figure out what's wrong with him, he *is* going to die."

The doctor might as well have stabbed her in the heart. She could feel the pain, feel the blood draining from her body, feel her heart struggling to beat. Even breathing was difficult. "Isn't there something you can do for him?" Her voice sounded weak and far away.

"I haven't given up, but you should prepare yourself. And Kitty. The child appears to adore him." The doctor paused before asking, "Are you in love with him?"

Sibyl was so surprised at the question she couldn't answer.

"He seems to be a fine man, but he's a stranger whose face is so swollen you can't begin to know what he looks like."

Sibyl could see no reason to continue to deny

what everyone seemed to know. "I don't care about his looks. I never have. If you ask why I fell in love with him, I doubt I can give you a reason you can understand. I don't really understand it myself. I guess it's partly because he's the first person in my life who's ever gone out of his way to do things for me, who's ever tried to make me happy, who has any confidence in me. It's partly because Kitty and that miserable dog adore him. Who can argue against the wisdom of a child and a dog?"

"I can."

"Well, you can't argue against Cassie. Everybody knows she has the best instincts about people."

"I'm not arguing *against* anybody. I'm worried about you. You had a difficult marriage. You've been widowed less than two months. It disturbs me that you could fall in love with anyone so quickly."

"Well, you won't have to worry long. How much time does he have?"

"I don't know, but that's not what I was talking about. I don't want to see you hurt again. You've lost a husband and a father within a month."

It was on her tongue to tell him about Raymond Sinclair, but she held back. That was her tragedy alone. "I know this makes me sound heartless, but any fondness I had for either man disappeared long ago. My heart was free. Norman's death opened the door, and Logan walked in. Neither one of us expected what happened. We tried to stop it. When we couldn't, we tried to deny it. When Logan almost died, we decided it was time to stop pretending. I don't know how much time we have left, but I'm going to use every minute to immerse myself in the kind of love I'd come to believe I'd never know."

"Do you know Kitty wants me to make Logan well so he can marry you?"

Sibyl felt tears gather. "I know she's very fond of him, but I had no idea she'd thought of my marrying again."

"She said she loves him."

"I'm not surprised. I've never seen her take to anyone the way she's taken to Logan. It makes me angry all over again that Norman was so cold to her." She had told herself she was not going to think of Norman ever again. All of that was behind her. "I'll have to talk to Kitty, explain what might happen. She's got to be prepared."

"What about you?"

What about her? Was she strong enough to endure his death? Her love for Raymond had been more the idealistic daydreams of an impressionable young girl than a deep and abiding love. She had known Logan less than two months, yet she knew that's exactly the kind of love they shared. It would hurt more than anything ever had, but she could endure it because she would have known great love even if for a short time. She *would* endure it because Kitty's future was more important that her own.

A knock at the front door interrupted their conversation.

"I'll get it," the doctor offered. "It's probably someone nosing around for information about Logan. Or even you. You realize that having a man in your house is going to start rumors."

Sibyl laughed even though it wasn't funny. "Anyone who thinks I can be having an affair with a man who can barely sit up in bed is too stupid to worry about." She stood. "It's my door so I'll answer it."

But when she opened the door, she found herself facing a woman she'd never seen. "Can I help you?"

"Are you Sibyl Spencer?"

"Yes, but I don't know you."

"I'm Bridgette Lowe, Elliot Lowe's fiancée."

"I'm sorry, but I don't know anyone by that name."

"He's calling himself Logan Holstock now, and I'm told he's living in your house."

Thirteen

SIBYL MIGHT AS WELL HAVE BEEN TURNED TO STONE. She was unable to move, unable to speak, barely able to breathe. Either her mind had gone blank, or it was spinning so fast she couldn't hold on to a thought. This couldn't be true. There had to be some misunderstanding. Yet the woman standing on her porch didn't look like the kind of person to make such a colossal mistake. Confident to the point of haughtiness, she looked like someone out of a fashion magazine. She wore a walking dress of pale green silk. The upper part was cut as a polonaise with the shirt kilted under the sash. The silk sleeves and trimming were black.

"May I come in?"

Sibyl snapped out of her paralysis. "Of course. You'll have to forgive my surprise. Logan has told us nothing about his past except that he came from Chicago." She stepped back to let the woman enter. "Did you know Logan has been ill?"

"What other reason could I have for making this journey?"

Sibyl tried to forgive the woman's irritation. She

could imagine how difficult the journey must have been for a woman who, from the clothes she wore, was used to wealth, privilege, and a life completely different from anything she would find in Cactus Corner. Sibyl struggled to find something to say. "The doctor has been to see him this morning. Would you like to speak to him?"

"Elliot was a patient of the finest doctor in Chicago. Why should I want to speak to a doctor in this place?"

Whatever sympathy Sibyl had for this woman vanished. "You don't need to speak to anyone, me included. You can go straight back to Chicago. If Logan wants to get in contact with you, I'm sure he will."

Apparently realizing she'd gone too far, Bridgette unbent a little. "I'm sorry if I seem less than civil, but I've never suffered so much in my life as I have on the journey from Chicago. And the whole time I've been worried sick about Elliot. He has a mansion staffed with servants whose only job is to take care of him. He's a wealthy businessman and respected member of Chicago society. Why would he come out here?"

Her disclosure stunned Sibyl, but on reflection she realized she shouldn't have been too surprised. She had known Logan was more than the drifter he pretended to be, but she'd never imagined anything like this. "Only *Logan* can answer that." Maybe it was stubbornness, but she refused to call him Elliot.

"I want to see him immediately."

"He's sleeping. He's recovering from a particularly severe attack. Where are you staying?" There was only one hotel in Cactus Corner, and Sibyl owned it.

"At the only hotel in town." Bridgette's scornful tone indicated her opinion of her accommodations.

"Maybe you should go back and wait. I'll let you know when the doctor says it's okay to see Logan."

"I came over a thousand miles to see the man who's to become my husband. I won't be able to rest until I've seen Elliot."

The word *husband* caused Sibyl's throat to constrict. That was much more stunning than learning Logan was wealthy or that he was a member of society, but she pulled herself together.

"I'll speak to the doctor. Make yourself comfortable here."

The moment Sibyl left the parlor, her backbone seemed to dissolve, leaving her weak and nauseated. It took all her willpower to summon the courage to face the doctor. She was thankful he was waiting in her sitting room rather than the parlor.

"What nosy neighbor was that?" the doctor asked when she entered the room.

"No neighbor," she managed to say. "A woman who calls herself Bridgette Lowe. She says she's engaged to Elliot Lowe. She also says Logan's real name is Elliot Lowe."

The doctor was suddenly rigid with attention. "Has she come all the way from Chicago?"

"That's what she says. And she's dressed like it. She certainly wouldn't have traveled this far if she wasn't telling the truth."

"There's one way to find out," the doctor said. "Ask Logan."

Sibyl knew that. What she didn't want to admit was she was afraid of what she might hear. Why had she let herself fall in love with a man she knew nothing about? "She says Logan is a wealthy businessman, a respected member of society with a mansion full of servants. If that's true, why would he have come to Cactus Corner? I know. I should ask Logan," she said before the words could come out of the doctor's mouth.

"I'm surprised you didn't go straight to him instead of coming to me," the doctor said.

"I needed time to absorb the shock."

"And the realization that you've fallen in love with a man who's lied about himself."

Sibyl wasn't ready to admit that yet. She didn't know much about Logan's past, but she didn't believe he was a liar. Why would he? He didn't need money. If he was dying, what could he have to gain?

"Do you want me to go with you?" the doctor asked.

"Thanks, but I'm not some weak female who's afraid of the truth. Okay, I am afraid I'll hear something I won't like, but I won't hide. I've done that for too long."

"I'll go talk to your visitor," the doctor said. "I'd like to know what kind of woman travels over a thousand miles through Indian country to chase down a man who apparently doesn't want to marry her."

As she climbed the steps to Logan's bedroom, Sibyl could easily understand why a man like Logan would want to marry a woman like Bridgette. She was beautiful and she was young. If her clothes and attitude were anything to go by, she was exactly the right kind of wife for a man who was a wealthy, respected member of Chicago society. How could Sibyl compare to such a woman? Why should Logan be in love with her?

Or Elliot! What a terrible name! How could any man let himself be called that for over thirty years?

She paused when she reached Logan's bedroom door. Her nerve threatened to leave her. She wished Naomi and Laurie could be with her. Yet in the same instant she knew she preferred to face this alone.

"Come in," Logan called to her knock. He smiled broadly when she entered the room and propped himself up against his pillow. "I didn't expect to see you until the afternoon. The doctor said I had to sleep, or he'd give me something to make me." He stopped, his smile gone, his gazed focused on her. "What's wrong? You look upset."

It was so like him to sense her mood right away. It was one of the things that had drawn her to him. "You have a visitor," she told him. "A woman."

Logan smiled. "I'm surprised Cassie isn't right behind you. Where is she?"

"It isn't Cassie. She says her name is Bridgette Lowe."

The swelling sometimes made it difficult to see Logan's expression, but there was no mistaking the anger that flashed in his eyes. He pulled himself up until he was sitting erect. "I told that Pinkerton to tell her I was never going back to Chicago. She had no reason to follow me."

"She says she's your fiancée. Why shouldn't she follow you?"

"She's not my fiancée. I broke the engagement when the doctor told me I had three months to live."

The relief that flooded through Sibyl was so great she sank down in a chair. There was still a lot she needed to know, but at least Logan hadn't been engaged to another woman when he said he loved her. "If she loves you—"

"Bridgette may like me, but it's my money she

loves. I should have told you about her before, but I never thought to see her again."

"Did you love her?" Right now, that was more important than anything Logan could tell her.

"No, and she never loved me. Her father was my father's brother. When he died and left Bridgette in a bad way, it was sort of assumed I would marry her. When I found out I was going to die, I released her from our understanding and made sure she was taken care of. Then I left Chicago."

"Then why is she here?"

"Money. Do you think anything else would make her leave Chicago to come to Arizona? She thinks she should have inherited all of her uncle's money. She has always considered me an interloper."

"What do you want me to tell her?"

"I don't want you to tell her anything. You'd better send her up."

"The doctor said you were to rest."

"Neither of us will get any rest as long as Bridgette Lowe is in Cactus Corner."

❧

Logan told himself he was a fool not to have made a will before he left Chicago. He'd always intended to leave Bridgette most of the money, but he'd put off making a will as long as there was the possibility Jared Smith might be his brother. Now he was in a quandary. He didn't know enough about his brothers to know if they could use his money, and he wanted to give Sibyl and Kitty something. Then there was Cassie, who had a son to support, and Horace, trying to raise a family on a bank teller's salary. He needed to make up his mind while his mind was relatively clear.

How like Bridgette to walk in without knocking first.

"What are you doing in this town?" she asked. "And in this house?"

"I should be asking you those questions."

"I'm here because you're my fiancé, and you're sick." She reached into her reticule. "I brought you some more medicine."

"You lied to Sibyl. Everybody in Chicago knows I'm not your fiancé. You never cared enough to visit me after I got sick while I was still in Chicago. As I recall, your excuse was that you were afraid you might get sick, too."

"How could I know? James had no idea what was wrong with you. Besides, he kept me informed of your condition so I had no need to see for myself."

Logan had agreed to marry Bridgette because he felt sorry for her. Her mother had died when she was a child, and her father was a drunken fool who treated her like a servant. Logan's father had tried to look out for his niece, giving her money when she needed it and intervening when her father was at his worst. She'd had a difficult life, but Logan's father had left his niece money in his will. She could live comfortably if she was careful.

But Bridgette had too much of her father in her to do that. She was greedy and ungrateful. She wouldn't hesitate to marry a sick, disfigured man she didn't love, especially if he would die soon, and she would have all of her uncle's fortune.

"Go back to Chicago, Bridgette. There's nothing you can do here."

"I can't go back and leave you in this godforsaken place. I couldn't forgive myself."

"You don't have to stay because of the money. I plan to leave you more than enough to take care of you for the rest of your life."

"I'm not here because of the money. I came because you're sick, and you need someone to take care of you. I'm taking you back to Chicago. James has promised not to leave your side until you're better. We'll hire nurses and anything else you need."

"I'm not going back to Chicago. I have a perfectly good doctor here, and Sibyl can provide all the care I need."

Bridgette stared at him in disbelief. "You must really be sick if you prefer a sawbones in a place like this to a man of James's reputation."

"James has already told me he's done all he can do, that I have only weeks to live. I doubt even a *sawbones* can do any harm."

"I spent the last fifteen minutes talking to him." Bridgette's voice was thick with scorn. "He's more interested in gossip than in figuring out how to cure you. You ought to be thankful I brought some new medicine."

"You shouldn't have wasted your money. All any of the medicines I've taken do is make me sick without making me better. I've decided not to take the pills any longer."

Bridgette went so white he thought she might faint. "You've got to take your medicine." She held out a small bottle to him. "This is a new prescription. James is certain this one will make you better."

Logan had never been under the illusion that there

was any love between him and Bridgette, but how could she appear so devastated if she didn't care for him? She looked like she might burst into tears any minute.

"Please, Elliot, you've got to take it," she pleaded. "What will I do if you die?"

"You'll have enough money to do whatever you want."

Some of her panic seemed to abate. "How can I inherit anything when you don't have a will? Your lawyer said I wasn't a relation since Uncle Samuel didn't adopt you officially."

"I'll make a will soon. There are a few people here in Cactus Corner I want to include."

Bridgette tried to hide it, but Logan spotted the flash of anger in her eyes. Her jaw tightened. "Why would you want to leave money to anyone here? They aren't related to you, and you don't know them."

"Actually, they are. I found both my brothers. They have families of their own."

Now there was no mistaking the anger mixed with fear. "How can you be sure? You haven't seen them in more than thirty years. They're probably just after your money."

That caused Logan to laugh. "I haven't told either of them yet. Besides, everyone here thinks I'm a penniless drifter who is so poor he has to live in a tent in the woods."

"Elliot, none of this makes sense. You are a wealthy man with a house full of servants, the best doctor in Chicago, and me to take care of you. Your recovery is our only concern. You'll get the finest care available anywhere. Please come back to Chicago with me."

"Going back to Chicago is what doesn't make sense. I'd probably die before I got there. I'm happy here, and there are people here who will take care of me."

"Does that include the woman who owns this house?"

Jealousy and anger aren't an attractive pair. They make the eyes go hard, the facial muscles tighten, and the voice become harsh. They also cause you to forget the positive impression you were trying to make. If Bridgette had been a cat, Logan would have expected to see her claws.

"Sibyl is one of several people who've offered to take care of me. I've never found so many wonderful people in one place before."

"Then they have to know about your money," Bridgette snapped. "Otherwise why would strangers care about a sick man with distorted features?"

"They care about everyone. A woman I don't even know made beef broth for me. I feel more at home than I ever did in Chicago."

"This has to be your fever talking," Bridgette insisted. "Let me give you some of this medicine. It'll make you feel much better."

"I've already told you I'm not taking any more medicine."

"You've got to. How do you expect to get well?"

"I don't."

"This is some new medicine. It will—"

A knock sounded on the door, and Sibyl entered without waiting to be invited. "The doctor said Logan has to rest. You can come back later, but we have to let him get some sleep now."

"I'll sit with him while he sleeps."

"I don't think that's a good idea."

"Well, I happen to think it's the *best* idea."

A change came over Sibyl. Logan couldn't say exactly what it was, but it was obvious that Sibyl had no intention of giving ground. "I needn't remind you that Logan is very sick and is under a doctor's care. It is the doctor's orders that he rest. Since he's my patient and this is my house, I intend to see that the doctor's orders are followed. If you will not leave voluntarily, I will have you removed."

Bridgette swung toward Logan. "Are you going to let her talk to me like that?"

Logan suppressed a smile. "It's her house. She can talk any way she wants."

Bridgette shook with fury. "I'll be back in an hour."

"It would be better if I send a note to your hotel letting you know when Logan is ready to see visitors."

Bridgette looked about ready to explode. "I'm his fiancée. I have every right—"

Logan interrupted her. "You are *not* my fiancée. Now go away, and take your medicine with you."

Bridgette plunked the bottle down on the table next to Logan's bed. "I'll be back. I'm not leaving until I talk some sense into you." She turned on Sibyl. "You and that *doctor* had better take good care of him. If anything happens to him, I'll see that you pay for it." With that, she stormed out of the room.

❧

Sibyl whispered to Logan, "I'll be back," and followed Bridgette downstairs. Bridgette stopped when she reached the hall and turned to confront Sibyl. "I know what you're trying to do," she said angrily, "and I won't let you get away with it."

"I'm trying to see that Logan gets better. That's all I care about."

"You don't have to pretend with me. I know you're after his money—you and everybody else in this town."

Sibyl didn't like this woman, but she couldn't repress a shred of sympathy. She couldn't know Bridgette's feelings for Logan, but it had to be difficult to find you were no longer engaged to the man you'd hoped to marry. Even worse, that he might be in love with another woman. "Logan deposited about five hundred dollars in my bank when he came to Cactus Corner. About half of that is gone. There's no money to be after."

"*Your* bank? A woman can't own a bank."

"I'm sure it's rare, but I do."

"What bank?"

"Spencer's Bank. You must have noticed it when you came into town."

It was clear Bridgette had noticed it, and that she didn't consider it good news. "It can't be a very *big* bank, but I suppose a little place like Cactus Corner is lucky to have even one bank."

"We have two. My cousins own Community Bank."

Bridgette suddenly dropped all pretenses of politeness. "Why are you taking care of Elliot? You can't expect me to believe you didn't know he's rich. Did that Pinkerton tell you?"

"I've never seen a Pinkerton. I don't even know what one is, but no one in Cactus Corner thinks Logan is anything other than a very sick man drifting from one place to the next. We've become very fond of him. He's a favorite of the children."

"Children? Elliot has never been around children

in his whole life. He wouldn't know what to say to one."

Sibyl studied Bridgette a moment before replying. "You don't know Logan very well, do you?"

"Will you stop calling him *Logan*! His name is Elliot. And I've known him all my life. I know everything there is to know about him. And that's more than enough to know he'd never fit in this miserable little town. Elliot is used to going to the theater, to socializing with wealthy and educated men. He's used to beautiful women in elegant gowns and dinner parties with foods you've never heard of."

"If he's going to die, as he's convinced he will, then all of that means nothing to him."

"I want him to go back to Chicago so he *won't* die," Bridgette insisted. "He needs better medical care than he can get here."

"Everyone in Cactus Corner has complete faith in Dr. Kessling."

"*Everyone in Cactus Corner*," Bridgette repeated derisively. "An insignificant little town in the middle of nowhere. We have more doctors in Chicago than you have people."

"Since Logan refuses to see any doctor, it wouldn't matter if you had twice that many. Now I have to prepare my daughter's lunch. I'll be sure to notify you when Dr. Kessling says Logan is able to see visitors."

"I will see him before this day is out with or without your permission," Bridgette stated. "And if you try to stop me, I'll have the law on you."

"We don't have any official law, but my cousin's husband is the unofficial sheriff."

Bridgette's expression hardened. "Is there anything in this town you and your family don't control?"

"Quite a lot, but many of us are from a small village in Kentucky. We're very supportive of each other."

"Chicagoans are also supportive of each other, which is why Elliot needs to go home."

"That will have to be his decision. Now, I really must see to my daughter's lunch."

"Make sure to send me a message as soon as Elliot wakes up."

Sibyl didn't answer, so Bridgette was forced to take her leave.

"Is she gone?" Logan asked when Sibyl entered his room.

"Yes, but she'd be back in an instant if she knew you weren't asleep."

"How could I sleep knowing Bridgette was downstairs probably filling your ears with lies. I don't know why I ever agreed to marry her. One of my friends jokingly told me she'd probably poison me after the wedding."

The words were hardly out of his mouth before Sibyl and Logan locked gazes.

"She wouldn't do that," Logan said. "I made no will so she'd get nothing. No one on my staff would have a reason to do that. Besides, I never got sick from anything I ate or drank. Only after I'd taken one of those pills."

"Your doctor certainly wouldn't try to poison you," Sibyl said. "Why did you start taking the pills in the first place?"

"I had been feeling off for a while, probably the consequences of my father's death. We were never separated, and I really missed him. I was working too much and let myself get run down. I went to the doctor because I didn't have time to be sick. I was better for a while, but then I started to get worse. He kept changing my medicine but nothing helped." He suddenly remembered that the doctor had said it was a shame he couldn't compare his medical history with family members to look for a similar condition. "Do you know if Colby or Jared have ever been sick?"

"They're two of the healthiest men I know. Colby had an Indian arrow in his back. He pulled it out and acted like it never happened. Jared had some war wounds, but he had no trouble recovering from them. Why do you want to know about them?"

Logan hesitated, then decided it was time to stop keeping secrets. "I believe they're my brothers. Colby looks exactly like I remember my real father. You can't tell it now, but he looks a lot like me."

Sibyl stared at him in disbelief. "Are you sure?"

"As sure as I can be without incontrovertible proof."

Excitement was added to the shock in her voice. "Have you told them?"

"No. But I didn't come to Cactus Corner by accident. I saw an article in the paper about a Jared Smith who'd been appointed a marshal in the Arizona Territory. It said he'd been born a Holstock. I knew my brother had been named Jared. Having been told I had just a few months to live, I decided to see if he could be my brother. When I saw Colby, I was certain."

"Then why didn't you say something?"

"I didn't want to be a burden to them just as I don't want to be a burden to you."

"You're not a burden to me, and you wouldn't be

to Colby and Jared. You should have seen them when they found out they were brothers. It's the only time I've ever seen Colby cry."

"Look at me! Who wants a brother who looks like this? They'll feel guilty about not being able to make me well. Besides, it would be difficult to find a brother only to lose him almost immediately."

"I don't believe they'll feel that way. Colby has been tending his parents' graves ever since he found them. Jared was looking for his brothers before he was assigned to Camp Verde. I think you ought to tell them. Especially if you don't have a lot of time left. It would be cruel for them to find out after you were gone."

Logan wasn't sure what to do, and lying here in bed frustrated him. He felt better than he had in a while, but he was still sick. It just didn't seem fair to tell his brothers now. Maybe right before the end would be better. That way they would know but wouldn't have long to deal with his illness.

"I'll think about it. What did you tell Bridgette?"

"I said I'll send her a message when you could see visitors."

Logan grinned. "I bet she didn't like that."

"I don't care what she likes. I won't have her badgering you while you're sick. Once you get well, you can have her all to yourself."

"She just wants me to get well."

"Then she should be anxious for you to get your rest. I am, too, so I'm going to leave you alone."

"Not for too long, I hope."

"If I had my choice, I'd never leave you alone." She seemed to choke up. When she spoke again, her words were unsteady. "You have to promise you'll do everything you can to get well. I don't know if I can stand to lose you."

She left the room before Logan could think of anything to say.

❧

Bridget paced her hotel room like a caged animal. Rage churned through her like steam through a boiler. Nobody was fooling her. Sibyl Spencer was a beautiful woman, exactly the kind of woman a man like Elliot would be attracted to. What man could resist falling in love with his beautiful nurse? Sibyl couldn't fool Bridgette. She didn't know how she'd found out, but that woman knew Elliot was rich. No woman in her right mind, especially not a beautiful one who said she owned a bank, would fall in love with a penniless drifter who looked like Elliot. But how did they find out about the money? Was it from the Pinkerton agent? Had they hired him to investigate *her*?

A momentary panic subsided. She had nothing to hide. James was her doctor and a family friend. It was only natural they would be seen with each other. They had been very careful not to be seen together in public, except at gatherings to which they'd both been invited.

How was she going to make sure Elliot took the medicine? She couldn't force it down his throat. She couldn't put it in his food. She wondered if it might not be better to let him recover. He would surely return to Chicago. This time she wouldn't have to do it gradually. After his prolonged illness, no one would be surprised if he died suddenly.

She flopped down in the chair, then got up immediately. Before she left this hotel, she was going to burn that chair. She walked to the window and looked out. Why would anyone who had lived in Chicago want to come to a place like this? If Sibyl had all the money she pretended to have, she'd have left this miserable town years ago. The streets were nothing but dirt churned up by hooves and wagon wheels. The buildings were pitiful wooden structures that looked like they'd blow over in a strong wind. Children dressed like ragamuffins played in the streets. She doubted the town could boast of anything that could be called a school. Worst of all, there were Indians in the area. Who knew when they might revert to their savage nature and kill everybody in their beds?

She stared at her room in disgust. It wasn't fit for her servants. The uncomfortable bed was covered with a thin quilt that could only be described as rustic by an uncritical person. Bad prints of unrealistic western scenes decorated the plain walls. That ladderback chair and a table with a basin and pitcher were the only other furniture besides a wardrobe that couldn't hold half of the clothes she'd brought with her. Even worse, she'd have to take her meals in what passed for a restaurant. The only good thing about it was that she could recognize the food. That way she could make certain never to put anything like it in her mouth again.

She *had* to convince Elliot to return to Chicago. Then she would be in control rather than Sibyl Spencer.

❧

Logan was nervous. He'd asked Sibyl to bring Colby and Jared to see him. He had no idea how they would respond to being told he was their brother. He still wasn't sure how he felt about it. In a way, keeping it a secret from them had kept him from fully accepting it. What was he going to do once he'd told them? More importantly, what would they do?

In truth, what was there that could be done other than recognize a relationship that his impending death made virtually meaningless? It was like something that was written down on paper yet would have no effect on their lives. What was he hoping to gain? He was sick and dying, so he couldn't expect to be incorporated into their families. There couldn't be any emotional bonds between men who'd never known each other. They had no shared experiences because their lives had been completely different and lived in different parts of the country.

He didn't know why he was even bothering. It was probably going to end up being a problem for all of them. They would feel that they ought to do something for him, but there was nothing they could do. It would probably end up being an awkward situation for everyone when they all would have been better off if he'd never said anything. Well, he hadn't said anything yet. Sibyl wouldn't if he asked her not to, but she would feel compelled to tell them after he died. How else could she explain their being included in his will? No matter how difficult things might be now, that would be worse.

He heard footsteps he knew didn't belong to Sibyl or the doctor. Trusty, who'd been asleep next to his bed, got to his feet, a growl low in his throat.

"Be quiet," Logan told the dog. "If I have the guts to tell them we're brothers, you're going to have to get used to them. I can't have you growling at members of my family."

My family. Logan didn't think he'd ever used those words before. They sounded a little alarming. As much as he'd loved his father, he'd always been aware that he'd never been officially adopted, that he lacked the blood bond that everyone else accepted as a natural state of being. Nobody *had* to love him.

But there was an unbreakable bond between siblings. No matter how different, no matter how terrible, they always felt a responsibility to each other. He'd seen that firsthand between his father and his brother. Aaron Lowe had been a drunk, a liar, and a cheat, but Samuel Lowe had never turned his back on his brother no matter now ungrateful or underhanded he was. But they had grown up together. What could Jared and Colby feel for him?

Sibyl was the first to enter the room. "You only have so much time before the children will demand to come up," she warned him. "Peter can't wait for you and his father to compare stories."

Colby, who had entered right behind Sibyl, laughed. "He's sure I have better stories than you," he told Logan. "Ever since you got to town, he's remembered every snippet of conversation he's ever heard about me and been convinced there's a story behind it if I'd just tell him. I would never want any child of mine to know about half the things I did. You have a lot to answer for."

"If you'd been a perfect son like me," Jared kidded his brother, "you wouldn't have to be so worried about your past coming to light. By the way, what *are* some of those terrible things you did?"

"You don't need to know. Not even Naomi knows everything."

"I should hope not. How is a woman to respect a man with a past as black as night?"

As Logan listened to the two men take swipes at each other, he was nearly overcome with envy and a terrible sense of loss. This kind of relationship could have been his if he'd been able to live longer. They hadn't known each other until two years ago, but in that short time— and despite what Jared had claimed—they'd managed to forge a relationship much like that of brothers who'd grown up together. It was painful to see something up close that he knew was beyond his grasp. It was all the harder because it was something he wanted so much.

"You sound like squabbling children," Sibyl told the brothers. "Even Trusty thinks so." The dog hadn't relaxed his guard. "If you can stop long enough, Logan wants to talk to you."

"You've made Naomi terribly curious," Colby told Logan. "She's convinced you're about to disclose some mysterious secret about your past. Why else would you break your engagement to a woman like Bridgette Lowe?"

"Laurie says it's about money," Jared said. "Ever since Bridgette came to town, you being a rich member of Chicago society is all anyone wants to talk about."

"I'll leave you three alone," Sibyl said, "but don't forget the children are waiting. Peter isn't noted for his patience."

"Could you tell your dog we're not here to murder you?" Colby said. "He hasn't stopped growling since we got here."

"Take a seat. He'll relax then."

"Does he treat Miss Lowe like this?" Jared asked.

"Worse," Logan said with a chuckle. "It makes her furious."

"She must love you a lot to have followed you all the way from Chicago," Colby said. "I'm surprised she hasn't convinced you to go back."

"There's not much point," Logan said. "I can die here just as dead as in Chicago."

That put a damper on the mood, and both men concentrated on settling into two of the several chairs in the room. He'd had so many visitors in the last two days Sibyl had said she was considering putting his bed in the parlor.

"What did you want to talk to us about?" Colby asked.

Logan made a quick decision to start with something he hadn't even thought of until now. "I think you ought to consider combining your bank with Sibyl's. I know why it was started, but Sibyl is nothing like Norman. Besides, the doctor doesn't like being the head of the bank. Even though his son does most of the work, he finds it distracting and thinks it's not good for the town because it perpetuates friction that no long exists. I think having Sibyl and Ethan manage the bank together would be best for everyone."

"How do you know all of this?" Jared asked.

"The doctor's determined to figure out what's wrong with me so we spend a lot of time together. I get tired of talking about my illness, so I ask him questions. Since Sibyl and her bank are what interests me most, it's what I asked about."

"Why do you care about that happens with our banks?" Colby wanted to know.

"Sibyl is a very intelligent woman who can manage her bank on her own, but she's caught between her desire to be a success and her dislike of being in competition with her own family. You've got to know that Sibyl will treat her customers fairly. Besides, this town doesn't need two banks."

"Have you talked to Sibyl about this?" Jared asked.

"No, and I never will if either of you is against it."

"I'm not against it," Colby said. "In fact, the same thought had occurred to me, too, but I haven't wanted to say anything just yet."

"My family's business is already divided between the two banks," Jared said, "so I wouldn't have any objection."

"How do you propose to bring this up?" Colby asked.

"Since your wife's family runs the bank and you're its major backer, I think you ought to broach the subject with them. If they're against it, I won't say anything to Sibyl."

"What makes you think they'll listen to me?"

Logan laughed softly. "I hadn't been here more than one week before I learned everybody listens to you. Sibyl says Norman was jealous. Cassie said he couldn't stand your guts."

All three men laughed.

"I doubt Ethan will object," Colby said, "and I know Dr. Kessling will be relieved. He only headed the bank because no one else could have convinced people to turn over their money to a new bank with no experienced staff and limited capital assets. I'll talk with them tonight. I should be able to let you know something by tomorrow." He started to rise. "I'm sure the children are anxious to come up."

"I'm not through yet," Logan said. "I have something else I want to talk about."

Fourteen

"Is this this going to be a surprise?" Colby asked, an amused glint in his eye.

"I expect it will be." Logan didn't know how best to say what he had to say, so he just said it. "I was called Elliot Lowe growing up in Chicago, but my father told me my name had been Logan Holstock and that I had two brothers, Jared and Kevin. Our parents had died on the Santa Fe Trail, and we'd been adopted by three different families. I'm your older brother."

The two men stared at him in stunned silence. Afraid of what they might be thinking, Logan hurried on.

"I didn't come to Cactus Corner by accident. I read an article in the Chicago paper about a man named Jared Smith who'd been born a Holstock. When my doctor told me I had only a few months to live, I decided to find out if that Jared was my brother. Even though a lot of facts seemed to fit, I wasn't sure until I saw you," he said to Colby.

"Why me?" Colby asked.

"Because you look exactly as I remember my father. Before I got sick and my face swelled up, we looked a lot alike."

"This can't be right." Colby looked shell-shocked. "I know my birth name was Kevin, but the odds against us finding each other are enormous. Why should an article about Jared be in the Chicago newspaper?"

"The article implied that Jared had become a marshal so he could recommend the appointment be given to Loomis Drucker, a man he'd served with during the war. Loomis grew up in Illinois just outside of Chicago. He was something of a local boy made good."

"I knew there was something about you from the first," Jared said. "I had no idea what it was, but I knew there was something. Why didn't you tell us before now?"

"I wasn't sure you'd want to know," Logan confessed. "I'm not going to be around much longer. I wouldn't have said anything, but Sibyl convinced me it would have been cruel for you to learn this only after my death. In any case, you only have my word that what I say is true. I could be after your money."

"What about Bridgette?"

"She could be in on it. You're both rich."

"Not as rich as you," Colby pointed out.

"You only have Bridgette's word for that. I could be the drifter I look like and Bridgette my accomplice. I could wiggle into your confidence, somehow gain access to your money, and make off with it."

Both men looked at him like he was crazy, then burst out laughing simultaneously. "I don't know which story is more fantastic," Colby said. "I spent half my life hoping to find my brothers. Then after I'd given up, they found me. I find it hard to believe."

"I don't," Jared said. "It's no more unbelievable than me finding you."

"Do you have anything to back up what you say?"

Logan shook his head. "I'm not expecting you to do anything. I hope you'll believe me, but I have no way to prove it. I was taken in by Samuel Lowe. Bridgette was his niece, but he left everything to me. I'm a wealthy man. I plan to leave something to each of you."

Both men protested, but Logan didn't listen.

"The money won't do me any good, and I have no one else to leave it to."

"What about Bridgette?"

"I won't forget her, but I intend to make some other bequests."

"How much money do you have?" Jared asked.

"Quite a lot."

"I think he must be our brother," Colby said with a seriousness Logan could tell wasn't genuine. "How much do you plan to leave me? I hope it's a lot. Peter wants to own a ranch as big as the whole territory. He intends to enact every story you've ever told him."

"Stop fighting against what you want to believe," Jared told Colby. "We both knew we had an older brother, and I knew his name was Logan—it was only because we thought he'd lived all his life in Chicago that we convinced ourselves to ignore what was staring us in the face all this time. We accepted each other with nothing more than a name to go on. Why can't you accept Logan?"

"Because I'm not sure I can stand to be that happy and heartbroken at the same time," Colby confessed. "After all these years, to find a brother, only to know I'm going to lose him before I can even get to know him. How can you stand it?"

"Because I'm not thinking of anything but having found him. I have faith Dr. Kessling will come up with something to keep us from losing him."

"How long have you known?" Colby asked Logan.

"When I looked up into your face that day I stopped the horses."

"Why didn't you say something then?"

"Like I said, I wasn't sure you'd want to know. Why would you want anything to do with a man in my condition?"

"Being my brother is more important than anything else," Colby said. "I wouldn't care if you had only one leg and were blind as a bat. For years I dreamed about finding the two of you. I imagined what we'd say to each other, how we'd spend the rest of our lives together."

"I didn't know."

"Well, you couldn't," Colby said, "but that's how I feel. Now before I start crying, I'm going to give you a hug. And if you aren't my brother, you'd better go to your grave without letting me find out, because if I do, the doctor won't get a chance to cure you."

Logan was just as choked up as Colby so he didn't try to say anything. He submitted willingly to a hug that was more deep-felt and prolonged than he could have dreamed. How could he have known Colby would feel this strongly about finding his brother? The man was a rock everybody looked up to, depended on, went to for advice.

"Don't let him fool you," Jared said in a voice not entirely clear of emotion. "He's just glad to know the only man who can outshoot him is his relative."

When Colby drew back from hugging Logan, his

eyes were swimming. "You'd better be glad I don't have that rifle now, or I'd shoot you," he said to Jared.

"If you could see me for the tears." Jared turned to Logan. "I'm not as emotional as Colby, but I'm just as happy as he is to have finally found you. I hope you can stand another hug."

"I think I can."

"We've got a lot of catching up to do, and not a lot of time to do it," Colby said. "I'm not leaving town until… Damn, I'm not going to deal with that until I have to. I hope you don't mind, but you're going to see more of me than of Peter."

"Me, too," Jared said. "Steve has been wanting the chance to prove he can run the ranch as well as I can."

"I don't want you to change your lives for me," Logan said.

"Of course we will," Colby said before Logan could protest further. "After thirty-one years, we're finally together again. What could be more important than that?"

Logan could think of one person, but he didn't think this was a good time to mention it.

Colby peppered Logan with questions about his life in Chicago, threatened to choke him for waiting so long to tell them he was their brother, and then eventually said he had to leave. "I've got to tell Naomi. She'll never forgive me if anyone else knows before she does."

"Laurie is just as bad," Jared said, "but I don't want you to think about leaving me any money. Finding you after all these years is the best possible legacy."

For several minutes after his brothers had left, Logan lay there listening to the mix of voices outside his door. He was relieved when Sibyl entered the room wearing a big smile.

"How did it go?" she asked.

"Okay. I think they were happy."

"You *think* they were happy," Sibyl repeated. "Colby's wearing a grin so wide I'm worried it'll split his face. He grabbed me and whirled me around until I was dizzy. Then he bounded down the steps three at a time. I was afraid he'd break his neck. Jared tried to act the mature older brother, but he's just as excited as Colby. Don't be surprised if they're back here tonight with their whole families. Oh my God!" she exclaimed. "Bridgette."

"She already knows. I want to see a lawyer as soon as possible," he told Sibyl. "I want to make a will."

∽

The lawyer stared at the notes he'd taken. "This will you're asking me to write up is a bit unusual," he said to Logan. "Are you sure this is what you want to do? I'm not divulging any secrets when I tell you that Miss Bridgette Lowe has told everyone that you're her cousin—that she's your *only* living relative—and that you were engaged before this illness caused you to behave in a manner entirely unlike your former self. I don't know the woman as well as you, but I expect she will challenge this will. I wouldn't like to bet against the possibility that she could be successful in getting it set aside in favor of an earlier will. You do have an earlier will, don't you?"

"No, but there's a secret codicil to my father's will."

"Who was the beneficiary?"

"Bridgette."

"Anyone else?"

"No one other than some small bequests to my servants and a few of the men who work for me. They were the same ones I've asked you to put in the new will."

"So Miss Lowe was essentially the heir to the whole estate?"

"Yes, but she doesn't know that."

"And what is your reason for setting her aside for people you've known for only a matter of weeks?"

"Why do you want to know?"

"If I'm going to be able to defend this will, I have to know why you changed it. She's likely to claim undue influence because of your illness."

Logan should have anticipated this, but he was so busy being happy he hadn't wanted to think of anything that would change that. "Colby and Jared are my brothers. We were adopted by different families after our parents died."

The lawyer was clearly surprised. "What about your other bequests?"

"Sibyl Spencer gave me a job and has taken care of me since I arrived. Cassie and Horace are friends."

The lawyer didn't appear reassured. "I'll write this up and have it ready for your signature when you're sure this is what you want to do."

"I'm sure," Logan said. "More sure than I've ever been."

❧

"You've done what?" Bridgette's shriek could probably be heard all the way to the outskirts of town.

"I've made a new will leaving money to my

brothers and some people here who need it." Logan was feeling well enough to sit in a chair. He'd refused to meet Bridgette lying on his back.

"That was my uncle's money, not yours!" she screamed. "You have no right to give a penny of it to anyone but me."

"I worked with my father all my life," Logan reminded her. "It's as much my money as his."

"He wasn't your father. You're not even adopted. You're no blood relation at all."

Logan had expected Bridgette to be upset, but this surprised him. Her father, not Bridgette, had always been the one to attack him for not being a blood relation. "Since I spent my whole life working with my father to build the company, I was the logical heir. And he did leave you a monthly allowance." Bridgette had claimed it was too small, but Logan had thought it more than adequate.

Bridgette struggled visibly to gain control of her emotions. It was several moments before she was able to speak. When she did, it was obvious she was barely in control. "I can understand why you might want to leave a small sum to Mrs. Spencer for taking care of you. I can even understand a token bequest for the people you worked with, but I don't understand the amounts. Nor do I understand why you want to leave so much money to men who claim to be your brothers."

"They didn't make that claim. I did."

Again, Bridgette struggled to control herself. "I know you wanted to find your brothers, but what proof do you have? Do they have birth certificates or any other records?"

"No, but I don't need anything like that."

"You're not thinking clearly," Bridgette said. "Your illness has made you susceptible to outside influences. This is what happens when you don't take your medicine."

"No one has tried to influence me. The lawyer is the only one who knows anything about the will or what's in it."

"How can you know that? He's the only lawyer in town, and everybody is related to everyone else. I expect everyone knew what you intended to do ten minutes after the lawyer left."

"It wouldn't matter if they did. No one influenced what I put in it."

"You ought to go back to Chicago as soon as you're strong enough to travel. That will give you plenty of time to decide if this is really what you want to do. I'm not thinking just about the money," Bridgette added. "I'm thinking about you getting well. You need the best medical treatment available, and you can't get it here."

"James Pittman is reputed to be one of the best doctors in the country. He's already told me there's nothing he can do for me. How would going back to Chicago change that?"

"We can go to New York, Boston, or anywhere else you want. With all the excellent doctors back east, one is sure to know a way to cure you."

"Dr. Pittman consulted several of his colleagues months ago. He tried some of their suggestions, but nothing worked."

"Things are always changing. You never know when something new will come along."

"Nothing is going to come along fast enough for me. We have to accept things as they are."

"I can't," Bridgette protested. "I can't accept that you're going to die and will do nothing about it."

"Everything that can be done *has* been done. All I want to do now is make the most of the time I have left."

"Then come back to Chicago."

"My family is here."

"I'm your family!"

The people in Cactus Corner felt more like family than Bridgette. Cassie asked about his health every day. Horace kept an eye on him in case he had an attack. People he didn't know had dropped by the house to ask how he was doing. That didn't even include Sibyl or the children who'd made him part of their everyday lives. In Chicago, he'd go weeks without seeing Bridgette. After he got sick, he hadn't seen her at all. Her father had always considered Logan an interloper and an opportunist and had rarely missed a chance to say so.

"I can't expect you to understand how I feel about finding my brothers. It's like finding a part of me that's been missing. They're really fine men. I'm proud to be their brother."

"I'm sure they are," Bridgette said, struggling to keep her voice calm, "but you can't have anything in common with them. Have they ever been to the theater, read a book, or consorted with educated men? You're part of a social elite they know nothing about."

"Much to my surprise, I feel very comfortable here. I often felt I didn't belong in Chicago or in the *social elite*. I know my father didn't. Maybe you've forgotten, but he found me when he was traveling the Santa Fe Trail. For years we slept on the ground, fought Indians and flood-swollen rivers, and cooked our meals over an open fire. I was over twenty before we stopped."

"That doesn't mean you have to do anything like that now."

"I don't know how much time I have left, but I intend to enjoy it. And I've been happier here than anywhere since my father died."

"You have friends in Chicago who'll help you enjoy your time," Bridgette said.

"No, they won't. They'll be horrified by the way I look and worried I might get sick in front of them. They won't know what to say and will end up avoiding me. Besides, I don't have friends, just business acquaintances. That's my own fault, but it's also true."

A soft knock preceded Sibyl's entrance.

"Sorry to interrupt, but it time for Logan to rest," she said to Bridgette. "You can come back tomorrow."

Bridgette ignored Sibyl. "I'm not giving up. You belong in Chicago, not here. I'll be back as soon as I'm allowed." With that, she turned and sailed through the door without acknowledging Sibyl's presence.

"What was that about?" Sibyl asked. "I've never seen her so angry."

"I told her something she didn't want to hear."

"Warn me next time. When she started screaming, Kitty was sure she was going to attack you."

"Tell Kitty I'm perfectly safe."

"You can tell her yourself, but only after your nap. Is there anything I can get you before I go?"

"More time with you."

Sibyl's expression softened. "That's why I'm taking such good care of you. I want the same thing."

Instead of leaving, she pulled a chair next to his, sat down, and clasped his hands in hers. "I know she's your cousin, but I don't like Bridgette coming here. She thinks she's doing the right thing, but she always upsets you."

"She can't understand why I don't want to go back to Chicago."

"You mean she can't understand why you want to be around people like us. She thinks we're hardly better than savages."

"Bridgette can't imagine anything better than being part of Chicago's social scene. I can because I've found what I want right here." Logan pulled Sibyl close enough for a quick kiss. "The swelling is going down. Soon you won't have to close your eyes when I kiss you."

Sibyl pinched him. "I've never closed my eyes."

"I know. That's just one more thing that has happened to me since I came to this magical town that I don't understand."

Sibyl smiled and kissed him. "You don't have to understand. Just accept it. Now I want you to get your rest. Bridgette would wear down a saint. I want you here as long as possible."

&c&

"Are you sure you're feeling up to this?" Sibyl asked for the third time in the last fifteen minutes. "Having all three families here at once will be exhausting."

"I'm feeling fine. I wouldn't have missed a minute of this."

Having learned that their husbands were Logan's brothers, Naomi and Laurie arranged a gathering of the clan at Sibyl's house to properly celebrate the brothers being together at last. All the children were included so they could be introduced to Logan as their new uncle. Peter and Esther were delighted, but Kitty was unhappy because she thought that somehow made Logan belong more to them than to her. He was sure the feeling grew stronger when Peter said they all ought to have the same name.

"We haven't talked about that," his father told him.

"How can you be brothers if you all have different names?" he asked. "We changed our names when you got to be our papa."

"The poor kids," Sibyl said. "First they were Stuarts then Blaines. Now you want them to become Holstocks. They won't know who they are."

"It would be strange calling myself Naomi Holstock," Naomi said to Colby, "but not half as weird as calling you Kevin. I don't think I could do that."

"Colby Holstock wouldn't be a bad compromise," Laurie said. "I think I'd like being Laurie Holstock better than Laurie Smith."

"Nobody needs to change their names," Logan said. "You've gotten along just fine as Blaines and Smiths for the last two years. Don't change that because of me."

"I don't agree," Colby said. "I don't think I could ever get used to being called Kevin, but I would be proud to be called Colby Holstock. I spent years looking for my brothers. Now that I've found both of you, I want us to *feel* like brothers. I think changing my name to Holstock is one way to do that."

"I feel the same," Jared said to Logan. "I've always known I was a Holstock, so it won't be much of a change for me."

"I don't see why it's such a problem," Sibyl said. "Women have to change their names all the time."

"I've had three names," Laurie said, "and now you're thinking of giving me a fourth. I don't want to hear complaints from any of you men."

"I'm hungry," Peter announced. "When are we going to eat?"

"Leave it to Peter to remind us of the really important things in life," his proud father said.

For Logan, the most important thing in his life right then was their coming together as a family. Eating together was just one more way to celebrate it.

&

"What are you doing out of bed?" Cassie was waiting at the bank door the next morning when Sibyl and Logan came to open up. "I'm sure the doctor thinks you're still in bed."

Sibyl gave Logan a stern look. "He's here because he's too stubborn to listen to good advice, no matter where it comes from. I managed one small victory. He's not going back to his camp on the Rim. Colby said animals have destroyed it, and the doctor has absolutely forbidden it."

"I can't see why you would want to go back there when you can stay in a perfectly good house with someone to wait on you hand and foot."

Sibyl looked slightly discomfited.

"I feel fine, much better than I have on some days when I've come to work."

"That's not a good excuse to go back to your camp or be out of bed," Cassie said as she followed them into the bank. "The fact that you're feeling better just proves you should have stayed in bed. You didn't start feeling better when you were running all over town making a hero of yourself."

Logan decided there was nothing he could do to stop people calling him a hero other than to ignore it. They didn't understand that when one was going to die, one didn't fear death. "I was bored, and Sibyl felt she couldn't leave me to come to work."

"I even got Kitty to beg him to stay home," Sibyl said. "She has more influence over him than I have."

Cassie settled at her desk and began arranging the flowers she'd brought. "Don't try pulling that wool over my eyes," she said. "I know you're in love with each other. Half the town knows it, and the other half suspects."

Sibyl paled, but Logan experienced a sense of relief. If everybody knew or suspected, there was no need to hide his feelings any longer.

"They've been polite enough not to say anything—they're waiting for you to say it—but I don't think that'll last much longer."

Horace breezed through the doors. "There's a crowd gathering already," he told them. "The news is around town that Logan is out of bed, and they want to see what he looks like. It seems Peter has been telling everyone that you've seen God."

Logan couldn't repress a chuckle. "I can't wait for that boy to grow up. The Territory will never be the same again."

"That's what Naomi's afraid of," Cassie said. "It's got me worried because Little Abe wants to be just like him."

"I might as well be on one of the windows with

Horace," Logan said to Sibyl. "That way everybody can see that I'm alive without having to disturb you."

"Most of the ones I saw have their accounts at the Community Bank," Horace informed them. "They're just here to look."

"Think we ought to charge them?" Logan asked. "What is it worth to see the local freak? Two bits? Half a dollar? Better yet, let's require them to make a deposit first."

Sibyl failed to see any humor in Logan's remarks. "Don't you *ever* say anything like that again! And if anyone in this town dares, they'll never again set foot in my bank or my home."

"Mine, either," Cassie echoed.

Logan had been half serious—he still couldn't look in a mirror without feeling like a circus sideshow attraction—but it did his heart good to see how angry that made Sibyl. It was further proof that she didn't care how he looked.

"I wasn't serious," he said, "but I should work one of the windows. That will leave Horace free to deal with the people who really do want to do business."

Sibyl reluctantly agreed, but she made an angry remark about people treating Logan like a spectacle.

"I don't think that's it," Cassie said. "People really like him. Besides, anyone who can stop a runaway wagon and shoot better than Colby is a celebrity in this town."

Hearing that tempted Logan to hide in his office, but he resisted the urge. The only way to get this over with was to deal with it right now. People's curiosity never lasted long. Peter was bound to do something that would oust him from public attention soon.

"Okay," Sibyl said before turning to her office, "but if anyone says anything rude or asks any question that's none of their business, let me know. I'm not going to allow anyone working for me to be harassed."

"Are you ready for me to open the doors?" Horace asked.

"Let me do it," Cassie said. "They might run right over you."

There wasn't much of a crowd outside, just a few who went directly to Logan. After the first few, Logan was able to relax and enjoy it. It became clear that people were genuinely interested in him, not just as a curiosity.

One visitor in particular interested him—the Pinkerton who'd traced him from Chicago. The man spent a long time talking to Cassie before coming over to Logan—so long that Logan began to wonder if Cassie wasn't of more interest to the man than he was.

"What are you doing here?" Logan asked when the man came to his window.

"I want to open an account and make a deposit."

"You should see Horace."

"I'd rather see you."

"Why?"

"I have some information I think you might want."

"You worked for Bridgette Lowe. Doesn't it seem dishonest to you to turn around and offer information about her to me?"

"No. I did what she asked. The information I'm offering to you I gathered after I completed the job for her."

"I'd rather not have it," Logan said. "Now, if you really do want to open an account, I'll help you."

After the agent opened his account and made his deposit, he said to Logan, "I'll be around for a while in case you change your mind."

He left without waiting for an answer.

A steady flow of visitors came into the bank, more than any day since Logan had been there. Horace was tied up with a customer when a man wearing an army uniform entered. A number of people were in the bank, but all but one of them were gathered in small groups talking. Seeing Logan's window free, the man walked over.

"How can I help you?" Logan asked.

"My name is Major Killoran. I'd like to see Mrs. Sibyl Spencer."

"Could I ask what about?"

"I'm looking into the disappearance of Raymond Sinclair. I'd like to see if she is able to help me."

"I don't know anyone by that name in Cactus Corner."

"I doubt he'd be here. He disappeared in Kentucky seven years ago."

"Then why are you here?"

"The man's father thinks he was murdered, and he thinks Mrs. Spencer knows who did it."

Logan hadn't realized it at first, but except for the voices of Horace and Cassie, the bank had fallen eerily silent. Several women were staring at the army officer with a look of horror on their faces. Others turned abruptly and left so hurriedly Logan could only think they were fleeing something that had frightened them.

"I'll get Mrs. Spencer," Logan told the man.

Fifteen

Sibyl struggled not to show the panic that had her brain in a whirl and her heart beating much too rapidly. "I'm sorry, but I can't help you," she told the major. "It's true that Raymond and I were seeing each other, but I don't know what happened to him."

"His father said you were engaged."

"That's not true. Raymond *did* want to marry me, but my father thought I was too young to marry a man ten years older, especially a soldier in the middle of the war."

"His father says Raymond was willing to wait until after the war. Wouldn't that have removed your father's objections?"

Sibyl had done her best to erase the events of that momentous year from her mind. It had caused nothing but pain, horror, and a persistent fear that she would be accused of murder. It didn't matter that she was guiltless. She had been entangled in events she was unable to control. Now this man was forcing her to reveal information she had hoped would remain buried forever.

"That's not true, either. Raymond might have been willing to wait until the end of the war if he'd had no choice, but he tried to convince me to run away with him. I was a remarkably naive and romantic girl of fifteen, too foolish to understand what running away meant. My father found out and told Raymond he was never to come to our house again." Sibyl paused only briefly because she'd known what to say for seven years. "I never saw him again."

"His father doesn't believe that's true. He's never stopped trying to clear his name."

"I think it's easy to understand why he would prefer to believe someone in Spencer's Clearing was responsible for his son's disappearance rather than be forced to admit he was a thief and a deserter."

"Who told you that?"

"The army sent people to investigate right after Raymond disappeared. They came to see me for the same reason you're here. They're the ones who said Raymond stole an army payroll, and they're the ones who said he'd deserted. I'm sure there's an official record somewhere that says that."

"There is, but his father doesn't believe that's what happened."

"Then how does he explain the stolen payroll?"

"Another soldier deserted that night. He believes that soldier stole the money."

"The army people said Raymond and that soldier were friends. That's why they believed they had stolen the money and deserted together. The last anybody heard, they never found either of them. I can't think of any reason they would have had for coming to Spencer's Clearing. I would have thought both men would have wanted to get as far away from the army as possible, as quickly as possible."

"The army report said they traced them to your village."

"It also said they found no proof that they'd ever been there. They found their horses a long way from Spencer's Clearing. The horses weren't together, so they figured they split up. I know this because my father was angry about the accusations and followed the investigation until it was over."

Sibyl had told more lies in the last few minutes than she'd told in her whole life, but she wasn't about to stop now. Anything that hurt her would also hurt Kitty, and she would do anything to protect her daughter.

"I'm going to talk to other people in town. If I hear anything different, I'm coming back."

The door to her office opened, and Logan walked in.

"You're going to leave this office right now," he said. "And if you come back without making an apology for the way you've spoken to Mrs. Spencer, the army is going to think it has another deserter on its hands."

The major stood, rising to his full height, which was several inches shorter than Logan's. "Are you threatening me?"

"Not at all. I'm merely stating a fact."

"The army wouldn't stop until they found out what happened to me. A major is a person of importance."

"That wouldn't help you if you were dead."

The major looked as though he couldn't believe his ears. "I can report this."

"Do as you please. I can also report *you*—or we can both deny the threat. Whichever appears to be most to our advantage."

"I don't believe you."

Logan didn't answer, merely drew a pistol and put a hole in the major's hat, which he'd been rude enough to leave on his head.

The hat having been blown off his head, the major clamped his hand down on his baldpate. His look of astonishment was comical. Recovering himself, he crossed the room, picked up his hat, and stared at the hole in it. He looked up at Logan, his expression a mixture of cold fury and shock. "You could have killed me."

"Could have, but didn't," Logan said.

Cassie burst into the office. "Did that army man shoot either one of you?"

"*Me*, shoot!" the major shouted, goggle-eyed. "That man tried to kill me."

"If he'd wanted you dead, you'd be dead," Cassie told him. "He can put three bullets into a hole so small it looks like just one. Ask anybody in town. They'll tell you."

"The major is leaving," Logan told Cassie. "See that he doesn't get lost on his way out."

"Be glad to." Cassie turned to the major. "I don't know what you're doing in this town, but you're not the first person to be shot at in this bank. All the others are dead. I suggest you don't come back."

The major stared at his hat before putting it back on his head. "You haven't heard the last of this."

"I hadn't expected to be that lucky," Logan said. "Next time, I suggest you talk to the marshal before you go around threatening people."

"There's an army post just up the river. I'm sure they won't look favorably on a fellow officer being shot at."

"Jared Smith used to be the commander there. He can tell you all about it. He has a ranch between here and the fort. It'll be on your way. By the way, he's married to Mrs. Spencer's cousin. It's a very close family."

The major looked about ready to say something else. Instead, he turned and marched toward the door. Horace practically fell into the room when he opened it. The major was momentarily stymied by the crowd gathered outside the office door. Then, with a look of determination, he charged through and out of the bank.

"I wasn't trying to listen," Horace hastened to explain. "I was trying to keep everybody out. A couple of men raced off to get their guns."

"All the excitement's over," Cassie announced, "so everybody can go home." With that, she firmly closed the door on all the curious glances.

Sibyl remained standing for a moment then slowly sank into her chair. "You're crazy," she said when she managed to find her voice. "You do realize you just shot at a major in the United States Army."

"I merely tried to teach a lesson to a brute who thinks a uniform gives him the right to mistreat a lady."

"What if Jared can't get you out of this?"

"I'm not depending on Jared to do anything. I can defend myself."

"*You shot at an army officer!*"

"I know, but he was a very poor example of one."

Sibyl gripped the edge of her desk. "Are you trying to give Bridgette proof that your illness has made you act crazy?"

Logan lost a little of his imperturbability. "I won't allow anyone to treat you like that. I don't care who he is."

"He wasn't going to hurt me. He was just annoyed I didn't give him the answers he wanted."

Logan came closer, took Sibyl's hands in his. "I don't care whether he was annoyed or mad as hell. I won't let him treat you like that." He pulled her closer. "I mean to protect you."

Sibyl looked up at him. "I wasn't in any danger, and I'm not now."

"That isn't the point. I won't let—"

"I understand," Sibyl said, "but please don't do it again. I nearly had heart failure." A slow smile appeared. "You really are a remarkable man. How did you ever manage to be tame enough to live in Chicago?"

Some of the tension left Logan, and he smiled. "I traveled the Santa Fe Trail until I was twenty-five. After that, I took up target shooting. Maybe that explains it. I don't know, but I intend to see you don't have to defend yourself."

He didn't know what he was getting into, and she couldn't tell him. It was her past, and she had no right to draw him into it. "Thank you. Now you'd better spend the rest of the day in your office well out of sight. I don't know what I'm going to tell people when they ask why they heard a pistol shot in my office."

"Why not tell them the truth? That major was being rude, and I thought a hole in his hat was the best way to make the point."

She might as well. After the things he'd done, no one would question it. She hoped he was truly better. The world couldn't afford to lose a man like Logan Holstock.

"I don't know what's wrong," Cassie announced to no one in particular, "but everybody's acting really weird. Anytime someone mentions that major's name, people act like they've seen a ghost. When he tries to talk to people, they turn into gobbling idiots. What's wrong with them?"

More than a dozen adults had gathered in Sibyl's parlor to discuss an event that had turned the whole town on its ear. The U.S. Army major had kept his promise and had started asking questions of everyone about the disappearance of Raymond Sinclair. Most of the people barely knew Raymond or his family, which had sided with the North during the war. Being on the dividing line between the two armies, the people of Spencer's Clearing had remained neutral. Both armies had claimed the surrounding territory from time to time, but no one had been killed.

"Before the war, Raymond Sinclair was sweet on Sibyl," Dr. Kessling told Cassie. "He wanted to marry her, but her parents insisted she was too young. When he tried to convince her to run away with him, her father told him never to come back."

Logan's gaze hadn't left Sibyl from the moment he joined the meeting. Sibyl had said there was no reason for him to be here, that he ought to rest, but he could tell from the change in her after the major's visit that something very important had taken place, or was about to. He was spending more time out of the bed than in it and was determined to protect her no matter what he had to do.

"In 1863, Raymond and another soldier disappeared about the same time an army payroll went missing," the doctor continued. "The army investigated at the time, but they were never able to find either man or the money. However, Raymond's father was convinced he had gone to Spencer's Clearing, and that somebody there knew what had happened to him and the money."

"What did happen?" Cassie asked.

"Nobody's sure," the doctor said, "but we're sure something *did* happen. The problem is that only Norman Spencer and Vernon Edwards knew if Raymond Sinclair was involved and what might have happened to him. Everybody was sworn to secrecy and told never to divulge what they knew. Since they're both dead, we'll never know what really happened."

"I think it's time everybody told what they do know," Colby said. "I'm sure nobody here is guilty of a crime, but we need to come up with some answers. The major told me Raymond's father has become one of the richest men in Kentucky. He has enough influence to keep this going for years." He turned to his wife. "You might as well start."

Naomi didn't look happy, but she spoke with a firm voice. "I don't know anything about Raymond, but I know something about the other man. When my Grandfather Brown caught that man trying to steal from him, the soldier killed my grandfather. I came in at that moment. I barely remember what happened, but I know I shot the soldier. I don't know what happened to him or the money."

Frank Oliver spoke up. "I know nothing about the money, but I know what happened to the body. We were afraid the Union Army would never believe we knew nothing about the stolen payroll or why the soldier had died, so we buried him in the bottom of the grave we used for Grandpa Brown."

There was a long silence. Finally, Laurie spoke up. "I know nothing about either man, but I know what happened to some of the money. I took it."

There was an audible gasp.

"I didn't know it was part of an army payroll, or I'd never have touched it. I found it in the soldier's saddlebags when I was helping clean up Grandpa Brown's house. I was desperate to get out of my marriage to Noah. I hid it in case I could use it someday."

"Do you still have it?" Dr. Kessling asked.

"When I found out Norman intended to exercise even more control over me than Noah, I used it to buy a partnership in Jared's ranch. I can pay it back if it would help."

"From what the major says, the payroll isn't the issue," Colby said. "He's only interested in what happened to Raymond Sinclair because his father is putting a lot of pressure on the army to find out."

One after another, everyone present said they knew nothing about Raymond.

"There was nobody out and about that night," Virgil Johnson said. "All the men were off hunting, the women were at a sewing bee, and the children were with Flora Hill and Pearl Sumner. If Naomi hadn't gone home for some scraps she wanted to put in the quilt, nobody would have known about the other soldier."

"Are you saying that if Raymond Sinclair was in Spencer's Clearing that night, nobody saw him?" Logan asked.

There were nods from all around the room, but

Logan noticed Sibyl didn't respond with the others. Worse than that, she'd looked like she was about to faint all evening. She knew something, but she was too afraid to tell it. He didn't believe she had done anything wrong, but he was convinced she knew someone who had. She was a strong, sensible woman who didn't let herself panic when things went wrong. Now she looked as though she'd like nothing better than to run from the room and stay hidden until this whole thing blew over.

"So what do you think we ought to do?" Frank Oliver asked Colby.

"Do you think Naomi ought to tell him about the other soldier?" his wife asked.

"I don't like the idea of hiding things," Colby said. "In my opinion, you should have told the army what happened to the other soldier. If he deserted after stealing a payroll, the army would have hanged him. I think they would have commended Naomi for shooting a deserter who'd robbed and killed her grandfather. But it's too late to bring it up now. Besides, the major isn't asking about him. He's only interested in Raymond. As long as no one knows anything about him, there's nothing we can say."

"So we just say we don't know anything?" Mae Oliver asked.

"You don't know anything, do you?" Colby asked.

"No."

"Then you can't say anything else."

"But he doesn't believe you. Don't look at me like that," she said as several heads turned in her direction. "I've told the man I never saw anybody from Spencer's Clearing until we left Missouri, but I haven't said a word against anyone here. You've been like a family to me after my husband was killed. I don't know what I would have done without you."

Logan marveled that Cassie could tear up without losing a jot of her beauty.

"What has he said to you?" Colby asked.

"There's nothing like a pretty woman to get a man talking, especially when he's a thousand miles from his wife. I didn't like what his being here was doing to everybody, so I decided to find out what I could."

Every eye was on Cassie, the tension in the room even greater.

"He doesn't care what happened to Raymond Sinclair," Cassie said, "but it's his job to find out, and he wants to look good. He says he doesn't believe people, but I think he just doesn't want to go back without being able to tell his boss something."

"We can't tell him anything if we don't know anything," Mae insisted. "I never left my house that night. I didn't know Grandpa Brown had died until the next day. I didn't learn he'd been shot until Naomi's nightmares caused her to remember."

"I'm just telling you what I found out," Cassie said. "I don't know what to do." She grinned. "That's a job for the men. Aren't they always telling us women to leave everything to them?"

Laughter was able to break some of the tension, but it didn't last long.

"Does the army have any proof that Raymond and the thief were traveling together?" Colby asked.

"Not that I ever heard," Dr. Kessling said. "The only connection I know of is that they seemed to have disappeared at the same time."

"I think they were together."

Everyone turned to Horace in surprise.

"What do you know?" Colby asked.

"Nothing about two men, but Norman Spencer asked me to take two horses and let them loose in separate places as far away as I could ride to and back from in one night. He wouldn't tell me why, but he said the safety of the village depended on it. I wasn't going to do it—I didn't like Norman—but Sibyl's papa said I had to do it, that I'd be the same as a traitor if I didn't."

"You never told me," the young man's father said.

"Or me," his brother added. "I always wondered where you went that night. I didn't believe your story about possum hunting. I wasn't too young to go with you, and you knew it."

"I was sworn to secrecy," Horace said.

"So it looks like Raymond was there that night," Colby said. "Does anybody know anything else?"

"I always thought it was peculiar that Vernon Edwards insisted Grandpa Brown's grave had to be so deep," Morely Sumner said, "but I never wasted my time asking why to anything he and Norman Spencer came up with."

"Anything else?" Colby asked. "Even a small detail might be important."

No one had any information to offer. Logan doubted they would have spoken up if they had. Horace's confirmation that there had been two horses had frightened many of them. They might not know anything about that night, but there was a pervasive fear that something terrible *had* happened.

"If there's nothing more, I say we all go home,"

Colby said. "Be as polite and helpful to the major as you can, but you have nothing to tell him, so stop worrying. If anything did happen, the only two people who know about it are dead. There's nothing we can do about that."

Usually people were slow to leave neighborhood gatherings in a small town like Cactus Corner, but the rooms cleared in a matter of minutes.

"I don't think we helped anybody," Dr. Kessling said.

"No," Colby agreed. "Looks like we ended up making them more nervous."

"Still, I think it was good to clear the air. We've been keeping secrets for too long."

"I know I don't live here, and I probably have no right to speak," Logan said, "but there's more to this than we know."

Everyone turned to him with an attention that wasn't entirely friendly.

"Look at this as an outsider would see it," he said. "Something mysterious happens in a small community. Two years later, the whole community picks up and moves west. That's bound to arouse suspicion."

"I asked the same questions," Colby said, "but Norman said they agreed to move because the countryside had been virtually destroyed by the fighting armies. Most moved because so many families were related. The others came along because they didn't want to be left behind."

That did seem like a logical explanation, but Logan couldn't rid himself of the feeling that there was something more behind it than the shooting of a deserter.

"You," Dr. Kessling said, turning to Logan, "are to

go to bed and go to sleep immediately. I don't know why Sibyl let you get out of bed."

"Because I refused to stay upstairs when so much was going on down here. I now have an interest in what happens to this town."

"Well, if you want to live long enough to find out, you've got to take care of yourself so you can get well."

When Logan started to get to his feet, his brothers were at his side immediately. "I can walk on my own," he insisted.

"Probably, but we want to help," Colby said. "It's the brotherly thing to do."

Logan couldn't tell whether Colby was serious or making a joke—it seemed a little of both—but he accepted the offer of assistance. He'd gotten so much stronger that even climbing stairs didn't wear him out, but it meant to lot to him that they were eager to help.

"Make sure you tuck him into bed," the doctor joked.

"That's my job," Sibyl said with a wink.

She didn't appear quite so upset now, but she was far from her usual cheerful, confident self.

"I'll check on you after everyone has gone," Sibyl told him before she left the room.

Logan didn't feel tired, but he didn't object. He had a lot to think about.

He didn't really care about what might have happened to Raymond Sinclair. He'd never heard of the man before tonight. If he was a thief and a deserter, he deserved whatever fate had in store for him. He was, however, very worried about the effect of all this on Sibyl. Not even the deaths of her husband and father had affected her so dramatically. It wouldn't do him any good to search for answers when he knew nothing about what had happened, but he couldn't stop himself.

The most logical answer seemed to be that Raymond had fled with the rest of the money and was alive and well somewhere far from Kentucky. The only problem with that was Horace's story about two horses. If Raymond had come to Spencer's Clearing, why would he have left without his horse? Maybe he talked Norman into giving him another horse and hiding his own horse to throw the army off his trail. That would have been even more important after the other soldier had been killed. But what was he doing in Spencer's Clearing in the first place? As a thief and a deserter, he should have been trying to put as much distance between himself and the army as possible. Had the two men gone there with the intention of changing horses, and had the other soldier taken the opportunity to rob Grandpa Brown? Once a thief, why stop when you came upon easy pickings?

He didn't want to clutter up his mind with possible explanations for Raymond Sinclair's disappearance, and he wouldn't have if it weren't obvious that something about that night had Sibyl scared nearly out of her mind. He couldn't allow that to continue. One way or the other, he was going to rid Sibyl of that terrible fear.

She took so long to return that he had started to worry that something had happened. When she entered the room, he could tell something else had happened to upset her.

"Is everything all right?" he asked.

"It's nothing for you to worry about." When she avoided meeting his gaze, he knew something was seriously wrong. She focused on rearranging some tiny statues on a table and shaking out a doily that had become wrinkled.

Logan walked over to her and took her hands to stop her fiddling needlessly. "Whatever it is, it has upset you. That makes it something for me to worry about."

She turned to him. "There's nothing you or anyone else can do to change the past."

"It's not the past that concerns me. It's the future, and right now, you look like you don't want to see tomorrow come."

Sibyl tried to put on a brave face. Freeing one hand, she moved a picture that didn't need straightening. "You forget I've lived through a wagon trip from Kentucky to the Arizona Territory. There's nothing about tomorrow or the next day that scares me."

"You've never been anything but truthful with me, so I assume it's something in the past that has you looking as though you'd like to go into your room and hide."

Sibyl laughed with something of her old spirit. "Do I look that poor-spirited? I should be ashamed of myself."

"You don't look poor-spirited, but you look worried." He put his arms around her. "I like it when you're near me. I like it when we hold hands. I can't get enough of looking at you. I love knowing that, as incredible as it seems, you love me. Having you near makes me feel like I'm a part of your life."

"You are a part of it. A very important part."

"I love you," Logan told her. "More than I ever

thought possible. There's nothing I wouldn't do to make you happy. I would even have Bridgette kidnapped and sent back to Chicago in a large wooden box." He was relieved when Sibyl smiled. "That makes it all the more important that I know what has upset you so badly. You have to tell me so I can make sure whatever it is never bothers you again."

"You can't do that."

"Why?"

"Because I know what happened to Raymond Sinclair."

Sixteen

It took Sibyl several moments to gather her thoughts. Though it was difficult, Logan waited in silence.

"My mama and her sisters were known for their looks, but Mama said I was more beautiful than any of them. She said one day a handsome man would come along who would sweep me off my feet, and I would have a wonderful life. My father never paid me much attention. He wanted a son and was angry with Mama for not giving him one, and me for not being one. By the time I was fifteen, I was a silly girl infatuated with her own looks and waiting eagerly for the Prince Charming who would whisk me off to an enchanted world. Can you believe I was ever such a fool?"

Logan gave Sibyl's hands a squeeze. "There's nothing wrong with dreams, no matter how fanciful, if they help us get through the bad times."

Sibyl returned his gesture. "It made me susceptible when Raymond Sinclair came calling. He was so handsome in his army uniform I was sure he was the man who was meant for me. I fell so deeply in love I was sure no one had ever loved like I did. When Raymond fell in love with me, I was certain this was how it was meant to be. When he said he wanted to marry me, I was delirious with happiness."

"How old was he?"

"Twenty-five."

"That's too old for a fifteen-year-old girl."

"That's what my father said. I don't think he liked Raymond, but he didn't forbid him from seeing me. Mama didn't want me marrying a soldier. She was afraid he'd be killed, and I'd be left a penniless widow. I didn't care about any of that. When Raymond asked me to run away with him, I couldn't wait."

"He was in the army. That would have been desertion."

"I couldn't be bothered by a detail like that. Besides, he was sure he'd be pardoned as soon as they knew he'd run away only so he could marry me."

"He doesn't sound like the kind of man who would make a good husband."

"That's what my father said when he told Raymond to leave and never to return. He said if he did, he'd shoot him."

"What happened next?"

"Exactly what you'd expect. What little sense I had went out the window. I cried, I shouted, I would close myself in my room and not speak for days. I was sure my life was ruined and nothing good would happen to me ever again. By the time Raymond returned, I was ready to do anything he wanted."

Logan didn't know what was coming next, but he knew it wouldn't be good.

"You already know that the men were out hunting, the women were at a sewing bee, and the children were at Pearl Sumner's house. I was home alone because I was still sulking. I couldn't believe it when

I answered a knock at the door, and Raymond was standing there. I threw myself into his arms. I knew he'd come to take me away."

"Had he stolen the army payroll?"

"I didn't know about that then, but I'm not sure it would have stopped me from running away with him if I had known. I thought he was perfect, that he could make anything right. I wanted to pack a few things, but Raymond wanted me to leave the way I was." Sibyl's gaze dropped to her lap. "I'm not sure how it happened, but our passions got out of hand, and we ended up making love."

Logan knew the jealousy he was feeling was irrational, but that didn't make it less real. Even greater was his anger that a grown man would take such advantage of a young girl. How could he pretend to love her when he would do something like that? Apparently, Sibyl's father's judgment of Raymond had been correct. "What happened?"

Sibyl looked at him once again. "My father returned from the hunt early, I don't remember why, but he found us in bed. Raymond came to his feet immediately. He told my father that we were going to run away and get married. My father grabbed Raymond's sword that was lying with his uniform and ran it though his body. I was so stunned I couldn't scream. Instead I fainted."

At last Logan understood the reason for her fear, but he was relieved. However naive and suggestible she may have been at the time, she was in no way responsible for Raymond's death or his theft of the payroll. Later they could decide if, when, or what to tell the major, but right now, he had to make her understand that nothing that happened was her responsibility. "What happened to Raymond's body?"

"I didn't find out until years later. My father hid his body and that of the other soldier in the smokehouse until my grandfather's grave was dug. Then during the night, he and Norman put both men in the grave and covered them. When the soldiers came looking for Raymond, the whole village was in mourning and burying my grandfather. No one had any idea there were two extra bodies in the grave."

"What happened to you?"

"I went from being half crazy with shock and grief to not caring if I lived or died. I probably wished I would die. My parents were horrified that I'd slept with Raymond and insisted I get married as soon as possible. Right then, I didn't care what happened to me. I probably thought being forced to marry a man I didn't like was just punishment for what I had done. I didn't argue when they told me I was going to marry Norman Spencer. My father was relieved to have me off his hands, and my mother was pleased I was going to have a wealthy husband."

"Didn't other people think it was strange you were marrying a man you didn't like so abruptly?"

"Several people tried to change my mind, but I wouldn't listen. I really didn't care what happened to me. I might have listened to Naomi, but she was sick."

"So you married Norman. When?"

"The day after we buried Grandpa Brown."

Logan had never been in love as a teenager so he couldn't imagine the kind of emotions Sibyl had suffered from. It had taken him years to feel secure in his father's love, so he could imagine how a young girl whose father resented her could have been so desperate for love she would take almost any chance to win it. He could also imagine the shock and desolation she must have felt when her own father killed the man she loved.

"Was Norman ever good to you?"

"He was in the beginning."

"What caused him to change?"

"My father had urged Norman to get me pregnant as soon as possible. He said it was good for a young wife to have something to occupy her time while her husband was at work. I did get pregnant. Kitty was born nine months later, but from the moment he saw her, Norman was certain he wasn't her father. He never touched me again."

"What made him so certain? I don't know anything about infants, but don't they all look the same?"

Sibyl laughed. "Only to a man who's never been a father."

"Still, babies don't look like adults."

"I don't know how he knew, but he was right. Kitty looks a lot like Raymond. She's going to be a beautiful woman when she grows up."

So that's why Norman treated his wife and daughter so badly. "Didn't Norman want any children of his own?"

"I thought so at first, but I don't believe Norman had any room in his heart to love anyone but his mother and himself."

"What happened to the money?"

Sibyl's expression was bleak. "My father gave it to Norman so he would marry me. No man who thought as much of himself as Norman did would marry a ruined woman without sufficient inducement.

Norman was already rich, but he could never resist the chance to get more money."

"So that's where the money in the safe came from."

"I guess. Now you need to go to bed. You need to rest."

"Not until I've convinced you that you weren't responsible for what happened to Raymond."

"How are you going to do that?"

"You didn't make Raymond do any of the things he did. I don't know if he truly loved you, but a responsible man his age would have been willing to wait to marry you, especially since you were so young. There was a war going on. More important, a man of integrity wouldn't have stolen an army payroll. Why did he think he needed so much money?"

"He was going to get back at my father by planting some of it in the house and telling the army where to look for it. I'm sorry to say I didn't try to talk him out of it. It would have been terrible for the whole community."

"You were fifteen—"

"Sixteen by then."

"You were sixteen, young, and in love. You had every right to expect Raymond to take care of you instead of putting you and your community in danger. I'm sure if everything hadn't happened so fast, and if your father's objection hadn't been so severe, you would have acted differently."

It was an effort, but Sibyl smiled. "You're sweet to think so well of me, but I'm not sure it would have made any difference. No matter how much in love I thought I was, I should have had the good sense to tell Raymond we couldn't run away. I had to know it would only lead to trouble."

"Did you know about the army's rules on desertion?"

"I didn't think of it as desertion. He was coming to marry me. That made everything all right."

"Still, nothing that happened is your responsibility. The decisions were all made by Raymond and your father. You couldn't have stopped them, and you couldn't have done anything to change the consequences."

"But what about the major? Should I tell him what happened? I don't want to, but Raymond's father deserves to know what happened to his son."

Logan couldn't think of a way to bare all the truth that wouldn't have dire consequences for people in Cactus Corner who'd had nothing to do with Raymond's death. "We need to think about this for a while."

"I wish you wouldn't burden yourself worrying about this," Sibyl said. "You need to concentrate on getting well."

"I have to think about it because it would kill me if anything happened to you. I'm thankful to have found my brothers, but you and Kitty are the two most important people in my life. I'm not going to let anything happen to either of you."

Tears appeared in Sibyl's eyes. "Why couldn't you have been the man to find me when I was fifteen? None of this would have happened, and I wouldn't have wasted so many years."

"But you wouldn't have Kitty."

"She's all that made those years bearable. She's so serious. There are times I wonder if she isn't really Norman's daughter."

"You told me Colby's twins were very serious

before they came to live with him. From what you've said, it was Norman's treatment of Kitty that has made her so serious. I expect she could give Peter a run for his money if she wanted."

Sibyl laughed and went up on her tiptoes to give Logan a kiss—on his lips. "You are the kindest man in the world. Instead of resting so you can get better, you've spent all this time trying to make me feel better."

"Have I succeeded?"

"Yes, though I hope you're wrong about Kitty being like Peter. I'm too young to have gray hair."

"You'll be beautiful even then."

"Are you sure you didn't leave Chicago to escape all the women chasing after you? I've never met a man with such a silver tongue."

Logan felt warmth spread all through him. "My tongue must have been made of rusted iron because there wasn't a single woman chasing me. You must be the one who caused it to turn to silver. I never have to *think* of things to say to you. They're just there already."

Sibyl shook her head. "I'm beginning to feel as lightheaded as I did when I was sixteen, and that's not a good thing. I'm going to leave you to get some rest. And I mean sleep. I don't want you lying awake trying to think of what I should tell the major. I'll talk to Colby, and then we'll both talk to you. Among the three of us, maybe we can come up with the right thing to say." She kissed him once more. "I love you, Logan Holstock. One of these days, when you're well and have hours and hours with nothing to do, I'll tell you all the reasons. Just know that there're too many for me ever to change my mind."

Logan was beginning to feel a little lightheaded himself. "I feel the same way. And if I don't get well, know that loving you has made it all worthwhile."

Sibyl's facial muscles tightened. "Then get well. I'll never forgive you if you don't."

But Logan knew that his future was not in his hands. He didn't want to die, but he'd been given so much in the last two months that he couldn't feel his life had been incomplete.

Logan walked with purposeful steps, his anger lending steadiness to his step. Major Killoran was back in Cactus Corner. He hadn't attempted to question Sibyl—yet—but he was questioning other people, especially women. Did he somehow think that because they were women, they'd be so awed by his military rank that they'd tell him what he wanted to know? If so, he had a lot to learn about women, especially women strong and brave enough to leave Kentucky to come to a strange and difficult land. Still, Logan wasn't going to wait around for the major to decide what he was going to do next. Logan had every intention that the major's "next" was going to be leaving Cactus Corner as quickly as possible, never to return.

Mae Oliver stepped out of the mercantile just as Logan was passing. Never one to be subtle, she stepped in front of him so he couldn't pass without speaking. "You're looking mighty sour," she said. "I hope that doesn't mean you're feeling worse."

Logan had learned that coming to the point right away saved time and aggravation. "The major is back questioning people even though we've told him we don't know anything. I thought it was time we did something about it."

"If Colby was here, he'd be out on his ear already."

"I'm sure I'm not as good as Colby, but I'll see what I can do."

"Nobody's telling him anything because there's nothing to tell."

"I know that, but he doesn't believe it. I'm here to convince him."

Mae eyed him with speculation in her gaze. "There are times you're so sick you can hardly stand up, but somehow I think you'll find a way to convince him." Her mouth twisted in a grin. "I see you've brought your pistol."

Logan was well aware of the weight of the pistol in a holster at his side. It made him self-conscious. He hadn't worn a gun since his days on the Santa Fe Trail. "I don't intend to use it."

"A silent persuader?"

"Maybe."

Mae nodded. "Too bad you weren't in Kentucky eight years ago."

"Why then?"

"Sibyl wouldn't have married Norman Spencer." With that, Mae stepped aside and went on her way.

Taking only a moment to recover from the shock of knowing that apparently everybody knew of his feelings for Sibyl, Logan quickly reached the hotel.

"I think he's in his room," the clerk told Logan. "I haven't seen him come down, but he sometimes uses the back entrance."

Logan preferred to meet the major in private. It

would be easier for both of them. The major answered his knock, but he was clearly not happy when he saw who was at the door.

"I'm not letting you in," he said, "not with that gun. You nearly killed me the last time."

"I've never killed anyone by mistake," he said—a statement that didn't reassure the major. Logan pushed his way into the room and closed the door. "I've come to talk, not to shoot you."

"Why am I supposed to believe that?"

"Because I told you so. My father taught me that a man of honor never breaks his word."

"And how do I know you're a man of honor?"

"Because I didn't shoot you the first time."

The major didn't look convinced, but he said, "Why are you here?"

"To tell you there's nothing to find out about Raymond Sinclair's death that you don't already know, and that it's time for you to leave Cactus Corner."

"I think that's for me to decide. Besides, you're a civilian. You have no control of anything the army might do."

"Maybe you've forgotten that we have telegraphs even in remote places like the Arizona Territory. While you were stomping around Fort Verde trying to throw your influence around, Jared Holstock asked the commander of the fort to telegraph the general in charge of the army in Kentucky to ask about the progress of the investigation."

The major lost some color and a lot of his attitude.

"The investigation was closed years ago. The official report says that Raymond Sinclair and a friend stole an army payroll and deserted. Their horses were found far away from Spencer's Clearing. They were not together, and there was no sign of the men. There was also no sign that they had ever been in Spencer's Clearing. Do you know what that means?"

The major didn't answer.

"I'll tell you what it means." Logan didn't try to hide the menace in his voice. "It means this is *not* an official investigation. It means you have no authority to be here or to question anyone. It means this is probably an investigation being paid for by Josiah Sinclair, but that you're using your military rank as a means to force people to answer your questions. I believe it means you don't plan to leave until you get the kind of information Josiah Sinclair wants because he'll pay more for it."

"You don't know that," the major blustered, but his protests lacked conviction.

"It will be easy to verify," Logan said. "I don't know your commanding officer—I expect you don't have one because you're retired—but that'll be easy to determine. Whether you're still in the army or not, I doubt they'll look kindly on your using them to squeeze information out of innocent people."

"I don't think they're innocent."

"What you think doesn't matter. The army's investigation does matter, and according to them, the investigation is closed. Now it's time for you to leave town."

"You can't force me to do anything."

"Have you ever heard of Lowe, Inc. in Chicago?"

"Of course. They do a lot of work with the army."

"I own that company."

"I don't believe you."

"It doesn't matter what you believe because I can prove it. Do you know a Brigadier General Owen Scott?"

"Of course. He was in charge of an army division under General Grant."

"He was Jared Smith's commanding officer. They're personal friends. He had Jared appointed marshal of the Territory. Jared Smith is my brother. His wife is Sibyl's cousin."

The major looked shell-shocked.

"You have a choice. You can leave quietly, tell Josiah Sinclair there's nothing more to be learned, and you'll never hear from me again."

"And if I don't leave?"

"I'll use every means I have to ruin you financially, socially, and politically. If Josiah Sinclair is unsatisfied with the official report, he should get the army to reopen its investigation. Until that happens, you have nothing to do here."

"What can I tell Mr. Sinclair?"

"Have you found anything to add to the army's report while you've been here?"

"No."

"Then that's what you'll tell him."

"Would you have shot me if I'd refused to leave?"

"No. There are better ways to stop you without endangering myself. Now I'll leave you to pack. I'll tell the hotel clerk to have your horse ready. You will need to speak with Colby Blaine before you leave. Will an hour be enough time?"

"More than enough," the major replied.

"Then I wish you a safe return journey."

"Do you really hope I have a safe journey?"

"Certainly. That way there won't be any question that something could have happened to you here."

❧

"The major has left," Colby said to Sibyl. "He told me he didn't believe anybody here knew anything about Raymond Sinclair's disappearance so there was no reason to stay any longer."

Sibyl's sense of relief was so great she felt dizzy. She had dreaded having to see the major again. He had a way of making her feel guiltier than she did already. Logan's step-by-step logical reasoning of why she wasn't responsible for Raymond's death had helped, but it couldn't erase from her mind the horror of seeing her father kill the man she loved right before her eyes. That would remain with her forever.

"Do you believe him?" Logan asked.

"Why shouldn't I?" Colby wanted to know.

"I didn't like the way he questioned Sibyl. I got the feeling that even though he had no facts, he was certain she knew something she wasn't telling."

"Maybe, but Jared says it wasn't an official investigation, that it was being done as a favor for Raymond's father." Colby chuckled. "Your putting a bullet in his hat punched a hole in his enthusiasm for the job. The lack of support he got from the commander at Camp Verde must have finished it off. I think he was only too glad to decide that there was no information to be found here." Colby turned to Sibyl. "I'm sorry you were put through this."

"I'm just glad it's over. Raymond was very impetuous, but he was a nice man." She wanted to tell Colby the truth. The community owed so much to him, she felt he had a right to know, but she knew she'd be trying to unburden her conscience rather than helping Colby. In fairness to him, she would have to bear this burden. But it helped that Logan knew.

Colby turned back to Logan. "You, Jared, and I have to decide what we're going to do about being brothers."

"What do you mean?" Logan asked.

"Well, there's the question of having the same name. Who ever heard of three brothers with Blaine, Smith, and Lowe for surnames?"

"That's not a problem. I've already shed Lowe. What else?"

"Jared thinks we ought to go on a camping trip so we can sit around the campfire and catch up on our lives. I'd like to know what you were like when you were Peter's age. Not as wild, I hope. We might even go into business together. We've got to find some way to spend your money. Neither one of us wants it."

Sibyl could have kissed Colby. She could see how much his acceptance meant to Logan. Even after telling Colby and Jared that they were brothers, Logan had been holding back. He'd told Sibyl that the next move was up to them. She was thrilled that Colby and Jared wanted to include Logan in their lives. She didn't know what they could do together, but that Colby would talk this way with a death sentence hanging over Logan showed that they really did accept him as their brother.

"You're welcome to come to the house any time you want," Sibyl said, "but he's not going on a camping trip until he's much better."

"He looks healthy to me," Colby said.

"That's what I thought before the last attack," Sibyl

said. "I'm not taking any chances, and the doctor will back me up."

"I'll have a horse below your window at midnight." Colby pretended Sibyl couldn't hear him whisper. "I'll have you out of that bed and half the way to Prescott before she knows you're missing."

"The moment you crack that window, Trusty will howl the house down," Sibyl told him.

The dog, recognizing his name, raised his head. When nothing in the way of food or a threat was forthcoming, he put it down again.

"Then you'll just have to get well," Colby told Logan. "Jared and I need a break from too much domestic bliss. I haven't had to swim a river or fight off Indians in years."

The happiness in Logan's face caused warmth to flood through Sibyl. Colby had managed to make him feel included, genuinely accepted. Having been surrounded by family all her life, she was unable to comprehend the kind of loneliness these three men must have felt, but the extent of their happiness told her it must have been a long, bleak journey. These were men who feared noth-ing and backed away from no challenge, yet coming together as a family had reduced them to tears, had made them act like schoolboys. It was painful to think they might not be together much longer.

❧

Logan didn't think there was any purpose it in, but he subjected himself to the doctor's examination. This had happened at least once a day since his attack, and the doctor hadn't done anything but shake his head and go away mumbling under his breath.

"I told you it was a waste of time," Logan told him.

"It's my time, and I'll be the one to decide how I waste it."

Taking care of Logan had had a negative effect on the doctor's temperament. He was famous for his ability to handle the most difficult patient, but he was more prone to snap at Logan than exercise his famous patience.

"Leave the doctor alone," Sibyl said. "He's only trying to help you."

"I know, but nothing can help me."

"Don't say that. There must be something that will make you well. If anyone can find it, Dr. Kessling can."

"You've been listening to Naomi again," the doctor grumbled. "You'd think a man's own daughter would know he's not infallible."

"Oh, she thinks you're very fallible," Sibyl said with a smile that caused Logan's heart to skip a beat. "She just thinks you're the greatest doctor in the world."

The doctor grunted, twisted his mouth from one side to another, and then looked up at Logan. "I don't understand it."

"What don't you understand?"

"Your illness, or whatever it is."

"My doctor in Chicago didn't understand it. Neither did all the doctors back east that he consulted."

"That's not what I mean," the doctor said.

"What do you mean?" Sibyl asked.

"I mean I haven't done a single thing. Prescribed no medicine and laid out no regimen. You've ignored my advice to stay in bed by going to work and letting these children treat your room like their own. You've got that Bridgette woman nagging at you at least once a day to go back to Chicago, and you've had the lawyers in here working on a will."

"I can't stay in bed when I feel so much better," Logan said.

"That's the point," the doctor said. "You are better. In fact, I would say you're getting well."

Logan's heart skipped a beat. Then another one. He refused to let himself believe it. There was too much he hoped for to have it snatched from his grasp. "What do you mean?"

"I'm not sure," the doctor confessed. "I've said from the beginning it was like you were being poisoned, but not with a poison that would kill you. Or maybe not enough of the poison to kill you. I don't know. I've never seen symptoms like yours. At times you were strong enough to stop runaway horses. At other times you were too weak to stand up. It's like nothing is permanently damaged, just made too weak to function."

"That doesn't make any sense."

"That's what I've been saying," the doctor said, his patience running out. "None of this makes sense."

"But he is better?" Sibyl asked. She sat through every examination barely breathing until the doctor was finished.

"Definitely. And I don't see any reason why he should have a relapse."

"He's cured?"

Her hope was so intense it hurt Logan. What if the doctor was wrong?

"I'd say he was on the way to a full recovery."

The sense of relief, the flood of hope, was so enormous Logan was dizzy with it. He'd struggled so hard to accept his death that having to reverse all those feelings was disorienting. He couldn't let go of the fear just yet. He had to make sure before he let himself believe.

"How can you say that when you don't know what was wrong?" he asked the doctor.

"Because all the things that weren't working right before seem to be working right now. Your heartbeat is slower and regular. You're breathing without difficulty. You haven't complained of fatigue even though you've been working a full day."

"Desk work isn't hard."

"It would be for a man who was dying."

Still, he wouldn't let himself hope. "What about my face? I still look like a gargoyle."

The doctor laughed. "I like a man who can look at a face like that and joke about it."

"I didn't like the other choice," Logan told him.

"I can't be sure," the doctor said, "but I think some of the swelling has gone down. However, I expect Sibyl is a better judge of that."

Sibyl was getting used to people knowing how she felt about Logan, but she still blushed. "I think you're right, but I was afraid I was seeing what I wanted to see."

"We can give it a week to make sure the swelling is going down," the doctor said, "but he's definitely on the mend."

But Logan couldn't wait a week to hope, to dream, and to plan. He wanted to start right now. He had two brothers who were eager to build on their relationship. He had a beautiful woman in love with him, and a town that cared more for him than Chicago ever had. He had a dog that refused to leave his side, and four children who alternated between hanging on his every word and worrying that he was going to die. How could he possibly wait a whole week to look toward such a future?

The doctor gathered up his instruments. "I doubt we'll ever know what caused your illness, but you appear to have been strong enough to survive it. Being Jared and Colby's brother, I'm not surprised. They're two of the healthiest men I've ever known. I can find my way out," he said to Sibyl. "I expect you'll want to celebrate Logan's recovery."

"Thank you for everything you've done," she told the doctor.

"That's just it. I didn't do anything. He did it all."

Sibyl turned to Logan after the door closed behind the doctor, happiness radiating from her entire being. "You'll going to get well. I know you're going to get well because I can feel it." She hugged herself. "I'm so happy I could run down the middle of the street shouting to everybody that you're going to live. I can't wait to tell Kitty."

"Peter will be unhappy I won't get a chance to see God."

"Don't tease. You know Peter's been upset at the thought you might die. All of us have. The whole town has." She went to the door, opened it, and called downstairs. "Kitty, come to Logan's room. We have something wonderful to tell you."

"Sibyl, the doctor said we wouldn't know for another week."

"You're going to be fine. I just know it."

The way Kitty came racing into the room, Logan decided she was taking lessons from Peter.

"What is it, Mama? Logan isn't sick anymore, is he?"

"No, darling. The doctor says Logan is going to get well." Sibyl paused. "How did you know what I was going to tell you?"

"Dr. Kessling winked at me. He said you had some good news for me. I knew it had to be that, because that's the very best news." She turned to Logan. "Now you and Mama can get married."

"Kitty! You can't say things like that to Logan."

"I already asked him. You said you loved him."

Sibyl turned pink. "It's impossible to keep any secret in this town. When children know what I'm thinking, I have to be so obvious I might as well announce it in church."

"It's nothing to be ashamed of," Logan said.

"I know, but I'd like to have a few things in my life that aren't known to everyone in town."

"Can I go tell Peter?" Kitty asked. "Aunt Naomi said Peter prays for Logan. Peter never prays for anything but a horse."

"Of course you can. And while you're at it, you can tell Aunt Naomi, too. Between the two of them, everybody in town will know by bedtime. Take Trusty with you. It's about time for him to go out."

Trusty didn't agree, but Kitty was insistent. It helped that Sibyl pushed from behind.

Sibyl turned back to Logan. "I know we haven't spoken of it, but I would like to marry you. Kitty needs a father like you, and *I* need you for my husband. I know a woman isn't supposed to ask a man to marry her, but I was afraid you never would."

Things were moving faster than Logan had ever imagined. He still hadn't gotten used to knowing he would soon be completely well. He knew he was in love with Sibyl, but he'd never thought of marrying her. How could he when he'd been certain he wouldn't live through the summer?

"You can't marry a man who looks like I do."

"I fell in love with you looking like that, so I don't see why it should make any difference now."

"You should marry a man you can be proud of, not one who causes people to snicker or look away when he walks by."

"Nobody in Cactus Corner is going to snicker or look away when you walk by, but it wouldn't change my feelings if they did."

"I don't think we should talk about this until the doctor says I'm completely recovered. That will give you time to decide if you really do want to marry a gargoyle. It's also something you'll want to talk to your family about."

Sibyl looked insulted. "I don't need anybody's permission to marry you. Don't you think I'm capable of making up my own mind?"

"Of course I do, but not everybody is going to agree with you. There might be lots of things you haven't taken into consideration."

Sibyl faced him, hands on hips. "Such as?"

Logan's father had often told him not to make statements when he wasn't ready for the consequences, but there were so many thoughts whirling about in his brain he couldn't think clearly. He'd already mentioned all the obvious obstacles, and he didn't know her family well enough to predict how they would feel about such a marriage.

"You don't know me very well," he said. "I haven't told you very much about my past."

"If anyone as condescending as Bridgette thinks you're husband material, there can't be anything really terrible in your past. Besides, you're a member of Chicago's *elite society*. I doubt they accept members who have a questionable past."

Logan laughed. "They'd accept the devil himself if he had enough money."

"Well, I might accept the devil himself if I felt about him the way I feel about you."

It was a good thing Logan heard someone thundering up the steps because he couldn't think of a thing to say to that. Peter burst into the room and almost ran into Sibyl in his hurry to reach Logan.

"Kitty says you're not sick anymore."

"That's what the doctor says."

"Does that mean you're going back to Chicago with that lady? I want you to stay here. I don't like her."

"I'm not going back to Chicago. I like it here."

"Papa says you're really rich. Would you buy me a horse?"

Both Logan and Sibyl laughed. "Why won't your father buy you a horse?"

"He says I can't have one until I'm responsible enough to take care of it. Mama says they'll both die of old age first."

More laughter and more pounding up the stairs followed by Kitty leading a procession of Esther and Little Abe into the room. Trusty slipped in between their legs. "You didn't wait for us," Kitty accused.

"He wanted to get here first," Esther complained. "He *always* wants to be first."

"I think we ought to go downstairs," Sibyl said. "This room is getting a little crowded."

Getting everyone downstairs wasn't easy. Getting them quiet enough to hear himself think was something else, but Logan didn't care. This was a celebration of life, *his* life, and the noisier the better.

It got considerably noisier before the evening got much older. It was apparent the village grapevine was in full cry because it seemed nearly everyone in town wanted to tell Logan how happy they were. Even Bridgette came over but didn't stay long. No one was willing to yield their position to a woman who was intent on stealing one of their favorite people. The looks she received would have penetrated a skin much tougher than Bridgette's. After Sibyl and the children, the best part of the evening for Logan was his two brothers. Neither attempted to speak to him while the room was crowded. They were content to keep their distance, but they watched the proceedings with broad grins that never flagged. From time to time, one would say something to the other and both would laugh. Logan wanted to know what they were saying, but he would wait. When he found out, he wanted to have a quiet space to enjoy it.

But no evening can last forever, and gradually the last of the well-wishers said their good-byes and left. Naomi took the children home to bed, but Colby stayed until everyone else had gone.

"I think I'm angry with you," he said to Logan.

Logan had a moment of panic before he realized Colby was smiling. "And why is that?"

"I saved the lives of half the people who were in this room tonight. I dragged their inexperienced hides across a wilderness and practically built a town for them. You arrive two months ago, get sick all

over everybody, and they like you better than me."
He turned to Sibyl, who was trying not to laugh. "Is
that fair?"

"I don't think they like Logan better than you.
You're just so healthy nobody thinks you'll ever die.
Logan was a pathetic wreck. Who couldn't be sorry
for him? Even the children tried to take care of him."

Logan had never been the butt of a joke. Nothing
had ever happened that would make him think he
would like it, but he found himself laughing just as
hard as Sibyl and Colby. He had laughed many times
before for many reasons, but this time it was different.
It was better. It felt good inside, deep inside to places
he wasn't sure had been reached before. In a short time,
the two people with him had become more important
than anyone in his life except the man who'd been his
father for nearly thirty years. Still, there was an extra
dimension to this relationship that hadn't existed before.
One was the first woman he'd ever truly loved. The
other was his brother. It was hard to get better than that.

"I'd better be getting home," Colby said. "Peter is
probably still awake waiting for me to tell him if he
missed anything exciting. You realize you're not going
to be quite as interesting to him in the future. Now
that you're no longer dying, you'll probably end up
being boring like the rest of us adults."

"Then I'd better work harder on my stories."

"Are any of those true?" Colby asked. "Because if
they are, you're probably going to have to adopt him.
I'm not so special anymore."

"I don't think you have to worry about that. Every
time I finish, he wants to tell me something you've
done. He still idolizes you."

Colby was about to leave, then turned back. "Did he ask you to buy him a horse?"

Logan laughed. "Why?"

"I made the mistake of telling him you were richer than I am. Before he opened his mouth, I knew what he was going to say. I told him if he mentioned a horse to you, I'd gag him."

"We had a nice visit," Logan said. "There were so many children in the room I couldn't understand half of what they said."

"Let's get something straight right now," Colby said. "If you're going to be Peter's uncle, you've got to be on my side."

"I thought it was an uncle's job to sympathize with the nephew then send him home so his father could deal with the heavy stuff."

"You're already worse than Jared," Colby said in disgust, "but he's got his reward coming. Those adorable babies of his will turn into boys who will run him ragged before they're big enough to be kicked out of the house."

"Stop talking nonsense," Sibyl said. "You're nuts about Peter."

"Well, yeah, but the trouble is he knows it."

"Don't change," Logan said. "I wish I had a son like Peter."

Logan couldn't put his finger on Colby's expression, but it looked a lot like Peter's when he was about to say something naughty.

"I'd say there's a good chance you might have a son, but let's hope he isn't like Peter. I don't think Cactus Corner could stand two of them."

He seemed pleased to leave Logan and Sibyl staring at each other, neither quite knowing what to say.

"Do you think he was hinting that he thinks we'll get married?" Sibyl asked.

"Sounds like it to me."

"Then *will* you marry me?"

Seventeen

LOGAN DIDN'T KNOW HOW TO ANSWER THAT question. So many different responses collided in his throat that he was unable to utter any of them. How did a man say that the dearest wish of his heart was the one thing his heart wouldn't allow him to do, especially when he wasn't sure *why* his heart wouldn't allow it? How could he say no and make it sound like a yes?

"You know I can't."

"No, I don't know that. Tell me."

"For the same reasons I've already given. Nothing has changed."

"Yes, it has. You're going to get well."

"Even if I do recover completely—"

"I'm not going to sit here and listen to you give me the same excuses again." Sibyl rose to her feet. "I'm going to bed. You ought to do the same. Maybe your mind will be working better in the morning."

"It's not that I don't *want* to marry you. There's nothing I want more."

"It doesn't sound like it to me. It sounds like, now that the possibility exists, you're getting cold feet. Or maybe you didn't really love me in the first place. A dying man can say anything he wants because he knows he won't be around to have to live up to his words."

Logan sprang up from his chair. A momentary dizziness didn't slow him down. He reached for Sibyl's hands, but she pulled them behind her. When he gripped her shoulders, she turned her head aside.

"Look at me."

"Why should I want to look at a man who swears he loves me but doesn't want to marry me?"

"I *do* want to marry you."

"Words are easy. I'm only interested in deeds. I want to go to bed."

"I can't let you go like this."

"You *let me go* when you refused to marry me. All that remains for you to do is move out. That ought to be easy since you have nothing but the clothes on your back. I'm sure Bridgette will be happy to let you share her room if the hotel is full. Oh, I forgot your dog, but he follows you everywhere. What are you going to do with him now that you're going to get well? Give him back to that brute in Camp Verde? I doubt he'd fit in with the socially elite in Chicago."

Unable to think of anything to say that would stem this flow of disappointment and anger, Logan took the easy way and kissed Sibyl. She resisted for a moment, then simply went limp, offering no resistance, but no participation, either. It had to be like kissing a life-sized doll. All the passion was on his side. He could feel a chill spread though him as he pulled away. The look in her eyes deepened it until he actually felt cold.

"I do love you. You must believe that."

"Maybe you did, but things aren't the same now that you're going to live. You're a rich, prominent citizen of a very important city. You have a business that has been the focus of your life for as long as you can remember. You have a way of life in Chicago that has nothing to do with a little town in the middle of a desert. You have a beautiful woman who shares your kind of life who wants to marry you. Why should you love a widow with a very questionable past? What if it came out that I slept with a man who my father killed and buried in secret? It would be a social disaster. People might stop speaking to you."

"I don't care about any of that."

"Of course you do. That was your life. Now that you're going to live, it's only natural that you'd want it back."

"But I don't want it back."

"You'll find it hard to explain to your brothers why you're leaving, especially to Colby. He's had the roughest life, so finding his family means the most to him. You don't know it, but he lost his family twice. He didn't get to see Peter and Esther until they were four. Having you leave will break his heart."

"What about your heart?"

"I thought you knew I didn't have one. I went straight from the bed of the man I loved to marrying a rich man I didn't like without saying a word. A woman who could do that has a cash register for a heart."

"You can say what you want about me, but I won't let you talk about yourself like that. You were young, frightened, and in shock. It's your father who was to blame."

"I'm his daughter. There's no reason I shouldn't be just like him."

This sudden flurry of sharp words and hurt feelings

wasn't like Sibyl. Logan was certain she was acting this way out of fear of rejection. But he hadn't rejected her. He just wasn't sufficiently over the shock of being told he would live to think clearly.

"You're not like your father," he told her. "You're warm and honest and brave."

"But not warm enough, honest enough, or brave enough for you to marry."

"I *want* to marry you."

"But you won't. Are you afraid I'll be disappointed, or that I'll decide it was a mistake? I fell in love with Raymond. That was a mistake. I married Norman. Another mistake. I fell in love with you. I thought this was the first time I'd gotten it right, but apparently I was wrong. So you see, I'm very experienced in mistakes. I don't know anything else."

"Will you stop talking like this? You've managed to survive all the misfortunes that have befallen you. You've made a success of your life."

"So you're such a colossal misfortune that I can't make a success of being married to you? If that's an example of your reasoning powers, you clearly aren't well yet. Now I *am* going to bed. I'll see you in the morning."

But as Sibyl disappeared up the stairs, so did Logan's objections to marriage. What had he been thinking? Marrying Sibyl had been all he'd thought about for weeks. He'd spent a month in agony believing she couldn't possibly love him. Once he learned that she did, he was content for the two of them to keep their love a secret for the time he had left. But now he was going to live. Why should he now be afraid to do the one thing he'd been wanting to do for weeks?

Was he afraid of too much happiness?

That didn't even make sense. People spent their whole lives chasing happiness, and he was running away from it when it was virtually handed to him? Maybe the sickness had gone to his brain. Maybe so much had happened so quickly, his mind hadn't had time to process it all. Finding his brothers, knowing Sibyl loved him, learning he wasn't going to die was all good news. He should have been bursting with energy to take advantage of all his good fortune.

He *was* crazy. There couldn't be any other explanation, and if he didn't go up those stairs right now and beg Sibyl to marry him as soon as possible, he was too big a fool to deserve his good fortune. When he reached her room, the door was closed. He went in without knocking.

Sibyl was sitting in a slipcovered chair next to the window. Her head was bowed, and her shoulders shook.

She was crying.

Logan felt like a dirty dog. The most wonderful woman in the world, and he'd been the idiot who reduced her to tears.

She spoke without looking up. "If you have something else to say, save it for tomorrow."

"It's not much, but I've got to say it now. I've been a fool. I don't know what I was thinking—I guess the problem is I *wasn't* thinking—but I love you very much, and I do want to marry you. I've always wanted to marry you. If you're willing to marry a man who looks like I do, I'm willing to take the chance that I'll have at least one son like Peter."

Sibyl turned toward him and raised her head, a weak smile breaking through her sadness. She was the most beautiful woman in the world to him. "How about a daughter like Kitty?"

"I love her already. Why wouldn't I want more?"

"She's not Norman's daughter. I'm glad of that, but you may not be."

"I don't really know anything about Raymond Sinclair, but from what I know of Norman, I'm glad she's not his daughter. But it doesn't matter either way because she has your personality."

"I was a fallen woman when I married a man I didn't love. I'd be lying if I said I mourned his passing."

Logan paused. "Now that I've come to my senses, are you trying to give me reasons *not* to marry you?"

"I'm trying to make sure you know the kind of woman who'd be your wife. I've never been to a city like Chicago. I know nothing about high society or music and art and theater. I can sing and dance a little, but I have no accomplishments. I don't have fancy dresses, and I don't want any if it means I have to wear a corset. I'll probably die without traveling more than twenty miles from Cactus Corner. The most important things in my life are my family and the people I love. As long as I have them, I don't need anything else."

"That's quite a speech. Are you expecting a similar one from me?"

"Now that I've practically thrown myself at your feet, I would like to know if you can spend the rest of your life married to a woman like me."

"I'd never met anyone I really wanted to marry, anyone I really loved, until I met you. I never wondered what it would be like if we moved to Chicago. I don't care about the terrible things that happened to you in the past. I only care about the woman you are today. And that woman comes with a daughter, a family, a whole town—and a future right here in the Arizona Territory. That's the woman I fell in love with, and that's the woman I want to marry. I don't want you to be anything but what you are."

"Are you sure? Just minutes ago—"

He crossed the room toward her. "I was out of my mind. So much has happened so quickly I couldn't think straight."

Sibyl let Logan pull her into his arms. "I shouldn't have said all those things, but I was afraid I'd lost you. I've been scared you were going to die for so long I was desperately trying to hold on to you for the future."

"And I've believed for so long that I was going to die I couldn't think straight. But my head is clear now. Forget everything I said except that I love you and want to marry you. Nothing else is important."

"Are you sure?" she asked again.

"Yes. What can I do to make you believe me?"

"You can make love to me."

Logan felt like he'd just run into a wall. Other than in his dreams, he'd never let himself think about making love to Sibyl. He'd told himself that Sibyl being in love with him was enough, more, in fact, than a dying man could expect. Never having been in love before, he'd always connected physical love with physical attractiveness. Even though the swelling in his face was going down, he couldn't imagine a woman wanting to make love to a man who looked like he did.

But falling in love had changed that. For the first time, he realized that a person could see beyond the surface, could even ignore physical imperfections, because the inner beauty shone so brightly nothing else mattered. He still found it difficult to understand how Sibyl could feel that way about him, but he no longer thought it was impossible.

"You haven't said anything."

"That's because the thought of making love to you has left me speechless."

"Then you don't have to talk."

Odd that after having made love to many women in his thirty-five years, he didn't know how to begin with Sibyl. In all the times before, there had been a ritual to follow. Both parties knew the rules because they'd played the game before.

But this wasn't a game. It was nothing like anything he'd experienced before. How could he have known that never having been in love could put him at such a disadvantage when the real thing came along?

Yet the confusion of his mind didn't extend to his body or his heart. Together they moved him across the room. Sibyl rose to meet him, and he took her in his arms. He didn't need rules or a ritual. Everything happened naturally. She slipped into his embrace like she'd been made to be there. His arms closed around her with strength combined with tenderness. He hadn't known such a combination existed. When she slipped her arms around his waist and leaned her head against his chest, he feared he might expire from happiness. How could anything so ordinary feel so life-changing? How could he have held off from doing this for so long?

"All my life I've dreamed of being held like this," she said. "Raymond wasn't allowed to do this, and Norman wouldn't."

Another reason Norman Spencer was one of the biggest fools ever born. His mother should have been ashamed of herself.

"I'd have held you in my arms long ago if I'd thought it was possible."

Sibyl turned so she could look up at him. "For an aggressive businessman, you're surprisingly hesitant when it comes to love."

That had been when he thought he was dying. It had taken a few moments to change his mental gears, but that was done now. He knew what he wanted, and he intended to have it. "I have years of experience in business, but none at being in love."

"Then it's time we changed that." She pulled his head down so she could kiss him. "Is that better?"

Rather than state the obvious, Logan pulled Sibyl into a tight embrace and kissed her with a passion than had been building inside him for the past month. It wasn't a tender kiss or a polite one. It was a little rough, very greedy, and the most thrilling thing he'd ever done. He couldn't imagine how he'd lived so long without suspecting how kissing a woman he loved deeply would affect him. It was like he'd been going through life with blinders on, his emotions cut off or neatly boxed up, his mind operating on neutral, his body going through the motions of a learned ritual.

This kiss was nothing like that. For the first time, he realized that making love to a woman could be an emotional as well as a physical experience. This wasn't solely about his physical gratification. In fact, he couldn't separate the physical from the emotional and the spiritual. This was something without precedent, unique in his experience, the first time for something about which he thought he knew all there was to know.

His hold on Sibyl tightened. He wanted to hold her forever, to make her an inseparable part of him, bind her so thoroughly they could never be separated.

"Not so tight," she said. "I still need to breathe."

His muscles were reluctant to respond to a message his brain sent but which his heart and emotions wanted to ignore. He was afraid if he relaxed his hold even a little, she would escape, and he might never hold her in his embrace again. He was acting like a boy with his first crush.

"Sorry. I've wanted to do this for so long, I can't let go."

"I'm not going to escape. I want this as much as you."

He wasn't sure that was possible, but he hoped it was. He was much more than the sick man she'd come to know. But this was no time for talk, especially not revelations from his past. Now was the time to cement a relationship he hoped would endure for the rest of their lives.

"I dreamed of you the first night after I saw you. You were like something out of my imagination suddenly come to life."

"I don't want to be in your dreams or your imagination. I want to be very real, so real you can reach out and touch me."

As if he could ever get enough of touching her. She was warm and soft, yet strong, a dream that had come true and taken substance in his arms. He didn't know why he'd been so fortunate, but he was grateful love had come along when he was old enough to realize how wonderful and rare it was.

"Nothing has ever been more real to me than you.
Loving you as I do, I don't know how I could ever
have believed I could be happy married to Bridgette
or anyone else. You've awakened emotions I've never
experienced, depths of feeling of which I didn't know
I was capable."

Sibyl put her hand over his mouth. "Kiss me again.
You can tell me about all this later."

That was an easy request to grant. Still, talking had
been important because it brought into focus things
that had been feeling random and unconnected.
Putting his feelings into words had not only clarified
them, but had deepened them as well. He wasn't
moving blindly or acting on pure instinct. As he did in
all his business transactions, he had his wits about him.
He had his objective clearly in mind. From this point
on, nothing was going to stop him.

❧

Sibyl was glad to know she had been responsible for
bringing about a transformation in Logan's life, but
that wasn't uppermost in her mind right now. She
hadn't known a man's embrace since before Kitty was
born. While she had never done more than tolerate
Norman's embraces, she hadn't ceased to long for the
feel of a man's arms around her. Lonely days and years
of nights in a cold bed had left her feeling unlovable.
Her reflection in the mirror had done nothing to
change that. Seeing Naomi and Laurie make happy
marriages had only resigned her to a bleak future.

Logan had changed all of that.

She didn't know when it started, but she had fought
it. It wasn't until Logan's collapse and the fear that he

would die within hours that she realized how pointless it was to deny what she felt, to refuse to reach for what she wanted and needed. Now that she had her arms around him, she would never let him go.

She had forgotten how wonderful it was to be held and kissed. She felt like a desert plant brought into flower by life-giving rain. She hadn't let herself think too much on a future with Logan, but the hope had never been long out of her mind. Now that the possible had become a reality, she could let herself go, let her imagination conjure up all the things she'd dreamed about but had believed would never happen. Most important, at the moment, was his arms around her. It had been so long she'd forgotten how much she needed that.

"Hold me tight again," she begged.

"I don't want to hurt you."

What a joy to know Logan needed her so desperately that he feared his embrace could be painful.

His arms pulled her ever closer. His weakness must make it difficult to hold her so close, but that was further proof of his need for her, of her importance to him. After so many years of cold rebuffs, it was hard to believe this was really happening. She had spent so many years trying to accustom herself to the acceptance that this would never happen, that it was going to take more than this night to believe this wasn't some kind of dream.

"I want you to make love to me," she reminded Logan.

"Are you sure?"

"When a woman works up the courage to make such a request, you can be sure she means it."

"But what if——?"

"No *what ifs*. No tomorrows and no yesterdays. I don't want to think of anything but the two of us at this very moment."

The pressure inside her was greater than she could have imagined. When Logan kissed her again, she strove to match him in intensity. She didn't care if it was unladylike or too forward, even inappropriate. Nothing was out of bounds.

"I wouldn't let myself believe this could happen," Logan whispered.

"Then kiss me so neither of us will ever forget this moment."

When Logan took her mouth again, she was afraid it wasn't going to be the kind of kiss she would remember for the rest of her life. He was too gentle, too polite. Before her disappointment could make itself felt, Logan kissed her with a ferocity she hadn't thought possible. She was certain her lips would be bruised, her ribs nearly broken, her body lifted from the floor. It was exactly what she craved.

Logan's tongue invaded her mouth like the fierce charge of a longhorn bull, determined and powerful enough to carry all before him. He ravaged her mouth, plunging into its depths, seeking out her sweetness and claiming it for his own. Beyond anything Sibyl had experienced, the assault left her breathless. She felt her strength drain away, leaving her defenseless in Logan's arms. But even as the feeling of helplessness flowed over her, she felt a countercurrent of strength emerge from somewhere in her depths. Passion, which had lain in wait for so many years, had cast off its slumber and exploded with the force accumulated during six years of waiting. She was suddenly brimming with more than enough energy to respond to Logan's advances, with a desire to experience his body as completely as he experienced hers.

Neither Raymond nor Norman had ever used his tongue when he kissed her. It was a novel and unanticipated experience, but it was tremendously exciting. Rising to her tiptoes to gain a better advantage, she returned Logan's kiss with a passion she hadn't known she possessed. His possession of her mouth had unleashed desires and needs that she hadn't known she still had after years spent trying to deny them. Now she was free to let them loose, to allow herself to ask for what she wanted, to become the passionate woman nature had intended her to be.

Logan deserted her lips to scatter kisses on the side of her neck. Each kiss sent sparks skittering through her like bolts of lightning. Who knew her neck—and now her throat—could be so sensitive? It was difficult to plan her own attack when Logan was slowly dismantling her ability to think, or her desire to do anything more than give herself up to him. Even through the thickness of her clothes, his hands were like branding irons, leaving a trail of fire wherever they moved. If her skin was so alive to his touch through her clothes, she wasn't sure she could endure his hands on her bare skin.

But Logan was about to put it to the test. The ease with which he undid the buttons down the back of her dress informed her that he was no novice when it came to making love, and that pleased her. After waiting so long, she wanted an experience that would wipe everything that came before it from her mind.

His hands played across her back, caressing her skin, circling her shoulder blades, and singling out each vertebra in her spine. By the time he finished, she was ready to melt into a puddle at his feet. When he slid her dress off her shoulders and covered them with kisses, she was certain she would. Her bones seemed to melt. Her muscles lost their tension. Even the air around her took on a soft, purple hue. It was a delicious feeling, a seductive feeling that was hard to resist, but she *did* resist. She wanted to be a full participant, so she tightened her arms around Logan's neck to keep upright.

She wasn't quite sure how Logan removed her dress. It just disappeared, and she found herself standing in her shift with Logan paying particular attention to her breasts. Raymond had been a clumsy lover, Norman an indifferent one. Logan was neither. Long before Logan removed her dress, her breasts had become highly sensitive, her nipples pressing against the restraining fabric. Now they stood out against the thin fabric, a perfect target for Logan's hungry tongue.

Shudders shook Sibyl as Logan teased her nipples with his teeth and lips. The groan that seemed to come from someone else had to be hers, the moans hers as well. She couldn't keep still, her body alternately pressing against Logan before pulling away, then pressing forward again. She wanted to open his shirt, but she couldn't force her mind and fingers to concentrate on their task. Just splaying her hand against his chest was enough to make her weak-kneed.

Determined to know if his body was as sensitive as her own, she managed to concentrate long enough to undo four buttons on his shirt. However, progress came to an abrupt halt when Logan untied her shift and refocused his attention on her bare breasts. When he nipped her nipple with his teeth, a tiny shriek escaped her.

"Did I hurt you?"

Unable to speak, she barely managed to shake her head. Her muscles—indeed, her whole body—were beyond her control. She wasn't sure how she managed to stand. When Logan picked her up and laid her on the bed, she didn't have to worry about it anymore. Just that he now had access to her whole body and was taking full advantage of it.

She managed to say, "You've got to undress. I feel foolish lying here almost naked while you're fully clothed."

"Would you like to undress me?"

Sibyl was afraid she might faint. She'd never been allowed to touch a man's body in that way. Her fingers trembled as she finished opening Logan's shirt. Almost unable to breathe, she pushed the shirt over his shoulders. Logan pulled his arms out of the sleeves and dropped the shirt to the floor because Sibyl was incapable of movement. The sight of his bare chest before her, the feel of his skin under her fingers, the heavy scent of male musk that filled her nostrils, mesmerized her.

"What's wrong?" Logan asked.

"I've never touched a man like this." She'd never been *invited* to touch a man, to have a man give her unfettered access to his whole body.

"I look forward to touching your body," Logan said. "It seemed natural to me that you'd feel the same way about mine."

She would have if she'd known it was possible. She

could ask Naomi and Laurie just about anything she wanted to know. Why hadn't she thought to ask them about this?

Because she didn't know it was possible. Her mother had said it was a woman's duty to allow her husband access to her body. She hadn't said anything about it being pleasurable or about it working both ways.

"I do feel the same," she said. "I just didn't know it was allowed." She was grateful Logan didn't ask her why she felt that way. She didn't want anything to destroy the magic of this moment.

"I want you to touch me," Logan told her. "I want you to enjoy my body as much as I hope to enjoy yours."

That was something else that was a new concept to her. She had been taught that a physical relationship between a man and a woman was what married couples did because they wanted children. Nothing was ever said about *enjoying* the relationship, not even that the relationship could have extra meaning if the two people were in love. It's what Naomi and Laurie claimed to have, but it was something Sibyl had never understood until now. She hardly knew where to begin.

Logan's skin didn't feel like she expected. It wasn't exactly rough, but it wasn't smooth or feminine. She could feel his ribs, but she could also feel the cords of muscle that had enabled him to stop the runaway horses. His shoulders were bigger than she'd expected, his arms equally stout. Norman had been as hairless as a piglet, but Logan had a nest of hair that covered his chest with a tantalizing trail that disappeared below his belt. Sibyl would never have had the nerve to explore farther, but her instincts showed no hesitation. The bulge in Logan's pants was as impressive as it was frightening. Her fingers traced its outline, tested its firmness.

"Careful," Logan warned. "If you keep that up, I'm liable to explode."

Sibyl froze. Had she hurt Logan or made him uncomfortable? She felt foolish. She'd been married for years but knew virtually nothing about how having sex affected a man. Norman had never said anything, and she'd been too afraid to ask. When he stopped wanting her, she assumed it was her fault.

"You don't have to stop touching me," Logan told her. "Just think of that part of me as a loaded rifle with a hair trigger."

His explanation caused Sibyl to chuckle, a reaction she doubted was suitable under the circumstances, but it did release the tension. "I don't know what to do."

"Just about anything you want."

And she knew exactly what she wanted. She wanted Logan naked. With trembling fingers, she undid his belt. She fumbled with the buttons of his pants, but she managed to get them undone thus allowing his pants to fall to the floor. The sight that met her eyes caused her breath to catch in her throat. That part of him that was "liable to explode" had pushed against his underwear until it appeared about to burst through the restraining fabric. For an instant, she froze. She'd never seen a man in this state before. Norman had come to her only in the dark. She was quick to banish the memory of Norman's awkward lovemaking from her mind. With Logan it would be altogether different. Gathering her courage, she grasped his underwear and pulled them down.

Now she doubted she'd ever breathe normally again. It looked like a weapon. Surely it was impossible she could accommodate it.

"You can touch me if you're careful," Logan whispered.

There was a brief struggle with ingrained inhibitions doing battle with basic need. Need won out. Her hand moved forward until she touched him. He was warm and amazingly soft yet so hard he was nearly rigid.

"I've never been this eager before," Logan murmured. "I don't know how long I can hold out. You can't imagine how beautiful you are."

Logan obviously didn't know how beautiful he was. Sibyl didn't know how a man who'd been so sick could be so vibrantly alive.

"I can't be the only one naked," Logan said. "I've spent so many nights dreaming of what you would look like I can hardly wait to see how close I came."

Sibyl was reluctant to give up her exploration of Logan's body, but his hands on her destroyed her concentration. She could only think of what he was doing to her. Up until now, she'd never experienced anything but youthful fumbling and the nearly impersonal union of two bodies in a ritual that felt like a surrender to a requirement of being married. Naomi and Laurie had told her everything was different when the two people were in love, that it was an expression of love that transcended words, but she found it hard to imagine. She loved Logan and he loved her, so she wondered if it could be that way for her.

The feel of his hands on her body made her skin ultra-sensitive. His feathery touch left trails of fire across her shoulders and down her arms that caused her to shiver with delight and anticipation. If merely touching her arms could create such a sensation, what would more intimate contact do? When Logan's hands cupped her breasts, she found out.

His hands were cold and hot, his skin rough and soft, his touch firm and gentle. She felt uneasy yet eager, fearful yet confident, cowardly yet courageous. Never had she experienced so many contradictions. When Logan slipped her shift under her and let it drop to the floor, she felt panic.

Would he find her as beautiful as he dreamed she would be? Would she be as desirable as the women in his past? Would she do something—or *not* do something—that could destroy his love for her?

His hands on her breasts were making it hard for her to think. When he took her nipple into his mouth, she ceased to be able to think at all. She could only experience the flood of sensations that threatened to overwhelm her. She fought to keep her wits about her. If this was going to be the most incredible experience of her life, she didn't want to miss one second of it.

It shocked her to find that her hands had gone to the back of Logan's head, pressing him more firmly against her, but she was feeling a need that had taken control of her. She didn't panic when he nipped at her with his teeth or laved her with his tongue. It merely fed the fiery need that was gradually consuming her. There was no longer space in her mind for fear, for reluctance, for holding back. She wanted more. She could hear herself beg for it. She didn't know what that *more* might be, but she knew it was there. At last she was beginning to understand.

Their bodies pressed hard against each other while

they shared a kiss the likes of which Sibyl had never dreamed was possible. The emotional riches of Logan's kiss penetrated deep inside her and opened up hidden treasures of love and warmth and need and giving and still more Sibyl couldn't name. Her soul was opening for the first time. Nourishment had reached a part of her that had been starved until it had come close to withering into a small, hard knot of insignificance. She was revitalized. Even more than that, she was infused with a rainbow of emotions and a breadth of understanding that had been beyond her grasp until now.

Yet nothing could put her beyond the effect of Logan's nearness or her body's response to his touch. It was like a fire that didn't burn, a flame that didn't scorch, but there was nothing cool about it. She felt ablaze with desire that would not be reined in or controlled. The heat of his erection against her abdomen stoked a fire in her belly that spread through her with the speed of a conflagration. When his lips deserted her mouth and found their way once more to her breasts, it threatened to consume her.

"I didn't think it was possible, but you're more beautiful than I dreamed," Logan murmured. "I thought I knew what it was like to be with a woman, but I had no idea anything like this was possible."

Neither had she, but she couldn't summon the words to tell him. He was moving down her body, his lips and tongue leaving trails of desire over her skin, stoking the fire in her abdomen to greater intensity. His hands moved down her back, over her hips, and along her thighs. She felt enmeshed, ensnared, entangled until she couldn't separate his body from her own. The fires kindled in their separate bodies flamed higher and wider until they merged into a single inferno of need and desire so powerful she could think of nothing but to feed it until it consumed her.

Logan touched her between her legs and a bolt shot through her with the force of a lightning strike. Was that his finger? No, it was his tongue! Shock and amazement were followed by an indescribable feeling that reduced her brain to mush. Her body writhed against him, which only drove him deeper inside her. Could this be real? How was it possible that her body could overpower her mind, evaporate all conscious thought? It had turned her into its slave, desirous of nothing more than complete subjugation to her desires.

When Logan backed away and moved up her body, she felt like she'd been pulled from a boiling cauldron and plunged into icy water.

"I'm going to enter you now," Logan murmured. "Let me know if anything is uncomfortable."

His abandoning her body was uncomfortable. The loss of being caught up in delight so intense it was beyond her imagination was uncomfortable. The feeling that she had been transported to the doorway of unimagined rapture only to be denied entrance was uncomfortable.

"This will be better than anything," he promised.

How could she believe him? It had never been more than tolerable with Norman.

"We love each other," Logan told her. "That will make all the difference."

She wanted to believe him, she *tried* to believe him, but it didn't seem possible.

Still, his kisses could make her forget everything else.

They claimed more than her mouth. They demanded all of her, a willing sacrifice on her part.

"I'll go slowly."

She didn't want *slow*. She wanted everything, and she wanted it now. She wanted it so powerful and overwhelming that everything that had gone before would be obliterated from her memory. She wrapped her arms around him and pulled him to her with all her might. She felt him begin to enter her. Impatient with his progress, she thrust her body against his, driving him deep inside her.

She gasped at the feeling of fullness, of being impaled by a velvet sword. Galvanized by the feeling of being physically joined with Logan, she fell away then rose to meet him.

"So that's how you want it," Logan said.

"Yes!" It was a sigh of fulfillment, a plea for more, and a challenge he had to meet.

"I didn't know you would be so eager." His voice was rough with desire.

"Neither did I. I don't know what's gotten into me. I've never been like this."

"I think you're seeing your real self for the first time."

She didn't know, and right now she couldn't find the energy to care. She only wanted more. She held him closer, kissed him harder, and encouraged him to reach places inside her that had never been touched before. As his rhythm increased, so did hers. When the waves began to build inside her abdomen and spread to the rest of her body, she threw herself against him, wrapped her legs around him, pulled him toward her depths. Something incredible was just out of reach. If he could get her just a little bit farther, something unbelievable would happen.

Yet when it did, she was unprepared for the impact. Her entire being was transformed into one enormous pulse of throbbing energy. This fusion of lust and need and naked desire coiled itself around her like a cocoon that separated her from her corporeal being. In this moment, nothing existed but the two of them joined in the throes of a passion greater and more wonderful than she could have imagined. They rose and fell together in perfect symmetry. Sibyl felt like they were floating, drawn toward a place in time where only they existed.

Yet even as she felt removed from substance and form, the forces building inside her brought her back to earth. The need became so real, so tangible, that she could follow its movement through her body until every part of her had merged into a single driving desire for fulfillment. And that fulfillment could only come from Logan.

She attacked him with a fierceness born of desperation, driving him deeper with every thrust. Her nails tore at his skin without regard for his pain. She thought she heard his breath coming in harsh gasps only to realize she was hearing her own breathing. His frantic movement was hers as well. They were nearing the precipice together. As they did so, his movement became erratic, his body rigid. A moment later, movement and breathing stopped altogether. Then she felt the heat of his seed deep inside her.

That's when she went over the precipice and into the abyss.

Eighteen

SIBYL LAY AWAKE LONG AFTER LOGAN HAD FALLEN asleep. Her heartbeat, though steady, was too strong to allow for sleep. Disbelief kept her brain spinning. Tender nerve endings amplified every feeling. She was alive in ways that had never been breached before. She was so acutely conscious of her physical nature that she kept touching herself to make sure her body was unchanged because everything else about her had undergone a transformation. It didn't seem possible that there wouldn't be some outward manifestation of the inward changes, but there were none. She'd even gotten out of bed and checked her reflection in the mirror.

But when she asked herself what changes she had expected to see, the only answer she could come up with was that she felt like a different person. She now knew what it was like to love and be loved. Love had nourished her soul and her body. Not since she was sixteen had she felt so excited about the future. She was impatient for the night to be over and the day to dawn. Everything about her life was new, exciting, filled with anticipation. She couldn't wait to get started.

Logan was going to live, and that put a different complexion on everything. It didn't affect his love for Sibyl or his desire to marry her, but every decision he'd made since leaving Chicago had been based on the assumption that he would die within a few months. Now that wasn't going to happen, so how did it affect everything else?

He supposed the first question was what did he want to do about his business and whether that would require him to return to Chicago. Did he want to go back? Other than work, what did he have there to draw him back? He knew hundreds of people—business associates, competitors, social acquaintances, and casual friends—but none of them were the kind of friends who were necessary to his life and happiness. Other than some of the men who worked for him, he couldn't think of a single person he'd missed in the months he'd been gone. If he didn't go back, what would he do about the company he and his father had worked more than twenty years to build? He couldn't just turn his back on it. It represented too much of his life. Besides, creating that company had been his father's lifelong ambition. One of the last things his father talked about before he died was what he thought Logan could do to make the company bigger and stronger. Logan had realized long ago that his father had never married because he didn't love any woman as much as he loved his work.

But if Logan went back to Chicago, would Sibyl go with him? Would she be happy if she did? Her life was closely tied to her friends and family. She loved them so deeply it would be like asking her to divide her soul. She wouldn't know anyone in Chicago, nor would she have anything in common with the people he knew. More than that, he was certain Bridgette would do everything in her power to make sure society turned its back on her. How could he do that to the woman he loved?

And what about his brothers? He had just found them and was looking forward to becoming part of their lives, but there was no question of them moving to Chicago. Could he turn his back on them?

Fortunately, he didn't have to decide right away. He would talk to Sibyl and his brothers. They might have some ideas. They knew more about Arizona than he did. He turned to Trusty, who'd been watching him as he got dressed.

"I haven't forgotten about you," he told the dog, "but I doubt you'd like Chicago. You're not fashionable enough, and you're too big to be a lap dog."

Trusty thumped his tail and whined softly.

"I guess you can't make up your mind either. Your tail says yes, but your whine says no."

That was very much how he felt about Chicago. It had been his home for most of his life. He'd never felt at home there, but that was probably his fault. He'd been too busy working to give it a chance.

❧

Sibyl knew something was wrong the moment Logan stepped through the kitchen door. "What's wrong?" she asked.

Logan looked startled. "Nothing. Why do you ask?"

"He doesn't look sicker to me," Kitty told her mother.

"He looks healthier than I've ever seen him," Sibyl told her daughter, "but he's worried about something."

"Are you worried about Trusty?" Kitty asked. The dog followed on Logan's heels.

"I'm not worried about Trusty," Logan told Kitty, "but the doctor says I'm going to get well. I hadn't planned on that."

"Aren't you glad you're going to get well?" Kitty asked.

"Yes, I am."

"Then there's nothing to worry about. I'll take Trusty out. Mama said we had to wait for breakfast until you got up."

There were times when Sibyl wished she had her daughter's black-and-white view of the world. It would make decision-making so much easier. When the door closed behind Kitty and Trusty, Sibyl said, "Now you can tell me what's bothering you." The only thing that had changed was that they had made love. She was petrified that was the problem.

Logan rounded the table, took the spoon from Sibyl's hand, and put his arms around her. Putting his hand under her chin, he tilted her head up until she was looking directly into his eyes. Then he kissed her. Sibyl felt much of her tension ease, but not all of it. She knew something was wrong, and a kiss wasn't going to change that.

"You look especially lovely this morning," Logan said. "It seems that making love agrees with you."

Sibyl couldn't believe she was blushing, but she was. "That's not something I'm used to talking about—certainly not at the breakfast table."

"Then that's something we have to change."

"Not as long as Kitty is within earshot."

Logan grinned. "Okay, but I love you every hour of the day, and I want to be free to talk about it."

"Love and sex are two different things."

"Not in my mind."

She could tell he knew he'd made a mistake as soon as the words were out of his mouth, but she couldn't resist the chance to tease him. "If you've loved every woman you've ever had sex with, how far down the line does that put me? And if you mention Bridgette's name, you can leave my house right now."

Logan wasn't taken in. "Love and sex are the same only with you. With everyone else, it was just scratching nature's itch."

"Did we scratch your itch last night?"

Logan burst out laughing. "Not so much that it can't use a little more scratching."

Sibyl laughed but sobered quickly. "You're not going to avoid answering me. Something has changed since last night. What is it?"

Logan led her over to the table, and both sat down. "Everything I've done in the last several months, every decision I made, was based on the expectation that I would be dead before the end of the summer. Knowing that I might live has changed everything except that I love you and want to marry you."

Sibyl breathed a sigh of relief. As long as Logan still loved her, everything else could be worked around. "As long as you still love me, we can figure out everything else. Do you want to go back to Chicago?"

"I haven't had time to think about it, but that's where the company my father spent his life building is. On the other hand, I've just found my brothers. I want to get to know them, to become part of their lives, but it's out of the question that they would want to move to Chicago. I'd certainly never ask it of them. I've loved being in Cactus Corner, but what would I do if I stayed here? You don't need me at the bank. Besides, it's *your* bank. I want you to run it by yourself."

Sibyl laughed. "If Norman knew I was running his bank, he'd rise from his grave. Seriously, we could run the bank together, but I can tell that you want your own business. You're used to being in control. It would be hard to work for a boss."

"I worked for my father until he died. It would be hard to find a more demanding boss than he was."

"Maybe, but he's dead and you've grown used to being in charge. I understand, but I feel the same way. I'd never want to go back to doing nothing more complicated than figuring out what to make for supper. Things have changed so suddenly you haven't had time to figure out what you want to do—but you will."

"There's one more thing, and it can't be *figured out*. I'm not the man everybody thinks. I'm not a brave hero who scoffs at danger. I knew I could be shot when I faced those bank robbers. I was certain I'd end up a mangled bunch of bones when I tried to stop the runaway horses, but I didn't care because I was going to die anyway. If it happened sooner than expected, I'd be spared a lot of suffering. I'm no braver than anyone else. I certainly can't compare to Colby."

Sibyl had already faced the possibility that Logan might want to return to Chicago, but she hadn't thought about how he would see himself, because he was a real hero to her.

"That's ridiculous. Are any of those stories you tell Peter true?"

"Yes, but—"

"No buts. You forget I went down the Santa Fe Trail, so I know how dangerous it is. You and your father did it dozens of times, facing Indians, bandits, and terrible storms. It takes lots of courage to do something like that."

"There were other men along. I didn't have to depend on myself."

"Did anyone take over your responsibilities for the safety of the group? Did you wait in your wagon until it was safe to come out?"

"Of course not! What kind of coward do you think I am?"

Sibyl reached across the table to take his hand. "I think you're the bravest man I've ever met. Okay, one of the *two* bravest men I've ever met. You might have thought a second or two longer before facing four gunmen, but you would have done it. And you'll never convince me you wouldn't have tried to stop the runaway horses, not with children playing in the street."

"I suppose I would have done those things, but I would have felt differently about it. People can't expect me to keep taking chances with my life. I have you and Kitty to think about. Just the idea of missing one minute of the rest of your life gives me cold chills."

Sibyl squeezed his hand. "As long as you feel like that, you have nothing to worry about."

Kitty and Trusty came in from outside. The dog went to his bowl of water and drank. "That woman is coming," Kitty told her mother.

Sibyl knew *that woman* referred to Bridgette Lowe. "Are you sure? She's never come this early before."

"If you don't believe me, ask Peter. He threw a stick at her when she walked by. She called him a name. It wasn't nice."

Sibyl stood and brought Logan to his feet. "She's all yours. I can't put up with her this early in the morning."

"I want you to go with me. I'm going to tell her that we're going to be married."

"You are?" Kitty asked. "Why didn't you tell me? I've been asking for ages."

"I'm sorry," Logan said to Kitty. "It would have been unforgivable of me to tell Bridgette before I told you. But I have to tell her before we tell anyone else. We were engaged to be married."

"Trusty doesn't like her."

Bridgette felt the same way about him. Watching them together was the only pleasure Sibyl found in her visits. Trusty would move to Logan's side and growl if Bridgette attempted to approach him. Bridgette disliked dogs in general, but particularly mutts like Trusty. She always said she couldn't understand why Sibyl allowed him in the house.

"We'll keep Trusty in the kitchen with us while we have breakfast. Maybe she'll be gone by the time we're done."

"You're really going to make me do this by myself, aren't you?" Logan asked.

"I'm glad she's not really related to you because I wouldn't want to dislike your kinfolks that much."

"Put your fingers in your ears," Logan warned. "If you can still hear her screaming, hum really loud."

Kitty giggled, and Sibyl tried not to smile. She was about to get everything she wanted. She could afford to be charitable.

Bridgette was surprised she didn't fall down in a screaming fit. She probably would have if she hadn't been sitting down. Logan couldn't be doing this. It was insane. If he married that woman, he would regret it for the rest of his life. She couldn't let him make such a fool of himself, but she had to control her anger. Logan had always been difficult to manage. Despite her beauty, he'd always been annoyingly indifferent to her attempts to influence him by cajolery, flattery, or flirting with other men. She'd learned from the first that pouting would send him straight out the door with a heartless request to let him know when she was in a better humor. It took all of her self-control to speak in a voice that sounded just shy of hysterical.

"Do you think you've had enough time to think this through properly? After all, you've only known her"—Bridgette couldn't bring herself to use Sibyl's name—"for a short time. And you've been very sick the whole time."

"I haven't been so sick that I couldn't tell I was falling in love with her. I've wanted to marry her for weeks. I didn't say anything because I thought I was dying, but now that I'm going to get well, there's no reason to hold back."

Why wasn't he dying? Why wasn't he already dead? James said he'd given him enough medicine to kill him several times over, yet here he was looking like he really was getting better. She had to find a way to get him to take his medicine again. "I'm glad the doctor thinks you're going to recover, but it might be dangerous to put too much faith in his opinion. After all, if he were a really good doctor, he wouldn't be in this place."

"I have faith in him."

"That's because he's telling you what you want to hear. Now that he knows you're rich, he might be hoping you'll take him back to Chicago and help him set up a practice."

"He'd never leave. He's related to half the people in this town."

She didn't know how these people could stand having brothers, sisters, aunts, cousins, nieces, and nephews around every corner. They always knew all the things about you that you hoped other people would never know. And no matter how beautiful you were, how rich your husband, or how high you rose in society, they still thought they were your equal. She'd always been thankful she didn't have any siblings. "I still think it's foolish to rely on his opinion. I think you ought to start taking your medicine again and go back to Chicago with me. Now that you're feeling better, I'm sure James can find a cure."

"For a long time the medicine didn't have much effect on me. After James changed it again, I had my worst attacks after taking a dose."

"James said he was trying different medicines. I'm sure he can find something that won't make you sick. Besides, now that you have a chance of getting well, you'll have to go back to Chicago. You won't want to sell your company now. And it was my uncle's work of a lifetime. He never considered letting it out of the family." She knew how much Logan revered his father. She hoped that would be enough to counterbalance this momentary lunacy.

"I don't know what I'm going to do about Chicago or the company. Now that I'm going to get well, I have to think through everything again, but I do know that I *am* going to marry Sibyl. And if we're lucky, we'll have a couple of children. That means I'll have to make a new will. You'll have to learn to live on your allowance. That's a very stylish dress you're wearing, but I doubt you have paid for it yet. You're a beautiful woman, Bridgette. I know a dozen men who'd be happy to marry you. Go back to Chicago, look around a bit, and then settle on one of them."

She wasn't going back to Chicago, and she wasn't going to settle for a husband who would give her an allowance when she ought to have a fortune of her own. She would not see the Lowe money go to support the spawn of *that woman*. She didn't know what she was going to do, but Elliot Lowe was going to his grave whether or not he went back to Chicago with her. One way or another, the Lowe fortune would be hers.

❧

"I hate to think of you going back to Chicago just after we've found each other," Jared said to Logan, "but there's no reason we can't visit Chicago or why you can't come here. They already have trains in the southern part of the Territory. As soon as trains reach Prescott it'll be easy to get to Chicago and back."

Logan could tell that despite Jared's words, he was not happy. Colby wasn't as diplomatic.

"I'm going to take advantage of my position as baby of the family to say I'll be mad as hell if you disappear after I spent most of my life hoping to find the two of

you. Every time I went to our parents' grave, I swore
to them I'd never stop looking. I'm ashamed to say
I *did* stop looking. I was so sure I would never find
either of you that I wouldn't listen to anything Jared
said. I was afraid to let myself believe. When you told
me you were my brother, my first thought was that
I wished I could tell our parents that we were finally
together again. I know this sounds a little gruesome,
but since everybody expected you to die and be buried
here, I was thinking about moving our parents' graves
here so we could all be together."

"That's not fair," Sibyl protested. "You're putting
unfair pressure on Logan."

But nobody attacked Naomi's husband and got off
scot-free. "I don't think wanting to have his family
close to him is unfair or unreasonable," she said.
"Colby is just telling Logan what's important to him."

"What about you?" Colby asked Sibyl. "Are you
willing to move to Chicago? All your family is here.
This is your home."

"I will go wherever Logan goes," Sibyl said. "His
home will be my home."

"What will you do about the bank?" Laurie asked.

"I haven't had time to think about that," Sibyl
confessed. "I've been so afraid Logan might not get
well I hadn't thought of what to do if he did. Besides,
I wasn't always in love with him."

"Nonsense," Naomi said. "You were in love with
him for weeks before you would admit it."

"I was in love with her even before that," Logan
confessed, "but I didn't think about the future, either."

"I don't see why anybody has to make any decisions right away," Laurie said. "Logan can go back to

Chicago and decide what he needs to do. Sibyl can go with him and see if she can be happy there."

"I'll be happy anywhere as long as I'm with Logan," Sibyl insisted.

"But would you be as happy with him in Chicago as you would with him in Cactus Corner?" Colby asked.

"No, but that's not the question."

"It ought to be," Naomi said. "You have family and friends here, people who love you, who've been part of your life since you were born. For goodness sakes, Sibyl, my father delivered you and Kitty."

"I know that, but—"

"I haven't finished," Naomi said. "Logan has no family in Chicago, but he has two brothers here. You worry about his business in Chicago, but you have a business here. The way I see it, you're giving up friends, family, and your business while Logan would be giving up only his business. That doesn't look like a fair exchange to me."

Logan had never intended to do anything that would cause friction between Sibyl and her family, but his saying that he might have to go back to Chicago had put the cat amongst the pigeons. Worse than that, he'd put Sibyl squarely in the middle. "Look," he said before anyone could say anything else, "I haven't made up my mind what I have to do."

"I think you have," Naomi said. "You just haven't said so."

"I agree," Laurie said. "And you've put Sibyl in the position of having no choice."

"I *do* have a choice," Sibyl declared. "I have a choice to love him or not love him. I chose love. I have a choice to marry him and follow him wherever

he goes, or not marry him and stay here. I've chosen
to follow him wherever he goes. That's not a choice
either of you had to make, so you don't know what
it's like. And if you tried for one minute, Naomi
Blaine, to tell me you wouldn't follow Colby if he
decided to move to Prescott or Tucson, I'd be forced
to say something very unkind about you."

"Of course I'd follow Colby wherever he went,"
Naomi said, "but I'd make him suffer for it."

Logan breathed a sigh of relief when everyone
laughed. Things had gotten entirely too heated.

"Everything he's ever worked for is in Chicago,"
Sibyl said. "I have Kitty to take care of, and I hope
to have more children. I'll miss the bank, and I'll miss
everybody here more than I could ever say. But if I
can be Logan's wife, and hopefully the mother of his
children, I'll count it worth the cost."

It appeared that Sibyl's cousins had said all they
were going to say, but he could tell Colby wasn't
through yet.

"Maybe I was a fool, but I never let myself believe
you would die," he said to Logan. "From that day
you told me you were my brother, I've been trying to
think of ways the three of us could work together."

"Did you come up with anything?"

"You could tell us more about your business.
Could you bring it to Arizona? That way you'd have
something to do, and Sibyl wouldn't be forced to lose
her job. I've even planned a couple of hunting trips.
We have so many years to make up for I thought we'd
need to have as much time as possible to be together.
If you go back to Chicago, we might as well give up
on being a family."

If Colby had been trying to make Logan feel like a rat, he'd succeeded.

"Colby is obsessed with family," Naomi explained. "For him, nothing is more important than that."

"It's important to Logan, too," Sibyl said, "but he's just found his family. He's got thirty years with another family to balance against that."

"Don't you dare tell me that he considers Bridgette Lowe's claim equal to that of Colby and Logan," Naomi said in a flash of temper. "Because if that's the way he feels, he ought to go back to Chicago."

"Even though I've known Bridgette my whole life, and I've just come to know Colby and Jared, I'd never think of her as family in the same way," Logan said. "What I decide to do will have nothing to do with her."

"If you do decide to go back to Chicago," Naomi said, "you've got to take her with you. She doesn't like us any better than we like her."

Logan was certain Bridgette would demand to leave with him. "I haven't decided what I'll do," he told everyone. "As I said, I never expected to be in a position to have to make this decision, but I wanted to talk with you, to find out how you felt. I feel like all of you are my family."

"Family is about more than blood," Colby said.

"I know that. I see it every day in this town."

Colby rose abruptly. "I'd better go. I've said more than enough already."

"I'd better go, too," Naomi said. "The children know something is up. I wouldn't be surprised to find Peter has been listening at the window."

"Don't leave yet," Jared said. "I have something I

want to say." He turned to Logan. "I understand some of how you feel. I had some of the same doubts when Steve and I decided to sell up and leave Texas. All I can tell you is that it was the best decision of my life. After asking Laurie to marry me, that is. I found a kind of happiness here that I would never have had if I'd stayed in Texas. I know Texas is nothing like Chicago, but it's the people who make the difference. You won't find any better than right here in Cactus Corner. Now I've said enough. What about you, Laurie?"

"I'll miss Sibyl terribly if she leaves. The three of us have been like sisters ever since we were born, but her happiness is what's important. If that means going to Chicago, then I think that's what she should do." Tears started to gather in her eyes. "That doesn't mean I won't think some mean things about Logan for taking her away, but it doesn't mean I won't think you did the right thing."

The two women embraced, both shedding a few tears.

"That is a lot harder than I expected," Logan said. "I feel like I'm tearing your family apart."

Sibyl put her arms around him. "It will put some distance between us, but it will never destroy the bonds we've built throughout our lives."

"I know, but can you be happy in Chicago?"

"I don't know anything about Chicago, but I will be happy anywhere as long as Kitty and I are with you."

Logan never doubted that Sibyl was the most wonderful woman in the world, but she'd just added another to the list of reasons why he couldn't envision living another moment of his life without her. He couldn't imagine why he'd ever considered marrying a woman like Bridgette when everything was always about what *she* wanted. All Sibyl asked was that he love her and that they spend the rest of their lives together.

But that's all Colby and Jared had asked. Could he balance that against the loyalty he felt toward his father's company? The answer came immediately and with undisputable clarity. His father's life might have been centered on the company, but his wasn't. What was the company anyway but an impersonal enterprise that didn't care whether he lived or died? To everyone in this room, his life was something precious they wanted to be a part of. In return, they wanted to share their lives with him. What could his company offer in comparison to that?

Nothing.

"I've made up my mind," he said. "I'm not going back to Chicago. This is where I belong. I've finally come home."

❧

Bridgette was so furious she could barely think. She'd already broken her mirror by throwing her water pitcher at it. She'd driven the landlord from her room by throwing the ewer at him. He hadn't come up when she'd thrown every shoe within reach, as well as a bottle of scent that was so strong it nearly overpowered her. Nothing was enough to assuage her fury.

Elliot had decided to stay in Cactus Corner.

He'd told her of his decision just like it was the most natural thing in the world. That was on top of telling her that he was going to change his will *again* and leave her nothing more than the miserable allowance Uncle Samuel had seen fit to give her. Even

worse, he was thinking about selling his company and
going into business with his brothers.

His brothers.

The very thought of strangers getting their hands
on money that should be hers nearly drove her to
the edge of madness. There wasn't a single person in
this miserable hellhole who was remotely related to
Samuel Lowe, but she was his niece, *his only living
relative*. Everything should have been left to her. Elliot
could have stayed in charge of the company. She'd
have seen that he got a good salary. But no, Uncle
Samuel had said Elliot was his *son* and that everything
would be left to him. Bridgette had been willing to
share with Elliot when he was going to marry her, but
now he deserved nothing. And his greedy relatives
deserved nothing as well. They pretended they didn't
want his money, but she knew better. No one who
could afford to leave this godforsaken spot would have
stayed if they'd had two coins to rub together.

What had to happen next was inevitable. Bridgette
felt a tiny twinge of regret, but she banished it as easily
as she would swat an annoying insect. Everything was
Elliot's fault. None of this would have happened if
he'd died like he was supposed to.

She'd have to take care of that.

&

When Bridgette saw so many strange men staring
at her with naked lust in their eyes, she knew she'd
come to the right place. When you wanted something
dangerous done, there was no better place to look for
someone to do it than among the men who'd been
dismissed from the army. They were used to danger,

had fewer morals than most, and were always in need of money. The only question was how to go about finding the right man.

She thought of approaching one of the women, but they had a tendency to be suspicious of other women, especially when they were beautiful and were where they weren't supposed to be. They also had an annoying habit of remembering the wrong details.

She decided to start by walking down the streets of Camp Verde. Thanks to her father being constantly in debt and always looking to make a buck by dubious means, she knew a great deal more about Chicago's underbelly than was usual for a woman of her position in society.

Her position in society! Just thinking about that made her angry. Chicago didn't even exist forty years ago. Her Uncle Samuel Lowe was practically a founding member of society, but thanks to her reprobate of a father, she wouldn't have had any position in that society if it hadn't been for her uncle and his money. Despite her beauty and her expensive clothes, she'd been subjected to snubs and slights. She'd only been welcomed into the upper reaches when her future engagement to Elliot Lowe became common knowledge. That was a position she was determined not to lose.

Thanks to some of the men who came to their house looking for her father, she knew enough to recognize the kind of man she wanted. She smiled to herself when a man who appeared to be that type approached her.

"Can I help you find something?" His words said one thing, but his eyes pored over her body.

"I'm looking for a man who wouldn't hesitate to cut your throat if the price was right."

The man's startled reaction told her he wasn't the man she wanted.

"What would a beautiful woman like you be wanting with a man like that?" He appeared to think she was teasing him or playing some kind of game. "I know half a dozen men who'd cut a throat just to be near you."

"Then give me the name of the man who'd cut the other five throats to have me to himself."

Apparently convinced she wasn't joking, the man drew back. "If murder's what you have in mind, the man you want is Wat Pfefferkorn. He'd slice his own mother for the price of a beer."

She gave him what she hoped was a reassuring smile. "I would never ask anyone to commit murder, but what I have in mind could possibly be very dangerous."

"If that's what you're after, there's lots of men who'd tackle danger for a woman who looks like you."

Bridgette couldn't understand why men were so stupid they never looked beyond a woman's face or her body. That made it easy to control them. "I'm sure you're right, but I want a man who would stop at nothing to defend me. Mr. Pfefferkorn sounds like that kind of man. Where might I find him?"

"Ask for him at Dyer's Saloon. But if you'll take my advice, you won't go near that place. Wat is the worst of the lot that hangs out there."

"What harm could come to me on the grounds of an army fort?"

"From the looks of you, more than you can guess."

"Don't make the mistake of judging a woman by her looks," Bridgette told him.

"Seems I just have," the man said and turned away.

His reaction annoyed Bridgette, but she wasn't about to let vanity get in her way. She had come here on a mission, and this clueless man had just delivered the weapon she needed into her hands.

❦

Sibyl was relieved she didn't have to feel bad about not inviting Bridgette to the gathering in her home that evening. The get-together was just for Logan's brothers, their wives, and their children. Cassie and her Pinkerton admirer were included because one never seemed able to exclude her from anything. The excuse for the gathering was to come up with ideas for a business the brothers could go into together, but the real reason was to celebrate Logan's decision to stay in Cactus Corner. If it had been possible for Sibyl to love Logan more than she already did, she'd have been out of her mind over him.

She was making one last check on the food laid out in the kitchen when Kitty asked, "What's in that bottle?"

"What bottle?" It seemed every inch of the counters and the table was covered with platters of meat, dishes of vegetables, plates waiting to be loaded up, and glasses waiting to be filled. How could she be expected to notice one little bottle?

"That one." Kitty pointed to a dark blue bottle that was almost hidden between the flour and sugar bins. "It's been there a long time."

It took Sibyl a moment before she remembered.

"It's the medicine Bridgette brought for Logan, but he had already stopped taking anything."

"Do you think she wants it back?"

"I'm sure she doesn't."

"Do you want me to throw it away?"

"If you want."

When Kitty reached for the bottle, Trusty jumped up from where he'd been lying under the table. He knew he wasn't allowed to touch anything on the table or counters, but anything in a person's hands was open for inspection. He pressed his nose to the bottle the minute Kitty lowered it from the counter.

"Stop it, Trusty. You don't need medicine. You're not sick."

Apparently Trusty didn't understand or didn't care because he nudged the bottle so hard Kitty dropped it. The stopper came out, and the dark brown liquid spilled onto the floor. Trusty managed to get his tongue into the liquid before Kitty shoved him aside.

"Bad dog!" Kitty scolded. "Look what you've done. Aren't you ashamed?"

Sibyl laughed. "I don't think it's possible to shame that dog. You hold him, and I'll clean up the spill."

"I'm going to take you outside," Kitty said to Trusty. "You don't deserve to be allowed inside."

Sibyl chuckled to herself as she poured the rest of the medicine down the drain and chucked the bottle into the waste bin. Kitty was almost more grown-up than her mother, but in a way that made her sad. Norman's treatment of the child had forced her to be mature beyond her years. Kitty came back as Sibyl was cleaning the last of the spill from the floor.

"Peter says he'll play with Trusty," she said with

a disapproving frown that had Sibyl chuckling again. "How is Trusty going to know he's being punished?"

"I don't think it matters. If Peter is here, that means the rest of his family is at the front door. Come on. We can't be caught in the kitchen."

With the arrival of her guests, Sibyl forgot all about Bridgette's medicine and thoroughly enjoyed herself. She listened to Naomi and Laurie talk about their children and watched the three brothers talking over ideas of what they might do together. It had already been decided that the two banks would be joined, but it appeared that Logan had to find ways to invest a lot more money.

"It looks like you're going from being the richest woman in Cactus Corner," Naomi said, "to the wife of the richest man west of the Mississippi. No wonder Bridgette is upset he's not going to marry her."

"A least no one can accuse me of marrying him for his money," Sibyl said.

"Not since you fell in love with him when everybody thought he was a drifter on his deathbed and his face was so swollen it looked like it could pop at any moment," Cassie told them.

Sibyl laughed. "He never looked that bad."

"Only in your eyes," Laurie said. "The rest of us thought you'd lost your mind." She looked to where Logan was standing with his brothers. "He's looking a lot better. His face doesn't look nearly as swollen. I think I can see the resemblance to Colby. What do you think?"

"I agree, but it wouldn't matter if nothing had changed. The rest of him is so beautiful I don't think about his face."

"Can't we talk about something else?" Logan asked.

"It feels like I've been the subject of every conversation in this town since I arrived."

"You have to admit you haven't exactly kept a low profile," Colby said. "Did you think *minor* events like stopping a bank robbery, throwing yourself at runaway horses, and beating me at shooting were going to go unnoticed?"

"I hadn't planned to do any of that," Logan pointed out.

Colby laughed. "I hadn't planned to rescue half of this town from an Indian attack, but I did, and look what happened."

Naomi elbowed her husband. "That was the luckiest day of your life."

"Have you forgotten about the arrow in my back?"

"If you even hint that you regret it, I'll do something so terrible you'll wish it was just an arrow."

Sibyl shook her head. After five years, it still amazed her that two people as deeply in love as Colby and Naomi should still battle like teenagers.

"Could you two cut it out?" Jared asked. "It's enough to make Logan want to go back to Chicago."

"Nothing could be that bad," Logan said.

"Wait until you've been here a couple of years. By the way, did you hear about the break-in at the lawyer's office?"

"I heard it this morning," Naomi said. "The lawyer was at my door before we finished breakfast."

"Does he know what was taken?"

"He said everything had been pulled out, and papers were strewn all over the office. It'll probably take him a couple of weeks before he can straighten things up enough to begin to figure out what was taken."

"No one has ever broken into an office in Cactus Corner," Colby said. "We'll have to contact the marshal. He's your friend, Jared, so it's up to you."

"He's over in Prescott right now, but I'll talk to him when he gets back."

"That'll be too late. I think we should—"

The door from the back parlor burst open, and Peter rushed in. "Something's wrong with Trusty. I think he's dead."

Nineteen

"HE'S BEEN POISONED," DR. KESSLING ANNOUNCED after a brief examination, "but I can't find any sign of a rattlesnake bite."

Everyone had crowded into the kitchen. In the wake of this tragedy, even the children had forgotten it was time to eat.

"A snake didn't bite him," Peter said. "I was there when Kitty brought him outside. We stayed in the yard the whole time."

"Could he have gotten hold of some rotten meat?"

"Not in my kitchen," Sibyl insisted, "and he hasn't been fed since this morning. I haven't given him anything but water since."

"He didn't lick up much of the medicine," Kitty said.

"What medicine?" the doctor asked.

"It was the medicine Bridgette brought for Logan," Sibyl said, "but he never took any of it. Kitty was going to throw it out, but Trusty knocked it out of her hands. The stopper came out, and he lapped up some before we could stop him."

"No medicine I know of could make a dog this sick," the doctor said, "or cause these symptoms.

This dog has been poisoned. I'd stake my reputation on it."

For a moment the room was in complete silence as the implication began to sink in.

"I have never liked the woman," Naomi said, "but why would she try to poison Logan? She said she was in love with him, that she wanted to marry him."

The Pinkerton agent spoke up. "If she brought the medicine herself, that means it was in her possession for a period of time."

"What are you trying to say?" Sibyl asked.

"He's trying to say Bridgette could have poisoned Logan," Cassie said. "That woman hates every one of us. She's determined to get Logan's money for herself."

"But she wouldn't poison him," Sibyl protested. "She's in love with him."

"Tell them what you found," Cassie said to the Pinkerton.

"Is this the information you tried to give me earlier?" Logan asked.

The Pinkerton nodded. "I always like to make sure the work I do doesn't have any unfortunate results," the agent began, "so I also investigate my clients. That's how I learned that Miss Lowe was seeing Doctor James Pittman on a regular basis. I also learned that Miss Lowe was asking through certain connections of her late father for information about a forger."

"She wouldn't need a forger," Logan said. "According to a codicil to my father's will, she would get everything if I died."

"Which you almost did," the agent pointed out.

"Are you saying you think the doctor was poisoning him?" Dr. Kessling asked.

"You're the one who insisted he was acting like he was poisoned," Naomi reminded her father.

"Yes, but by his own doctor?"

"Bridgette is a beautiful woman," Cassie said. "A face like hers has driven more than one man to commit murder."

"The lawyer's office," Logan said. "Now it all makes sense."

"What has the break-in got to do with Bridgette?" Sibyl asked.

"I'm certain the lawyer will find the only document missing is my new will. An expert forger would be able to make a new one."

"But if you were dead, she wouldn't need a new one," Sibyl pointed out.

"I didn't make a will before I left Chicago, and she didn't know about the codicil. I didn't understand it at the time, but I'm beginning to believe my uncle didn't trust her. In any case, she would have wanted a will that gave her unquestioned control of everything."

"I say we find out just what she's been doing," Colby said.

"What about Trusty?" Kitty asked. "Is he going to die?"

"I don't think so," the doctor told her. "He didn't swallow much, and he threw it up. He's tough."

"Come on," Colby said. "Sibyl said Bridgette told her she was leaving town soon."

Sibyl had wanted to come with them, but Logan had convinced her to stay with their guests. He was glad that he did because when they got to the hotel, the place was in an uproar.

"There was a lot of shouting in her room," the

manager told Logan. "When I went to see what was wrong, a man told me to go away, or he'd put a bullet between my eyes." The manager straightened himself. "I'm not a coward, but I didn't have a gun. I never liked that woman, but I didn't suspect her of keeping that kind of company. The man was Wat Pfefferkorn. He's as close to being a murderer as makes no difference."

"We'll go up and see what's going on," Colby said.

"I wouldn't recommend it, Mr. Colby, sir."

"There are three of us," Colby said.

"Why don't you and Jared stay down here?" Logan said to Colby. "There's no point in all three of us going, and I'm the one Bridgette apparently wants dead."

"You have brothers now," Colby said. "We're going with you."

"Is there a back door?" Jared asked the manager.

"Yes, but you have to come through the lobby to reach it."

"Then I'll stay here in case either of them tries to sneak out."

"Okay, let's go." Logan had always known Bridgette thought she should have inherited her uncle's money, but he couldn't believe she would go to the extreme of convincing his doctor to poison him to get it. Nor could he imagine why Dr. Pittman would take a chance on ruining a sterling career by poisoning one of his patients.

"I told Norman not to build a hotel with two floors," Colby said as they climbed the stairs. "We never had enough visitors to fill half the rooms."

"Does Sibyl own this hotel?"

"There's not much in Cactus Corner that isn't owned by someone in their family."

The carpet in the hall deadened their footsteps, so

the sound of Logan knocking on the door sounded like a small explosion of sound. "Bridgette, it's Logan. I've come to talk to you."

The only response was the muffled sound of footsteps and harsh whispers.

Colby elbowed Logan aside. "You might as well open the door. We're not going away until we talk to you."

The response was a pistol shot that splintered the door and narrowly missed Logan. Colby pushed his brother aside only to have two more pistol shots send bullets that buried themselves in his body.

Logan forgot all about Bridgette. The horrible realization that he'd gotten his brother killed nearly incapacitated him. Dropping to his knees, he ripped open Colby's shirt. One bullet had gone through his upper arm. The other had entered his chest.

Jared came racing up the stairs. "What happened?" he shouted even as he dropped to the floor beside Colby.

"Somebody shot at us through the door. Colby wouldn't have been hit if he hadn't pushed me aside to protect me."

"Colby's still breathing," Jared said, "but he's badly wounded. We've got to get him to the doctor as quickly as possible."

By now the manager had come up the stairs, and one of the lodgers had come out of his room.

"We need to get him to the doctor before he bleeds to death," Jared told them.

Getting Colby down the steps was awkward, but the pistol shots had brought people running. In seconds there were more than enough hands to carry Colby.

"What happened?"

"Who shot him?"

"Where are they? We ought to go after them."

Logan's only concern was doing everything possible to save Colby's life, but the hotel manager was more than happy to tell everything he knew. In moments a small posse had formed and was headed back to the hotel. Logan was worried that, even if Bridgette was innocent, she might never get a chance to prove it.

News travels faster than the speed of galloping hooves in a small town. Before they reached Sibyl's house, Naomi was running toward them. She lost color when she saw Colby, but she didn't lose her head.

"Take him to my father's house. It's only two doors away."

Naomi led them into the house and through to her father's office. The doctor was already laying out implements.

"Place him on the table," he directed as he reached for a pair of scissors. In no time, he'd cut away Colby's shirt. Logan could tell from the slight intake of breath that Colby was in great danger of dying.

"Naomi is going to help me," the doctor said. "The rest of you wait outside in case I need you." With that, the doctor gave his full attention to the patient. As far as he was concerned, they had already left.

The scene that met Logan's gaze when he entered the doctor's parlor was the most painful he'd ever seen. Sibyl was trying to comfort a hysterically crying Esther while Kitty stood glued to her mother's side. Naomi's brother, Ethan, was holding his nephew Jonathan. Cassie was trying to comfort Annabelle, who was too young to understand what was going on. The Pinkerton had been delegated to take care of Little Abe. Laurie was fully occupied with her small son and the baby. Ben, Naomi's young brother, had been trying to reassure Peter, but the boy rushed toward Logan when he came into the room, his face ashen, tears having streaked his cheeks, as he struggled not to cry.

"My papa isn't dead." He said it like saying it would make it true. "I know he isn't dead."

Logan knelt down and put his arms around the stiff, trembling body. "He's not dead, but he's very sick right now. Your mama and grandpapa are going to do everything they can to make him better."

"He didn't die in the war, and he didn't die when the Indians shot him," Peter said. "Mama said now that we live in Cactus Corner, nobody was going to shoot at him ever again. Why did that man do it?"

"I don't know, but as soon as we know your papa is going to be okay, I promise I'm going to find out. Nobody is going to shoot my brother and get away with it."

Jared had gone to his wife's side. Jere left his Uncle Steve and climbed into his father's lap. Steve got up and came over to Logan.

"When you go after that man, I'm going with you."

"Thanks, but this is something I have to do alone. I brought this tragedy on this family, so I have to be the one to find the man who did it."

"Are you sure it was a man? No one saw who fired the shots. It could have been that Bridgette woman."

"When the manager went to see why people were shouting in Bridgette's room, he said Wat Pfefferkorn threatened to shoot him. The man has a very bad reputation. I know Bridgette hasn't been nice to people here, but this doesn't sound like her."

"Sibyl says she tried to poison you."

"The doctor said he thought that's what happened to Trusty, but there's no way to know until I talk to Bridgette."

"I don't like her," Peter said. "She said I was a filthy little boy, and that my papa was nothing but a money-grubber."

"I'm sorry she said those things."

"Papa said I wasn't to pay any attention to her, that some people weren't nice." The boy started to cry. "If she killed my papa, I'm going to take his rifle and shoot her."

"You're much too nice a boy to do anything like that."

"No, I'm not. Great-Aunt Mae says I'm a young hooligan. She says hooligans always end up no good."

Logan felt a wave of tenderness for the little boy's attempt to be brave and proud. He knew the child worshipped his father. For Peter's sake, if no other, he prayed the doctor could find a way to save Colby.

Time passed with agonizing slowness. Each second seemed to grow into a minute, each minute into an hour. People came to the house in a steady stream, but Steve attempted to turn them away saying they didn't know anything yet. Mae Oliver and Elsa Drummond used their kinship to Naomi to overrule the boy and took their places inside next to Sibyl and Laurie. At first the others went back home, but after a while some started to stay. They sat on the porch, stood in the yard, or gathered in the street. Before long, it seemed half the town had gathered outside the doctor's house.

When Mae took Esther into her lap, Sibyl came over to stand with Logan and Peter. "That's a testament to how the town feels about Colby," she told Logan. "Your brother is the most admired and respected man in town."

"And I may have gotten him killed."

"You didn't shoot him."

"If he hadn't gone with me, he wouldn't have been shot."

"From the moment we met Colby on the Santa Fe Trail, he has always been the first one to face danger. You wouldn't have been able to make him stay behind. It simply isn't something he could do."

"Bridgette is in Cactus Corner because of me. That man was in that room because of Bridgette. It's my fault that he was shot."

"If it's anybody's fault, it's Bridgette's. Now stop trying to blame yourself and think of what you're going to do about it."

"I'm going after that man."

"Mae says both of them have left town. Several men followed them, but they were shot at. One of the men was wounded. They said they'd try again in the morning."

Logan had been so focused on comforting Peter and listening for the slightest sound from the doctor's office that he hadn't realized the sun had gone down. "Was the man badly wounded?"

"It's not fatal, but it is serious."

"Why didn't someone bring him to the doctor?"

"No one will interrupt the doctor as long as he's with Colby."

So the vigil went on. But as it did, changes started

to occur. Laurie and Jared took their two children and Naomi's two youngest and left for Naomi's house. Jared said he would come back after they'd fed the children and put them to bed. Women from the town invaded the doctor's kitchen, and soon the aromas of food wafted into the parlor. The children didn't want to leave the room, but they were hungry and were soon persuaded to go to the kitchen. In twos and threes the adults left to eat before returning. When Logan refused to leave, Sibyl brought him a bowl of soup.

Esther and Little Abe fell asleep, but Peter remained wide awake. Kitty left her mother, came to sit next to Peter and took his hand. Three more hours passed before the doctor entered the parlor. He looked absolutely exhausted. He hadn't taken the time to change from his blood-smeared clothes.

"I've removed the bullets from Colby. One caused a loss of blood, but it wasn't serious. The other bullet, however, entered his lung. I was able to remove it and close the lung, but I don't know if it will be enough. Naomi will stay with him through the night. I'll sit with her. If he lives through the night, he's got a chance. Everybody should go home and pray."

Peter started to cry. "I want to stay."

"You need to sleep," Logan told him.

He rubbed his eyes. "I'm not sleepy."

"Well, I am. I want to be up early to see your father when he wakes up."

Peter looked toward the doctor's office. "Why can't I stay with Papa?"

"Your mother and grandfather are taking good care of your father. Maybe you can sit with him tomorrow while they take a nap."

That didn't make Peter any happier, but he was so sleepy he could hardly keep his head up.

"Let me take you home."

"I want to go with you," Peter said.

"I'm sure your Aunt Laurie has your bed all ready."

"I want to go with you," Peter repeated.

Logan had no idea how he'd come to be a substitute for Peter's parents, but apparently he had. "Come on, then. We'll check on Trusty then go to bed."

Sibyl was still up when Logan and Peter reached the house. "Is there any news about Colby?"

"No. The best news is that he's still alive."

"What's Peter doing here? Why isn't he in bed? Laurie must be worried about him."

"He insisted on coming with me," Logan explained. "I stopped by his house on the way and told Jared he was with me. I'll put him in the room next to me. How is Trusty doing?"

"He's fine. You'd never guess he was poisoned just hours ago. He wasn't happy when I wouldn't let him out to find you, so I closed him in your room."

"Go to bed. There's nothing more any of us can do tonight."

Sibyl gave Logan a quick kiss. "I hope you intend to take your own advice as soon as I put Peter to bed."

"I can put myself to bed," Peter announced. "I'm not a baby like Jonathan."

"Of course you aren't," Sibyl assured him. "You're the man of the family until your father gets well."

Peter teared up. "Why did that man shoot Papa? Mama said everybody likes him."

"Wat Pfefferkorn isn't a nice man," Sibyl said.

"Now go to bed. You'll want to see your father in the morning."

Logan barely got Peter undressed before the boy had fallen asleep. In complete repose, he looked younger than his nine years, more like an angel than the terror of the neighborhood. Logan could see a young version of Colby in his son. The restless energy, the complete confidence in himself, the willingness to tackle any challenge without hesitation, the passion with which he faced life were so much like his father. Logan wished he could have known Colby when he was growing up. From what Sibyl had told him, Colby hadn't had an easy time. Logan hoped Colby would have many decades ahead of him to make up for that rough beginning.

~⁂~

Dawn had yet to break when Logan stepped out of the house. He'd taken great care not to wake anyone except Trusty. They had a job to do. Apparently he hadn't been as quiet as he thought because Sibyl came into the kitchen just as he was trying to ease the back door open.

"I knew you'd try to go after Bridgette and Wat by yourself," she said. "Why can't you wait? There're at least a half-dozen men in town who'd be willing to go with you."

"All this trouble is because of me. Trusty wouldn't have been poisoned and Bridgette wouldn't have teamed up with Wat if it hadn't been for me. Colby wouldn't be fighting for his life if he hadn't pushed me out of the line of fire. I can't be responsible for anyone else getting hurt. I *have* to do this by myself."

"I understand, but that doesn't mean I have to like

it or agree with it. They've gone away so maybe that means she's given up and won't come back."

"Bridgette persuaded my doctor to poison me. When that didn't work, she tried to poison me herself. When *that* didn't work, she hired a dangerous killer to steal my will so she could forge a new one after I was dead. Does that sound like she's giving up?"

Sibyl leaned against Logan and wrapped her arms around him. "You could give her the money. I have enough for both of us."

"I think it's too late for that. She's gone too far to stop now."

"Is there anything I can say to change your mind?"

"There are a lot of things you could say, but I hope you won't say any of them. This is something I have to do."

"I was sure you'd say that, but I had to try. You will be careful, won't you?"

Logan folded Sibyl into his embrace. "I've fallen in love for the first time in my life. I have a *real* family for the first time in my life. I promise I'm coming back to you and Kitty. I'm a Holstock. We don't go back on our promises."

Sibyl stood on tiptoes so she could kiss him. "I'll have a lot more of these waiting for you when you get back."

Logan kissed her back. "And I'll have a lot more of these for you. Now I have to go. It'll be light soon."

Yet he couldn't resist one last kiss before he left.

The hotel was dark when he arrived, but the front door was unlocked. There was no one to tell him not to go to Bridgette's room. He managed to get up the stairs without stumbling in the dark. The door to

Bridgette's room was unlocked so he entered. Trusty growled softly.

"I thought that's how you'd feel about scenting the man who treated you so badly. I'm counting on you to help me find him."

It was difficult to tell in the dark, but it looked as though Bridgette hadn't taken anything when she left with Wat. Logan wondered whether she'd been forced or had gone willingly. She'd become such a different person he didn't really know what she might do. He had Trusty sniff several of her garments. "You have to find her," he told the dog. Trusty seemed more distracted by the scent of his former owner, but Logan figured it didn't matter. If he found one, he'd find the other.

Outside again, he mounted up. "Okay, Trusty, find the scent." Trusty was only part bloodhound, but Logan hoped his nose would be keen enough to follow Bridgette's trail. The dog sniffed round the entrance to the hotel for so long Logan was afraid he wasn't going to be able to find a scent to follow. Without Trusty, he would have to go to Camp Verde and hope someone there had seen Wat and Bridgette. "Hurry up, boy. I want to be gone before people start to wake up." It wasn't long before Trusty growled and started running toward the west. With a sigh of relief, Logan followed.

Logan had spent many years traveling the Santa Fe Trail, but he'd never really paid attention to the landscape in the morning. He thought he knew what it was like, but sunrise in the Verde River Valley was completely different.

In the dead quiet before dawn, he could hear the

murmur of the river as it flowed slowly over rocks or around the roots of the massive cottonwoods that lined its shores. Their thick canopy formed great black blotches against the lightening sky. Three white-tailed deer, a buck and two does, had come down to the river to drink. Apparently hearing his horse's hoofbeats, the buck raised his head, water dripping from his muzzle. He stood silent for a moment before turning and bounding away. The does followed quickly. A moment later a cougar emerged from the trees farther down and came to the river to drink. He paused when he caught sight of Logan. Trusty had been uninterested in the deer, but he took a strong exception to the mountain lion. Barking furiously, he started toward the cat.

"Get back here," Logan called. "That cat can tear you to pieces."

Trusty stopped in his tracks, but he kept barking. The cougar bared its teeth before melting back into a thick stand of cottonwoods, sycamore, black walnut, box elder, and willows.

"Keep your mind on your business," Logan told Trusty.

The sky gradually turned from a deep gray to dusty blue to a pale backdrop for the red-gold sphere of the sun as it rose over the surrounding mountains, turning the river into an ever-changing ribbon of shimmering silver and burnished gold. Morning mist rose from the surface of the water, spiraling upward in crazy patterns affected by the cool air drifting down from the Rim above. Birds awoke, filling the air with their chatter as they fluttered among the bulrushes lining the shore. A lone bald eagle's gaze followed them as they wended their way along the riverbank. In one spot, Logan saw the sharp-edged footprints of javelinas that had come down to the river to drink.

The river truly was the ribbon of life for the valley. Everything in nature revolved around it.

A deep-throated growl from Trusty caught Logan's attention. "What did you find?"

It was a battered hat. Logan didn't know why it lay alongside the trail, but Trusty's actions told him it belonged to Pfefferkorn. Did that mean Bridgette had struggled with Wat? Logan couldn't imagine her going willingly with such a man.

"Let's keep moving," he said to Trusty. "We're getting close to Camp Verde."

Logan wasn't sure whether that was good or bad. If there was to be any shooting—and from what he knew of Wat Pfefferkorn there *would* be shooting—it would be better not to endanger innocent bystanders. On the other hand, it was possible the army would be willing to help find Bridgette. Out here, the abduction of a woman was just about the most serious crime a man could commit. They must be getting close because the hair on Trusty's back was standing so upright he looked like a porcupine.

They had reached the outskirts of town when Trusty drew his attention to a small cabin-like structure standing back in a dense stand of sycamore and black walnut. From the dog's action, Wat was either inside or had been recently.

"You've done your job," he told the dog. "Now stay here and let me do mine."

The first thing would be to search the area around the cabin for signs that Wat and Bridgette were inside. Once he knew that, he'd decide what to do next. He dismounted, but hadn't gone more than a dozen feet when he heard the sound of an approaching horse. "Damn!" he muttered. "I'd hoped to get this done before anybody from town caught up with me."

His annoyance turned to blood-chilling horror when he saw Peter approaching on his father's gigantic Appaloosa. He didn't feel any better when he saw Peter was carrying his father's rifle. Running toward the child, Logan demanded, "What are you doing here?"

"I've come after the man who shot Papa," Peter explained. "I'm going to shoot him."

A dozen questions crowded each other in Logan's mind. "Why aren't you still asleep?"

"I heard you get up," Peter told him. "I knew you were going after the bad man."

"But the horse? The rifle? How did you get away without anyone seeing you?"

"I was very quiet," Peter said.

Logan was in a quandary. He had to take Peter home, but he didn't want to lose track of Wat. He would have to go to the fort and report what he was doing to the commander and hope he could capture Pfefferkorn before any of the men from Cactus Corner could arrive and risk their lives.

"I have to take you back," Logan said to Peter.

"No!" Peter shouted. "I want to shoot the man who shot Papa."

"I'm sorry, Peter, but you can't—"

Logan didn't get a chance to finish before Peter turned his horse in the direction of the cabin and started toward it. Logan shouted for him to stop as he ran over to his own horse and mounted up. Instead of stopping, Peter whipped the big Appaloosa into a gallop. By the time Logan got into the saddle and got his horse headed toward the cabin, Peter was almost there. Logan experienced fear like he'd never known when Wat Pfefferkorn suddenly burst from the door of the cabin, ran toward Peter, dragged the struggling boy off the horse, and ran back inside the house so fast there was nothing Logan could do to stop it.

The man now had a hostage Logan would have given his life to protect. He had to rescue the boy, but how?

A bullet whistled by Logan's head. Ducking low in the saddle, he turned his horse into the trees and dismounted. He had to get close to the house. That shouldn't be too hard to do because the trees provided good cover, but he didn't know what he could do after that. Being inside the house with two hostages, Wat had the advantage.

Trusty had followed Logan. As they got closer to the cabin, he could hear raised voices. He recognized Bridgette's voice, but he couldn't tell what she was saying. Peter was shouting, too. Logan was petrified of what might happen to the boy, but he had to give the child credit. He wasn't intimidated by Wat Pfefferkorn.

Trusty continued to growl, the hair on his back still standing.

"I wish you could talk and shoot a gun," Logan said to the dog. "I feel at a disadvantage out here."

"You out there."

Pfefferkorn was shouting at him from inside the cabin.

"I don't want to hurt this kid," he told Logan, "but Bridgette and I have to get away."

"Don't listen to him," Bridgette shouted. "I didn't want to come with him."

Logan heard what sounded like someone being hit.

After a moment, Wat shouted again. "We're coming out, and we're taking the boy with us. If you make any attempt to stop us, the boy dies. Once we're far enough away that I think we're safe, I'll let the boy go."

Logan didn't trust Wat's word any more than he would trust a cougar not to attack a deer, but his best chance for getting Peter and Bridgette away safely was to get Wat out of the cabin. As long as he was inside, he was basically invulnerable.

"Come on out," he called to Wat.

"We're not leaving until you come out where I can see you and you throw down your gun."

"The man isn't as stupid as I thought," Logan said to Trusty. "You're going to have to help me out here. I don't think he's seen you, so stay in the woods. When I call you, go straight for Wat. If we're lucky, that'll give me time to reach for my gun. If we're not…well, I don't want to think about that."

"I'm not going to wait much longer," Wat shouted.

"I'm coming out," Logan called back.

Walking slowly with his hands out from his sides, Logan emerged from the woods. "I left my rifle with my horse." He reached down, pulled his gun from its holster, and tossed it on the ground. "Now it's time to keep your part of the bargain. Just know that if you hurt that boy, you won't be safe anywhere in the world because I'll follow you until one of us is dead."

Wat didn't respond. It seemed to Logan that he'd waited a long time before the door opened. A moment later, Wat and Peter emerged with Wat holding a gun to Peter's head.

The boy struggled, but he was too small, and Wat was too big and powerful. "My father will kill you when he gets well," Peter hollered.

The Bridgette Lowe that emerged from the cabin was unlike the woman Logan remembered. Her hair was in complete disarray. The part of it hanging over her face only partly covered a cheek that was swollen and red. What had once been a beautiful dress was soiled in places and had suffered several tears. It was clear even from a distance that she was extremely angry. She attempted to pull Peter from Wat's grasp, but he shoved her aside without once taking his eyes off Logan.

"Get the horses," he ordered.

"I'm not leaving here on a horse," Bridgette shouted. "Look at me! This is what your horse did. You can let that wretched child go and find me a respectable carriage. There's got to be at least one in this miserable corner of the world."

"Get the horses," Wat growled. "You can get your damned carriage once we get away safely."

"If you hadn't been stupid enough to shoot through that door, you wouldn't have to worry about *getting away safely*. I only wanted you to steal a will, not shoot the best-liked man in town."

"Stop arguing and get the horses," Wat shouted.

"I didn't shoot anybody so I don't have to run away. I won't get myself hanged because you murdered a child who didn't have enough sense to stay in bed."

"I'm not going to shoot the boy. I'm just using him as a hostage until I get away."

"You're a liar, and a stupid one at that. I was dumb

to think you could do something as simple as break into a lawyer's office without messing it up. I was told you were the most dangerous man in town. You're not dangerous. You're just too stupid to know what not to do."

Logan wanted to shout to Bridgette to be quiet, that it was dangerous to goad a man like Wat when he was in trouble.

"Shut up and get the horses!" Wat shouted again.

Bridgette glared at him. "What are you going to do if don't?" She laughed at him. "Nothing. That's what I thought. You're a pathetic excuse for a man. In Chicago we have more dangerous men than you sweeping the streets. Do women actually like to be with you, or do you have to kidnap them like you did me?"

Logan had been worried what Wat would do, but he was still caught by surprise when the man simply turned his gun on Bridgette and shot her. Logan felt a flash of concern, but he put that aside to focus on what had to be done.

"Trusty, now!" he shouted.

Twenty

WITH A HEART-STOPPING GROWL, TRUSTY EXPLODED from the trees. Wat was already off balance from shooting Bridgette, but he was thrown further off when he whirled to see Trusty coming at him with fangs bared. The moment Wat turned to shoot Bridgette, Logan had dived for his gun. Wat fired once at Logan and missed. Rolling away from Wat, Logan came to his knees. Just as he drew his gun into firing position, Trusty flung himself at Wat and sank his teeth into the man's thigh. Before Wat could take aim at the dog, Logan shot him in the center of his forehead.

Wat sank to the ground dead.

Logan ran to where Bridgette lay on the ground. He felt for a pulse, found it, but it was very weak. "I'm going to get you to a doctor," he told her.

Bridgette pushed him away. "I hate you," she said. "I've hated you from the day Uncle Samuel brought you to Chicago until this very moment. You ruined my life."

"There's a doctor at the fort. It won't take long to get you there."

Bridgette coughed up blood. "Why couldn't you

die like you were supposed to? James said he gave you enough poison to kill a horse."

"You can talk about all of this later."

"There isn't going to be any *later*." Bridgette coughed up more blood. "Get me inside. I don't want to die lying on the ground."

Logan picked her up and started toward the cabin. "Are you hurt?" he asked Peter.

"No, but these ropes hurt."

"I'll take them off as soon as I've made Bridgette comfortable."

"She didn't want him to hurt me," Peter said. "She wanted him to leave me behind."

Logan thought that might have been the only kind thing Bridgette had done since she left Chicago. "Leave the man alone," Logan told Trusty, who was worrying Wat's clothing. "He can't do anything to hurt anybody ever again."

By the time Logan got Bridgette inside the building and on a bed, her eyes had closed. From the position of the bullet hole in her dress, she'd been shot in virtually the same spot as Colby. "I want you to stay here with Bridgette," Logan said to Peter as he untied him. "I'm going to the camp to look for a doctor. I'll leave Trusty with you."

He'd just untied the last rope when Bridgette had a paroxysm of coughing. Blood ran from both corners of her mouth. Once the coughing stopped, she took a deep breath, her body shuddered, and she died.

Thoughts and regrets chased each other around in his head as he stared at the body of the woman he once planned to marry. She'd destroyed her own life. She had beauty, wealth, social prominence—far more of all three than ninety-nine percent of the women in the world—and she couldn't be satisfied. She'd let greed, jealousy, and hate destroy what could have been a nearly perfect life. She'd learned nothing from the mistakes of her father or the sterling example of her uncle.

Yet Logan felt sorry for her. She'd never found the kind of love he had found with Sibyl. She'd never had the opportunity to realize that there were many things much more important than money and social position, that one didn't have to live in a bustling city like Chicago to find meaning in life. She'd never had the opportunity to work hard for something worthwhile and be able to feast on her success. She'd spent her life chasing an illusion.

"Is she dead?" Peter asked.

"Yes."

The child stared at Bridgette's body. "She wasn't nice."

"No," Logan agreed, "she wasn't nice, but she was very unhappy."

"I'm unhappy that Papa won't let me have my own horse, but I don't call people names."

That wasn't exactly how Logan would have expressed it, but Peter was nine. The sound of approaching horses caught Logan's attention. When he went to the door, he saw a group of men from Cactus Corner gathered around Wat's body.

Morely Sumner looked up when Logan and Peter emerged from the cabin.

"I'm sure glad you found that boy," he said. "The whole town was in an uproar when they found he was missing. Some people thought you'd taken him with you, but Jared told them not to be idiots."

"How's Colby?" Logan asked.

"No change when we left," Reece Hill said. "We didn't tell Naomi about Peter." He walked up to the boy. "What were you doing?"

Peter pointed to Wat. "I wanted to shoot that man."

"Jared almost had a heart attack when he found the boy had taken Colby's favorite horse and his rifle. He'd be here now if we hadn't forced him to stay in case something happened to Colby."

"Where's that woman?" Morely asked.

"She's inside the cabin," Logan said.

"She's dead," Peter said. "The bad man shot her."

Both men turned to Logan. "I'm sorry for you," Reece said, "but I can't say I'm sorry she's dead."

"We need to get the bodies to the fort," Logan said. He would decide later what to do about Bridgette. Right now he wanted to get Peter back to town and find out how Colby was doing.

&

"She won't leave him," Sibyl told Logan. "We've all tried to get her to rest, but she won't listen to anybody."

"How about the doctor?" Colby asked.

"He won't leave, either. He says he can't do anything useful in bed."

Peter was safely home and asleep in his room. Laurie had given him a severe dressing down for scaring them all to death, but she'd ruined it by hugging him and shedding enough tears over him to soak his shirt. Kitty, acting at least fifteen years older than her age, told Peter that he was an annoying boy and that he would have to change before any woman would consider marrying him.

Sibyl kept touching Logan—holding his hand, putting her arm around him, leaning against him—as though constant contact would keep him safe and at her side. Logan seemed equally in need of reassurance that they wouldn't be parted again.

They had left Wat Pfefferkorn's body at Camp Verde, but Logan had insisted that they let him bring Bridgette's body back to Cactus Corner, as there was no way he could get her back to Chicago for burial. She would be buried the next day. They still had to answer questions when the marshal arrived, but Jared had assured him there wouldn't be a problem.

The town was still keeping a vigil for Colby, but life had to go on so most people went about their business, stopping from time to time to ask if there was any news and wanting to be told the minute there was. Sibyl had stayed home, but Cassie and Horace had opened the bank. Because of the impending merger, Ethan Kessling had moved his office from the Community Bank to Spencer's Bank. The Pinkerton agent, Dan Giles, had stopped in to say he was looking to buy a house. Since he'd been paying very conspicuous attention to Cassie, Sibyl had suggested he look into buying the house Cassie was renting. That would keep Cassie from having to move after the wedding.

"I'm sorry about Bridgette," Sibyl said to Logan. "I couldn't like her, and I'll never forgive her for trying to poison you, but I wouldn't have wished her to die the way she did."

Logan didn't tell her about Bridgette's last words to him. There didn't seem to be any point.

"I don't know what Naomi and Colby are going to

do when they find out what Peter did. I know that boy worships his father, but that was a crazy thing to do."

Logan agreed, but he could see himself having done something like that for his father. At that age, a child has no real understanding of death. "He is a brave little boy," Logan said. "Even after Wat had tied him up, he was threatening the man."

"If we have a boy like that, I'm sending him to live with Naomi. I wouldn't know what to do with him."

"Yes, you would. You'd love him as much as Naomi and Colby love Peter."

Sibyl laughed. "I wouldn't be the least bit surprised if he did something like what Peter did. That's because he'd be the son of a man who's selflessly brave without even realizing the significance of what he's done. It's the wife and mother who'd be quaking with fear."

"I've never seen you quake with fear, not even during the bank robbery."

"I quaked on the inside," Sibyl told him. "I wasn't about to let those men think I was afraid of them."

"Should I start worrying about our daughters taking after their mother?" Logan asked with a grin.

"Let's hope there's no need for either of us to do anything like that ever again. I wouldn't mind growing old quietly."

Logan kissed her. "Just as long as we do it together."

They spent the rest of the morning waiting for some news about Colby's condition. By the end of the day, there still had been no change. Sibyl had been able to convince Naomi to lie down for a bit, but she only agreed when they brought a cot so she could sleep next to Colby. Sibyl fed all the children, and Laurie put them to bed.

The next morning, the doctor told them Colby was still in a coma. There was no knowing when or if he would come out of it. Logan left everyone, becoming more and more despondent, to take care of Bridgette's funeral.

No one was in attendance except Logan, the preacher, and the men hired to move the casket. The service was brief, the remarks at the cemetery even shorter. Logan stayed while the grave was being filled in. When he turned away, he was stunned to see Dr. James Pittman walking toward him.

Many emotions flowed through him, but the primary one was rage. It was all he could do not to attack the man. "What are you doing here?" he demanded. "If you've come to see Bridgette, you're too late."

"So I was told." He looked to where the men were shoveling the dirt into the grave. "Thank you for giving her a decent burial. Would you tell me what happened to her?"

"Why should I?"

"Because I loved her. If I had loved her better, maybe I could have found a way to keep her from destroying herself."

Logan would never forgive the man, but having found love himself, he could understand what a powerful force that could be. "I doubt anyone could have helped Bridgette. Not even the man she loved."

"I know now she didn't love me, at least not the way I loved her," James said, "but I was so sure she did that I was willing to sell my soul. Looking back now, I don't know how I ever justified trying to poison you. I told Bridgette we didn't need your money. I could make enough to support us in any style she wanted. I made the first doses weak, hoping she'd have a change of heart when she saw what was happening to you."

"Then why did you give her the poison she used to try to kill me?"

"I didn't give her any more medicine or any poison. Before she left Chicago, I told her I was through."

"Then were did she get the poison? She said she had the medicine you had sent for me."

"I don't know, but she didn't get it from me. I've given up my practice and left Chicago for good."

"What are you going to do?"

"I was going to try to talk Bridgette into coming back to Chicago. Even knowing she didn't love me, I would have still married her. Now I have to find a way to restore my soul. I not only failed Bridgette and myself, I violated my Hippocratic oath."

"What do you have in mind?"

"I don't know where to start. It's possible none of that matters. You could turn me in to the police, and I could spend the rest of my life in jail."

"I could," Logan said, "but if you'd like to absolve yourself in my eyes, find a western town or community without a doctor. Go there, set up your practice, charge as little as you can, and do your damnedest to make sure every person lives a long and healthy life."

"I've given up medicine."

"Then take it up again. If you're half as good as everybody says you are, that's the best thing you can do with your life."

"You don't want to see me pay for what I did?"

"That wouldn't change anything, and it would deprive

some community of an excellent doctor. We can ask Colby. He knows—" Logan shook his head in disgust. "I'm a fool. The best doctor in Chicago is standing right in front of me, and I didn't think to tell him I have a brother who may die from a bullet wound. If you can do anything to save him, I'll forgive you anything you want."

"I'll see what I can do."

Naomi wasn't happy to have a second doctor introduced into the room regardless of his reputation, but her father told her not to be a fool. All that was important was saving Colby's life. Two heads were better than one, especially when the second head was much younger than his. Logan listened while the two doctors consulted.

"I know you said he's a famous doctor," Naomi said to Logan, "but who is he and what's he doing in Cactus Corner?"

"He was in love with Bridgette. He came hoping to convince her to return to Chicago and marry him."

"I thought you said he was brilliant."

"He is, but love can make anyone blind. Besides, Bridgette was a beautiful woman."

"Only a man could think so. What are you going to do?" Naomi asked the doctor.

"Nothing different," James said. "Your father has given your husband the best possible care. I've offered to sit with him while he gets some rest."

"You need some rest, too," Logan said to Naomi. "Why don't I sit with Dr. Pittman while you lie down."

"I don't want to leave Colby. I want to be here when he wakes up." She was choked by a sob. "He *will* wake up."

"And you won't make him feel any better looking

like something the cat dragged in," her father said. "You look terrible. Get some rest. I'll give you something to help you sleep."

After a while, her father convinced Naomi to go to a real bed and try to get some rest. "You'll call me at once if there's any change," the doctor said to Dr. Pittman.

"Absolutely," James said. "The first faces he'll want to see will be yours and his wife's."

The morning and afternoon passed slowly. Sibyl brought them some lunch and stayed to talk briefly. Peter haunted the house, begging to be allowed to see his father, even though he had been assured he'd be told the minute Colby woke. Jared and Laurie stuck their heads in, but Cassie insisted upon coming in and getting a good look at Colby for herself. "I wouldn't be alive if it wasn't for him," she said. "You've got to make him well."

Supper time passed, the children were all sent home to bed, and the house was so quiet Logan thought he could hear his own breathing. When James suddenly became alert, he realized it was Colby he heard. His first thought was that it was a death rattle.

"I think he may be regaining consciousness," James said. "You'd better get his wife and the doctor."

"Are you sure?" He didn't want to build Naomi's hopes only to have them dashed.

"You can never be sure in situations like this, but they'll want to be here either way."

Logan woke the doctor first, then Naomi.

"What's happened?" she asked, her eyes filled with fear.

"I don't know, but James wanted me to call you."

Naomi dashed past Logan and ran down the stairs. When Logan reached the doctor's office, all three of them were gathered around Colby's bed. Logan reached the bedside just in time to see Colby open his eyes.

"What's everybody staring at?" he asked. "Have I been sick?"

With a body-racking sob, Naomi fell back onto the cot next to Colby's bed. Dr. Kessling seemed incapable of speech, and Logan was too choked up to talk.

"You were shot," Dr. Pittman told him. "You've been unconscious for close to three days."

It seemed Colby hadn't realized until now that he was on a bed in the doctor's office. "I guess that's why I'm trussed up like a papoose. Did somebody get the bastard who shot me?"

"Yes. I believe it was Elliot who got him."

"Who the hell is Elliot?"

"I'm Elliot," Logan managed to say. "Or at least I was."

"Nobody's making much sense," Colby said. "Maybe I'd better go back to sleep and wake up again. Naomi, are you crying? Now I know something's wrong. Naomi never cries."

"You nearly died, you idiot," his loving wife told him. "I'm crying because I'm happy you survived."

"Where's Peter? At least I can depend on him not to act weird."

"I'll get him," Logan volunteered. "I'll get the rest of your family, too. They've been waiting as anxiously as the rest of us."

❧

It was close to midnight, but finally the excitement over Colby's recovery had quieted down, and everybody had gone home. Logan was relieved to be back in Sibyl's house with Kitty asleep upstairs. He and Sibyl had retreated to a bench in the backyard in a grove of young cottonwood trees. After the stress of the last few days, the soft evening air engendered a sense of well-being.

"This is the first time I've had you to myself in days," Sibyl said.

Logan kissed her on her nose. "You've had me all to yourself for weeks."

Sibyl giggled. "You know what I mean. We were worrying about Colby, Bridgette was a dark shadow over all of us, and you were pulled away by your brothers or one of the children. I was starting to feel like you were taking me for granted."

Logan put his arms around her and pulled her hard against him. "I can never take you for granted. I still can't believe you love me. The swelling in my face is nearly gone, but I'm far from handsome. Next to Ted Drummond I look like a gargoyle."

Sibyl elbowed him gently in the side. "So does every man in Cactus Corner, but you're my gargoyle. As long as you look a little scary, I don't have to worry about some hussy trying to steal you away from me."

Logan laughed softly. "There'll be a lot of things that will worry you from time to time, but you'll never have to worry that I'll stop loving you. I've never been half as happy in my life, and I don't mean to let anything change that."

"Kitty loves you as much as I do. I think it was her liking you that made me look beyond the surface. I decided what I found there was worth keeping."

They were silent for a few minutes.

"Will you really be happy not going back to Chicago? Your whole life was there for thirty years."

"I lived and worked in Chicago, but I hadn't found any real meaning or focus in my life until I came to Cactus Corner. My brothers and their families are here." He laughed. "Peter is here. How could I think of living anywhere where I couldn't be part of his unbounded enthusiasm for life? But most important, you and Kitty are here. The two of you are my family. I could be happy anywhere as long as I'm with you."

"I would have gone to Chicago."

"I know, and I love you for it, but I really do want to stay here. I feel like I've finally come home."

Sibyl snuggled deeper into Logan's embrace. "I can't wait to become your wife, but you know we have to wait until Colby is strong enough to attend the wedding. He'll want to stand up with you."

"Are you sure?"

"You should have seen how excited he was standing next to Jared when he married Laurie. You'd have thought he was marrying Naomi all over again."

"If both my brothers stand with me, Naomi and Laurie should stand with you."

"And Cassie. It would break her heart if we left her out."

"Kitty and Esther can be the flower girls, but can we trust Peter not to drop the rings?"

Sibyl sat up and faced Logan. "I never heard of a man who wanted to help plan his wedding."

"Marrying you is the most important step I've ever taken. I want to be part of every bit of it."

Sibyl sank back into his embrace. "You really are an unusual man."

"And forgetful." Logan pulled Sibyl into a sitting position. "There's one important step I completely forgot."

"What? I can't think of anything."

"If we're going to do this, we've got to do it right all the way." Logan slid off the bench and knelt before a very surprised Sibyl. "My dearest Sibyl, would you do me the honor of becoming my wife?"

There in the moonlight, kneeling before the woman he adored more than life, Logan received the perfect answer to the most important question of his life.

About the Author

Leigh Greenwood is the *USA Today* bestselling author of the popular Seven Brides, Cowboys, and Night Riders series. The proud father of three grown children, Leigh resides in Charlotte, North Carolina. He never intended to be a writer, but he found it hard to ignore the people in his head, and the only way to get them out was to write. Visit him at www.leigh-greenwood.com.

Read on for a special glimpse into the
lives of the Bachelors of Battle Creek by
New York Times bestselling author Linda Broday.

Forever His Texas Bride

FROM THE AUTHOR...

IT GIVES ME GREAT PLEASURE TO INTRODUCE YOU TO MY Bachelors of Battle Creek series. In it, I show how three ragged boys came together in the orphanage to form an unbreakable bond as brothers that forges their journey into adulthood. Tears still come into my eyes when I think of how they were so desperate for family that they created their own.

Brett Liberty's story goes to the very core of who I am, maybe who we all are, and what I stand for. Being a half-breed was the worst thing for a man in the 1800s because it meant he straddled two worlds with neither claiming him. In this story, Brett faces pure hatred to the point that others want him dead. He's never been with a woman, never known the softness of a woman's touch or the feel of her lips on his. But when he meets pickpocket Rayna Harper in the jail cell next to his, he finds a kindred spirit. The brush of her hand is almost unbearable in its tenderness, and when she curls up beside him on the narrow bunk, she curls up inside his heart as well.

This is a story of never giving up hope and reaching for a forbidden love that others are bent on denying. It's about how through compassion you *can* change. Brett and Rayna's deep love binds them together like a strip of the toughest rawhide and won't let them go.

Now, I'd like to share an excerpt of *Forever His Texas Bride*…

One

North Central Texas
Spring 1879

A PLAN? DEFINITELY *NOT DYING*. BEYOND THAT, HE didn't have one.

High on a hill, Brett Liberty lay in the short, bloodstained grass, watching the farm below. With each breath, pain shot through him like the jagged edge of a hot knife. The bullet had slammed into his back, near the shoulder blade from the feel of it.

If a plan was coming, it had better hurry. The Texas springtime morning was heating up and the men chasing him drew ever closer. Every second spent in indecision could cost him. He had two choices: try to seek help from the family in the little valley, or run as though chased by a devil dog.

The blood loss had weakened him though. He wouldn't get far on foot. About a half mile back, Brett's pursuers had shot his horse, a faithful mustang he'd loved more than his own life. Rage rippled through his chest and throbbed in his head. They could hurt him all they wanted, but messing with his beloved horses would buy them a spot in hell.

He forced his thoughts back to his current predicament.

Through a narrowed gaze, Brett surveyed the scene below. It seemed odd that no horses stood in the corral. The farmer who was chopping wood had a rifle within easy reach. The man's wife hung freshly washed clothes up on a line to dry under the golden sunshine while a couple of small children played at her feet. It was a tranquil day as far as appearances went.

Appearances deceived.

Help was so near yet so far away.

Brett *couldn't* seek their aid. The farmer would have that rifle in his hand before he made it halfway down the hill. The fact that Indian blood flowed through Brett's veins and colored his features definitely complicated things. With the Indian uprisings a few years ago fresh in everyone's minds, it would mean certain death.

No, he couldn't go forward. Neither could he go back.

They'd trapped him.

Why a posse dogged his trail, Brett couldn't say. He'd done nothing except take a remuda of the horses he raised to Fort Concho to sell. He could probably clear things up in two minutes if they'd just give him the opportunity. Yet the group, led by a man wearing a sheriff's star, seemed to adhere to the motto *shoot first and ask questions of the corpse*.

He was in a hell of a mess and wished he had his brothers, Cooper Thorne and Rand Sinclair, to stand with him.

Inside his head, he heard the ticking of a clock. Whatever he did, he'd better get to it.

The family below was his only chance. Brett straightened his bloodstained shirt as best he could and removed the long feather from his black hat. Except for his knee-high moccasins, the rest of his clothing was what any man on the frontier would wear.

At last he gathered his strength and struggled to his feet. He removed a bandana, a red one, from around his neck. On wobbly legs, he picked his way down the hill.

When the farmer saw him and started for his rifle, Brett waved the bandana over his head. "Help! I need help. Please don't shoot. I'm unarmed."

With the rifle firmly in hand, the farmer ordered his wife and children into the house, then cautiously advanced. Brett dropped to his knees in an effort to show he posed no threat. Or maybe it was that his legs simply gave out. Either way, it must've worked—he didn't hear the sound of a bullet exploding from the weapon.

The man's shadow fell across Brett. "Who are you and what do you want?" the farmer asked.

"I'm shot. Name's Brett Liberty. I have a horse ranch seventy miles east of here." When he started to stand, the farmer jabbed the end of the rifle into his chest. Brett saw the wisdom in staying put.

"Who shot you?"

"Don't know. Never saw them before." A bee buzzed around Brett's face.

"How do I know you didn't hightail it off the reservation? Or maybe you're an outlaw. I've heard of Indian outlaws."

Brett sighed in frustration. "I've never seen a

reservation, and I assure you, I don't step outside the law. I'm respected in Battle Creek. My brother is the sheriff. If I took up outlawing ways, he'd be the first to arrest me." Likely throw him *under* the jail instead of putting him in a cell. But he didn't add that.

He glanced longingly toward the house, but the rifle barrel poking from a window told him asking for safety inside was out of the question. So was running. Their guns would cut him down before he'd gone a yard.

Maybe if he stalled, made sure he looked as unthreatening as possible and kept the man nearby, he might just make it. With a witness to the posse's actions, the sheriff might let him live. It was his only shot.

The ticking clock in Brett's head was getting louder, blocking out the buzz of the persistent bee. His pursuers would be here in a minute. His dry mouth couldn't even form spit. "Please, mister, could you at least give me some water?"

It was a gamble, but one that looked like it might pay off. Silently, the farmer backed up a step and motioned Brett toward the well with his rifle barrel.

"Thank you." Brett got to his feet and stumbled toward the water. He lowered the bucket and pulled it up, then filled a metal cup that hung nearby and guzzled it down. He was about to refill it when horses galloped into the yard and encircled him.

"Put up your hands or I'll shoot," a man barked, sparing an obvious glance toward the farmer.

Brett glanced up at the speaker and the shiny tin star on his leather vest. He set his empty cup on the ledge circling the well. "Your warning comes a little late, Sheriff. I would've appreciated it much earlier. Would you be so kind as to tell me what I did to warrant this arrest?"

The bearded sheriff dismounted. Hate glittered in his dark eyes, reminding Brett of others who harbored resentment for his kind. Jerking his hands behind his back, the middle-aged lawman secured them with rope. "You'll know soon enough."

Ignoring the sharp pain piercing his back, Brett tried to reason. "I can clear up this misunderstanding if you'll only tell me what you think I did wrong."

No one spoke.

Brett turned to the farmer. "I'll give you five of my best horses if you'll let my brothers know where I am. You can find them in Battle Creek. Cooper Thorne and Rand Sinclair."

The farmer stared straight ahead without even a flicker to indicate he'd heard. While the sheriff thanked the sodbuster for catching Brett, two of the other riders threw him onto a horse. With everyone mounted a few minutes later, the group made tracks toward Steele's Hollow.

Brett had passed through there before daybreak, anxious to get home to the Wild Horse Ranch. The town had been quieter than a blade of grass growing. He couldn't imagine what they thought he'd done. This was the first time he'd traveled through the community. Usually he took a more southerly tack returning home after driving a string of horses to Fort Concho, but this time he'd had to deliver a sorrel to a man on the Skipper Ranch near Chalk Mountain, so he'd decided to cut through.

He made a mental note to give Steele's Hollow a wide berth from now on.

Not that there would be a next time if things kept going the way they were.

The combination of blood loss and the hot sun made Brett see double. It was all he could do to stay in the saddle.

By the time they rode into the small town an hour later, Brett had doubled over and clung to the horse's mane with everything he had. The group halted in front of the jail, jerked him off the animal and into the rough wooden building.

"Please, I need a doctor," Brett murmured as they rifled through his pockets.

After taking the bank draft from the sale of the horses and his knife, they unlocked a door that led down a dark walkway. The smell of the earthen walls and the dim light told him the builder had dug into a hill. They unlocked a cell and threw him inside.

"A doctor," Brett repeated weakly as he huddled on the floor.

"Not sure he treats breeds." The sheriff slammed the iron door shut and locked it. "See what I can do, though. Reckon we don't want you to die before we hang you."

"That's awful considerate." Brett struggled to his feet and clung to the metal bars to keep from falling. "Once and for all, tell me…what did I do? What am I guilty of?"

"You were born," the sheriff snapped. Without more, he turned and walked to the front of the jail.

❧

Panic pounded in Brett's temples like a herd of stampeding mustangs long after the slamming of the two iron doors separating him from freedom. This proved that the sheriff had targeted him solely because of his Indian heritage; he had nothing to charge him with.

His crime was simply being born?

Dizzy, Brett collapsed onto the bunk as his hat fell to the crude plank floor.

Movement in the next cell caught his attention. Willing the room to keep from spinning, Brett turned his head. He could make out a woman's form in the dimness. Surely his pain had conjured her up. They didn't put women in jail.

He couldn't tell what she looked like because she had two faces blurring together, distorting her features—but he could hear her pretty voice clear enough.

"You're in pitiful shape, mister."

Since his bunk butted up to the bars of her cell, she could easily reach through. He felt her cautiously touch one of his moccasins.

"Checking to see if I'm dead?" he murmured.

"Nope. Do you mind if I have your shoes after they hang you?"

Brett raised up on an elbow, then immediately regretted it when the cell whirled. He lay back down. "That's not a nice thing to ask a man."

"Well, you won't be needing them. I might as well get some good out of them."

"They aren't going to hang me."

"That's not what Sheriff Oldham said."

"He can't hang me because I didn't do anything wrong." It was best to keep believing that. Maybe he could convince someone, even if only himself. "I think he was joking."

"Humor and Sheriff Oldham parted company long ago. He's serious all the time. And mean. You don't want to get on his bad side."

"Wish I'd known this sooner. You sure know how to make a man feel better," Brett said dryly, draping his arm across his eyes and willing his stomach to quit churning. "What is your name?"

"Rayna."

"Who stuck that on you? I've never heard it before."

"It's a made-up name. My father is Raymond and my mother is Elna. My mama stuck 'em together and came up with Rayna. I've always hated it."

"Got a last name, or did they use it all on the first one?"

"Harper. Rayna Harper."

"Forgive me if I don't get up to shake hands, but I'm a little indisposed. I'm Brett Liberty."

With that, blessed silence filled the space, leaving him to fight waves of dizziness and a rebellious stomach. Keeping down the contents seemed all he could manage at present.

But Rayna wasn't quiet for long. "Where did you get those Indian shoes, Brett? I'd sure like to have them."

"My brother." His words came out sounding shorter than he intended.

"Sorry. I've been in here for a while by myself, and I guess I just have a lot of words stored up. Sometimes I feel they're just going to explode out the top of my head if I don't let some out. What are you in here for? I couldn't hear too well."

"For being born, I'm told." Brett was still trying to digest that.

"Me too." Rayna sounded astonished. "Isn't that amazing?"

Brett had a feeling that no matter what he'd said, she would say the same thing. He wished he could see her better so he could put a face to the voice. Even though the conversation taxed him, it was nice to know he wasn't alone. Maybe she'd even hold his hand if he died.

That is, if she wasn't too busy trying to get his moccasins off instead.

"Why do you think it's amazing?"

"Because it makes perfect sense. I figure if I hadn't been born, I wouldn't be in here for picking old Mr. Vickery's pockets."

"So you're a pickpocket?" Surprise rippled through him.

"Nope. I'm a spreader of good. I don't ever keep any of it. I take from those who have and give to the have-nots. Makes everyone happy. Except me when I get thrown in the calaboose."

"You're a Robin Hood." Brett had seen a copy of the book about the legendary figure at Fort Concho. He'd learned it so he could share the tale with Toby, Rand's adopted son. Brett had taken the six-year-old into his heart and loved spending time with the boy.

"I'm a what?"

"A person who goes around doing good things for the poor."

"Oh. I guess I am. It makes me so sad that some people have to do without things they need and no one helps them. This past winter, my friend Davy froze to death because the only place he had to sleep was under a porch. He was just a kid with no one except me to care."

Rayna's unexpectedly big heart touched Brett. She seemed to speak from a good bit of experience. "Do you have a place to sleep whenever you're not in here?"

"I get along. Don't need you to fret about me. Worrying about them putting a rope around your neck is all you can handle. Do you reckon it hurts a lot, Brett?"

"I wouldn't know." Hopefully, he wouldn't find out.

"I'll say a prayer for you."

"Appreciate that, Miss Rayna Harper." She was wrong about him only having to worry about getting his neck stretched, though. He could feel himself getting weaker.

He could also feel her eyeing his moccasins again.

Pressure on the bottom of his foot made him jump. He raised his head and saw that she'd stuck one bare foot through the bars and was measuring it to his.

"Stop that," he said with a painful huff of laughter. "The doctor'll be along soon. I'm not going to be dead enough for you to get them."

The next sound to reach his ears was sawing and her soft, "Oh dear."

"Why did you say that? What's wrong?"

"The sawbones had best hurry or you won't be needing him. They've started building the gallows."

That ticking clock in his head had taken on the sound of tolling bells.

We hope you've enjoyed this special look into Linda Broday's The Bachelors of Battle Creek.

Texas Mail Order Bride now available
Twice a Texas Bride now available
Forever His Texas Bride available December 2015